About the Authors

L⬚ ⬚ielding was born with itchy feet. She made it to Z⬚bia before her twenty-first birthday and, gathering he⬚wn special hero and a couple of children on the wa⬚ ⬚ved in Botswana, Kenya and Bahrain. Seven of her t⬚es have been nominated for RWA's Rita®; and she ⬚ won the Best Traditional Romance in 2000, the ⬚sh Romance Prize in 2005 and the Best Short Con⬚orary Romance in 2006.

City ⬚ng, book addict, peony obsessive, **Katrina Cud⬚** lives in Cork, Ireland with her husband, fou⬚ ⬚ children and a very daft dog. A psychology gra⬚ with a M.Sc. in Human Resources Katrina sp⬚ ny years working in multinational companies an⬚ ⬚t believe she is lucky enough now to have a job th⬚olves daydreaming about love and handsome ⬚u can visit Katrina at www.katrinacudmore.com

⬚winning author **Jennifer Faye** pens fun ⬚porary romances. Internationally published with ⬚ranslated into more than a dozen languages, she is ⬚ime winner of the RT Book Reviews Reviewers' ⬚e Award and the CataRomance Reviewers' Choice A⬚. Now living her dream, she resides with her very p⬚ husband and Writer Kitty. When she's not plotting o⬚ next romance, you can find her with a mug of tea ⬚book. Learn more at https://jenniferfaye.com

Ever After

COLLECTION

Enchanted
Ever After

LIZ FIELDING

KATRINA CUDMORE

JENNIFER FAYE

MILLS & BOON

Harmonisation in the Internal Market and in other countries.

First Published in Great Britain 2021
by Mills & Boon, an imprint of HarperCollins*Publishers* Ltd,
1 London Bridge Street, London, SE1 9GF

www.harpercollins.co.uk

HarperCollins*Publishers*
1st Floor, Watermarque Building,
Ringsend Road, Dublin 4, Ireland

ENCHANTED EVER AFTER © 2021 Harlequin Books S.A.

Vettori's Damsel in Distress © 2015 Liz Fielding
Her First-Date Honeymoon © 2017 Katrina Cudmore
Beauty and Her Boss © 2018 Jennifer F. Stroka

ISBN: 978-0-263-29944-1

MIX
Paper from
responsible sources
FSC™ C007454

This book is produced from independently certified FSC™ paper
to ensure responsible forest management.

For more information visit: www.harpercollins.co.uk/green

Printed and bound in Spain
by CPI, Barcelona

VETTORI'S DAMSEL
IN DISTRESS

LIZ FIELDING

This book is dedicated to the authors I hang out with online. They are the best support group in the world – always up for a brainstorming session when the plot wobbles, ready to celebrate the good stuff and reach out through cyber space with comfort when fate lobs lemons.

They know who they are.

CHAPTER ONE

'Life is like ice cream on a hot day. Enjoy it before it melts.'
—from *Rosie's Little Book of Ice Cream*

IT WAS LATE and throwing down a sleety rain when Geli emerged from the Metro at Porta Garibaldi into the Milan night. Her plan had been to take a taxi for the last short leg of her journey but it was par for the course, on a day when everything had conspired to keep her from her destination, that there wasn't one in sight.

Terrific.

The weather had been mild with a promise of spring in the air when she'd left Longbourne and, optimistically, she'd assumed Italy would be warmer; something to do with all those sun-soaked travel programmes on the television, no doubt. If she'd had the sense to check the local weather she'd have been wearing thermals instead of lace beneath her dress, leggings over her ultra-sheer black tights and a lot more than a lace choker around her neck.

Not the most practical outfit for travelling but she was going to Milan, style capital of Europe, where the inhabitants didn't wear joggers unless they were jogging and policewomen wore high heels.

In her determination to make a fashionable impression

she had overlooked the fact that Milan was in the north of Italy. Where there were mountains. And, apparently, sleet.

Okaaay...

According to the details she'd downloaded from the Internet, her apartment was no more than a ten-minute stroll from the Metro. She could handle a bit of sleet. In style.

She checked her map and, having orientated herself, she pulled the wide hood of her coat over ears that were beginning to tingle, shouldered her roomy leather tote and, hauling her suitcase behind her, set off.

New country, new start, new life.

Unlike her sisters, who were married, raising families and, with their rapidly expanding ice cream events business, had life all sewn up and sorted, she was throwing herself into the dark—literally.

With little more than an Italian phrasebook and a head full of ideas, she was setting out to grab every experience that life offered her. If, as she crossed the railway bridge into the unknown, the thrill of nervous excitement that shot through her was edged with a ripple of apprehension, a shiver of fear—well, that was perfectly natural. She was the baby of the family.

She might be the one with the weird clothes, the 'attitude', but they knew it was all front; that this was her first time out in the world. Okay, she'd been to Italy before, but that was on a student study trip and she'd been with a group of people she knew. This time she was on her own, without the family safety net of loving hands reaching out to steady her if she stumbled. To catch her if she fell. Testing herself...

'Scusi!'

'Sorry...um...*scusi*...' She steered her case to one side to let someone in a hurry pass her and then, as she looked up, she saw the colourful street art gleaming under the street lights—bright tropical scenes that lit up dull concrete—and caught her breath.

Despite the icy stuff stinging her face, excitement won out as she remembered why she had chosen Italy, Milan... Isola.

The minute she'd opened a magazine, seen the photographs, read about this enclave of artists, musicians, designers all doing their own thing, she'd been hooked. This was a place where she could spread her wings, explore her love of fashion, seek new ways of making art and maybe, just maybe fall in love. Nothing serious, not for keeps, but for fun.

Twenty minutes later, her face stiff with cold, the freezing stuff finding its way into a hood designed more for glamour than protection, and totally lost, the bounce had left her step.

She could almost see her oldest sister, Elle, shaking her head and saying, *You're so impatient, Geli! Why didn't you wait for a taxi?*

Because it was an *adventure*! And the directions had been simple enough. She'd counted the turnings, checked the name of the street, turned right and her apartment should be there, right in front of her, on the corner.

Except it wasn't.

Instead of the pink-painted five-storey house on the corner of a street of equally pretty houses that overlooked the twice-weekly market, she was faced with eight-feet-high wooden barriers surrounding a construction site.

No need to panic. Obviously she'd missed a turning. There had been a couple of narrow openings—more alleys than streets—that she'd thought were too small to be the turnings on her map. Obviously she was wrong.

She backtracked, recounted and headed down one just about wide enough to take a Fiat 500. It ended in a tiny courtyard piled up with crates and lit by a dim lamp over what looked like the back entrance to a shop. In the dark something moved, a box fell, and she beat a hasty retreat.

The few people about had their heads down and her, *'Scusi...'* was blown away on wind that was driving the sleet, thicker now, into her face.

It was time to take another look at the map.

Ducking into the shelter of the doorway of a shuttered shop, she searched her tote for the powerful mini torch given to her by her explorer brother-in-law as a parting gift.

She'd reminded him that she was going to one of the world's great cities rather than venturing into the jungle. His response was that in his experience there was little difference and as something wet and hairy brushed against her leg she let out a nervous shriek.

Make that one for the explorer.

A plaintive mew reassured her and the bright beam of her torch picked out a tiny kitten, wet fur sticking to its skin, cowering in the doorway.

'Hey, sweetie,' she said softly, reaching out to it, but it backed away nervously. She knew how it felt. 'You're much too little to be out by yourself on a night like this.'

The poor creature, wetter and certainly colder than she was, mewed pitifully in agreement. She'd bought a cheese sandwich on the plane but had been too churned up with nerves and excitement to eat it and she opened it up, broke a piece off and offered it to the kitten. Hunger beat fear and it snatched the food from her fingers, desperately licking at the butter.

Geli broke off another piece and then turned her attention to the simple street map. Clearly she'd taken a wrong turn and wandered into the commercial district, now closed for the night, but for the life of her couldn't see where she'd gone wrong.

Phoning Signora Franco, her landlady, was not an option. The *signora*'s English was about on a par with her own Italian—enthusiastic, but short on delivery. What she needed was one of Isola's famous cafés or bars, somewhere warm and dry with people who would know the area and, bracing herself to face to what was now whiter, more solid than mere sleet, she peered along the street.

Behind her, the kitten mewed and she sighed. There were a few lights on in upper floors but down here everything was shut up. The tiny creature was on its own and was too small to survive the night without shelter. The location might be new, but some things never changed.

Inevitably, having begged for help, the kitten panicked when she bent and scooped it up but she eased it into one of the concealed seam pockets hidden amongst the full layers of her coat.

She'd come back tomorrow and see if she could find someone who'd take responsibility for it but right now it was time to put her Italian to the test. She'd memorised the question and could rattle off '*Dov'è* Via Pepone?' without a second thought. Understanding the answers might be more of a problem.

She stuffed her torch, along with the useless map, in her bag and began to retrace her steps back to the road from the station, this time carrying straight on instead of turning off.

In the photographs she'd seen it had been summer; there were open-air jazz concerts, the communal garden and collective 'bring a dish' lunches where every Tuesday the local people gathered to share food and reinforce the community ties. People sitting outside trendy cafés. Perfect.

This was the wrong time of day, the wrong time of year. Even the famous Milan 'promenade' was on hold but, encouraged by a sudden snatch of music—as if someone had opened a door very briefly—she hurried to the corner and there, on the far side of a piazza, lights shone through a steamy window.

It was Café Rosa, famous for jazz, cocktails and being a hangout of local artists who used the walls as a gallery. More relieved than she cared to admit, she slithered across the cobbles and pushed open the door.

She was immediately swathed in warmth, the rich scent of luscious food and cool music from a combo on a tiny stage in the corner mingling with bursts of steam from the expresso machine. Tables of all shapes and sizes were filled with people eating, drinking, gossiping, and a tall dark-haired man was leaning against the counter talking to the barista.

If the scene had been posed by the Italian Tourist Board it couldn't have been more perfect and, despite the cold, she felt a happy little rush of anticipation.

A few people had turned when the door opened and the chatter died away until the only sound was the low thrum of a double bass.

The man standing at the bar, curious about what had caught everyone's attention, half turned and anticipation whooshed off the scale in an atavistic charge of raw desire; instant, bone-deep need for a man before you heard his voice, felt his touch, knew his name.

For a moment, while she remembered how to breathe, it felt as if someone had pressed the pause button on the scene, freezing the moment in soft focus. Muted colours reflected in polished steel, lights shimmering off the bottles and glasses behind the bar, her face reflected, ghost-like, behind the advertisement on a mirror. And Mr Italy with his kiss-me mouth and come-to-bed eyes.

Forget the thick dark hair and cheekbones sharp enough to write their own modelling contract, it was those chocolate-dark eyes that held her transfixed. If they had been looking out of a tourist poster there would be a stampede to book holidays in Italy.

He straightened, drawing attention to the way his hair

curled onto his neck, a pair of scandalously broad shoulders, strong wrists emerging from folded-back cuffs.

'*Signora...*' he murmured as he moved back a little to make room for her at the counter and, oh, joy, his voice matched the face, the body.

She might have passed out for lack of oxygen at that moment but a tall, athletic-looking blonde placed a tiny cup of espresso in front of him before—apparently unaware that she was serving a god—turning to her.

'*Sta nevicando? E brutto tempo.*'

What?

Oh...

Flustered at being confronted with phrases that hadn't featured so far on the Italian course she'd downloaded onto her iPod, she took the safe option and, having sucked in a snowflake that was clinging to her lip, she lowered her hood. The chatter gradually resumed and, finally getting a *move it* message through to her legs, she parked her suitcase and crossed to the bar.

'*Cosa prendi, signora?*'

Oh, whew, something she understood. 'Um...*Vorrai un espresso...s'il vous plait...*' Her answer emerged in a mangled mixture of English, Italian and French. 'No...I mean...' *Oh, heck.*

The blonde grinned. 'Don't worry. I got the gist,' she replied, her English spiced with an Australian accent.

'Oh, thank goodness you're English. No! Sorry, Australian—' Achingly conscious of the man leaning against the counter, an impressive thigh stretching the cloth of his jeans just inches from her hip, she attempted to recover the cool, sophisticated woman of the world image with which she'd intended to storm Milan. 'Shall I go out, walk around the block and try that again?'

The woman grinned. 'Stay right where you are. I'll get

that espresso. You've just arrived in Isola?' she asked as she measured the coffee.

'In Isola, in Milan, in Italy. I've been working on my Italian—I picked some up when I spent a month in Tuscany as a student—but I learned French at school and it seems to be my brain's foreign language default setting when I panic.'

Her brain was too busy drooling over Mr Italy to give a toot.

'Give it a week,' the woman said. 'Can I get you anything else?'

'A side order of directions?' she asked hopefully, doing her best to ignore the fact that it wasn't just her brain; her entire body was responding on a visceral level to the overdose of pheromones wafting in her direction. It was like being bombarded by butterflies. Naked…

She was doing her level best not to stare at him.

Was he looking at her?

'You are lost, *signora*?' he asked.

In Italian, his voice was just about the sexiest thing she'd ever heard, but his perfect, lusciously accented English sent a shiver rippling down her spine that had nothing to do with the snow dripping from her hair. That was trickling between her breasts and turning to steam.

She took a breath and, doing her best to remember why she was there, said, 'Not lost exactly…' Retrieving the apartment details from her tote, she placed it, map side up, on the counter and turned to him, intending to explain what had happened. He was definitely looking and, confronted with those eyes, the questioning kink of his brow, language of any description deserted her.

'No?' he prompted.

Clearly he was used to women losing the power of speech in his presence. From the relaxed way he was leaning against the bar, to eyes that, with one look made her feel as if he owned her, everything about him screamed danger.

First day in Isola and she could imagine having a lot of fun with Mr Italy and, from the way he was looking at her, he was thinking much the same thing about her.

Was that how it had been for her mother that first time? One look from some brawny roustabout at the annual village fair and she'd been toast?

'I know exactly where I am, *signor*,' she said, looking into those lusciously dark eyes. To emphasise the point she eased off the fine leather glove that had done little to keep her hand warm and tapped the piazza with the tip of a crimson nail.

'No,' he repeated, and this time it wasn't a question as, never taking his eyes from hers, he wrapped long fingers around her hand and moved her finger two inches to the right. 'You are here.'

His hand was warm against her cold skin. On the surface everything was deceptively still but inside, like a volcano on the point of blowing, she was liquid heat.

She fought the urge to swallow. 'I am?'

She was used to people staring at her. From the age of nine she had been the focus of raised eyebrows and she'd revelled in it.

This man's look was different. It sizzled through her and, afraid that the puddle of snow melting at her feet was about to turn to steam, she turned to the map.

It didn't help. Not one bit. His hand was still covering hers, long ringless fingers darkly masculine against her own pale skin, and she found herself wondering how they would look against her breast. How they would feel...

Under the layers of black—coat, dress, the lace of her bra—her nipples hardened in response to her imagination, sending touch-me messages to all parts south and she bit on her lower lip to stop herself from whimpering.

Breathe, breathe...

She cleared the cobwebs from her throat and, hoping she sounded a lot more in control than she was, said, 'One piazza looks very much like another on a map. Unfortunately, neither of them is where I was going.'

'And yet here you are.'

And yet here she was, falling into eyes as dark as the espresso in his cup.

The café retreated. The bright labels on bottles behind the bar, the clatter of cutlery, the low thrum of a double bass became no more than a blur of colour, sound. All her senses were focused on the touch of his fingers curling about her hand, his molten eyes reflecting back her own image. For a moment nothing moved until, abruptly, he turned away and used the hand that had been covering hers to pick up his espresso and drain it in one swallow.

He'd looked away first and she waited for the rush of power that always gave her but it didn't come. For the first time in her life it didn't feel like a victory.

Toast...

'Where are you going, *signora*?' He carefully replaced the tiny cup on its saucer.

'Here...' She looked down but the ink had run, leaving a dirty splodge where the name of the street had been.

'Tell him the address and Dante will point you in the right direction,' the barista said, putting an espresso in front of her. 'He knows every inch of Isola.'

'Dante?' Geli repeated. 'As in the *Inferno*?' No wonder he was so hot... Catching the barista's knowing grin, she quickly added, 'Or perhaps your mother is an admirer of the Pre-Raphaelites?'

'Are you visiting someone?' he asked, ignoring the question.

'No.' Mentally kicking herself for speaking before her brain was in gear—he must have heard that one a thousand times—she shook her head. 'I'm here to work. I've leased an apartment for a year. Geli Amery,' she added, offering him her hand without a thought for the consequences.

He wrapped his hand around hers and held it.

'Dante Vettori.' Rolled out in that sexy Italian accent, his name was a symphony of seduction. 'Your name is Jelly?' He lifted an eyebrow, but not like the disapproving old biddies in the village shop. Not at all. 'Like the wobbly stuff the British inflict on small children at birthday parties?'

Okay, so she'd probably asked for that with her stupid *'Inferno'* remark, but he wasn't the only one to have heard it all before.

'Or add to peanut butter in a sandwich if you're American?' She lifted an eyebrow right back at him, which was asking for trouble but who knew if he'd ever lift his eyebrow at her like that again? This was definitely one of those 'live for the day' moments she had vowed to grab with both hands and she was going for it.

'é possibile,' he said, the lines bracketing his mouth deepening into a smile. 'But I suspect not.'

He could call her what he liked as long as he kept smiling like that…

'You suspect right. Geli is short for Angelica—as in *angelica archangelica*, which I'm told is a very handsome plant.' And she smiled back. 'You may be more familiar with its crystallised stem. The British use it to decorate the cakes and trifles that they inflict on small children at birthday parties.'

His laugh was rich and warm, creating a fan of creases around his eyes, emphasising those amazing cheekbones, widening his mouth and drawing attention to a lower lip that she wanted to lick…

Make that burnt toast…

In an attempt to regain control of her vital organs, Geli

picked up her espresso and downed it in a single swallow, Italian style. It was hotter than she expected, shocking her out of the lusty mist.

'I had intended to take a taxi—' Her vocal cords were still screaming from the hot coffee and the words came out as little more than a squeak. She cleared her throat and tried again. 'Unfortunately, there were none at the Porta Garibaldi and on the apartment details it said that Via Pepone was only a ten-minute walk.'

'Taxis are always in short supply when the weather's bad,' the barista said, as Dante, frowning now, turned the details over to look at the picture of the pretty pink house where she'd be living for the next year. 'Welcome to Isola, Geli. Lisa Vettori—I'm from the Australian branch of the family. Dante's my cousin and, although you wouldn't know it from the way he's lounging around on the wrong side of the counter, Café Rosa is his bar.'

'I pay you handsomely so that I can stay on this side of the bar,' he reminded her, without looking up.

'Make the most of it, mate. I have a fitting for a brides-maid dress in Melbourne on Tuesday. Unless you get your backside in gear and find a temp to take my place, come Sunday you'll be the one getting up close and personal with the Gaggia.' She took a swipe at the marble counter top with a cloth to remove an invisible mark. 'Have you got a job lined up, Geli?' she asked.

'A job?'

'You said you were here to work. Have you ever worked in a bar? Only there's a temporary—'

'If you've been travelling all day you must be hungry,' Dante said, cutting his cousin off in mid-sentence. 'We'll have the risotto, Lisa.' And, holding onto the details of her apartment and, more importantly, the map, he headed for a table for two that was tucked away in a quiet corner.

CHAPTER TWO

'There's nothing more cheering than a good friend when you're in trouble—except a good friend with ice cream.'

—from *Rosie's Little Book of Ice Cream*

TOO SURPRISED TO REACT, Geli didn't move. Okay, so there had been some fairly heavy-duty flirting going on, but that was a bit arrogant—

Dante pulled out a chair and waited for her to join him.

Make that quite a lot arrogant. Did he really think she would simply follow him?

'Angelica?'

No one used her full name, but he said it with a 'g' so soft that it felt like chocolate melting on her tongue and while her head was still saying, *Oh, please...*her body went to him as if he'd tugged a chain.

'Give me your coat,' he said, 'and I'll hang it up to dry.'

She swallowed.

It was late. She should be on her way but for that she needed directions, which was a good, practical reason to do as he said. Then again, nothing that had happened since she'd walked through the door of Café Rosa had been about the practicalities and, letting her tote slide from her shoulder onto the chair, she dropped her glove on the table and began to tug at its pair.

Warm now, the fine leather clung to her skin and as she removed her glove, one finger at a time, Geli discovered that there was more than one way of being in control.

A chain had two ends and now Dante was the one being hauled in as she slowly revealed her hand with each unintentionally provocative tug.

She dropped the glove beside its pair and everything— the heartbeat pounding in her ears, her breathing—slowed right down as, never taking her eyes off his, she lowered her hand and, one by one, began to slip the small jet buttons that nipped her coat into her waist.

There were a dozen of them and, taking her time, she started at the bottom. One, two, three... His gaze never wavered for a second until the bias cut swathes of velvet, cashmere and butter-soft suede—flaring out in layers that curved from just below her knees at the front to her heels at the back—fell open to reveal the black scoop-necked mini-dress that stopped four inches above her knees.

She waited a heartbeat and then turned and let the coat slip from her shoulders, leaving him to catch it.

An arch *got you* lift of an eyebrow as she thanked him should leave him in no doubt that the next move was up to him and she was more than ready for anything he had to offer, but as she glanced over her shoulder, fell into the velvet softness of his eyes, she forgot the plot.

He was so close. His breath was warm on her cheek, his mouth was inches away and her eyebrow stayed put as she imagined closing the gap and taking his delicious lower lip between hers.

Make that burned to a crisp toast. Toast about to burst into flames...

She blinked as a clatter of cutlery shattered the moment and Dante looked down at her coat as if wondering where it had come from.

'I'll hang this by the heater to dry,' he said.

'Are you mad?' Lisa, the table swiftly laid, took it from him. 'You don't hang something like this over a radiator as if it's any old chain store raincoat. This kind of quality costs a fortune and it needs tender loving care.' She checked the label. 'Dark Angel.' She looked up. 'Angel?' she repeated and then, with a look of open admiration, 'Is that you, Geli?'

'What? Oh, yes,' she said, grateful for the distraction. Falling into bed for fun with a man was one thing. Falling into anything else was definitely off the agenda… 'Dark Angel is my label.'

'You're a fashion designer?'

'Not exactly. I make one-off pieces. I studied art but I've been making clothes all my life and somehow I've ended up combining the two.'

'Clothes as art?' She grinned. 'I like it.'

'Let's hope you're not the only one.'

'Not a chance. This is absolutely lush. Did you make the choker, too?' she asked. 'Or is that an original?'

'If only…' Geli touched the ornate Victorian-style lace and jet band at her throat. 'It's recycled from stuff in my odds and ends box. I cut my dress from something I found on the "worn once" rack at the church jumble sale and—' if she kept talking she wouldn't grab Dante Vettori '—my coat was made from stuff I've collected over the years.'

'Well…wow. You are so going to fit in here. Upcycling is big in Isola.'

'It's one of the reasons I'm here. I want to work with people who are doing the same kind of thing.'

'And I suggested you might want a job behind the bar.' She rolled her eyes. 'If you've got something you want to exhibit I'm sure Dan will find space for it.' She glanced at him, but he offered no encouragement. 'Right, well, I'll go and find a hanger for this,' she said, holding the coat up so that it didn't touch the floor. She'd only gone a couple of steps when she stopped. 'Geli, there's something moving... Omigod!' She screamed and, forgetting all about its lushness, dropped the coat and leapt back. 'It's a rat!'

The musicians stopped playing mid-note. The patrons of the café, who had resumed chatting, laughing, eating, turned as one.

Then the kitten, confused, frightened, bolted across the floor and pandemonium broke out as men leapt to their feet and women leapt on chairs.

'It's all right!' Geli yelled as she dived under a table to grab the kitten before some heavy-footed male stamped on the poor creature. Terrified, it scratched and sank its little needle teeth deep into the soft pad of her thumb before she emerged with it grasped in her hand. 'It's a kitten!' Then, in desperation when that didn't have any effect, *'Uno kitty!'*

She held it up so that everyone could see. It had dried a little in the shelter of her pocket but it was a scrawny grey scrap, not much bigger than her hand. No one looked convinced and, when a woman let loose a nervous scream, Dante hooked his arm around her waist and swept her and the kitten through the café to a door that led to the rear.

As it swung shut behind him the sudden silence was brutal.

'Uno kitty?' Dante demanded, looming over her. Much too close.

'I don't know the Italian for kitten,' she said, shaken by the speed at which events had overtaken her.

'It's *gattino*, but Lisa is right, that wretched creature looks more like a drowned rat.'

And the one word you didn't want to hear if you were in the catering business was *rat*.

'I'm sorry but I found it shivering in a doorway. It was soaking wet. Freezing. I couldn't leave it there.'

'Maybe not—' he didn't look convinced '—but rats, cats, it's all the same to the health police.'

'I understand. My sisters are in the catering business.' And in similar circumstances they would have killed her. 'I only stopped to ask for directions. I didn't mean to stay for more than a minute or two.'

Epic distraction…

She was about to repeat her apology when the door opened behind them. Dante dropped his arm from her waist as Lisa appeared with her coat and bag over one arm and trailing her suitcase, leaving a cold space.

'Have you calmed them down?' he asked.

'Nothing like free drinks all round to lighten the mood. Bruno is dealing with it.'

Geli groaned. 'It's my fault. I'll pay for them.'

'No…' Lisa and Dante spoke as one then Lisa added, 'The first rule of catering is that if you see a rat, you don't scream. The second is that you don't shout, *It's a rat*… Unfortunately, when I felt something move and that something was grey and furry I totally— Omigod, Geli, you're bleeding!'

Geli glanced at the trickle of blood running down her palm. 'It's nothing. The poor thing panicked.'

'A poor thing that's been who knows where,' Lisa replied, 'eating who knows what filth. Come on, we'll go upstairs and I'll clean it up for you.'

'It's okay, honestly,' Geli protested, now seriously embarrassed. 'It's late and Signora Franco, the woman who owns the apartment I've rented, will be waiting for me with the key. I would have called her to let her know my plane had been delayed but her English is even worse than my Italian.'

Geli glanced at her watch. She'd promised to let her sisters know when she was safely in her apartment and it was well past ten o'clock. She'd warned them that her plane had been delayed but if she didn't text them soon they'd be imagining all sorts.

'There's no need to worry about Signora Franco,' Dante said.

'Oh, but—'

'Via Pepone has been demolished to make way for an office block,' he said, his expression grim. 'I hoped to break it to you rather more gently, but I'm afraid the apartment you have rented no longer exists.'

It took a moment for what Dante had said to sink in. There was no Via Pepone? No apartment? 'But I spoke to Signora Franco…'

'Find a box for Rattino, Lis, before he does any more damage.' Dante took her coat and bag from his cousin and ushered her towards the stairs.

Geli didn't move. This had to be a mistake. 'Maybe I have the name of the street wrong?' she said, trying not to think about how the directions on the map she'd been sent had taken her to a construction site. 'Maybe it's a typo—'

'Let's get your hand cleaned up. Are your tetanus shots up to date?' he asked.

'What? Oh, yes…' She stood her ground for another ten seconds but she couldn't go back into the restaurant with the kitten and if there was a problem with the apartment she had to know. And Lisa was right—the last thing she needed was an infected hand.

Concentrate on that. And repeating her apology wouldn't hurt.

'I really am sorry about the rat thing,' she said as she began to climb the stairs. 'The kitten really would have died if I'd left it out there.'

'So you picked it up and put it in the pocket of your beautiful coat?' He liked her coat… 'Do you do that often?'

'All the time,' she admitted. 'Coat pockets, bags, the basket of my bicycle. My sisters did their best to discourage me, but eventually they gave it up as a lost cause.'

'And are they always this ungrateful? Your little strays?'

As they reached the landing he took her hand in his to check the damage and Geli forgot about the kitten, her apartment, pretty much everything as the warmth of his fingers seeped beneath her skin and into the bone.

When she didn't answer, he looked up and the temperature rose to the point where she was blushing to her toes.

Toast in flames. Smoke alarm hurting her eardrums...

'Frightened animals lash out,' she said quickly, waiting for him to open one of the doors, but he kept her hand in his and headed up a second flight of stairs.

There was only one door at the top. He let go of her hand, took a key from his pocket, unlocked it and pushed it open, standing back so that she could go ahead of him.

Geli wasn't sure what she'd expected; she hadn't actually been doing a lot of thinking since he'd turned and looked at her. Her brain had been working overtime dealing with the bombardment of her senses—new sights, new scents, a whole new level of physical response to a man.

Maybe a staff restroom...

Or maybe not.

There was a small entrance hall with hooks for coats, a rack for boots. Dante hung her coat beside a worn waxed jacket then opened an inner door to a distinctly masculine apartment.

There were tribal rugs from North Africa on the broad planks of a timber floor gleaming with the patina of age, splashes of brilliantly coloured modern art on the walls, shelves crammed with books. There was the warm glow and welcoming scent of logs burning in a wood stove and an enormous old leather sofa pulled up invitingly in front of it. The kind with big rounded arms—perfect for curling up against—and thick squashy cushions.

'You live here,' she said stupidly.

'Yes.' His face was expressionless as he tossed her bag

onto the sofa. 'I'm told that it's very lower middle class to live over the shop but it suits me.'

'Well, that's just a load of tosh.'

'Tosh?' he repeated, as if he'd never heard the word before. Maybe he hadn't but it hardly needed explaining. It was all there in the sound.

'Total tosh. One day I'm going to live in a house exactly like this,' she said, turning around so that she could take in every detail. 'The top floor for me, workshops on the floor below me and a showroom on the ground floor—' she came to halt, facing him '—and my great-grandfather was the younger son of an earl.'

'An earl?'

Realising just how pompous that must have sounded, Geli said, 'Of course my grandmother defied her father and married beneath her, so we're not on His Lordship's Christmas card list, which may very well prove the point. Not that they're on ours,' she added.

'They disowned her?'

She shrugged. 'Apparently they had other, more obedient children.'

And that was more personal information than she'd shared with anyone, ever, but she didn't want him to think any of them gave a fig for their aristocratic relations. Even *in extremis* they'd never turned to them for help.

'The family, narrow-minded and full of secrets, is the source of all our discontents,' Dante replied, clearly quoting someone.

'Who said that?' she asked.

'I just did.'

'No, I meant…' She shook her head. He knew exactly what she meant. 'I have a great family.' For years it had just been the four of them. Her sisters, Elle and Sorrel, and their grandmother. They'd been solid. A tight-knit unit standing against the world. That had all changed the day a stranger had arrived on the doorstep with an ice cream van. Now her sisters were not only successful business-women, but married and producing babies as if they were going out of fashion, while Great-Uncle Basil—who'd sent the van—and Grandma were warming their old bones in the south of France.

'You are very fortunate.'

'Yes…' If you ignored the empty space left by her mother. By an unknown father. By the legions of aunts, uncles, cousins that she didn't know. Who didn't know her.

'The bathroom is through here,' Dante said, opening a door to an inner hall.

'*Il bagno…*' she said brightly, making an effort to think in Italian as she followed him. Making an effort to think.

His *bagno* would, in estate agent speak, have been de-scribed as a 'roomy vintage-style' bathroom. In this case she was pretty certain the fittings—a stately roll-top bath with claw feet and gleaming brass taps, a loo with a high tank and a wide, deep washbasin—were the real deal.

'I'll shut the door so that you can put the kitten down,' he said, and the roominess shrank in direct proportion to the width of his shoulders as he shut the door. 'He can't escape.'

'I wouldn't bank on it,' she said as, carefully unhook-ing the creature's claws from the front of her dress, she set it down in the bath. 'And if it went under the *bagno…*' She left him to imagine what fun it would be trying to tempt him out.

Dante glanced down as the kitten, a tiny front paw rest-ing against the steep side of the bath, protested at this in-dignity. 'Smart thinking.'

'When you've taken a room apart looking for a kitten that's managed to squeeze through a crack in the skirting board,' she told him, 'you learn to keep them confined.'

'You live an interesting life, Angelica Amery,' he said,

watching as she attempted to slip the buttons at her wrist
without getting blood on her dress.

'Isn't that a curse in China?' she asked.

'I believe that would be "May you live in interesting
times",' he said, 'but you'll forgive me if I say that you
don't dress like a woman in search of a quiet life.'

'Well, you know what they say,' she replied. 'Life is
short. Eat ice cream every day.'

A smile deepened the lines bracketing his mouth,
fanned out from his eyes. 'What "they" would that be?'

'More of an "it", actually. It's Rosie, our vintage ice
cream van. In her *Little Book of Ice Cream*.' He looked
confused—who wouldn't? 'Of course she has a vested
interest.'

'Right…'

'It's the sentiment that matters, Dante. You can sub-
stitute whatever lifts your spirits. Chocolate? Cherries?'
No response. 'Cheese?' she offered, hoping to make him
laugh. Or at least smile.

'Permesso?' He indicated her continuing struggle with
shaky fingers and fiddly buttons.

Okay, it wasn't that funny and, giving up on the buttons, she surrendered her hand. *'Prego.'*

He carefully unfastened the loops holding the cuff together, folded the sleeve back out of the way, then, taking hold of her wrist, he pumped a little liquid soap into
her palm.

Her heart rate, which was already going well over the
speed limit, accelerated and, on the point of telling him
that she could handle it from here, she took her own advice. Okay, it wasn't ice cream or even chocolate, but how
often was a seriously scrumptious man going to take her
hand between his and—?

'Coraggio,' he murmured as his thumb brushed her
palm and a tiny whimper escaped her lips.

'Mmm…'

He turned to look at her, the edge of his faintly stubbled jaw an enticing whisper away from her lips. 'Does that sting?'

'No…' She shook her head. 'That's not…stinging.'

She was feeling no pain as he gently massaged the soap between her fingers, around her thumb, wrist and into her palm. All sensation was centred much lower as he rinsed off the soap, pulled a thick white towel from a pile and carefully dried her hand.

'*Va bene?*' he asked.

'*Va bene,*' she repeated. Very, very *bene* indeed. He was so deliciously gentle. So very *thorough*.

'Hold on. This *will* sting,' he warned as he took a box of antiseptic wipes from the cupboard over the sink and opened a pouch.

'I'll try not to scream,' she said but, taking no chances— her knees were in a pitifully weak state—she did as she was told and, putting her other hand on his shoulder, hung on.

She'd feel such a fool if she collapsed at his feet.

Really.

His shoulder felt wonderfully solid beneath the soft wool shirt. He was so close that she was breathing in the scent of coffee, warm male skin and, as his hair slid in a thick silky wedge over his forehead, she took a hit of the herby shampoo he used. It completely obliterated the sharp smell of antiseptic.

He opened a dressing and applied it carefully to the soft mound of flesh beneath her thumb.

'All done.'

'No…'

Dante looked up, a silent query buckling the space between his brows and her mouth dried. He'd been right about the need to hang on. The word had slipped through her lips while her brain was fully occupied in keeping her vertical.

'There's something else?' he asked.

'Yes… No…' She hadn't been criticising his first aid skills; she just hadn't wanted him to stop. 'It's nothing.'

'Tell me,' he pressed her, all concern.

What on earth could she say? The answer that instantly popped into her mind was totally outrageous but Dante was waiting and she managed a careless little shrug and waited for him to catch on.

Nothing…

For heaven's sake, everyone knew what you did when someone hurt themselves. Did she have to spell it out for him?

'Un bacio?' she prompted.

'A kiss?' he repeated, no doubt wondering if she had the least clue what she was saying.

'Sì…' It was in an Italian phrasebook that her middle sister, Sorrel, had bought her. Under 'People', sub-section 'Getting Intimate', which she'd found far more engrossing than the section on buying a train ticket.

Posso baciarti?—Can I kiss you?—was there, along with other such useful phrases as *Can I buy you a drink?*, *Let's go somewhere quieter* and *Stop bothering me!*

There hadn't been a phrase for kissing it better. Perhaps it was in the 'Health' section.

'This is considered beneficial?' Dante asked.

He was regarding her with such earnestness that Geli wished the floor would just open up and swallow her. Then the flicker of a muscle at the corner of his mouth betrayed him and she knew that Dante Vettori had been teasing her. That he'd known exactly what she meant. That it was going to be all right. Better than all right—the man wasn't just fabulous to look at; he had a sense of humour.

'Not just beneficial,' she assured him. 'It's absolutely essential.'

'Forgive me. I couldn't have been paying attention when this was covered in first aid,' he said, the muscle working overtime to contain the smile fighting to break out. 'You may have to show me.'

Show him? Excitement rippled through her at the thought. It was outrageous but a woman in search of an interesting life had to seize the day. Lick the ice cream—

Coraggio, Geli—

'It's very simple, Dante. You just put your lips together—'

'Like this?'

She caught her breath as he raised her hand and, never taking his eyes from hers, touched his lips to the soft mound of her palm, just below the dressing he'd applied with such care.

'Exactly like that,' she managed through a throat that felt as if it had been stuffed with silk chiffon. 'I'm not sure why it works—'

'I imagine it's to do with the application of heat,' he said, his voice as soft as the second warm kiss he breathed into her palm. Her knees turned to water and her hand slid from his shoulder to clutch a handful of shirt. Beneath it, she could feel the thud of his heartbeat—a slow, steady counterpoint to her own racing pulse. 'Is that hot enough?'

Was he still teasing? The threatened smile had never appeared but his mouth was closer. Much closer.

'The more heat,' she murmured, her words little more than a whisper, 'the more effective the cure.'

'How hot do you want it to be, Angelica?' His voice trickled over her skin like warm honey and his eyes were asking the question that had been there since he'd turned and looked at her. Since he'd put his hand on hers and moved it across the map.

His hand was at her back now, supporting her, his breath soft against her lips and her answer was to lift the hand he'd kissed, slide her fingers through his dark silky hair. This close, she could see that the velvet dark of his irises was shot through with tiny gold sparks, sparks that arced between them, igniting some primitive part of her brain.

'Hot,' she murmured. *'Molto, molto caldo...'* And she touched his luscious lower lip with her mouth, her tongue, sucking in the taste of rich dark coffee that lingered there. Maybe it was the caffeine—on her tongue on his—but, as she closed her eyes and he angled his mouth to deepen the kiss, cradled her head, she felt a zingy hyper-tingle of heat lick through her veins, seep into her skin, warming her, giving her life.

'Hello?' Lisa's voice filtered through the golden mist. 'Everything okay?' she called, just feet from the bathroom door and, from the urgency with which she said it, Geli suspected that it wasn't the first time she'd asked.

Geli opened her eyes as Dante raised his head, took a step back, steadying her as a cold space opened up between them where before there had been closeness, heat.

'Don't open the door or the kitten will escape,' he warned sharply.

'Right... I just meant to tell you that there are antiseptic wipes in the cabinet.'

'I found them.' His hand slid from her shoulder and he reached for the door handle. 'We're all done.'

Noooo... But he'd already opened the door and stepped through it, closing it behind him. Leaving her alone to catch her breath, put some stiffeners in her knees and recover what little dignity remained after she'd flung herself at a total stranger.

Okay, there had been some heavy-duty flirting going on, but most of it had been on her side. Dante, realising that she was in a mess, had tried to sit her down and quietly explain about the apartment while she had put on a display that wouldn't have disgraced a burlesque dancer. One minute she'd been struggling with her glove and the next...

Where on earth had that performance come from? She wasn't that woman.

Bad enough, but when he'd told her that she'd been the victim of some Internet con she'd practically thrown herself at him.

What on earth had she been *thinking*?

What on earth must *he* be thinking?

Well, that was easy. He had to be thinking that she'd do anything in return for a bed for the night and who could blame him?

As for her, she hadn't been thinking at all. She might have been telling herself that she was going to grab every moment, live her mother's 'seize the day' philosophy, but it was like learning how to parachute: you had to make practice jumps first—learn how to fall before you leapt out of a plane or the landing was going to be painful.

Cheeks burning, her mouth throbbing with heat, she dampened the corner of the towel he'd used to dry her hand and laid it against her hot face before, legs shaking, she sank down onto the side of the bath.

'Mum,' she whispered, her head on her knees. 'Help...'

CHAPTER THREE

'Ice cream is cheaper than therapy and you don't need an appointment.'
—from *Rosie's Little Book of Ice Cream*

DANTE WALKED INTO the kitchen, filled a glass with ice-cold water from the fridge and downed it in one. The only effect was to make him feel as if he had steam coming out of his ears and, from the way Lisa was looking at him, he very well might have.

Angelica...

Her name suggested something white and gold in a Renaissance painting, but no Renaissance angel ever had a body, legs like that. A mouth that felt like a kiss from across the room. A kiss that obliterated every thought but to possess her.

He hadn't looked at a woman in that way, touched a woman in that way for over a year but when he'd turned, seen her crimson mouth, the one jolt of colour against the unrelieved black of her clothes, her hair, against skin that looked as if it had never seen the sun, every cell in his body had sat up and begged to go to hell.

Someone must have been listening...

Dark Angel was right.

Aware that Lisa was regarding him with undisguised amusement, brows raised a fraction, he stared right back at her, daring her to say a word. She grinned knowingly then turned away as Angelica finally joined them.

'How did he do?' Lisa asked. 'Has he earned his first aid badge?'

'Gold star,' Angelica replied, holding out her hand for inspection. She was doing a good job of matching Lisa's jokey tone but she wasn't looking at him and there was a betraying pink flush across her cheekbones.

'Did you find a box, Lis?' he asked sharply.

'I have *this* box,' she said, 'thoroughly lined with news-paper.' She looked down at the deep box she was holding and then up at him, her brows a *got you* millimetre higher and he could have kicked himself. So much for attempt-ing to distract her. 'Chef gave me some minced chicken for Rattino. I assumed you'd have milk up here.'

'I have, but it'll be cold,' he said, grabbing the excuse to escape. 'I'll put a drop in the microwave to take the chill off.'

'Thank you. That's very kind,' Angelica replied qui-etly as she took the box from Lisa and retreated to the bathroom. He watched her walk away, trying not to think about what her legs were doing to him. What he wanted to do to her legs…

He turned abruptly, opened the fridge door, poured some milk into a saucer and put it in the microwave for a few seconds.

'Haven't you got something to do downstairs?' he asked as, feeling like an idiot with Lisa watching, he put a finger in to test the temperature.

'It's snowing hard now. Everyone's making a move and I've told the staff to go home.' She leaned against the door frame. 'What are you going to do about Geli?'

'Do?'

'If it's true about her apartment.'

'It's true about Via Pepone,' he said. 'My father demolished it last year. He's about to put a glass box in its place.'

'That's the place—?'

'Yes,' he said, cutting her off before she said any more.

'Right.' She waited a moment and then glanced towards the bathroom. 'So?'

'So what?' he snapped.

'So what are you going to do about Geli?'

'Why should I do anything?' he demanded. 'My father may have demolished the street but he didn't con her out of rent for an apartment that no longer exists.' Lisa didn't say anything but her body language was very loud. 'What do you expect me to do, Lis? Pick her up and put her in my pocket like one of her strays? Have we got a cardboard box big enough?'

'No,' she said. 'But she's been travelling all day, it's late and, in case you hadn't noticed, it's snowing out there.'

'I'd noticed.' Snowflakes had been clinging to Angelica's hair and face when she'd arrived. She'd licked one off her upper lip as she'd walked towards him.

'That's it?' Lisa asked. 'That's all you've got?'

'Lis…'

'It's okay; don't worry about it.' She raised a hand in a gesture that was pure Italian. 'I've got a room she can have.'

'A room?'

'Four walls, ceiling, bed—'

'I wasn't asking for a definition,' he said, 'I was questioning the reality. You and Baldacci live in a one-bedroom flat and Angelica's legs would hang over the end of your sofa.' He could picture them. Long legs, short skirt, sexy boots—

'The sofa is a non-starter,' she agreed, 'but the room is here, just along the corridor. Right next to yours.'

That jolted him out of his fantasy. 'That's not your room!'

'No? Whose clothes are hanging in the wardrobe? Whose book is on the bedside table? Nonnina Rosa believes that it's my room and that, my dear cousin, makes it a fact.'

'Nonnina Rosa is on the other side of the world.'

'She's just a second away in cyber space. You wouldn't want her to discover that when I selflessly volunteered—'

'Selflessly? *Madonna!*'

'—when I selflessly volunteered to come halfway across the world to pick up the pieces and glue you back together, you did nothing to stop me from moving in with a Baldacci?' She mimed her grandmother spitting at the mention of the hated name. 'Would you?'

'The only reason you're here is because Vanni Baldacci's father sent him to his Milan office to keep him out of the scheming clutches of a Vettori.'

'Epic fail. The darling man has just texted me to say he's on his way with my gumboots and a brolly.'

'Lisa, please…'

'Nonnina was desperately worried about you, Dan. She felt responsible—'

'What happened had nothing to do with her. It was my choice. And you were about as much use as a chocolate teapot,' he added before she could rerun what had happened. It was over, done with. 'The only reason I keep you on is because no one else will employ you.'

She lifted her shoulders in a theatrical shrug. 'Whatever,' she said, not bothering to challenge him. 'Of course, if you object so strongly to Geli having my room you could always invite her to share yours.'

'Go away, Lisa, or I swear I'll call Nonnina myself. Or maybe I should speak to Nicolo Baldacci.'

'How long is it, exactly, since you got laid, Dan?' she asked, not in the least bothered by a threat that they both knew he would never carry out. 'It's time to forget Valentina. You need to get back on the horse.'

He picked up the saucer of milk and waited for her to move.

'I mean it. You've been looking at Geli like a starving man who's been offered hot food ever since she walked through the door,' she said, staying right where she was. 'In fact, if I were a betting woman I'd be offering straight odds that you were taking the first mouthful when I interrupted you.'

'I met her less than an hour ago,' he reminded her, trying not to think about the feel of Angelica's tongue on his lip even as he sucked it in to taste her. Coffee, honey, life…

'An hour can be a lifetime when lightning strikes. I wanted to rip Vanni's clothes off the minute I set eyes on him,' she said with the kind of smile that suggested it hadn't been much longer than that.

'I'm not about to take advantage of a damsel in distress.'

'Not even if she wants you to take advantage of her? She looked…interested.'

'Not even then,' he said, trying not to think about her crimson lips whispering *'caldo...'*, her breath against his mouth, the way she'd leaned into him, how her body fitted against his.

'You are so damned English under that Italian exterior,' she said. 'Always the perfect gentleman. Never betraying so much as a quiver of emotion, even when the damsel in question is stomping all over you in her designer stilettos.'

'Valentina knew what she wanted. I was the one who moved the goalposts.'

'Don't be so damned noble. You fall in love with the man, Dan, not some fancy penthouse, the villa at Lake Como, the A-list lifestyle. I'd live in a cave with Vanni.'

'Then talk to your parents before your secret blows up

in your faces.' Dante had experienced that pain at first-hand... 'It won't go away, Lis.'

'No.' She pulled a face, muttered, 'Stupid feud...' Then she reached out and touched his arm. 'I'll leave you to it. Good luck with finding a hotel that'll take Rattino,' she said, heading towards the door. She didn't get more than a couple of steps before she stopped, turned round. 'I suppose Geli could put him back in her coat pocket and sneak him in—'

'Are you done?' he asked, losing patience.

'—but it will only be a temporary solution. Tonight's scene in the bar will be the talk of the market tomorrow.'

'The snow will be the talk of the market tomorrow.'

She shook her head. 'It snows every year but the combination of a head-turning woman, the rare sound of Dante Vettori laughing and a rat? Now that is something worth talking about.'

'Lis,' he warned.

'Never mind. I'm sure you'll think of something.'

'You don't want to know what I'm thinking.'

She grinned. 'I know exactly what you're thinking. You and every man in the bar when she arrived in a flurry of snowflakes. How to make an entrance! Tra-la-la...' Lisa blew on her fingers and then shook them. 'Seriously, Dan, I don't know if Geli needs a job but she will need space to show her stuff and having her around will be very good for business.'

'Are you done now?'

'As for the other thing, my advice is to get in quickly or you're going to be at the back of a very long queue.' She almost made it to the door before she said, 'You won't forget that you offered her supper? Have you got anything up here or do you want me to look in the fridge?'

'Just lock up and go home.'

'Okay.' She opened the door, looked back over her

shoulder. 'I've brought up Geli's suitcase, by the way. It's in her room.'

'Basta! Andare!'

'And you have lipstick—' she pointed to the corner of her own mouth '—just here.'

Geli's hands were shaking as she scooped out a tiny portion of chicken for the kitten, her whole body trembling as she sank to her knees beside the bath, resting her chin on her arms as she watched him practically inhale it. Trying to decide which was most disturbing—kissing a man she'd only just met or being told that the flat she'd paid good money to rent did not exist.

It should be the flat. Obviously.

Elle was going to be furious with her for being so careless. Her grandmother had lost everything but the roof over their heads to a con man not long after their mother died. Without their big sister putting her own life on hold to take care of them all, she and Sorrel would have ended up in care.

Fortunately, there was the width of France and Switzerland between them. Unless she told them what had happened they would never know that she'd messed up.

Which left the kiss. Which was ridiculous. It wasn't as if it was her first kiss—her first anything—but for a moment she'd felt as if she'd been on the brink of something rare, something life-changing.

As she leaned against the edge of the bath watching the kitten, she remembered the moment when she'd caught her sister on the point of kissing Sean McElroy. Their closeness, the intensity of their focus on each other, had terrified her. Elle was hers—surrogate mother, surrogate father, big sister, carer—but suddenly there was someone else, this man, a total stranger, getting all her attention.

For a moment, with Dante's arm around her waist, his

lips a millimetre from her own, she'd known how Elle had felt, had wanted it for herself. That was why she was shaking. For a moment she had been utterly defenceless...

'I'm sorry I took so long to bring the milk. I was arranging with Lisa to lock up for me.' Dante placed the saucer in the bath but, instead of joining her, he stood back, keeping his distance.

Which was a very good thing, she told herself. Just because she wanted him here, kneeling beside her, didn't make it a good idea...

'We're putting you to a lot of trouble,' she said, keeping her eyes fixed on the kitten as he stepped in the saucer and lapped clumsily at the milk.

'He's looking better already,' he said, his voice as distant as his body.

'He's fluffed up a bit now he's dry but he hasn't learned to wash.' Keep it impersonal. Talk about the cat... 'He's much too young to be separated from his mother. I'll take him back to where I found him tomorrow and see if I can reunite them.'

'How do you think that will work out?' he asked.

'About as well as it usually does.' She reached out and ran a finger over the kitten's tiny domed head. 'About as well as my escape to Isola is working out.'

'Escape? What are you running away from?'

She looked up. He was frowning, evidently concerned. 'Just life in a small village,' she said quickly before he began wondering which asylum she'd broken out of. 'Conformity. I very nearly succumbed to the temptation to buckle down to reality and become the design director for my sisters' ice cream parlour franchise.' She did a little mock shiver. 'Can you *imagine*? All that *pink*!'

He snorted with laughter.

'You see? You only met me half an hour ago but even you can see that's ridiculous.'

'Let's just say that I find it unlikely.'

'Thank you, Dante. You couldn't have paid me a nicer compliment.' She hooked her hair behind her ear, stood up and faced him. *Forget the kiss...* 'And thank you for trying to break the news about my apartment gently over supper.'

He shrugged. 'I wanted more information before I leapt in with the bad news,' he said, turning away to reach for a towel. 'You could have made a mistake with the address.'

'But you didn't believe I had.'

'No.' He stopped looking down at the towel and looked at her. 'The map you had was out of date. If you had followed the directions you were given, you would have ended up at a construction site.'

'Which I did,' she admitted. 'Lisa was right when she said you know Isola like the back of your hand.'

'I spent a lot of my childhood here but it's changing fast. We're struggling to hang on to what's left.'

'You'll forgive me if I say that I wish you'd struggled a little harder.' He didn't exactly flinch but clearly she'd said the wrong thing. 'I'm sorry. It's not your fault.'

'Here, Rattino will be more comfortable on this,' he said. 'Bring the box through to the fire when he's settled.'

She looked down at the towel he'd thrust into her hand and then at the space where, a moment before, Dante Vettori had been standing.

What had she said?

Everything about Dante was still except the hand holding the wooden spoon as he stirred something in a saucepan. The light glinting off the heavy steel band of his wristwatch was mesmerising and Geli could have stood in the doorway and watched him for ever.

'Is he settled?' he asked without looking up.

'Asleep and dreaming he's in heaven,' she said. 'Life

is so simple when you're a cat.' She held up the lease that was currently severely complicating hers.

He turned down the heat and took it from her. 'There's no mistake about the address,' he said.

'No. I have Signora Franco's number,' she said, clutching the phone she'd used to tell her sisters that she'd arrived safely. Well, she'd arrived... 'If I call her will you talk to her?'

'Of course.'

The wait to connect seemed endless but, in the end, was nowhere near long enough.

'No reply?' he asked when she let the phone drop to her side.

She shook her head. 'The message was in Italian, but "number unavailable" sounds the same in any language.'

He shook his head. 'Tell me, Angelica, how did you learn such impressive self-control?'

She held her breath momentarily. Let it out slowly. 'Self-control?'

'Few women I know—few men, come to that—would have taken the news about the apartment without throwing something, even if it was just a tantrum.'

'Oh...' Momentarily thrown, she said, 'I don't do tantrums.'

'Is there a secret to that? Anything you're prepared to share with Lisa?' he asked.

'Yoga?' she offered. 'It's all in the breathing.'

He turned back to the sauce without a word, stirring it very slowly.

Damn it, she didn't know him... He might regret kissing her but he'd been kind when he didn't have to be. He hadn't yelled at her, or thrown her or the kitten out when they'd caused a near riot in his café.

She took one of those yoga breaths.

'I cried a lot when my mother died. It made things difficult at school and my sisters sad because there was nothing they could do to make things better.' This was something she never talked about and the words escaped in a soft rush of breath. 'I wanted to stop but I didn't know how.'

'How old were you?' He continued to stir the sauce, not looking at her.

'Eight.' Two days short of her ninth birthday.

'Eight?' He swung round. *Madre de Dio...*

'It was cancer,' she said before he asked. 'The aggressive kind, where the diagnosis comes with weeks to live.'

Non c'è niente che posso dire,' he said. And then, in English, 'There are no words…'

'No.' She shook her head. 'There's nothing anyone can say. No words, not an entire river of tears… Nothing can change what happened.'

'Is that when you stopped crying?' he asked. 'When you realised it made no difference?'

'I was eight, Dante!' So much for her self-control…

'So?' he prompted, 'you were too young for philosophy but clearly something happened.'

'What? Oh, yes… My grandmother found an old black hat in the attic. With a floppy brim,' she said, describing in with a wavy gesture. 'Crocheted. Very Sixties. My grandmother was something of a style icon in her day.'

'And that helped?' he asked, ignoring the fashion note that was meant to draw a thick black line under the subject.

'She said that when I was sad I could hide behind the brim.' She still remembered the moment she'd put it on. The feeling of a great burden being lifted from her shoulders. 'It showed the world what I was feeling without the red eyes and snot and was a lot easier for everyone to live with. I wore that hat until it fell apart.'

'And then what did you do?'

'I found a black cloche in a charity shop. And a black

dress. It was too big for me but my grandmother helped me cut it down. Then, when I was twelve, I dyed my hair.'

'Let me guess. Black.'

'Actually, it was nearer green but my grandmother took me to the hairdressers' and had it sorted out and dyed properly.' The memory of the moment when she'd looked in the mirror and seen herself still made her smile. 'My sisters were furious.'

'Because of the colour or because they hadn't had the same treat?'

'Because Grandma had blown all the housekeeping money on rescuing me from the nightmare of going to school with green hair. They thought eating was more important.'

'Hunger has a tendency to shorten the temper,' he agreed, turning the sauce down to minimum and pouring two glasses of wine from a bottle, dewed with moisture, that stood on the china-laden dresser that took up most of one wall.

'Where was your father in all this?' he asked as he handed a glass to her.

'I don't have one. None of us do.'

His eyebrows rose a fraction. 'Unless there's been a major leap forward in evolution that passed me by,' he said, leaning back against the dresser, 'that's not possible.'

'Biologically perhaps, but while my mother loved babies, she didn't want a man underfoot, being moody when his dinner wasn't ready.' She turned and, glass in hand, leaned back against the dresser. It was easier being beside him than looking at him. 'My grandparents' marriage was not a happy one.' She took a mouthful of the rich, fruity wine. 'I imagine the first time she got pregnant it was an accident, but after that, whenever she was broody, she helped herself to a sperm donation from some man she took a fancy to. A travelling fair visits the village every year for the Late Spring Bank Holiday,' she said. 'Our fathers were setting up in the next county before the egg divided.'

'She lived dangerously.'

'She lived for the moment.'

'"Take what you want," says God, "take it and pay for it…"' He glanced sideways at her. 'It's an old Spanish proverb. So? What colour is your hair?'

She picked up a strand, looked at it, then up at him. 'Black.'

He grinned and it wasn't just the wine that was warming her.

'How did you find it?' he asked. 'The apartment.'

'What? Oh…' Well, that was short-lived… 'On the internet.' He didn't have to say what he thought about that. A muscle tightening at the corner of his mouth wrote an entire essay on the subject. 'It was an international agency,' she protested, 'affiliated to goodness knows how many associations.' Not that she'd checked on any of them. Who did? 'There were comments from previous tenants. Some who'd enjoyed their stay in the apartment and couldn't wait to come back, and a few disgruntled remarks about the heat and the lack of air conditioning. Exactly what you'd expect. Look, I'll show you,' she said, clicking the link on her smartphone.

Like the phone line, the web link was no longer available.

Until that moment she hadn't believed that she'd been conned, had been sure that it was all a mistake, but now the air was sucked right out of her and Dante caught her as her knees buckled, rescued her glass, turned her into his chest.

His arm was around her, her head against his shoulder and the temptation to stay there and allow him to hold her, comfort her, almost overwhelmed her. It felt so right, he was such a perfect fit, but she'd already made a fool of herself once today. She dragged in a deep breath, straightened her shoulders and stepped away.

'Are you okay?' he said, his hand still outstretched to steady her.

'Fine. Really.'

He didn't look convinced. 'When did you last have something to eat?'

'I don't know. I had a sandwich at the airport when they announced that my flight had been delayed.'

'Nothing since then?' He looked horrified. 'No wonder you're trembling. Sit down while the pasta cooks.' He tested it. 'Another minute or two. It's nothing fancy—*pasta al funghi*. Pasta with mushroom sauce,' he added in case her Italian wasn't up to it.

She shook her head. 'I'm sure it's wonderful but, honestly, I couldn't eat a thing.' He didn't argue but reached for a couple of dishes. 'The apartment looked so perfect and the rent was so reasonable...' *Stupid, stupid, stupid!* 'I assumed it was because it was the middle of winter, off-season, but it was a trap for the gullible. No, make that the cheap.' She'd had it hammered into her by Elle that if something looked too good... But she'd been enchanted.

'Did you give them details of your bank account?' Dante asked.

'What? No... At least...I set up a direct debit for the rent...' As she realised what he was getting at, she blinked, looked down at her phone and then swiftly keyed in her password.

As she saw the balance she felt the blood leave her head.

CHAPTER FOUR

*'When things are bad, send ice cream. With hot
fudge sauce, sprinkles and mini-marshmallows.'*
—from *Rosie's Little Book of Ice Cream*

'MADONNA...'

Dante caught her before she hit the floor and carried
her through to the living room. He placed her gently on
the sofa, her head flat and her feet propped up on the arm,
and knelt beside her until she opened her eyes.

For a moment they were blank as she tried to work out
what had happened, where she was.

'Angelica...' She blinked, focused, saw him, tried to sit
up but he put a hand on her shoulder. 'Lie still for a moment. Breathe...'

He'd thought she was pale before but now she was white,
emphasising the size of those extraordinary silver fox eyes,
the splendour of her luscious crimson mouth.

'What happened?'

'You fainted.'

She groaned. 'How unutterably pathetic.'

'The combination of shock and a lack of food,' he suggested. Then, as she made an effort to sit up, 'No. Stay
there. I'll get you some water.'

'Dante—' For a moment she challenged him, but then

sank back against the cushion. 'Why do you call me Angelica?'

'Geli is not a name for a grown woman.'

'Oh…' She thought about it for a moment. 'Right.'

Once he was sure that she was going to stay put, he fetched a glass of water from the kitchen. Angelica had dropped her phone and, as he bent to pick it up, he saw why she'd fainted. The con artists had cleaned her out.

He half expected her to be sitting up, fretting when he returned but she was exactly where he'd left her, flat on her back but with one arm thrown across her eyes. The gesture had pulled up her dress, exposing even more of her thighs, and it was a toss-up whether he gave her the water or threw it over himself.

'Here,' he said, 'take a sip of this.'

She removed her arm, turned her head to look up at him. 'Your first aid skills are being thoroughly tested this evening.'

'I may have been a bit slow on the kissing-it-better cure,' he assured her, 'but I remembered the head down, feet up recovery position for a faint.'

'Gold star. I said so…' She made a move to sit up and take the glass.

'Don't sit up too quickly,' he said, slipping his arm beneath her shoulders to support her while he held it to her lips.

'Sì, dottore…' She managed a smile which, under the circumstances, was pretty brave but drew unnecessary attention to her mouth. The temptation to see just how much kissing it would take to make this better was almost irresistible. So much for his declaration to Lisa about not taking advantage…

Putting the glass down on the end table, he moved to the safety of her feet.

'What are you doing?' she asked when he slid a hand beneath her ankle and reached for the zip of her boot.

'Taking off your boots. Didn't they teach you that at your very comprehensive first aid course?'

'Absolutely. It came right after kissing it better, but I thought you were absent that day.'

'It's just common sense. Everyone feels better with their boots off.'

'That's true,' she said, stretching her foot and wiggling her long toes. Apparently there was no 'safe end' when it came to Angelica Amery, and he quickly dispensed with the second boot and took a step away.

'Okay. You can sit up when you feel up to it,' he said, 'but slowly. Take your time.'

She eased herself up into the corner of the sofa, smoothing her skirt down and tucking her feet beneath her. 'What happened to my phone, Dante? I have to call the bank.'

He took it from his pocket and handed it to her.

'You saw?' she asked.

'When I picked it up. Will they refund you?'

She sighed. 'Not the first month's rent and deposit, that's for sure. I created the direct debit so that was a legitimate withdrawal as far as they're concerned. The rest would appear to be straightforward fraud so I should get that back. Eventually.' She found the number in her contact list and hit call. 'After they've done everything in their power to imply that it's my fault.' She looked up at him. 'Dante…'

'Angelica?'

'Thank you. For catching me.'

'Any time.'

The jet brooch at her throat moved as she swallowed down her emotions. 'You rate a gold star while I'm a triple chocolate idiot. With fudge topping. And sprinkles.'

'You won't be the only one who's been caught.'

'That doesn't make me feel any less stupid.' She shook

her head then winced, clearly wishing she hadn't, and he had a hand out to comfort her before he could stop himself. Fortunately, she was listening to the prompts and didn't see. 'I should have run some checks, but we'd found a short-term tenant for the house and it was all a bit of a rush.'

'You've let your home in England?'

'Yes.' So, even if she wanted to, she couldn't run for home… 'My sisters moved out when they married so it was just me, Grandma and Great-Uncle Basil. Grandma's arthritis was playing up and Basil wanted to take her somewhere warm for the winter so we decided to let the house to finance it—'

'And you were in a rush to escape from the horror of all that pink and white ice cream.'

'I shouldn't mock it.' She managed a somewhat watery smile. 'Ice cream has been very good to my family and, let's face it, art and fashion have never been safe career choices.'

'We do what we have to.'

'Yes…'

Leaving her to speak to the bank, he returned to the kitchen. She might think she had no appetite, but if it was put in front of her it was possible that she would be tempted.

When he returned, with a tray containing two bowls of *pasta al funghi*, a couple of forks and some napkins, she was staring into the fire.

'Sorted?' he asked, and she surprised him with a grin. 'What?'

'"*Sorted…*" You sound so Italian and yet you use English as if it was your first language. It sounds odd.'

'Not that odd. My mother is English.'

'That has to help,' she said.

'That and the fact that when she left my father she took

me with her to England and refused to speak another word
of Italian for as long as she lives.'

'Tough on you.'

He shrugged but there was nothing like a reminder of
that first endless cold, wet English summer hearing, speaking only an alien language, to dampen his libido.

Her eyes softened. 'How old were you?'

He handed her a fork, wishing he'd kept his mouth shut.
'Twelve, just coming up to my thirteenth birthday.'

'A bad age.'

'Is there a good one?'

She shook her head. 'I guess not, but it was tough
enough to be faced with your parents splitting up without
losing your home, your language.'

'My mother was angry, hurt...' He shrugged. 'She'd
discovered that my father had been having an affair with
the woman she thought was her best friend. She offered
me the choice to go with her or to stay in Italy.'

'And you chose her.'

'She needed me more than he did.' He passed her a
bowl of pasta. 'Eat...'

She looked at the dish she was holding as if unsure how
it had got there but, as he'd hoped, she was too well-man-
nered not to eat food put in front of her. 'It smells very
good,' she said politely and took a mouthful.

'Life is short,' he said as he settled at the far end of the
sofa. 'Eat pasta every day.'

'I have to admit that on a cold, snowy Milan night it's
the perfect comfort food.' Her brave attempt at a smile
lit up her eyes, fringed with thick lashes and set in a soft
smudge of charcoal. It went straight to his groin and he
propped his foot on one knee in an attempt to keep that
fact to himself. The kiss had been a mistake. Kissing anyone was a mistake... 'Of course, come spring I might be

persuaded to make you a Bellini sorbet and then it would be a close run thing,' she added.

'A Bellini sorbet?' he repeated, mentally grabbing onto the thought of something ice-cold slipping down his throat.

'Fresh peach juice, Prosecco… The real thing, sparkling on the tongue, but frozen.' She raised her eyebrows. 'Oh, I see. You thought my sisters use mass-produced vegetable fat goo for their events business.'

He shrugged. 'The British are not famous for their ice cream.'

'Unlike Italians?'

'I believe you mentioned an ice cream van? If it's one of those stop-me-and-buy-one vans it won't be loaded up with Bellini sorbet.'

'True, but Rosie is a bit special. She goes to children's parties, hen nights, weddings…any fun bash that ice cream is going to enhance.'

'Is there a demand for that?'

'Huge. Of course, the fact that she makes the occasional appearance in a popular television soap opera means that we could book her three times over. We…they…my sisters…also make bespoke ices for weddings, corporate events and the like—that's the Bellini sorbet market—and now Sorrel, she's the sister with the business brain, is franchising a chain of retro American-style ice cream parlours.'

'And you design the interiors?'

With luck, talking would keep her mind off the non-existent flat until she'd finished the pasta. He prompted her to talk about how the business had evolved, looked at the photographs on her phone of the ice cream parlours she'd designed. She was very talented…

'So, you're a designer, an ice cream maker and you rescue kittens in your spare time?' he asked.

'Rescue is a two-way thing, Dante. People think that

cats are selfish, but I've seen them respond to need in their owners and in other animals.'

As she looked up at him from under those heavy lashes he found himself wondering who, in the kitten scenario, was rescuing whom. He sensed something deeper than a desire to paint, design, experience Italy behind her 'escape', but they were already way too deep into personal territory; he had no wish to hear more.

Maybe she sensed it too because she took another mouthful of the pasta. 'This is really good.'

'Wait until you try chef's *Risotto alla Milanese*. Arborio rice from the Po Valley, butter, dry white wine, saffron and Parmigiano-Reggiano.' Food was always a safe topic. 'I'm sorry you missed it but, with the weather closing in, Lisa sent everyone home.'

'Now that is really impressive.'

'Sending staff home early on a bad night?'

She shook her head, then said, 'Well, yes, but I was referring to your ability to name the ingredients in the risotto recipe.'

He shrugged. 'Nonnina used to make it for me,' he said.

'Nonnina? That's your grandmother, right?'

'Actually, she's Lisa's grandmother, my great-aunt, but everyone calls her Nonnina,' he said. 'Café Rosa was her bar until she finally surrendered to pressure from her son to retire and join him and his family in Australia. She used to let me help in the kitchen when I was a boy.'

She smiled. 'That's a sweet picture, but I think you were wise not to step into her shoes and take over the cooking.'

'Oh? And why is that?'

'You forgot the chicken stock.'

'Did I?' He sensed a subtext, something he was missing. 'Does it matter?'

'It does if you're the chicken.'

'Don't tell me,' he said, 'you find them wandering, lost

or abandoned, and put them in your pocket—no, in the basket of your bicycle. Do you put them in the bath, too?'

She grinned. 'I wouldn't advise you to try that with a chicken. They can't fly, but they do a very energetic flap and a panicky bird in a confined space is going to make a heck of a mess.'

'You are a fount of wisdom on the animal welfare front. So, what do you do with them?' he asked. 'Should the occasion ever arise.'

'I take injured birds to the local animal sanctuary, to be cared for until they can be released or found a good home.'

'Not to the vet?'

She tilted her head in an awkward little movement. 'I found a pheasant once. It had been winged by a shotgun and had taken cover in our hedge. I picked it up and carried it across the village to the vet, expecting him to take care of it. He didn't even bother to look at it, just wrung its neck, handed it back to me and told me to make sure my mother hung it for a few days before she cooked it.'

'*Perdio!* How old were you?'

'Nine.' She sketched a shrug. 'Grandma and I gave the poor thing a very elaborate funeral and buried it in the garden.'

'I hope your grandmother tore a strip off the vet.'

'No. She told me that he was an old school farm vet who thought he was giving a useful life lesson to a girl who lived in the country. No sentiment there.' She stirred the pasta with her fork. 'At least he was honest. He could have sent me on my way, promising to take care of the bird, and then eaten it himself.'

With his head now filled with the picture of a motherless little girl clutching a dead pheasant, he really wished he hadn't asked. And then her comment about the chicken stock registered. 'Are you a vegetarian, Angelica?'

'I don't eat meat,' she said.

'Is there a difference?'

'I don't wear fur, but I wear leather and wool and use it in my clothes. I don't eat meat, but I eat fish and cheese and eggs and I pour milk over my cereals.' She circled her fork over the dish she was holding to prove her point. 'I am fully aware of the hypocrisy.'

'I think you're being a little hard on yourself,' he said. 'Why didn't you say something earlier? When I ordered the risotto for you?'

'I was about to when events overtook us and actually this is perfect. One of my favourites,' she said, making an effort to eat a little more. 'Is it a problem for you?'

'Of course not; why would it be? It's just I'm surprised, that's all.'

She raised an eyebrow. 'Surprised? Why?'

'You are aware that you dress like a vampire?'

'Oh *that*,' she said, the corner of her mouth twitching into a smile. 'That's what Sean called me, the first time he set eyes on me. A skinny vampire.'

Sean? Who was Sean? Don't ask... 'That must have been some time ago,' he said.

'I was sixteen. I've put on a bit of weight since then,' she said, looking down at the soft curves of her breasts and then up at him and caught him doing the same.

For a moment nothing seemed to move and in his head, above the drumming of his heartbeat, he could hear Lisa asking how long it had been since he'd been laid.

Until tonight he hadn't noticed, hadn't cared, but then Angelica Amery had walked into his bar and it was as if she'd hit the start button on the part of him that, for self-protection, he'd switched off months ago. The part that could rage, react, *feel*. The moment he'd turned, seen her sparkling with snow, he'd known that all he had to do was put out his hand, touch her, and the life would come flooding back. And, like blood returning to a numb limb, the pain would follow.

He'd spent the last months concentrating on work, using it to create an impermeable membrane between his public life—devoting himself to this community, *his* community—and the vacuum within.

In a vacuum no one could hear you scream...

'Who's Sean?' he asked. She frowned at his abruptness. 'You said Sean called you a skinny vampire.'

'Oh, right. He's my brother-in-law,' she said. 'He and Elle have three little girls.' Her smile was something else, lighting up her face, making him want to smile right back. 'As for the vampire thing, it's just a look, Dante. I don't bite. Well, not often.' She scooped up another forkful of pasta. 'Just a little nip here, a little nip there but, unlike the kitten, I make it a rule to never draw blood.'

'A pity. I suspect that having you kiss it better would be an unforgettable experience.' Then, before she could speak, 'I'm sorry, that was—'

'No. I'm the one who has to apologise.' The pasta never made it to her mouth. 'I don't normally fling myself at total strangers.' She gave up pretending to eat and put down her fork. 'What am I saying? I *never* fling myself at total strangers. It must have been the shock—'

'Don't!' Without thinking, he'd reached out and put his hand over hers to stop her and the pulse in the tip of his thumb began to pick up speed, thrum in his ears. His brain did a desperate drive-by of all the meaningless phrases one used to cover awkward moments. None fitted. 'Don't apologise.' He didn't want her to apologise for kissing him so he said the only thing in his head—the truth. 'It's quite the best thing that's happened to me in a while.'

And that rushing in his ears had to be the sound of life pouring through the gaping hole she'd punched through his impermeable membrane.

Removing his hand, he abandoned his own supper and then, because he had to do something, he got up and opened the doors of the wood burner. 'What did the bank say?' he asked as he tossed in a couple of logs.

She didn't answer and he half turned.

'They took the details,' she said quickly. 'Asked me a load of questions. I got the feeling they thought, or maybe just hoped, that I'd shared my password with a boyfriend who'd done the dirty and cleaned me out.'

'It happens.'

'Not to me!' Perhaps realising that she'd used rather more vehemence than necessary, she said, 'My grandmother lost everything to a con artist not long after my mother died. He was elegant, charming, endlessly patient with us girls. He even bought me some black hair ribbons. It wasn't just Grandma. We all fell for him, even the dog. It took us a long time to recover. Financially and emotionally.'

'Is that why you're so angry with yourself?' he asked, standing up. 'You shouldn't be. You're as much a victim as if you'd been mugged in the street.'

'I know, but damn it, Dante, it was just so *perfect*. The living room had French windows that opened onto a tiny balcony with a distant view of the Duomo and there was a small second bedroom that I was going to use as a workroom...' She shook her head. 'I'm sorry. I know it doesn't exist but I'm still having trouble getting my head around this.'

'You know what's happened, but it's taking some parts of your brain a while to catch up.'

He knew how it was. He still had sleepless night reruns of the day he'd laid everything out for Valentina, giving her the choice to stay or walk away. She'd used everything she had—soft words and scorching sex—in a last-ditch effort to persuade him to change his mind. Trying to rewrite the scene, behaved better. She pulled a face. 'I guess.'

'A delayed flight, bad weather and then discovering that you're a victim of fraud would be enough to cloud anyone's thoughts.'

'Mine appear to be denser than mud.'

'Have you any idea what you will do?' he asked. 'Stay or go home?'

She lifted her shoulders. 'If I go home I'll be in the same situation as if I stay. Nowhere to live, no job, no money until the bank sorts out a refund. *If* the bank sorts out a refund.'

'What about your sisters?'

'Oh, they'd give me a room and a job like a shot but then I'll be stepping back into the role of baby sister. A big black cuckoo in the happy families' nest.' She glanced at her watch. 'It's late. Is there a B&B close by? A *pensione*? Somewhere that would take me in at this time of night?'

'Close enough.' He turned back to the fire and gave it a prod with the poker, sending up a cloud of sparks. 'Lisa has given you her room. It's the one opposite the bathroom.'

'Bathroom?' She frowned as she tried to make sense of that. 'Do you mean her room here? In this apartment? But I couldn't possibly—'

'There's a lock on the door,' he said before she could finish.

'What? No…' He couldn't be sure whether she had blushed or it was the glow from the fire warming her cheeks. 'I meant I couldn't possibly impose on you.'

'I think you should try,' he said. 'As you said, it's late and there's the additional problem—'

'I have some cash. And a credit card for use in emergencies. I'd say this counts as an emergency, wouldn't you?'

'Undoubtedly, but if you'd let me finish? I was going to

say that there's a problem with the kitten. He's not going to find much of a welcome in a hotel.'

'I could—'

'No,' he said. 'You couldn't.'

'You don't know what I was going to say.'

'You were going to say that you could put him back in your pocket and no one would ever know.' He raised an eyebrow, daring her to deny it. 'We all know how that turned out this evening.'

'Okay, so the kitten is a problem,' she admitted, 'but what about Lisa?'

'What about her?'

'If I have her room, where will she sleep?'

'Where she always sleeps,' he said. 'She keeps a few things here just in case there's an unannounced visit from her family, but she actually lives with Giovanni.'

'Really?'

'You think she's a bit old to be worrying what her parents think about her living with her boyfriend?'

'Well, yes.'

Dante had avoided looking at Angelica when he'd told her about the room. Forget the kitten, there was no way he was letting her leave after fainting so dramatically, but the flash of heat between them had complicated what should have been a simple offer of hospitality. She had to believe that there were no strings attached. No expectation that she follow through on a kiss that had fall-into-bed written all over it from the first touch.

He really had to stop thinking about that kiss.

'It's complicated.'

'I can do complicated,' she said. 'I have a very complicated family.'

'True.' He wanted to know all about them. All about her. Almost as much as he didn't... 'But nowhere near as complicated as a hundred-year-old family feud over a goat.'

'A goat?' Angelica looked startled, those hot crimson lips ready to laugh. If she laughed…

'Have you ever taken home a stray goat, Angelica?'

'Oh, please. Even I know that a goat in a well-tended garden is a recipe for disaster. They are particularly partial to roses and my grandmother loves her roses.'

'Goats will eat anything, but it's a story for late at night after good food and too much wine,' he said.

'Mine too,' Angelica said. 'Maybe we should save them for another night?'

'It's a date…'

No. Not a date…

Madonna, this was difficult.

One minute they'd been on the point of ripping one another's clothes off and maybe, just maybe, if he hadn't had time to think, it would have been all right. Now—thanks to an internet con and a stray kitten —Angelica might as well have a 'Do Not Touch' sign around her neck.

'You must be tired. I'll show you the room.'

'Yes… No…' The lace at her throat moved as she swallowed, the light catching the facets of the jet brooch. 'You and Lisa have both been incredibly kind but you don't know anything about me.' Then, and rather more to the point if she was going to be his roommate for the night, 'I don't know anything about you.'

CHAPTER FIVE

'Eat spinach tomorrow; today is for ice cream.'
—from *Rosie's Little Book of Ice Cream*

'THAT'S NOT TRUE,' Dante said quickly. Too quickly. 'At least not the first part. I've learned a lot about you.' He shut the doors of the wood burner, carefully replaced the poker on its stand and propped his elbow on the mantelpiece, hoping that he looked a lot more relaxed about this than he felt. 'You're a talented designer. You have a wide knowledge of first aid. And ice cream. And you have a complicated family who you care deeply about.' It was there in her voice every time she mentioned them.

'That's not much to go on when you're opening your home to a total stranger.'

'Maybe not, but you're compassionate.' She had also turned every head when she'd walked into his bar—always a bonus—and was the first woman to make him feel like a man in over a year. He should focus on the compassion. 'Despite the fact that you were lost and it was beginning to snow, you still chose to rescue a helpless kitten. I am simply doing—'

'I am not helpless!' Geli said, shifting from calm to heat in a heartbeat, which brought a touch of colour to highlight those fine cheekbones.

'—doing my best to aid a damsel in distress,' he continued, rapidly editing out any reference to helpless or maiden. She was not helpless and no maiden kissed the way she had kissed him.

His reward was a snort of laughter, quickly suppressed. Whether it was at the thought of herself as a damsel or him as a knight errant, he had no way of knowing, but he was glad to have made her laugh, if only briefly.

'Sorry, Dante, but I don't believe in fairy tales.'

'No? All those orphans? All that abuse, abandonment, fear? What's not to believe?' he asked. 'You've just had a very close encounter with the hot breath of the wolf in disguise.'

'Nothing as beautiful as a wolf. Just the cold, unfeeling click of a mouse.' She straightened her back, sat a little taller. 'Okay, I've lost money that I worked hard for, but I'm not going to starve and I'm not going to be sleeping in a shop doorway.'

'Not tonight. And not while there's a room here.'

'I—'

'Tomorrow I'll take you to the *commissariato* so that you can report the fraud,' he said, hoping to distract her. 'You'll need some help with the language.'

'Is there any point? Catching Internet crooks is like trying to catch flies with chopsticks.'

'Made all the harder by the fact that those who've been caught often feel too foolish to report the crime. As if they are in some way to blame for their own misfortune. They're not. You're not,' he said, taking the half-eaten pasta from her.

The colour in her cheeks darkened. 'I know, but I was careless, forgot the basic rule and let my guard down. It will be tougher now to do what I planned, but I am not going to allow a low-life scumbag to steal my dreams and creep home with my tail between my legs.' She took a breath. 'I will not be a victim.'

Her words were heartfelt, passionate, and everything Italian in him wanted to cry out *Bravissima*, kiss her cheeks, wrap her in a warm embrace. His English genes knew better. She wasn't just angry with the criminals; she was angry with herself for falling for the con.

'Basic rule?' he asked.

'Always be suspicious of perfection. If it looks too good to be true, then it almost certainly is.'

'We fall for that one all the time, Angelica. The entire advertising industry is built on that premise. You were meant to fall in love with the apartment and it won't just have been you.'

She sighed. 'No. And it won't just be that apartment, will it? There'll be a host of perfect apartments and villas lined up for the unwary.'

'Undoubtedly. It's your public duty to warn the police that they are likely to be inundated with angry tourists who've paid good money for non-existent accommodation this summer. And maybe stop more people being caught.'

'I suppose…' She tilted her head a little. 'I read somewhere that in Milan the policewomen wear high heels. Is that true?'

'There's only one way to find out,' he said. 'Is it a date?'

'Another one? At this rate we'll be going steady…' Their eyes met and for a moment the air sizzled between them and he was the one swallowing hard. 'It's a date,' she said quickly.

'Can I offer you something else?' he asked. 'Tea, coffee, or do you want to go downstairs and raid the fridge for dessert?'

'Tea?' she repeated, grabbing onto something sane, something sensible. 'Proper tea?'

'Proper tea,' he confirmed.

'Well, now you're talking,' she said, uncurling herself from the corner of the sofa.

'What are you doing?' he asked as she gathered the dishes.

'Whoever cooks in our house is let off the washing-up,' she said, heading for the kitchen before he could tell her to sit down.

'It's a good system,' he said, 'but I do have a dishwasher.'

'You do?'

She looked around and her scepticism was understandable. Apart from the American retro-style fridge he'd installed when he moved in, the kitchen was pretty much as Nonnina had left it. A dresser, loaded with old plates, took up most of one wall, while a family-sized table dominated the centre and a couple of old armchairs stood by the wood stove in the corner—much used in the days when they could only afford to heat one room in winter and the main room was kept for best. It was comfortable, familiar and he liked it the way it was. Which didn't mean he was averse to modern domestic convenience.

'The twenty-first century is through here,' he said, opening the door into what had once been a large pantry but was now a fully fitted utility room. *'Il bagno di servizio.'*

'Magic! You have the best of both worlds.'

'I'm glad you approve.'

Valentina hadn't been impressed, but then his father had given her a personal tour of his apartment in the Quadrilatero d'Oro. He put the kettle on for tea while Angelica stacked the dishes in the machine. The light gleamed on glossy black hair that swung silkily about her shoulders as she moved. On the soft curve of her crimson lips as she turned and saw him watching her.

'It's snowing heavily now,' she said, looking out of the window. 'Will it last?'

'It could be gone by morning, or it could be set in for

days,' he said, but he wasn't looking at the snow piling up in the corners of the window. He was looking at her reflection. 'Whichever it is, there's nothing we can do about it.'

'Except enjoy it. If my mother were alive she'd go out and make a snowman.'

'Now?'

'Absolutely. It might turn to rain in the night and the moment would be lost.' The thought brought a smile to her lips. 'She got us all up in the middle of night once, when it had begun to snow. We made snowmen, had a snowball fight and afterwards she heated up tins of tomato soup to warm us up.'

'And was it all gone in the morning?'

'No, but we had a head start on all the other kids.' Her eyes were shining at the memory as she turned to him. 'She never let the chance for fun pass. Maybe she sensed that time was short and she had to make memories for us while she could.'

'Is that what you're doing? Following her example,' he added when she frowned.

'Always say goodbye as if it's for the last time. Live each day as if it's our last...'

'Are you saying that you want to go out and have a snowball fight?' he asked, not wanting to remember how he'd parted from his father.

'Would you come?' she asked but, before he could answer, she shook her head. 'Just kidding. It's been a long day.'

'And you've had a bad introduction to life in Isola,' he said, although, on reflection, it wasn't an evening which, given the option, he would have missed. 'On the other hand, a little excitement to raise the heartbeat is never a bad thing and you did say that you came to Italy for experience?'

As their eyes met in the reflection in the window he

wanted to rewind the clock, stop it at the moment her tongue had touched his lip… Then, as if it was too intimate, intense, she turned to look directly at him.

'Believe me,' she said, catching a yawn, 'it has delivered and then some.'

'You're tired.' She had neither accepted nor refused Lisa's room but, whatever doubts she might have had about staying, whatever doubts he might have about the wisdom of offering it to her, the weather had made the decision for them both. 'Lisa brought up your case,' he said, picking up the mug of tea he'd made her and leading the way to the room his cousin had dressed to make it look, to the casual glance, as if she was using it.

There was a basket of cosmetics on the dressing table, a book beside the bed. A pair of shoes beneath it, lying as if they'd just been kicked off.

'How long has she been living with Giovanni?'

'She followed him here from Melbourne just over a year ago,' he said, picking up Lisa's shoes and tossing them into the wardrobe. 'To be honest, I didn't think their relationship would survive the day-to-day irritations of living together.' Not that he'd cared one way or the other at the time.

'Is that the voice of experience?' she asked.

'I came close once.' He looked at her and she shook her head.

'Not even close,' she said.

'The village gossips?'

'They wouldn't have stopped me.'

'No…' He crossed to the shutters, stood for a moment looking down at the piazza. The snow was blanketing the city in silence, softening the edges, making everything look clean.

Angelica pressed her hands against the window and sighed. 'I love snow.' Her voice was as soft as one of the huge snowflakes sticking to the window and, unable to help himself, he turned and looked at her. 'It's like being in another world,' she said, 'in a place where time doesn't count.' And then she turned from the window and looked up at him.

Geli could feel Dante's warmth as they stood, not quite touching, in front of the cold window. Everything about the moment was heightened, her senses animal sharp; she could almost hear the thud of his pulse beating a counterpoint to her own, almost taste the pheromones clouding the air. She wanted to tug his shirt from his waistband and rub her cheek against his chest, scent marking him, catlike, as hers.

Lifting his hand in what felt like slow motion, Dante leaned in to her. Her skin tingled, anticipating his touch. Her lips throbbed, hot, feeling twice their normal size. The down on her cheek stirred, lifting to the heat of his hand, and she closed her eyes but his touch never came. Instead, there was the click as he reached over her head to pull shut one of the shutters and every cell in her body screamed *Noooo!*

'My room has an en suite, so the bathroom is all yours,' he said abruptly. 'There's plenty of hot water and no one will disturb you if want to soak off the day.'

No one would disturb her? Was he crazy? She was disturbed beyond reason.

She had nowhere to live, she'd lost her money but all she'd been thinking about was kissing Dante Vettori, ripping open the buttons of his shirt and exploring his warm skin. Imagining how his long fingers would feel curved around her breast—

Click went the second shutter and, released from the mesmerising drift of the snow, she was jolted back to reality and somehow managed a hoarse, 'Thank you.'

He nodded. 'If you need me for anything I'll be downstairs in the office, catching up with the paperwork.'

'I've been keeping you from your work?'

'I'd stopped to eat. That's why I was in the bar when you arrived. You know where everything is. Please…make yourself at home.'

'Dante…' He waited, hand on the door. 'Thank you.'

He responded with the briefest of nods. 'I'll see you in the morning.'

Geli didn't move until she heard the door to the flat close and then her shoulders slumped. How on earth had they come from the promise of a searing kiss to such awkwardness in the space of an hour, two at the most?

Halfway between the two, she discovered when she checked her watch, and that was the answer. Too much had happened too quickly.

If the kitten hadn't made such a dramatic appearance they would have been able to sit quietly over supper. Dante would have explained about the flat, helped her find a room for the night and then tomorrow she'd have come by to thank him and maybe, hopefully, pick up on the fizz of attraction that had sizzled between them.

Instead, they'd veered between meltdown lust and awkwardness and in an effort to cover that she'd revealed way too much about herself.

Her mother, black hats—where on earth had all that come from? And that pheasant… She hadn't talked about that since her sisters had arrived home on the school bus to find her and Grandma singing a heartfelt *All Things Bright and Beautiful* over its resting place beneath a climbing rose.

'*Dio…*' Dante, the image of Angelica with her hands pressed against the window burning a hole in his brain, pulled open the bottom drawer of his desk and took out a bottle of grappa.

He poured himself a shot, tossed it back and for a moment he let the heat of it seep through his veins.

Close. He'd been within a whisper of touching her, had almost felt the down on her cheek rising to meet him as, lips softened, eyes closed, she'd anticipated a rerun of that kiss. He clenched his hand in an attempt to eradicate the memory.

He might have stepped back, walked out of the apartment before he did something unforgivable, but it hadn't stopped his imagination reacting to what had been a non-stop blast to his senses ever since she'd walked into his bar and stopped the conversation dead. The steely fresh air smell of her hair, snowflakes melting on her cheek, on crimson lips, she'd looked like something from a fairy tale. A lost princess stumbling out of the darkness.

He'd turned, their eyes had met and in that first look he'd forgotten the pain. The heartache...

And then she'd said, 'Via Pepone.'

He should have let Lisa deal with her because by then the complications were piling up, but that first look had fired a lightning charge through his senses, jump-starting them from hibernation as she walked towards him. As he'd touched her hand. As she'd removed her glove, removed her coat in a slow, tantalising reveal of the briefest little black dress.

His hand at her waist as he'd swept her out of the bar had sent a shock wave of heat surging through him and he hadn't been able to let it go.

He'd wanted to know how her cheek would feel beneath his fingers, wanted to taste her. He wanted to undress her, hold her against his naked skin, bury himself in her until he felt warm again.

What she'd said, how she'd looked at him when she'd stood by the window had been an invitation to take it all. Not a lost princess stumbling out of the night but something darker—an enchantress, a sorceress and if this had been a fairy tale he would already be doomed.

He shook his head.

Angelica Amery was simply a woman in need and that was the problem.

The spontaneity of that fall-into-bed moment had been real enough but Lisa's terrible—or possibly perfect—timing had wrecked that. They'd both had time to think about it and they'd lost the moment when a simple, unplanned elemental explosion of lust might have led anywhere or nowhere.

Worse, because she didn't know him, Angelica might well have thought he expected to share the bed he'd offered her.

Anything now would be tainted by that uncertainty and while his body, jolted out of stasis, might be giving him hell for walking away, he had to face himself in the shaving mirror in the morning.

Work. That had been the answer when Valentina had demanded that he forget Isola, that he walk away from what he couldn't change because, sooner or later, the old houses would come down and his father, or someone like him, would replace them with high-rise flats and office blocks. Work had been the answer when he'd allowed himself to be seduced by her sensual inducement to change his mind when he'd known in his heart that it was already over.

He called up the paper he'd been working on, his plan for the future of Isola, but the words on the screen kept dissolving into images that had nothing to do with preservation orders or affordable housing.

Angelica's hands—tapping the map with a blood-red nail...slowly unfastening tiny buttons...a fingertip stroking the head of the kitten.

Angelica's mouth lifted to kiss him, the black lace choker emphasising the length of her white neck.

Angelica's face as she stood beside him at the window watching the snow blanketing the city—as she turned to him and he knew that all he had to do was reach out, touch her cheek and, for tonight at least, the dark emptiness of the void would be banished.

CHAPTER SIX

'In the winter dip your ice cream in sparkly rose-pink sprinkles.'
—from *Rosie's Little Book of Ice Cream*

CAFÉ ROSA WAS buzzing with morning activity. Men in working clothes were standing at the bar, a pastry in one hand, an espresso at their elbow. She was in Italy, where it cost more to sit down.

With so much whirling around in her mind Geli hadn't anticipated much sleep, but a soak in that huge bathtub with a splash of Lisa's luxurious lavender-scented bubbles and she'd gone out like a light the minute her head hit the pillow.

She'd taken the kitten's box into the bedroom with her in case it woke, hungry, in the night but it had been the sound of a distant door closing that woke her.

For a moment she hadn't known where she was but then the kitten had mewed and it had all come flooding back to her. The delayed flight, the non-existent apartment, Rattino. Dante...

She shook her head. Her life was complicated enough right now, without what might have become an awkward one-night stand. She might have inherited her mother's 'seize the day' genes—that she was feeling regret, the loss of something special missed, instead of relief proved that—but she'd had more sense.

She wrapped herself in her dressing gown, crossed to the window, rubbed the mist away with the edge of her hand. The early-morning sun was slanting across the city, lighting up colourful buildings—deep rose-pink, pale green, yellow; spotlighting a Madonna painted on a wall; glittering off the glass towers of high-rise blocks and snow-covered roofs.

Below her the pristine white of the snow had already been mashed to dirty slush by trucks bringing produce to the market stalls that had been erected along the street opposite. Everywhere there was colour, people wrapped up in thick coats and bright scarves, out and about getting on with their lives, and her heart gave a little skip of anticipation.

There was nothing like a good market to put a spring in the step!

She opened the bedroom door and stuck her head out. 'Dante?'

No response. Maybe he'd woken her when he'd left the flat. Not sure whether she was relieved or disappointed, she headed for the kitchen where she found a note pinned to the fridge door with a magnet.

Kitty comfort station in the utility room. Coffee and breakfast downstairs whenever you're ready. Lisa.

There was a litter tray ready and waiting for Rattino in the utility room, as well as two little plastic dishes filled with fresh minced chicken and milk and Geli found herself blinking rather rapidly at such thoughtfulness, such kindness. She'd read that in Isola she'd find the truest, most generous spirit of old Milan.

Clearly it was a fact.

She introduced Rattino to the first and watched as he dived into the second and then set his box on its side so that he could eat, sleep and do what came naturally at his leisure. Then she closed the door so that he couldn't wander and put the kettle on.

She found tea bags and dropped one in a mug and topped it up with boiling water. She found milk in the fridge and carried her must-have morning mug through to the bathroom. Hair dry, make-up in place, she layered herself in clothes that would see her through the day. A fine polo neck sweater, a narrow, high-waisted ankle-length skirt, stout Victorian-style lace-up boots, all black, which she topped with a rich burgundy velvet cut-away jacket that exactly matched her lipstick. She chose a steampunk-inspired pendant she'd made from the skeleton of a broken watch and, after a spin in front of the mirror to check that she was fluff-free, she went downstairs.

'Ciao, Geli!' Lisa called out as she spotted her. 'Come sta?'

The men standing at the bar turned as one and stared.

'Ciao, Lisa! Molto bene, grazie. And Rattino thanks you for the litter tray. What do I owe you?'

She waved the offer away. 'Tell him to thank Dan. He called and asked me to pick it up on my way to work. Now, what can I get you? A latte? Cappuccino? Or will you go hardcore with an espresso?'

'Vorrei un cappuccino, grazie,' she replied, testing her phrasebook Italian.

'Buona sceita!'

She called out the order to someone behind her, piled pastries on a plate and came out from behind the bar and headed for a table in the centre of the room.

'How are you this morning, Geli?'

'Pretty good, all things considered. I thought I'd be tossing and turning all night, but I'd be lying if I said I re-

member a thing after I closed my eyes.' She couldn't say
the same about Lisa who, up close, looked as if she'd had a
sleepless one. 'Thanks so much for offering me your spare
room. It was a lifesaver.'

'No point in paying for a hotel room when there's an
empty one going begging,' she said, pushing the pastries
towards her. *'La prima colazione,'* she said, taking one.
'Otherwise known as cornettos. The perfect breakfast
food.'

'Thanks.' Geli took one and her mouth was filled with
crisp pastry and cream. 'Oh, good grief,' she spluttered.
'That's sinful.'

Lisa grinned. 'Start the day the way you mean to go on,'
she said then called out something in Italian to the men
at the bar. They grinned, put down the empty cups they'd
been nursing and made a move to go.

'What did you say to them?' Geli asked.

'To close their mouths before they catch flies.' She
shook her head. 'You are going to be so good for business. Your make-up, your clothes—everything is perfect.
Do you always make this much effort?'

'It goes with the territory. When you're a designer, you
have to be your own walking advertisement.'

'It works for me. I'm no Milan fashionista, but I'd give
my eye teeth for a jacket like yours.'

'I'll design a Dark Angel original for you when you
come back from Australia. A very small thank you for
being such a friend in need.'

'You don't have to do that.'

'It will be a totally selfish gift,' she assured her. 'You'll
wear it and with those elegant shoulders you'll look fabulous.' She lifted her hands in a *job done* gesture.

'You're telling me that I'm going to be a walking shop
dummy,' she said, grinning broadly.

'Walking and talking.'

'Oh, right. Everyone will want to know—' She stopped as Dante pulled out a chair and joined them.

Geli had wondered, as she'd taken her wake-up shower, if she'd imagined the attraction, or if it had simply been heightened by the drama of her arrival. A combination of being in Isola, being lost, the weather. Could anyone really hit all her hot buttons with no more than a look?

Apparently they could, even if it was a slightly crumpled, unsmiling version this morning.

'*Buongiorno*, Angelica,' he said. 'Did you sleep well?'

'*Buongiorno*, Dante,' she replied, her voice remarkably steady. It was the rest of her that felt as if it was shaking like a leaf. 'I slept amazingly well, under the circumstances.'

Dante, on the other hand, looked as if he'd been working all night and the urge to reach out and smooth the creases from his face was almost overwhelming. Fortunately, before she could do anything that idiotic he turned to Lisa.

'What will everyone want to know?' he asked.

'How on earth you managed to convince Geli that she should work for you,' she replied without a blush.

'Oh? And what is the answer?'

'You'll know that when you've persuaded her,' she said, getting to her feet. 'Off you go.'

'Lisa,' Angelica protested. 'My Italian is on the basic side of basic.'

'*No problema.* I might have an Italian father but I could barely utter a word when I arrived. Tell her, Dante,' she urged, turning a smile on her cousin that was so sweet it would give you toothache. 'There'll be a queue of regulars lining up to help her with the language and anything else she needs to make her stay in Isola a memorable experience before she can say *ciao*. Isn't that so?'

Geli, who had two older sisters, recognised one of those exchanges which, on the surface were exquisitely polite, while underneath there were seething undercurrents of hidden meaning.

'But you're family,' Geli protested, not sure what was going on, but not wanting to be in the middle of it.

'Unfortunately,' Dante said, his face expressionless. 'You can't fire family. It wasn't just the language; it was weeks before she could get an order straight or produce a decent espresso without me standing over her—'

Lisa snorted derisively and when he looked up she lifted an eyebrow a mocking fraction right back at him. 'I'm sure Geli is *much* smarter than me.'

He looked thoughtful. 'But nowhere near as devious, it would seem.'

'It runs in the family,' Lisa replied, moving aside as the waiter arrived with a tray containing her cappuccino, an espresso for Dante and two bowls of something pale and creamy. 'I'll walk you through the job when you come back from the *commissariato*, Geli. *Buon appetito.*'

'*Sì...grazie...*' she said, then, unsure what to say to Dante, she indicated the bowl in front of her. 'What is this?'

'*Zabaglione.* Whipped eggs, cream, sugar, a little Marsala. I usually leave out the wine before midday,' he added, 'but it's bitter outside.'

'So this is antifreeze?'

He laughed and the tension, awkwardness was defused. 'Let's hope so.'

She dipped in her spoon and let a mouthful, sweet and warming, dissolve on her tongue. 'Oh, yum. Pastries and pudding for breakfast. My mother would have so approved.' He looked up. 'When anything bad happened she'd make us cupcakes for breakfast. With pink frosting and gold stars.'

'Pink?' His brow kinked in amusement. 'Really?'

'Black frosting is just creepy.' She shrugged. 'Except at Halloween.'

Dante looked as if he was about to say something but the bleep of an incoming text distracted her and she searched in her bag for her phone. 'Oh, no… '

'Problema?'

'You could say that. I shipped my heavy stuff before I left. Who knew it would get here so quickly?' She showed him the phone. 'I think the driver is trying to the find the non-existent address I gave them.'

Dante read the text then replied to it before handing it back. 'I told him to bring it here.'

'Oh… This is so embarrassing.'

'Why?'

'This was supposed to be me standing on my own two feet. Being grown-up. Self-sufficient.'

'Would you like me to tell them to leave it on the pavement?' he asked.

'No!' She shook her head. 'No…I'm sorry, I didn't mean to sound ungrateful but this is my first excursion into the unknown, the first time I've ever done anything totally on my own and it's all going wrong.'

'It's hardly your fault,' he assured her. 'And it's just until Monday.'

Monday? 'Yes, absolutely. I'll have found a room by then.'

'That's Monday, when you can move into the apartment I've found for you. I'm afraid that, like the job, it is only temporary, but it will give you a little breathing space while you get yourself sorted out.'

'You see? Like that,' Geli said and then swallowed. 'I'm sorry. That sounded so ungrateful.'

'Yes, it did.'

She groaned. 'I bet you wish you'd listened to the

weather forecast and closed an hour earlier last night.' He didn't answer and she said, 'You're supposed to say no.'

The creases bracketing his mouth deepened slightly in what might just have been the promise of a smile. 'I'm thinking about it.'

She rolled her eyes. 'Okay, how much is this temporary apartment you've found to go with my temporary job?'

'Just the utilities. It's only for a month while Lisa and Giovanni are at the wedding, but it will give you time to look around.'

'Lisa and Giovanni?' She frowned. 'But I thought—'

'She wants me to give you a job so I offered her a deal. You get the job if she takes Giovanni as her plus one to her sister's wedding. They will need someone responsible to keep the pipes from freezing, make the place look lived in and feed the goldfish,' he added matter-of-factly. As if it was nothing. 'You are responsible, aren't you?'

'No goldfish has ever gone hungry on my watch,' she said, 'but why didn't Lisa tell me herself?'

'Because she wants you to stay here.'

'So that she doesn't have to take Giovanni?'

'No. His flight is booked.'

She went back over the conversation then shook her head. 'I seem to be missing something.'

'Lis believes that if we share the same apartment we'll inevitably fall into the same bed.'

The *zabaglione* took a diversion down her nose and Dante calmly handed her a paper napkin from the tray.

'That is outrageous.'

'I agree. I told her I never sleep with the staff, but apparently temps don't count.'

Never...? 'I wouldn't try that on an employment tribunal.'

'No,' he agreed with the wryest of smiles. 'And I did

point out that, since you had nowhere else to go, any move on my part would be open to the worst interpretation.'

And any move on hers might be seen as...

'So you suggested moving me out so that I'm available?' She should be outraged. She was pretty sure she was outraged... 'I don't believe we're having this conversation. No, scrub that. I don't believe you had this conversation with Lisa.'

But it went a long way to explaining that edgy undercurrent between them this morning.

'*Mi dispiace*, Angelica. It is, as you say, quite outrageous.'

'So you applied a little pressure of your own?' And when, exactly, had he come up with that idea? 'How does Giovanni feel about that?'

'The man is in love. He'll do whatever she asks.' The thought did not appear to give him great pleasure.

'I imagine you're banking on the fact that after a day of joy and celebration her family will realise that he doesn't have horns and a tail.'

'You're not convinced?'

'I don't know your family,' she said, 'and I don't know Giovanni, but I do know that weddings tend to be emotional affairs. There's the risk that, after a few glasses of the bubbly stuff, tongues will be loosened and fists will fly.'

'Maybe. Then they'll all get drunk, fling their arms around one another, vow eternal friendship and cry.'

'Or they'll all land in jail.'

'Or that.' He sat back. 'You don't have to take the job but if you'll just play along until they leave I'd be grateful.'

'I get that. What I don't understand is why throwing us together is so important to her.'

'We're doing each other a favour, Angelica. Does it matter if Lisa has her own agenda?'

Did it?

Lisa wanted to get them into bed together. Okay, so she'd been way ahead of her on her own account, but that was different. This was different... 'If you'll excuse me,' she said, sliding off her chair and standing up. It was time to leave. 'I'll pay for my breakfast and then I'll go and pack—'

He was on his feet, had caught her hand before she could move. 'Angelica...' She didn't pull her hand away, but she didn't look up at him. 'I haven't dated since my fiancée broke off our engagement a little over a year ago. Lisa thinks it's time I got back on the horse.'

He'd been dumped by the woman he loved? How unlikely was that? Then her brain got past the fact that any woman would dump him and she heard what he'd actually said.

'And I'm the horse?' she asked very quietly, aware that they were now the object of a dozen pairs of eyes. 'Gee, *grazie*, Dante. Or do I mean gee-gee *grazie*?' And, as everything suddenly fell into place, she took a step back. 'Is that what this has been about?' she demanded.

He tightened his grip on her hand. 'This?'

He'd known within minutes of her arrival that she was in trouble. All she'd seen was a man who could melt her underwear at twenty paces. All he'd seen was an opportunity. 'You've been using me from the beginning. Damn it, I should have known. If it looks too good...' she muttered, hurt, angry and feeling stupid. Again. 'Tell me, Dante, what would you have done without the kitten?'

'More to the point, what would you have done?' He closed the gap between them. 'You would still have needed somewhere to stay.' He reached up, touched her cheek with the tips of his fingers and the heat trickled through her, sweet and seductive as warm honey. 'There were two of us in that bedroom last night, Angelica. Which of us walked away?'

She flushed with embarrassment, well aware that it hadn't been her. That she'd wanted him with all the 'hang the consequences' recklessness of her Amery genes.

'I suppose I should be grateful that you weren't prepared to go that far,' she said, fighting the urge to lean into his hand. 'Oh, no, I forgot. You couldn't make a move in your own apartment. You need me off the premises so that it's not some totally sordid exchange that's open to misinter—'

'Basta!' His fingers slid through her hair, captured her head, shocking her into silence.

Around them, the café went quiet. He looked up and instantly everyone found they had somewhere else they needed to be. Then he turned back to her.

'I'm sorry, Angelica. You're absolutely right. We are both using you for our own ends but here's the deal. You get an apartment rent-free for a month and a temporary job if you want it. And, no matter what my cousin hopes might happen, there are no strings attached to either offer.'

'No strings? Well, golly, that's all right then.'

'Lis thinks she's helping,' he said, 'but I'm not ready for any kind of relationship. I don't know if I ever will be.'

'I don't imagine she's envisaging a "relationship",' she replied, making ironic quote marks with her fingers. 'Just a quick gallop to shake out the cobwebs. I'm a temp, re-member?'

'Dio...' he said a touch raggedly. At her nape, his hand softened but he didn't remove it and, despite her anger, she didn't step away. 'I was trying to be honest with you, Angelica. Nothing hidden. No con—'

Behind her, the café door opened, letting in a blast of cold air. 'Signora Amery?'

'Would you rather I'd prettied it up?' he insisted. 'Lied to you?'

Behind Dante, she saw Lisa watching them anxiously. Above her, Dante's face was unreadable.

She had left Longbourne determined to shake up her life, grab every experience that came her way. So far, Isola was delivering on all fronts. Make that all fronts but one. Not a problem. She was here to work, to learn, to grow as a designer, an artist. A little hot sex would have been a bonus but she wasn't looking for anything as complicated, as involving as a relationship. She had that in common with her mother, too. And, apparently, Dante.

The man at the door called out something in Italian and Lisa said, 'Geli…someone wants you.'

'Oh, for heaven's sake,' she muttered, then turned to the man standing in the doorway, '*Sono* Angelica Amery.'

'I'll see your boxes safely stored while you get your coat,' Dante said as the driver went to unload them. 'We'll go to the police station as soon as it's done.' He needed a little breathing space to recover from the sensory overload of being in close proximity to Angelica. A little cold air in his lungs.

'Would you like me to bring your jacket?' she asked.

'*Grazie*, Angelica. Thank you.' For a moment neither of them moved and the long look that passed between them acknowledged that it wasn't just the jacket he was thanking her for.

The last of the boxes was being stacked in the room opposite his office when she returned, dressed for the weather in the head-turning coat with pockets big enough to conceal a small animal. She'd added a scarf which she'd coiled in some fashionable loop around her neck and a black velvet beret with a glittering spider hat pin to fasten it in place.

Lisa was right. She certainly knew how to make an entrance. She was going to be a sensation at the *commissariato*.

'What is all this stuff?' he asked, indicating the boxes as she handed him his jacket and scarf.

'My Mac. A couple of collapsible worktables,' she said, walking around the boxes, touching each one in turn as she identified the contents. 'My drawing board, easel, paints, brushes, sketch pads.' The long full skirt of her coat brushed against the cartons as she moved among them.

'You intend to paint as well as design clothes?' he asked.

'Maybe...I haven't done anything serious since I switched to fashion for my post-grad. And I've been busy with the ice cream parlour franchise.' She stopped and bent to check a label. 'My sewing machines are in this one. And my steamer.' She looked up. 'I'll need to unpack the fragile stuff to make sure it's all survived the journey.'

'No problem. What about these?' he asked, indicating some of the larger boxes.

'Material, trimmings, buttons. It looks a lot when you see it in a small space,' she said.

'Buttons? You brought buttons with you? You can buy them in Italy,' he pointed out.

She smiled at that. 'I know, and I can't wait to go shopping, but these are buttons I've collected over the years. Some are very old. Some, like these—' she touched one of the tiny jet buttons at her waist and he tried not to think about the way she'd unfastened them last night...one by one '—are quite valuable.'

'Right.' He struggled with a dry mouth. 'Well, the bad news is that you're never going to get all this into Lisa's tiny one-bed flat.'

'Is there any good news?'

'This room isn't being used. You can work here until you find workshop space. Or a flat large enough to accommodate all this.'

'But—'

'I'll move these out of your way.' He indicated the few dusty boxes he'd pushed to one side. 'Will it do?'

'It's perfect, Dante, but we have to discuss rent.'

He'd anticipated that. 'No discussion necessary. In return for a month's lease, you can design an ice cream parlour for me. Whether you consider that good news is for you to decide. Shall we go?'

CHAPTER SEVEN

'There are no recipes for leftover ice cream.'
—from *Rosie's Little Book of Ice Cream*

THE POLICE STATION was noisy, crowded, and Italian police-women, Geli discovered to her delight, really did wear high heels.

'How on earth do they run in them?' she asked. Anything to break the silence as she waited with Dante for a detective to come and talk to them.

'Run?'

'Never mind,' she said. 'Stupid question. They're all so glamorous I imagine the crooks put up their hands and surrender for the sheer pleasure of being handcuffed and patted down by them.'

She swallowed, unable to believe she'd actually said anything so sexist.

Dante said nothing. He'd said very little other than, 'Take care...' as they'd walked along the snow-packed street.

'Dante!' A detective approached them, shook him by the hand. *'Signora...?'*

'Giorgio, may I introduce Signora Angelica Amery?' Dante said, then, 'Angelica—Commissario Giorgio Rizzoli. Giorgio...' Dante explained the situation in Italian too rapid for her to catch more than a word or two. *'Inglese... Via Pepone...'*

'Signora Amery...' The Commissario placed his hand against his heart. *'Mi dispiace...'*

'He's desolate that you have had such a terrible experience,' Dante translated. 'We are to go through to his office, where he'll take the details, although he's sure you will understand that the chances of recovering your money are very small.'

'Tell him that I understand completely and that I'm very sorry to take up his valuable time.'

Reporting the crime took a very long time. Apart from the fact that everything had to be translated, it seemed that every officer on duty, from a cadet who was barely old enough to shave to one who was well past retiring age, had some pressing matter that only the Commissario could resolve. He was extraordinarily patient, introducing each of his men to her, explaining what had happened and smiling benevolently as each one welcomed her to Isola, offered whatever assistance was in their power to give and held her hand sympathetically while gazing into her eyes.

Dante, in the meantime, gazed out of the window as she repeated the well-rehearsed phrase, *'Mi dispiace, parli lentamente per favore...'*—begging them to speak slowly. If she didn't know better, she would have thought he was afraid to catch her eye in case he laughed. It gave her a warm feeling. As if they were partners in a private joke.

'Well, you promised me it would be an experience and I have to admit that it was almost worth being robbed,' she said as they paused on the steps, catching their breath as they hit the cold air. 'Tell me, are the women officers notably more efficient than the men?' He took her arm as they made their way down the steps, despite the fact that they had been cleared and gritted. 'Only I noticed none of them needed assistance.'

'I think you know the answer to that.'

He wasn't smiling and released her arm the moment

they hit the slushy, slippery pavement, keeping a clear distance between them as they walked back to the café, his face, his body so stiff that he looked as if he'd crack in two.

After about twenty paces she couldn't stand it another moment and stopped. 'Dante, last night...' He'd gone a couple of steps before he realised she wasn't with him and glanced back. 'This morning...' She swallowed. 'I just wanted you to know that I'm truly grateful for everything. I won't do or say anything to mess up Lisa's plans.'

He turned to face her. 'I appreciate that,' he said stiffly.

'And I'll design you the prettiest ice cream parlour imaginable. If you're serious about the workshop space?'

'It's yours, but this isn't the weather to be standing around in the street discussing interior decoration.'

She didn't move.

He shrugged. 'There's a small room at the back of Café Rosa that opens onto the garden. When I saw your designs it occurred to me that an American ice cream parlour might go down well with the younger element.'

'In that case, forget pretty—it had better be nineteen-fifties cool.'

'Maybe. Will your sister object to me borrowing her ideas?'

'There's no copyright in ideas,' she said. 'She borrowed the concept from the US after all and you won't be calling it Knickerbocker Gloria, using her branding or copying her ices. You'll be using gelato rather than ice cream, I imagine?'

'You're getting technical.'

'Just thinking ahead. Will you make your own *gelato* or buy it in, for instance? Is there anyone local who would make specials for you?'

'Good question. I'll think about it. Shall we go?'

'Yes...' She took a step, stopped again. 'No.' There was something she had to say. 'I want you to know that I understand why you were being completely—if rather brutally—honest with me this morning.'

'Do you?'

'You said it's no con—at least where I'm concerned. Lisa, well, that's between you and her.'

'Is that it?'

'Yes…' She rolled her eyes; he really wasn't helping… 'No.' He said nothing, although his eyebrows spoke volumes. But he waited. 'You might want to relax a little, walk a little closer, try and find a smile from somewhere because right now we look as if we're in the middle of a fight rather than about to fall into bed.'

'Do we?' And for a moment the question, loaded with unspoken reference to how close they'd come to the latter, hung there. Then he stuck his hands in his pockets, looked somewhere above her head. 'I owe you an apology, too.'

'If it's about the horse thing,' she said quickly as they continued walking, 'the least said the better.'

'Lisa put the words in my head last night and they leapt out when I wasn't paying attention,' he said and stuck out his elbow, inviting her to slide her arm beneath it. Her turn to do the thing with the eyebrows and he raised a wintry smile. 'You said it, Angelica—we're in this together.'

'Right.' She tucked her arm in his and he drew her closer, no doubt glad of warmth. 'And forget about the horse. I shouldn't be so touchy. I don't know what I'd have done last night if you hadn't been so kind.'

'You'd have managed,' he said as they walked back towards Café Rosa. 'You're a resourceful woman.'

'I'm glad you think so because I'd rather like to put my resourcefulness to the test,' she said as they reached the piazza. 'Will the bartending lesson keep for an hour?'

'Take all the time you need. Lisa managed to drag hers out for weeks.'

'How?' she asked. The fancy barista stuff might take time to master but the basics weren't exactly rocket science.

'I was too wrapped up in my own misery at the time to realise that she was playing the idiot in order to keep me busy. Doing her best to take my mind off Valentina.'

'Valentina? Your fiancée?'

'She's not my anything.' In the low slanting sun his face was all dark shadows. 'She's married to someone else.'

'So soon?' Not the most tactful response but the words had been shocked out of her.

'My father was ready to give her everything I would not.' Grey… His face was grey… 'And it seems that she was pregnant.'

His father?

They'd reached the first market stall and, while she was still trying to get her head around what he'd told her, he unhooked his arm and stepped away. 'Give me your phone and I'll put my number in your contacts.'

Geli handed over her phone but her brain was still processing his shocking revelation.

Valentina had been cheating on him with his father? No wonder he'd withdrawn into himself or that Lisa was so worried about him.

Dante slipped off a glove, programmed in his number and handed her back her phone. 'Give me a call if you need any help haggling over the price of designer clothes and shoes.'

'What…?'

He'd dropped an emotional bombshell and was now casually discussing the price of shoes. But there had been nothing casual or throwaway about his earlier remark. His mention of Valentina had been deliberate; he'd chosen to tell her what had happened before someone else—before Lisa—filled her in on the gossip. And then, just as deliberately because he didn't want to talk about it, he'd changed the subject.

'Oh, yes. *Grazie*,' she said, doing her best to sound equally casual as she dropped the phone back in her pocket. 'I love looking around a new market but I'm afraid that clothes and shoes are on hold until I find out if the bank is going to refund my money.' Concentrate on the most immediate problem. 'My first priority is to take a walk back to where I found Rattino and see if anyone is missing him. Do people put up "lost pet" notices around here?'

'I can't say I've noticed any. I suppose we could put up some "found" ones?'

'That's probably a lot wiser than knocking on strangers' doors when I barely speak a word of Italian,' she agreed.

'Not just wiser,' he said, 'it would be a whole lot safer. Do not, under any circumstances, do that on your own.'

'You could come with me.'

'Let's stick with the posters. Can I leave you to take a look around the market without getting into any trouble while I take a photograph of the rat and run off a few posters? I'll come and find you when they're done.'

'Trouble?' she repeated, looking around at the bustling market. 'What trouble?'

'If you see anything with four legs, looking lost, walk away.'

Geli explored the market, using her phone to take pictures of the colourful stalls and sending them to her sisters. Proof that she'd arrived, was safe and doing what came naturally.

She tried out her Italian, exchanging greetings, asking prices, struggling with the answers until her ear began to tune in to the language of the street as opposed to the carefully enunciated Italian on her teach yourself Italian course.

Despite her intention to simply browse, she was unable to resist some second-hand clothes made from the most gorgeous material and was browsing a luscious selection of ribbon and beads on a stall selling trimmings when Dante found her.

The stallholder, a small, plump middle-aged woman so bundled up that only her face was showing, screamed with delight and flung her arms around him, kissing his cheeks and rattling off something in rapid Italian. Dante laughed and then turned to introduce her.

'Livia, *questa è la mia amica*, Angelica. Angelica, this is Livia.'

Geli offered her hand. '*Piacere*, Livia.'

Her tentative Italian provoked a wide smile and another stream of unintelligible Italian as Livia closed both of her hands around the box of black beads she'd been looking at and indicated that she should put it in her bag.

'I sorted out her traders' licence a few months ago,' Dante explained. 'It's her way of saying thank you.'

'She should be thanking you.'

'I don't have a lot of use for beads and, since you are my friend, it would make her happy if you took them. You can buy something from her another day.'

'*Grazie mille*, Livia,' she said. 'Will you tell her I love her stall, Dante, and that I'll come back and buy from her very soon.'

He said something that earned her a huge smile then, after more hugs and kisses for both of them, Dante took the carrier she was holding and peered into it.

'You changed you mind about window-shopping, I see?'

She shrugged. 'I've got a job, rent-free accommodation for a month and a workshop that I'm paying for with my time. And now I've got some fabulous material to work with, just as soon as I unpack my sewing machine.'

'Do you need more time?' He looked around. 'I believe

there are still a few black things left—' She jabbed her elbow in his ribs and he grinned. 'I guess not.' He took a sheaf of papers from the roomy pocket of his waxed jacket. 'Shall we get this done?'

She took one and looked at the photograph Dante had taken of the kitten. 'He's quite presentable now that he's clean and dry. *Trovato*… Found?' He nodded. '*Contattare* Café Rosa. And the telephone number. Well, that's direct and to the point. Uh-oh…' She looked up as something wet landed on the paper and the colours of the ink began to run into one another as more snow began to fall. 'If we put them out now they'll be a soggy mess in no time,' Geli said. 'Have you got a laminator?'

'No.'

'Fortunately, I packed mine.'

While Dante, wrapped up against the weather, left on his mission to stick up the laminated posters of the lost kitten, Geli called her bank's fraud office and passed on the crime number the Commissario had given her.

'Okay?' Lisa asked, handing her a long black apron.

She shrugged. 'I've done everything I can.' She tied the apron over her clothes and watched Lisa's demonstration of the Gaggia and then produced, one after the other, a perfect espresso, latte and cappuccino.

Lisa, arms folded, watched her through narrowed eyes. 'You've done this before.'

'I was a student for four years. My sisters paid me for the work I did for them, but paints, material and professional sewing machines do not come cheap. Then, as now, I needed a job.'

'Right, Little Miss Clever Clogs, you've got your first customer.' She indicated a man standing at the counter. 'Go get him.'

Geli took a deep breath. *'Ciao, signor. Che cosa desidera?'* she asked.

He smiled. *'Ciao, signora...* Geli,*'* he added, leaning closer to read the name tag that Lisa had pinned to her apron. *'Il sono* Marco.*'*

'Ciao, Marco. *Piacere. Che cosa desidera?'* she repeated.

'Vorrei un espresso, per favore,' he said. Then, having thanked her for it, *'Che programme ha per stasera? Le va di andare a bere qualcosa?'*

The words might not have been familiar, but the look, the tone certainly were and she turned to Lisa. 'I think I'm being hit on. How do I say I'm washing my hair?'

'He wants to know if you have any plans for tonight and, if not, can he buy you a drink. So good for business...' she murmured.

'Definitely washing my hair.'

Lisa gave him the bad news and he smiled ruefully, shrugged and drank his coffee.

'What did you say?'

'That you're working tonight. Why?' she asked, thoughtfully. 'Have you changed your mind? He is rather cute.'

'Very cute.'

'Well, he knows where you'll be tonight. Maybe he'll come back.'

'Does that mean I've passed the interview?'

'When can you start?'

'It had better be this evening, don't you think? I wouldn't want Marco to think I was lying.'

'Heaven forbid. Come on, I'll run you through the routine and then you'd better go and put your feet up. It tends to get busy on a Saturday night.'

Half an hour later, Geli said, 'Can I make a hot chocolate to go? I'll pay for it.'

'There's no need. Staff get fed and watered.'

'It's not for me. One of the stallholders I met this morning is a friend of Dante's—'

'They're all his friends when they want something,' she said, pulling a face.

'Are they? Oh, well, anyway, she gave me some beads so I thought I'd take her a hot drink.'

'That's thoughtful, but it's on the house,' she said as Geli made the chocolate and poured it into a carry out cup with a lid. 'You don't know how grateful I am that you're staying, Geli. I really didn't want to leave Dante on his own.'

'Hardly on his own. He seems to know everyone.'

'Everyone knows him. They come to him for help because he'll stand up for them, fight their corner against bureaucracy and lead their campaigns to save this place from the developers. They don't care what it costs him. You're different.'

Geli shrugged, not wanting to get into exactly how different it was. The situation was already awkward enough.

'I mean it,' Lisa said. 'You're the first woman he's shown the slightest interest in for over a year and it hasn't been for lack of attention from women wanting to comfort him. He was engaged—'

'He told me what happened,' she said, cutting Lisa off mid gossip.

'You see? He never talks about that. I don't suppose he told you that they were both punishing him for not doing what they wanted?'

'Punishing him?' Geli shook her head. 'I...I imagined an affair.'

'Nothing so warm-blooded.' Lisa rubbed a cloth over the chrome. 'It hit him very hard.'

So hard that he couldn't envisage another relationship. That was why he'd told her. Not to forestall gossip, but so that she'd understand his reluctance to follow through on the obvious attraction. The classic 'It's not you, it's me…' defence.

'I'm just saying…' Lisa concentrated on polishing an invisible smudge. 'I wouldn't want you to be hurt.'

Really? A bit late to be worrying about that, Lisa…

Geli shook her head. 'I'm not interested in commitment. My sisters have all that happy-ever-after stuff, baby thing well covered. I'm my mother's child.'

She frowned. 'Your mother?'

'She didn't believe in long-term relationships. My sisters and I all have different fathers. At least we assume we do, since we all look quite different.'

'You don't know your father?'

'She used sperm donors.' It was her standard response to anyone interested enough to ask. Spilling out the truth to Dante had been a rare exposure. But then everything about Dante was rare. 'So much less bother, don't you think?'

'Um…' She'd rendered Lisa speechless? That had to be a first… 'Okay. Well, I suggest you come down at seven, while it's still quiet, and you can shadow Matteo. He'll look after you until you get the hang of things. Hold on…' She reached behind her. 'Take the menu to familiarise yourself with it.' She wrote something on the bottom. 'And that should deal with anyone pestering you for a date, although a shrug and *non capisco* will get you out of most situations.'

'Like this?' She shrugged and, putting on a breathy Italian accent, said, *'Non capisco.'*

Lisa grinned. 'Say it like that and I refuse to be responsible!'

Saturday night at Café Rosa was non-stop service of food and drink to the accompaniment of the jazz quartet from the night before. Everyone was very patient with her and Matteo caught any potential disasters before they happened. She had a couple more offers of a drink and dinner, which she managed to dodge without incident, although once Lisa was away there was no need to pretend that she and Dante might become an item—

'Geli...' She turned to find Lisa holding a tray loaded with coffee, water and a *panino*.

'You can take your break now. Will you give this to Dan on your way upstairs? And remind him that it's Saturday night. All work and no play...' She looked around. 'We seem to be between rushes at the moment. Take your time.'

Dante heard Angelica coming—it was disconcerting how quickly he'd come to recognise her quick, light step—but he didn't look up as she opened the door. If she saw he was busy she might not stop. His head might be telling him not to get involved, but his body wasn't listening and he needed to keep his distance.

'Lisa sent you some supper,' she said, placing it on the table behind his desk.

Of course she had. Any excuse that would throw them together...

He grunted an acknowledgement and continued to pound away at the keyboard.

'It's not good for you, you know.'

'What isn't?'

'Eating while you work.' Angelica backed up and propped herself on the edge of his desk. 'You'll get indigestion, heartburn and stomach ulcers.'

Nothing compared with what her bottom, inches from his hand, was doing to him. 'Haven't you got a café full of customers?'

'I'm on my break.' He continued typing, although it was unlikely he was making any sense. 'Lisa expects me to sit on your knee and ruffle your hair while I tell you about all the men who've hit on me this evening.'

'Did she say that?'

'Not in so many words, but she told me to remind you that all work and no play makes Dante very dull. And she told me to take my time. Of course, it could be that I'm so useless she's desperate to get me out of the way for half an hour.'

'Are you useless?'

'Not totally.'

No. He'd heard all about her virtuoso performance on the Gaggia from a very smug Lisa.

He stopped pretending to work and looked up. She'd swathed herself in one of the Café Rosa's long black aprons and her hair was tied back with a velvet ribbon. She looked cool and efficient but that full crimson mouth would turn heads at fifty paces.

'How many men?' he asked.

'Let's see. There was Roberto.' She held up her hand, fingers spread wide and ticked him off on a finger. 'Dark hair, blue eyes, leather biker jacket. *"Andiamo in un posto più tranquillo..."'* she said in a low, sexy voice.

'I'd advise against going anywhere with him, noisy or quiet.'

'He's bad?'

'His wife is away, looking after her sick mother.'

'What a jerk,' she said, using a very Italian gesture to dismiss him. 'What about Leo? He wanted to "friend" me on Facebook. Was that a euphemism for something else, do you think?'

'That you're thinking it suggests you already know.'

'Men! All they want is sex. Doesn't anyone ask a girl out on a proper date any more?'

'A proper date?' he asked.

'The kind where a man picks a girl up from her home, takes her to the movies, buys her popcorn and they hold hands in the dark—'

'Was that it?' He cut her off, trying not to think about Angelica in the dark with some man who might be holding her hand in the cinema but would have his mind on where else he was going to hold her when he got her home.

'What? Oh, no. Gennaro was very sweet, but I'm not looking for a father figure, and Nic, the guy who plays the saxophone, said *"Ti amo..."* in the most affecting way, but I think that was because I'd just taken him a beer.'

'That'll do it every time for Nic; even so, that's quite a fan club you've got there. Are any of them going to get lucky?'

'With Lisa keeping a close eye on me? She's doing a great job of protecting your interests.'

'She doesn't trust my personal charm to hold you in thrall?'

'I'm down there and you're up here working.' She lifted her shoulders, sketching a shrug. 'Out of sight, out of mind.' She blew away a wisp of hair that had escaped its tie. 'Did I mention Marco? He came in this afternoon when Lisa was showing me the ropes. I made him an espresso. He's downstairs now...' She stopped. 'You don't want to hear this when you're so obviously busy. I hadn't realised running a bar involved so much bureaucracy.'

'There's enough to keep me fully occupied, but I'm working on a development plan for Isola. One that doesn't involve pulling down historic streets,' he added.

'Oh, I see. Well, that's seriously important work and I'm disturbing you.'

Without a doubt...

'Don't forget your supper,' she said, rubbing the tip of her thumb across her lower lip. 'Is my lipstick convincingly smudged, do you think?' As she leaned forward so that he could give her his opinion, the top of her apron gaped to offer a glimpse of black lace beneath the scoop top of the black T-shirt she was wearing. It was clinging to soft white breasts and if that was the view that customers were getting as she served them it was hardly any wonder that she was getting hit on. 'Maybe I should muss up my hair a bit?'

'You want Lisa to think that we've been making out over my desk?'

'I'm doing my best to convince her that we're struggling to keep our hands off each other. Without a lot of help, I might add—'

As she reached up to tease out a strand, he caught her wrist.

'You want your hair mussed?' he asked, his voice sounding strange, as if he'd never heard it before.

She said nothing, but the tip of her tongue appeared briefly against softly parted lips, her pupils widened, black as her hair, swallowing up the silver-grey of her eyes and the catch in her breath was answered by his body's clamour to touch her, take her.

For a moment neither of them moved then he released her wrist, reached for the ribbon holding her hair and, as he tugged it loose, the silken mass fell forward, brushing against his face, enveloping him in the intimacy of its scent as she slid into his lap.

His fingers slipped through it as he cradled her head, angling his mouth to tease her lips open and, as he brushed against the sensitive nerve endings at her nape, a tiny moan—more vibration than sound—escaped her lips, her body softened against him and his tongue was swathed in hot sweet satin.

With one hand tangled in her hair, the other sought out the gap between her T-shirt and the black ankle-length skirt that hid her fabulous legs, sliding over satin skin to cradle her lace-covered breast, touch her candy-hard nipple.

She wanted this, he wanted it and he was a fool not to taste her, touch her, bury himself deep inside her—over his desk, on the floor, in his bed. It had nothing to do with emotion, feelings; this was raw, physical need.

It was just sex—

The four words slammed through his body like an ice storm. Colder than the snow-covered Dolomites.

'It was just sex...'

The last words Valentina had said to him.

'Okay, that should do it,' he said, lifting her from his lap and setting her on her feet before swinging his chair back to face his laptop. 'If that's all, I want this on the Minister's desk first thing on Monday.'

She didn't move but he didn't have to look to know that her hair was loose about her shoulders, her swollen lips open in a shocked O, her expression that of a kicked puppy. The image was imprinted indelibly on his brain.

He didn't expect or wait for an answer but began pounding on the keyboard as if nothing had happened while she backed out of the room, then turned and ran up the stairs. Kept pounding until he heard the door bang shut on the floor above and his fingers froze above the keyboard.

He stared at the screen, the cursor blinking an invitation to delete the rubbish he'd just written. Instead, he slumped back in the chair, dragging his hands over his face, rubbing hard to eradicate every trace of Angelica Amery. It didn't work. The scent of her skin, her hair was on his hands, in his lungs and, as he wiped the back of his hand over his mouth in an attempt to eradicate the honeyed taste of her lips, it came away bearing traces of crimson lipstick.

It would be two more days before Angelica moved out.

They were going to be two very long days and right now he needed air—fresh, clean, cold air—to blow her out of his head.

CHAPTER EIGHT

*'You can't buy happiness but you can buy ice cream...
which is much the same thing.'*
          —from *Rosie's Little Book of Ice Cream*

GELI'S RACING PULSE, pounding heartbeat said, *Run—run
for your life.* Falling in lust with a man who had made
it clear not once, not twice but three times that while he
might be aroused—and he had certainly been aroused—
he was not interested in any kind of relationship was a
recipe for disaster.

Sharing an apartment with that man, working with him
was never going to work.

She threw open her bedroom window, stuck her head
out and filled her lungs with icy air, hoping that it would
cool not just her skin but freeze the heat from the inside
out.

What was it about Dante Vettori that made her lose her
wits? What had started out as a little teasing had ended
with his arms around her, his mouth on hers, his hands
spread wide over her skin. She shivered and pressed her
hand hard against her breast, where his touch had created a
shock of pleasure that racketed around her body like a pin-
ball machine, lighting up every sensory receptor she had.

Maybe she should suggest some straightforward recre-
ational sex so they could both get it out of their systems.

No strings. Except if he'd been a 'no strings' kind of guy he'd have been out there, taking anything on offer in an attempt to obliterate the heartbreak. A man who looked like Dante would not have been short of offers.

If he'd been a 'no strings' kind of guy they would have been naked right now.

He needed something more than that. Or maybe something less. Someone who didn't want anything from him but was just there...

She was good at that. She'd been rescuing broken creatures ever since she'd picked up that injured pheasant. She'd never tried rescuing a broken person before but there was no difference. They were edgy, scared and you had to earn their trust, too. No sudden moves. No demands...

She checked on Rattino, sat on the floor rubbing his tiny domed head, while she sipped iced water, rolled the glass against her mouth to cool her swollen lips and heated libido.

Having stretched the taking her time instruction to the limit, she found a clip and fastened back her hair, straightened her clothes, applied a fresh coat of lipstick. It was time to get back to work...

Dante was standing in the middle of the sitting room. He was wearing his jacket, had a bright red scarf around his neck and in his hands he was holding a battered cardboard box.

For a moment they stared at one another, then he said, 'I found this on the back doorstep.'

'On the doorstep?' What was he doing on the doorstep when he was so busy writing a report...?

'I needed some fresh air,' he said.

You and me both, mister, she thought, taking a step closer so that she could see what was in the box.

'Oh, kittens.' Two of them, all eyes, huddled together in the corner. 'Your notice appears to have worked.'

'I was under the impression that its purpose was to find the owner of Rattino so that we could return him to the bosom of his family,' he said, unimpressed. 'Not have the rest of his family dumped on our doorstep.'

She looked up. *Our doorstep...*

'In an ideal world,' she said, returning to the kittens, picking each one up in turn and checking it over for any sign of injury before replacing it in the box. 'They're thin but otherwise seem in good shape.'

'I imagine their mother is a stray who didn't come back from a hunting trip.'

'It seems likely. And would explain why Rattino went looking for food. He is the biggest. So what do you think?'

'What do I think?'

'Shall we call the black one Mole and the one with stripes Badger? We already have Ratty?' she prompted. '*Wind in the Willows*? It's a classic English children's book,' she explained when he made no response. 'Or would you prefer Italian names?'

'I think...' He took a breath. 'I think I'll go and take down those notices before anyone else decides to leave a box of unwanted kittens on the doorstep.'

'Right. Good plan. I'll, um, feed these two,' she said as he headed for the door. 'Introduce them to the amenities. Will you keep an eye out for their mother, while you're out? She wouldn't have abandoned them.'

'If she's been hit by a car—'

'You're right. She may be lying hurt somewhere,' she said. 'Hang on while I see to these two and I'll come with you. I know the kind of places she'll crawl into.'

Geli had no doubt that Dante would rather be on his own but, rather than waste his breath, he said, 'I'll go and tell Lisa that she's going to have to manage without you.'

'You'll make her evening.'

'No doubt.' His tone left her under no illusion that she wasn't making his. 'Wrap up well. It's freezing out there.'

Twenty minutes later, having fed the kittens, reunited them with their brother and changed her flat working shoes for a pair of sturdy boots, she was walking with Dante along the street where she'd found Rattino.

'Urban cats have a fairly limited range,' she explained, stopping every few yards to check doorways and explore the narrow street that had given her a fright the night she'd arrived. 'They avoid fights by staying out of each other's way whenever possible. Will you hold this?'

'Where is your glove?' he demanded when she handed him her flashlight and began to turn over boxes with her bare hand.

'In my pocket. I held the kittens so she'd smell them on me but she's not here—'

She broke off as he took her icy hand and tucked it into his own roomy fleece-lined glove so that their hands were palm to palm. 'Now we'll both smell of her kittens.'

She looked up at him. 'Good thinking.'

'I'm glad you approve,' he said and the shadows from the street lights emphasised the creases as, unexpectedly, he smiled.

Oh, boy... She turned away to grab one of the notices from a nearby lamp post and saw the wooden barriers surrounding the construction site where Via Pepone used to be.

'There,' she said. 'If she's survived, she'll be in there.'

'Are you certain?'

'As certain as I can be. Disturbed ground, displaced rodents, workmen dropping food scraps, lots of places to hide. Perfect for a mother with three hungry kittens. Maybe someone working on the site knew they were there and when he saw the notice brought them to us.'

'That makes sense.' He walked across to the site entrance and tried the gate. It did not budge.

'Is there a night watchman?' she asked.

'It's the twenty-first century.' He looked up at the cameras mounted on high posts. 'It's all high-tech security systems and CCTV monitored from a warm office these days.'

'Okaaay.' She reluctantly removed her hand from his glove and fished in her pocket for her own. 'In that case you'll have to give me a bunk-up so that I can climb over.'

'Alarms?' he reminded her. 'CCTV.'

'Which will deal with the problem of how I'd climb back out again with an injured cat. And the local *polizia* are so helpful. I'm sure they'll drive me to the vet before they arrest me.'

'Drive you to the vet, send out for hot chocolate to keep you warm and raise a collection to pay the vet's bill, I have no doubt. But you've had your quota of excitement for this week.'

'Well, that's a mean thing to say.' Their breath mingled in the freezing air and she pulled on her glove before she did something really exciting, like grabbing his collar and pulling him down to warm their freezing lips. 'Okay, your turn. What do you suggest?'

'I suppose I could climb over the fence and get arrested.'

'Your life is that short of excitement?'

'Not since you and that wretched kitten arrived.'

'You can thank me later. Any other ideas?' She waited. 'I sensed an *or* in there somewhere.'

He shrugged, looked somewhere above her head. 'Or I could make a phone call and get the security people to let us in.'

'Maybe sooner rather than later,' she suggested, stamping her feet.

He looked down at her for a long moment, then took out his cellphone, thumbed a number on his fast dial list and walked away down the street as he spoke to whoever answered. The conversation was brief and he wasn't smiling as he rejoined her.

'Someone will be here in a few minutes.'

'Well, that's impressive.'

'You think so?'

He looked up at the floodlit boarding high above the fence with an artist's impression of the office block that would replace Via Pepone. It bore the name of the construction company in huge letters. Beneath, smaller, was the name of the developer.

Vettori SpA.

Oh... 'That's not a coincidence, is it?' she said.

'My great-grandfather started the business after the war, repairing bomb-damaged buildings, working every hour God gave to save enough money to buy some land and build a small block of flats. My grandfather took over a thriving construction company and continued to expand the business until a heart attack forced him to retire and he handed it over to my father.'

This was his father's project? 'Was that who you called just now? Your father?'

Before he could answer, a security patrol van drew up in a spray of dirty snow. The driver leapt out, exchanged a few words with Dante in rapid Italian and then unlocked the small personal door set in the gates.

'Take care, Angel,' Dante said, taking her hand as they stepped through after him.

Angel? She turned and looked up at him.

'A construction site is a hazardous place,' he said.

'Yes...' With the ground frozen, no work had been done in the last couple of days and, as the patrolman shone his flashlight slowly across the site, there were few footprints to mar the pristine snow. Then she saw something... 'There!' She snatched her hand away to point to where the light picked up a disturbance in the snow. Not paw prints but a wider trail marked by darker patches of blood where an animal had dragged herself across the ground, desperate to get back to her babies. 'She's hurt.'

'Wait…'

She ignored Dante, running across the yard, using her own small flashlight to follow the trail until she reached the place where the cat had wedged herself under pallets piled with building materials.

'Let me do this.' Dante knelt beside her, but she'd already stripped off her gloves and was holding out her hands so that the cat could smell her kittens. Crooning and chirruping, she dragged herself towards the scent until Geli could reach her and lift her gently from her hiding place. '*Dio*… She's a mess.'

'We need to keep her warm. Take my scarf,' she urged, but Dante pulled off his beautiful red cashmere scarf and wrapped it around the poor creature. 'We need to get her to a vet,' she said.

Dante looked at this angel, so passionate, so full of compassion.

He called the vet and then asked the security guard to drive them to his office. 'He'll meet us there. Come on; it'll be a squeeze, but it's not far,' he said, holding the door so that she could slide into the passenger seat, then squashing in after her, sitting sideways to give her as much room as possible. 'I'll breathe in when you breathe out and we should be okay,' he said, and she laughed. Such a good sound.

The vet was unlocking the door as they arrived, and Dante translated while Geli assisted him until his nurse arrived and they were no longer needed. Then they retired to the freezing waiting room.

'This is going to take a while,' she said, her breath a misty cloud. 'You should get back to your report.'

'It will keep.' He settled in the corner of the battered sofa and opened his jacket in invitation but she hesitated. Despite the last hour, she wasn't likely to forget the appalling way he'd behaved when she came up to his office. Okay, she'd been flirting a little but he should not have risen to it. Should not have kissed her, touched her and, when she'd responded with an eagerness that had wiped everything but need from his mind, he should not have rejected her.

He was a mess, he knew it, but the room was freezing and she wasn't going anywhere until she knew whether the cat was going to survive.

'Come on. You're shivering,' he said and, after what felt like for ever, she surrendered to the reality of the situation and sat down primly beside him. 'Snuggle up. You're letting out all the warmth,' he said, looping his arm around her and drawing her close, wrapping his coat around her.

She looked at him. 'Snuggle?'

'My mother used to say that. That's right, isn't it?'

'Yes.' She nodded and relaxed into him. 'My mother used to say that when we piled on the sofa to watch a movie on the television.'

'What movies did you watch together?'

'*Beauty and the Beast. Mary Poppins. The Jungle Book. White Fang…* We used an entire box of tissues between us when we watched that one.'

'Did White Fang die?' he asked, in an attempt to distract himself from the way her body was pressed against his, the tickle of her hair against his cheek.

'No, it was the scene where the boy had to send the wolf away for its own safety. He pretended he didn't love it any more. It was heartbreaking.'

'I can imagine.' He looked down at her. Or, rather, the top of her head. 'Is the cat going to make it, do you think?'

'It's hard to say. She seems to have taken a glancing

blow from a car. There's a lot of superficial damage, cuts and scrapes and a broken bone or two.' She turned her head and looked up at him and, despite his best intentions, it took all his strength not to kiss her again. 'It depends what internal damage has been done.'

'Yes, of course.' *Look away. Think about the cat.* 'How on earth did she manage to get under the fence and drag herself back across the site?'

'Cats are amazing and she's a mother. Her babies needed her.'

'They survived without her.'

Her face pressed against the collar of Dante's shirt, his neck, sharing his warmth, Geli heard a world of hurt in those few words.

'Only because I found Rattino and you put up that notice,' she said. 'Do you see your mother, Dante?'

He stared straight ahead and for a moment she didn't think he was going to answer her, but then he shrugged. 'Occasionally. She remarried, started a new family.'

'So you were able to return to Italy.'

'Just for the holidays. I was at school in England. Then I was away at university.'

'England or Italy?'

'Scotland. Then the US.'

Distancing himself from a father who was too busy with the new woman in his life to put him first, she thought. And from a mother who had found someone new to love and made a second family where he probably felt like a spare part...

She felt a bit like that, too, now that her sisters were married. It was no longer the three of them against the world.

'What did you read? At uni?' she asked. Anything to take away the bleakness in those dark eyes.

'Politics, philosophy and economics at St Andrews. Business management at Harvard.'

'St Andrews,' she repeated, with a teasing Scottish accent. 'And Harvard?'

He looked down at her, a smile creating a sunburst of creases around his eyes. 'Are you suggesting that I'm a little over-qualified to run a café?'

She made a performance of a shrug. 'What are you going to do with your degree except work as a researcher for a Member of Parliament? But business management at Harvard seems a little over the top. Unless you're planning world domination in the jazz café market?'

'Not ice cream and definitely not jazz cafés,' he said. 'The plan was that I gain some experience with companies in the United States before joining my father.'

'The fourth generation to run Vettori SpA?'

'Until Via Pepone got in the way.'

'Do you regret taking a stand?' she asked.

'Wrong question, Angel. The question is whether, given the same choices, I would do it again.'

'Would you?' she asked, shivering against him, not with the cold, where the snow had melted into her skirt and clung wetly to her legs, but at the thought of the boy who'd had his life torn apart, bouncing between adults who thought only of themselves.

'Maybe I was never meant to be the CEO of a big company,' he said, taking out his cellphone and thumbing in a text with the hand he didn't have around her shoulders. 'I hoped it would bring us closer together, but my father and I are very different. He thinks I'm soft, sentimental, trying to hang onto a past that is long gone. Incapable of holding onto a woman like Valentina Mazzolini.'

'When what you're actually trying to do is make a future for a place that you love.' A place where, sitting in Nonnina Rosa's kitchen as a boy, watching her cook, he'd been happy. Where he'd spent time as a youth on those long school holidays while his mother and father had been absorbed in new partnerships...

Isola was his home.

'Local politics seems to be calling me,' he admitted. 'There's no money in it, no A-list parties, just a lot of hard work, but maybe, in twenty or thirty years, if I've managed to hold back the march of the skyscraper and secure the spirit of old Isola in a modern world, they'll elect me mayor.'

'Tell me about Isola,' she urged. 'About your vision.'

'Vision?'

'Isn't that what the report you're writing is all about? Not just facts and figures, but your vision, your passion. The human scale?'

'That's the idea,' he said, 'but it's difficult to put all that into words that a politician can use. They need the facts and figures. It's dull stuff.'

'We're going to be here for a while and the only alternative is a pile of dog-eared Italian gossip magazines about people I've never heard of.' And she could have listened to Dante Vettori read the telephone directory. 'Go for it.'

'Go for it?'

'Tell me your plan, Dan.' He laughed—not some big ha-ha-ha laugh, it was no more than a sound on his breath, but it was the genuine article. 'Tell me why you love it so much,' she urged.

'It's real,' he said. 'This was a working class district with a strong sense of community. The park was closed and, with no green space, we made our own on a strip of abandoned land by the railway. The factories and the foundry are gone now, but people are still making things here because it's what they do, who they are. You know that, Angel. It's why you came.'

'Nothing stands still. There has to be change. Growth.'

'But you don't have to tear everything down. If they could just see—' He dismissed the thought with a gesture.

'What would you show them?' she pressed.

'The life, the music, the people.' And, at her urging, he poured out his love of Isola, his vision of the future.

'I don't think they'll wait twenty years,' she said when he fell silent. 'I think, given the chance, they'd elect you now.'

That raised one of his heart-stopping smiles. 'Maybe I should ask you to be my campaign manager.'

'Maybe you should.'

Their words hung in the air, full of possibilities, but she knew he hadn't meant it. It was just one of those things that slipped out when your mouth was working faster than your brain...

A tap on the outside door released them.

'I hope that's not another emergency.'

Dante didn't reply, but slipped out of his jacket and wrapped it around her while he went to investigate. He returned a few moments later with two carry-out drinks from Café Rosa and a box containing a pizza the size of a cartwheel.

'I didn't eat the supper you brought up,' he said, staring at the magazines for a moment before pushing them aside and opening the box to release the scent of tomatoes, cheese, basil. 'And you didn't get your break. It's a Margherita,' he added, glancing at her. 'No meat.' He checked the cups. 'This is yours. Hot chocolate.'

'*Posso abbracciarti,* Dante?' His only response was a frown. 'Did I mess that up?'

'That depends if you intended to ask if you could give me a hug.'

'You sent out for hot chocolate and my favourite pizza,' she pointed out. 'What do you think?' Then, grabbing a slice to cover her embarrassment, 'Don't fret. I was speaking metaphorically.'

'Metaphorically? Right.' Did he sound disappointed? She didn't dare look. 'Your Italian is coming along in leaps and bounds.'

'I'm memorising the phrasebook that Sorrel gave me.'

'Your sister?'

'The one who's married to an explorer.'

'And that was in it?'

'They've apparently moved on a bit since "my postilion was struck by lightning".' She took a bite of the pizza and groaned with pleasure.

'But they haven't got to grips with the metaphorical.'

She caught a trailing dribble of cheese with her finger and guided it into her mouth. 'It's a very small phrasebook.'

'Small but dangerous. Not everyone will get the subtleties of meaning.'

'Marco?' she suggested. 'He wasn't very subtle.'

'Nor was Roberto.'

'Oh, I've got him covered.' She adopted a pose. '*Non m'interessa*—I'm not interested. *Mi lasci in pace*—Leave me alone. *Smetta d'infastidirmi!*—Stop bothering me!'

'I take it all back. It is a most excellent phrasebook.'

'And this is the most excellent pizza. You texted Lisa?'

'I knew she'd worry when we didn't come back. And I thought you would welcome some warm food.'

'You thought right,' she said, helping herself to a second slice. Then she drank her chocolate, checked the time.

'Put your feet up,' Dante urged and, rather than unlace her boots, she picked up a magazine, placed it on the sofa and rested them on that. Then she eased the damp skirt away from her legs, tucked her feet up under her coat and invited him back into his jacket. He slipped his arms in and she leaned back against him as if it was the most natural thing in the world and, warm from the food, tired from what had been a very long day, she closed her eyes.

Dante watched with the envy of the insomniac as Angelica closed her eyes and was instantly asleep. Watched her as the silence grew deep around him and he closed his own eyes.

'Dante…'

He felt a touch to his shoulder and looked up to find the vet standing over him. He'd slept?

'It's over, Dante. She's in recovery.'

'The prognosis?'

'Fair. Cats are tough. We'll keep her here for a day or two and see how she does but, all things being equal, you can take her home in a couple of days.'

'Actually, she's a stray.'

'Good try,' he said, 'but she's going to need warmth, good food and care if she's going to make a full recovery. Tell the young lady that she saved her life. Another hour or two…' His gesture suggested that it would have been touch and go. 'You can see her if you want.'

'I'm sure she'll want to.'

'Come on through. Is there a spare slice of pizza?'

'It'll be cold.'

'My food usually is,' he said, helping himself to a slice and taking a bite.

'How much do I owe you?'

'My receptionist will send you a bill at the end of the month but I'll bring my family to the café at the weekend and you can give us all lunch. A small repayment for disturbing my evening.'

'My pleasure.'

Angelica stirred, opened her eyes, looked blank for a moment and then sat up in a rush as she saw the vet walking away with a slice of pizza in his hand. 'What's happened? How is she?'

'She's fine. We can take her home in a couple of days. Do you want to see her?'

'Please.' She stood up, picked up the magazine to return to the table and saw the front cover. An older man and a much younger woman arriving at some gala event. She didn't need to read Italian or check the names to know who they were.

He was Dante, twenty-five years on, just as she'd imagined him, with a touch of silver at the temple to lend gravitas. The woman, gold-blonde with ice-blue eyes, was wearing a designer gown that was a shade darker than her eyes and a Queen's ransom in diamonds.

He turned back to see what was keeping her and saw the magazine in her hand. He walked back to her and took it from her.

'The first time I saw her was at a party my father threw to welcome me to Vettori SpA. They were standing together but I was too self-absorbed to realise that he was in love with her. Even later, when he married her, I thought...'

'You thought he'd done it to hurt you.'

'Lisa told you that.' He shook his head. 'I was wrong. If I'd just taken a moment to look at him instead of her.' He looked bleak, utterly wretched and, unable to bear it, she touched his arm so that he looked up at her instead of the picture. 'He stood back and let me walk away with her.'

'Because he loved you both.'

'Maybe, but he chose her.'

Rejecting him for the second time. And yet Dante had called him tonight, asked him for help. For her.

Before she could think of the words to tell him that she knew how much it must have cost him, he tossed the magazine back on the pile at the end of the table. 'Shall we go and see how cat number four is doing?'

They went through to the recovery area where she was sleeping off the anaesthetic. Large patches of fur had been shaved off. There were stitches, her leg was in a cast and she'd lost most of her tail.

'She looks like Frankenstein's cat,' he said.

'It's temporary. She's been through the mill and she'll need a lot of TLC, but one day, when her fur has grown back and the pain has retreated, she'll smell a mouse or see a bird and, without thinking, she'll be up and away, purring with pleasure at being alive and on the hunt.'

He was very still beside her, not speaking, not moving. Then he said, 'My father took Valentina away and married her secretly in Las Vegas. No one knew about it for months.'

'Well, that makes sense. The gossip magazines would have gone to town. Paps following you around, hoping for some reaction. Speculation about whether you'd been invited to the wedding. Whether you'd show.'

He managed a wry smile. 'I suppose I should be grateful. In the end, their extended honeymoon was brought to an end when Valentina's grandmother died. The fact that she was very obviously pregnant made the front page of *Celebrità*.'

'That must have been a shock. Were you there? At the funeral?'

'No. My father sent me an email telling me that they were married, about the baby, asking me to stay away and I've done that.'

'Until tonight.'

He nodded.

'And he answered.'

'I imagine he's been waiting for my call.' He took out his gloves and pulled them on. 'When he realised that all I wanted was to get into the site to rescue a cat he was so relieved that he couldn't do enough.'

'Maybe he'll call you next.'

'If he doesn't, I'll call him.' He'd sounded matter-of-fact as he'd talked about what had happened but, when he turned to her, his normally expressive face was blank of all emotion. 'Shall we go?'

She paused on the step and, hunting for a way to change the subject, she looked up at the night sky. 'There are no stars.'

'It's the light pollution from the city.' Dante took her arm as her foot slipped on the freezing pavement. 'You have to go up into the mountains to see them.'

'In the snow? That would be magic.'

He looked down at her, his lips pulled into an unexpected smile. 'Would you like to go?'

Her heart squeezed in her chest. 'Now?'

'You're the advocate of seizing the day,' he reminded her. 'The forecast this evening suggested a warm front was coming in from the south. It could be raining tomorrow.'

For a dizzying moment she saw herself lying back in the snow, making angels with Dante, while all around them the world was sparkling-white, velvet-black and filled with diamonds...

This was why she'd come to Italy. For excitement, for moments like this. Her mother would grab the moment without a backward glance, without a thought for the consequences.

But she wasn't her mother.

'I have to check the kittens,' she said, sounding exactly like her responsible big sister, Elle. Elle who, just eighteen and with a college place waiting, had sacrificed her ambitions to stay at home and take a minimum-wage job so that she could feed her siblings, take care of her mentally fragile grandmother. Nurturing, caring, always there.

'Of course you do. And I have no confidence in the weather forecast. Experience suggests that we're going to be freezing for a while yet.'

They walked in silence for a while, their boots crunching against the frozen snow, their breath mingling in the bitter air, but Dante had offered her something special and she wanted to give him something in return. Something that would show him that she had not been rejecting him.

Something personal, something that she would only share with someone she— Someone she trusted.

'It's blonde,' she said.

'Blonde?' He glanced down at her.

'You wanted to know the natural colour of my hair. It's white-blonde.'

'Really?'

'I have to dye my brows and lashes or they'd be invisible. There must have been a Scandinavian roustabout with the Fair the year before I was born.'

'I can't imagine you as a blonde,' he said.

No, well, she'd seen the quality of blonde he was used to dating. 'I did once consider leaving a natural streak,' she said. 'For dramatic effect.'

'*Cara*...you are all the drama a man can take.'

'Is that a compliment? No, it's not... Anyway,' she said, rapidly moving on, 'Great-Uncle Basil said I'd look more like Lily Munster than Morticia Addams so that was that.'

'You are like no one, Angel. You are individual. Unique.'

Unique? 'Not exactly the kind of compliment a woman queues up to hear but I'll take it.'

'You don't need me to tell you that you're stunning, Angelica Amery. You have Roberto and Gennaro and Nic and Marco lining up to turn your head.' She laughed and he drew her closer to his side.

The café was closed when they arrived back and they went in the back way.

At the first landing Dante stopped. 'Go and tell the kittens that their *mamma* will be home soon. Have a warm bath. I've got a few things to do.'

'Do you ever sleep, Dante?'

'Not much,' he admitted.

'Not enough,' she said, lifting her cold hands to his face and smoothing her thumbs across the hollows under his eyes. 'You need to quieten your mind before you go to bed.'

The world stilled. 'How do I do that?' he asked.

'First you switch off your computer. Then you write a list of the things you have to do tomorrow so that you don't stay awake trying to remember them.'

'But I've turned off my computer,' he reminded her. 'How do I do that?'

'Use a notepad and a pen.'

'That's a bit old school.'

'Maybe, but that's the rule.'

'Okay, pen, paper, list. Then what?'

'You take a bath—don't have the water too hot; your body needs to be cool to sleep.'

He leaned against his office door, folded his arms. 'Go on.'

'Sprinkle a few drops of lavender oil on your pillow before you get into bed and, when you close your eyes, think about all the good things that happened to you today.'

'Good things? What do you suggest? Our trip to the police station? That I've been lumbered with two more kittens and their injured mother? Spent hours in a freezing—'

'Don't be such a grouch. You helped a stranger who was in a fix. Rescued a cat that would have died without you doing something big, something difficult. You spoke to your father.'

She rubbed her hand over his arm, a gesture of comfort to let him know that she was aware how hard it must have been to ask him for help.

He looked at her hand, small, white, with perfect crimson-tipped nails, lying against his shabby worn waxed jacket sleeve, and for a moment he couldn't think about anything but reaching out and wrapping his arms around her, just holding her.

'Think about how good that pizza tasted.'

He looked up, realised that she was looking at him with concern. He straightened, breaking the contact. 'Is that it?'

'No. Last thing of all, you should think about all the good things you're going to do tomorrow so that you wake up happy.'

'Is that more of your mother's wisdom?'

'Yes…' Her eyes sparkled a little too brightly. 'Can I give you that hug now, Dante?'

'A metaphorical one?'

'Actually, I think you deserve the real thing,' she said, stepping close and, before he could move, she'd wrapped her arms around him, her cheek was against his chest. 'You have been a one hundred per cent good guy today, Dante Vettori. Think about that.'

Dante closed his eyes and inhaled the scent of this woman who had blown into his life like a force of nature.

She smelled of pizza and chocolate, there was a hint of antiseptic where she'd washed after handling the cat. And something more that he was coming to recognise as indefinably his Angel…

'You can hug back,' she murmured after a moment. 'It doesn't hurt.'

How could she be so sure? How could you want something so much and dread it at the same time? But ever since she'd asked him to hug her while they were waiting for the vet, leaning against him as she'd put her feet up, he'd been thinking about how it would feel to really hold her, to kiss her, live for the moment. What would happen if he followed through on those kisses without any thought of the past or the future?

Selfish thoughts. Dangerous thoughts. But if anyone

deserved a hug it was Angelica and he tightened his arms
about her, holding her close for a long perfect minute, but
she was wrong about it not hurting. It hurt like hell when,
after a while, she pulled away.

CHAPTER NINE

*'If you licked the sunset, it would taste like Neapoli-
tan ice cream.'*

—from *Rosie's Little Book of Ice Cream*

GELI STOOD AT the top of the stairs hugging her arms around her, holding in how it felt to have Dante's arms around her. Not in some crazy mad moment when one or both of them had temporarily lost control, but the kind of hug you'd give a friend in a shared moment. Special, real…

He was special. She could not imagine how hard it must have been for him to call his father and ask for his help but he'd done it for her. Okay, he'd done it for the cat, but if it hadn't been for her he wouldn't have been out there in the freezing night looking for a stray cat in the first place.

He *was* special and she would be his friend and if that was all he could give then she'd ask for nothing more.

Dante watched as Angelica ran up to the top floor to check on her precious kittens then went into his office and sat down at his desk. He'd left his laptop on and the screensaver was drifting across the screen waiting for him to touch a key and continue with his dry, full of facts report that, despite all the promises and encouragement from the minister, would be filed and forgotten.

He turned the machine off, pulled a legal pad close, uncapped a pen and wrote the number one in the margin.

Quieten his mind. Make a list…

It began easily enough as he jotted down half a dozen of the most urgent things he had to do in the coming week. He added a note of something to include in his report. Crossed that through. Wrote: *vision, passion*… He underlined the last two words. What was it Angelica had asked him? *'What would you show them?'*

The life, the music but, above all, the people. Not some slick documentary film but real people talking straight into the camera, telling those who would tear this place down what was so great about it. Why they should think again.

He sent a text to Lisa, wishing them both *buon viaggia, buona fortuna,* so she'd see it when she woke. He hoped he'd done the right thing. That Lisa and Giovanni's love would heal the rift between their families. If it did they would have Angelica's crazy arrival to thank for that.

Angelica—

She had never had a father, had lost her mother at a pitifully early age. She might wear the protective black she'd hidden behind as a child but on the inside her world was richly coloured and filled with wonderful memories. Tragedy, need, had not shattered her family; it had bound it together.

She'd asked him if he saw his mother and he'd implied that she hadn't had time for him. The truth was that he'd been so angry that she'd found someone else—had *looked* for someone else when he'd sacrificed his world to stay with her—that he'd walked away. He could hear Angelica telling him that he should be grateful that his mother had been strong enough to look forward, move on. Be grateful for the small half-sisters she and her husband had given him and reach out to make them part of his world.

This evening, when he'd called his father to ask for a

favour, they'd spoken as if they were strangers and yet assistance had arrived within minutes. Angelica had assumed guilt, but all he'd heard was the fear of a man with his head buried in the sand.

He looked at the phone lying beside the pad, then picked it up, flicked through the photographs, staring at one he'd downloaded from *Celebrità* for a long time before he sighed, thumbed in a text to let his father know that they'd found the cat, adding his thanks for his prompt response. There was more, but some things had to be said face to face. He added his initial and pressed send then, with the phone still in his hand, he texted his mother to let her know that he'd call her in the morning.

He tapped the end of the pen on the pad for a moment, added one final item to his list and then went upstairs.

The apartment was quiet. The kittens were curled up together in the shelter of their box. And, hanging from the knob of his bedroom door, was a small linen drawstring bag with a hand-embroidered spray of purple lavender. It contained a little glass phial with a handwritten label—*lavender oil* and a date—and a note.

> *Gloria—as in Knickerbocker Gloria of ice cream fame—produces this from her own garden. It's a bit magic, but then she's a bit of a witch.*
>   *I've done with the bathroom so use the tub—a shower will only wake you up.*
>   *Dormi bene. Sogui dolci. G.*

Sleep well. Sweet dreams.

The café did not open on Sunday and Geli got up early to the sound of bells ringing across the city, fed the kittens, gathered cleaning stuff from the utility room and, with a sustaining mug of tea, went down to her workroom.

Dante had cleared out everything but her boxes and she set to work cleaning everything thoroughly before setting up her work tables and drawing board, putting together her stool. Her corkboard was hung and was waiting for the scraps of cloth, pictures—anything and everything that would inspire her.

Three hours later, everything was unpacked, her sewing machines tested, her Mac up and running and all the boxes flattened and neatly stacked away in the corner, ready to be reused when she found somewhere of her own. Not that she could hope to find somewhere as perfect as this.

It was a fabulous space, and she took a series of pictures on her phone which she sent to her sisters, attached to an email explaining that there had been a problem with the apartment she'd rented but that she had found temporary accommodation and everything was great. She might even make a snowman later.

Elle replied, asking for a picture of the snowman.

Sorrel wanted to know: *what problem?* And actually her sister was probably just the person to fight her battle with the bank if things got sticky. She'd chase them up on Monday.

Right now she just itched to sit at her drawing board and begin working on an idea for a design that had been forming in her head ever since she'd seen those black beads in the market. Dusty, hungry; it would have to wait until she'd had a shower and something more substantial than a pastry for breakfast.

She was heading for the bathroom when Dante, dishevelled and wearing only a robe, emerged from his room and her heart jumped as if hit by an electric current.

'Angel—' He was sleep-confused, barely awake, giving her a moment to catch her breath. Gather herself. 'What time is it?'

'*Buongiorno*, Dante,' she said with what, considering

the way her heart was banging away, was a pretty good stab at cool amusement. 'Did you sleep through your alarm?'

He dragged a hand through his hair and his robe gaped to expose a deep V of golden skin from his throat to his waist, the faint spatter of dark hair across his chest. Releasing the knee-weakening scent of warm skin.

'I don't have an alarm clock,' he said, leaning against the door frame as if standing up was still a work in progress, regarding her from beneath heavy lids. 'I don't need one.'

'No?' She knew what the time was, but raised her wrist and pointedly checked her watch. 'You intended to sleep until ten o'clock?'

'Ten? *Dio*, that lavender stuff is lethal.'

It wasn't just the lavender that was lethal. Wearing nothing but a carelessly tied robe, Dante Vettori was a danger not just to her heart, her head, but to just about every other part of her anatomy that was clamouring for attention... 'You had a late night,' she reminded him.

'So did you but it doesn't appear to have slowed you down.' He reached out and she twitched nervously as he picked a cobweb from her hair. 'What on earth have you been doing?'

'Giving the storeroom a good clear-out.' Forcing herself to break eye contact, she brushed a smear of dust from her shoulder. 'I wanted to set up my stuff so that I can start work.' She should move but the message didn't seem to be getting past the putty in her knees. 'Give me ten minutes to clean up and I'll make breakfast.'

'Ten minutes.' He retreated, closing the door, and she slumped against the wall. A woman should have some kind of warning before being confronted with so much unfettered male gorgeousness.

Really.

She had just about got some stiffeners in her knees

when he opened the door again. 'I took your advice and made a list,' he said.

He had? 'Good for you. Clearly, it helped.'

'That's to be seen. One item concerns you.'

'Oh?'

'You won't be moving.'

'I won't?' Her heart racketed around her chest. He wanted her to stay... And then reality kicked in. 'Did Lisa change her mind about taking Giovanni to the wedding?' she asked, concerned.

'No. They should be safely on their way by now.'

'Well, that's good. For them,' she added in case he thought her only worry was about having somewhere to live.

'Let's hope so but, in the meantime, you're going to be here all day, working a shift or on your designs and you can't keep rushing across town to look after an injured cat and a bunch of kittens.'

'It's a kindle,' she said. 'The collective noun. It's a kindle of kittens, a clowder of cats. Would it be necessary to move them? As you said, I'll be around in the day and you'll be here in the evening, at night.'

'Not all the time. I've had my head stuck in this damned report when I need to be out there, drumming up support. Making a noise. I'll be going to Rome some time this week. And I've decided to supplement the report with a DVD.'

'A picture says a thousand words?'

'That's the idea. I thought I'd put together a short film. There'll be library footage of people at last summer's jazz festival, the collective lunches at the *giardino condiviso*, the "green" construction projects and the creation of the street art.'

'That's a start but you'll need people. Interesting faces, characters.'

'Two minds with but a single thought... I'll intersperse

the clips with people talking about why they love this place. Not just the old guys who've been here for ever, but the young people who are drawn here. You, for instance.'

'Me?'

'You're so excited about it. And, as Lisa said, you're good for business.'

'Oh, I see. I'm going to be the hot totty that keeps the old guys watching.'

'Not just the old guys.' He straightened. 'Anyway, that's for next week. I was talking about the cats and it's going to be easier if you stay here and I move into Lisa's flat.'

'You...?' According to Lisa, the heating was on a thermostat, a cheap timer switch would turn the lights on and off and, in any case, she was going to have to go and feed the goldfish and check that everything was okay while he was away. 'Is that really necessary?'

'*Cara...*' He lifted a hand and, although his fingertips barely brushed her cheek, her body's leaping response was all the answer she needed. Of course it was necessary. She would be here, in his space, all day, all evening, either in the café or working on her designs.

He'd made no attempt to deny the frisson of heat, the desire that simmered whenever they were in the same room, but he'd made it clear in every way that, despite the attraction between them, he was still mourning the woman who'd abandoned him.

He might be mourning for Valentina, but right now he was there, leaning against the doorframe, arms folded and very much awake beneath those slumberous lids as he called her *'cara'* in that sexy, chocolate-smooth accent.

She'd probably be doing him a favour if she reached out, tugged on the tie that was struggling to hold his robe together, pushing him over the edge so that he could blame her for his 'fall'.

She wouldn't have to push very hard. He wanted it as

much as she did and she had him at a disadvantage. Once her hands were on his warm satiny skin, his resistance would hit the floor faster than his robe and neither of them would be thinking about anything except getting naked. But afterwards he'd feel guilty, there would be awkwardness and she didn't just want his body, luscious as it was. She was greedy. She wanted all of Dante Vettori.

'Are you sure you'll be able to handle the goldfish?' she asked, stepping back from the danger zone.

'Are you mocking me, Signora Amery?'

'Heaven forbid, Signor Vettori.'

She was mocking herself. She'd come to Isola looking for artistic and emotional freedom. Marco, gorgeously flirtatious, would have been perfect for the kind of sex without strings relationship she had envisaged. Or even the elegant Gennaro. Throwing Dante Vettori in her path on day one was Fate's cruel little joke.

'Now, if you'll excuse me, I have a litter tray to clean.'

Dante shut the door and leaned back against it. He'd made his list then soaked in a tub, filled with water that was not too hot, in a bathroom still steamy and scented with something herby that Angelica had used. Sprinkled a few drops of lavender oil on his pillow before lying back and recalling all the good things that had happened that day. He'd implied it would be hard but a dozen moments had crowded in...

The moment he'd walked into the café that morning, seen Angelica and experienced the same heart-stopping response as the night before. Watching her laugh. Avoiding her eyes as every male in the *commissariato* had paid court to her, knowing that they would be laughing just for him. The weight of her body against his as she'd slept while the vet operated on their stray...

And then he'd thought about all the good things he'd do today so that he'd wake up happy.

He'd have breakfast with Angelica. Bounce ideas off her, about his film. He'd call the vet for an update on the cat because she'd be anxious. Afterwards, they could go into the city for lunch and he'd show her the Duomo, wander through the Quadrilatero so that she could window-shop at the great fashion houses. Finally, supper in front of the fire. And bed. With her? Without her?

He'd have woken very happy if, when he'd opened his eyes, she had been lying beside him, her silky black hair spread across the pillow, her vivid mouth an invitation to kiss her awake...

He tightened his hand in an attempt to obliterate the peachy feel of her skin against his fingertips, the soft flush that warmed her cheeks, darkened her eyes, betraying her, even while she attempted to distance herself with words. They both knew that all he had to do was reach out to her and she would be in his arms.

It had been there from the moment he'd looked around and their eyes had met; in that first irresistible kiss. Romantics called it love at first sight, but it was no more than chemistry bypassing ten thousand years of civilisation, sparking the atavistic drive in all animals to procreate. A recognition that said, *This one. This female will bear strong children, protect your genes...*

That was how it had been with Valentina. She'd been at the party thrown to welcome him home, welcome him into the Vettori fold. She was there when he'd arrived, standing with his father, a golden, glittering prize, and he'd been felled by the metaphorical Stone Age club.

He was still suffering from the after-effects of the concussion and, whatever Lisa advised, whatever the temptation—and he'd been sorely tempted—he would not use Angelica as therapy.

Before he could weaken, he took a bag from his wardrobe, packed everything he was likely to need in the next week and then took a wake-up shower. An espresso, a quick run-through of the heating system and he'd be gone.

And then he opened his bedroom door and the smell of cooking stopped him in his tracks.

'An English breakfast,' he said, dropping his bag in the hall and walking into the kitchen. 'That takes me back to those first days when my mother rented a house in Wimbledon. Sunday mornings and everyone walking their dogs on the Common.'

'Pastries for breakfast are all very well,' Angelica said without turning around, 'but a long day should start with something more substantial.'

'I noticed that you'd bought oatmeal.'

'Oatmeal is for weekdays. Sunday demands *il uovo strapazzato, la pancetta e il pane tostado*.'

'You've been at that phrasebook again.'

'I've moved on to food and drink. Sadly, I can't offer you *la marmellata*. I forgot to buy a jar when I was in the shop.'

'Eggs, bacon and toast with marmalade? Really? I thought you were looking for new experiences, not clinging to the old.'

'So you don't want any of this?' she asked, looking back over her shoulder as she waved a wooden spoon over the scrambled eggs, crisp thin bacon.

'Did I say that?'

Her mouth widened in a teasing grin. 'That's what I thought. You can make the coffee while I dish up. Then you can tell me all about this ice cream parlour you want me to design.'

She was brisk, businesslike, keeping her distance, which should have made their enforced intimacy easier to handle. It didn't. 'You're eager to start?' he asked, concentrating on the espresso but intensely aware of her standing a few feet away.

'I imagine you want it to be open in time for the spring?' She turned to him, a frown buckling the clear space between her lovely brows. 'Or was it just something you said to shut me up about paying rent?'

'No...' He shrugged. 'Maybe. I didn't want an argument, or rent complicating the accounts, but I do have a room that isn't earning its keep and the more I think about it the more the idea grows on me. We'll take a look after breakfast if you've got time.'

Breakfast...

On the intimacy level, that word rang every bell.

'This is it.' Dante stood back and Geli stepped into a large square room with French windows that opened out onto a snow-covered courtyard. He'd warned her that the heating wouldn't be on and she was glad of a long cardigan that fell below her hips and the scarf she'd looped around her neck. 'What do you think?'

With an injured cat to nurse and three lively kittens to look after, an ice cream parlour to design, an inconvenient lust for a man who was locked in the past and snow, Geli thought that this was so not why she'd come to Italy.

She walked across to the window and looked out. There was the skeleton of a tree and a frosted scramble of bare vines on the walls that promised green shade in the summer. An assortment of tables, chairs and a small staged area in the corner were hidden beneath a thick coating of snow, undisturbed by anything other than a confused bird, floundering in an unexpectedly soft landing.

Dante joined her at the window. 'It looks bleak on a day like this but in the summer—'

'I can see,' she said.

The snow would melt, the vines would flower, the kittens would be found good homes and designing an ice cream parlour would be a small price to pay for a temporary workspace. She'd find somewhere to live and Dante... Maybe her heart would stop jumping every time she saw him, every time he came near.

Meanwhile, there was this very tired room to bring to life.

She drew a rough square on the pad she was carrying and then fed out a tape measure. 'Will you give me a hand measuring up?'

He took the end and held it while she read off the basic dimensions—length, width, height of the room. She made a note and then added detailed measurements of the positions of doors, windows, lighting and electrical sockets.

'Have you any thoughts on a colour scheme?' she asked.

'Anything but pink?' he volunteered.

'Good start,' she said. 'I thought we might carry through the dark green from the café. It will tie the two parts together and look cool in the summer. I'll add splashes of colour that we'll carry through to the courtyard with pots filled with flowering plants.'

'That's very different to the designs you showed me. Rather more sophisticated.'

'You're right. I see a space and I get carried away with my own ideas of how it should look.'

'But?'

She shrugged. 'This is a sophisticated venue. If I was doing this in a UK high street I'd be using bright colours to catch the eye. I'd want nineteen-fifties American cars, a vintage soda fountain and a jukebox with fifties-era records, but you have live music and Italy has a fabulous car industry,' she said as she gathered her stuff and headed for the door.

'Keep the jukebox. We can turn it off when there's live music.'

'Okay, but you need to think about who is actually going to use this space. Who do you want to attract? Young people looking for somewhere to hang out? I doubt ice cream and fifties pop is going to do it. Most of our sit-down customers in the UK are young teenage girls, families—birthday parties for kids do really well—and women meeting up for a chat over a treat.'

'And the stand-up ones?'

'That's the takeaway trade.'

'Of course.'

'Having second thoughts?'

'No…I can see a daytime and early evening market for this, but you're right. It needs to fit in with what's going on outside.'

'You'd better give me some idea of your budget. Are you thinking Ferrari or Fiat 500?'

'I hadn't given it much thought.'

She grinned. 'My ideal client.'

'Show me what you've got and I'll have a better idea of what it's likely to cost,' he said, heading back to the rear lobby where he'd left his bags.

'The major capital expenses will be the freezer counter for the ices, jukebox and, depending on the look you want, furniture.' She looked around, already seeing it on a summer evening with the doors thrown open, musicians on the stage. 'There'll undoubtedly be some rewiring needed, the floor will need sanding and refinishing and whatever wall treatment you decide on.'

'I'm going to have to sell an awful lot of ice cream to pay for that.'

'I'll draw this up on my CAD program today and put together some ideas for you to look at.'

'Great. Give me your pen.'

She gave it to him and he leaned in to jot something down on the corner of the pad she was holding. Too close—so close that she could see a single thread of silver in amongst the glossy dark hair.

'This is my email address...' He looked up, catching her staring. 'Send me your ideas. It'll be light relief from the politics. Is there anything else?'

Yes... 'No.'

He nodded. 'I'll leave you in peace, then.'

About as much chance of that as a hen laying a square egg, she thought. He might have slept like a log but she'd tossed and turned all night. Getting up had been a relief.

'You've got my number. Give me a call if you have any problems,' he said as he shrugged into his heavy jacket, found his gloves in the pockets, continued searching... Swore softly under his breath. 'I left my scarf at the vet's office.'

The soft, very expensive scarlet cashmere scarf that he'd wrapped around the injured cat. The kind that usually came gift-wrapped, with love, at Christmas... Not this last Christmas, she suspected, but the one before.

As he turned up his collar she took off her own scarf and draped it around his neck. 'Here. This will hold you.'

He opened his mouth as if to say something, clearly thought better of it and left it at, 'Thanks.' Then concentrated on tucking in the scarf and fastening the flap across his collar. 'I'll ring the vet later. To ask about the cat,' he added.

'I usually switch my phone off when I'm working, but you can leave a voicemail.'

'Angel...'

'Yes?'

'You know how to set the alarm? The kitchen staff will turn it off when they arrive.'

'Lisa took me through it. Matteo is in charge while she's away. I start at seven for the morning shift,' she added, 'and work until everyone goes home when I'm on the evening shift.'

'He'll probably close up early. Once people get home they won't come out in this.'

'Very wise of them, if not great for business.' He didn't move. 'Will you come in for breakfast?'

'If I have time.'

'How about if I suggest chef puts porridge on the menu as a cold weather special? With fruit, cream, a drizzle of honey and, to give it a little Italian panache, a dash of Marsala to keep you warm while you're out doing your Zeffirelli thing.'

'Hold that thought.' He reached for the door handle and, still holding it, said, 'Will you be in it? The film. It was your idea.'

'It was?'

'You said, "What would you show them?"'

'So I did.' She lifted her shoulders in an awkward little shrug. 'If it will help. Do you want me in English or Italian?'

'Either. Both. Whatever comes out. Nothing polished or rehearsed. Just you.'

She managed a wry smile. 'I think I can guarantee that. You'll need an editor to pull it together.'

'I don't want a slick tourist promo. I'm looking for something raw, something from the street.'

'Why don't you use a student? Does the university have a media school?'

'Another great idea.'

'I'm full of them,' she said and, since he didn't seem in any hurry, 'for instance, do you have any contacts in local television?' He seemed thrown by the question. 'An historic part of the city struggling to retain its identity?' she prompted. 'It's the sort of thing that would get airtime in the early evening magazine programmes at home.'

'I suppose so.' He did not sound enthusiastic and she didn't press it.

'Okay, what about the local press? And social media? Politicians use it to target supporters and make themselves look good, but it's a two-way street. You can target them. Put your film on YouTube, post a link on their Facebook page and Twitter account and get everyone involved to share, leave comments, retweet.' He was still looking at her as if she had two heads and she shrugged. 'I did all the early promo for Rosie, our ice cream van, and I learned a lot. Mostly about how desperate the media are for stories that will fill airtime and the big empty spaces in their pages.'

'I'm sorry. You're right, of course. I'll give it some thought.'

For a moment neither of them said anything.

'Angel…'

'Dante…'

'What?' he asked.

'You should go. The goldfish will be getting lonely.' Hungry… She meant hungry…

CHAPTER TEN

'Forget science. Put your trust in ice cream.'
—from *Rosie's Little Book of Ice Cream*

DANTE SLUNG HIS bag and laptop case on the passenger seat of his car. Then he undid the neck flap of his jacket and touched the scarf that Angelica had placed around his neck.

He had other scarves, and had been about to say so, but this one was warm from her body and as she'd draped it around his neck he'd caught that subtle scent that seemed to stay with him whenever he touched her. He stood in the cold garage, lifted it to his nose, breathed in, but it was nothing he could name—it was just Angelica.

And it made him smile.

Geli settled at her computer, called up the CAD program, put in the dimensions of the room then began to play with ideas, searching through her boxes for fabrics and colours to create mood boards.

Dante called and left a voicemail to let her know that Mamma Cat was recovering and that he'd pick her up first thing on Monday.

When she found herself picking up her phone and, like some needy teenager, listening to the message for the tenth time, she deleted it and drove herself crazy trying to find the right combination of words—in Italian—that would bring up freezer counters and jukeboxes. Something her phrasebook was singularly useless at providing. It would be the perfect excuse to call Dante, but she told herself not to be feeble and eventually she got it and printed out photographs of the ones that inspired her schemes.

That night she tried her own remedy, listing all the good things that had happened that day and could only come up with one. Dante had touched her... And that wasn't good. At all.

'I'll take over here,' Matteo said as she began to make yet another espresso. 'Dante's taken the cat upstairs and he wants to know what to do with her.'

'Oh, right. I won't be long.'

She took off her apron and took the stairs two at a time. A cat carrier had been left in the kitchen but there was no sign of Dante. No doubt he was picking up something he needed from his room.

She took a breath, knelt down to look through the grille at the cat. 'Oh, poor lovely. Shall I take you to see your babies?'

'The vet sent antibiotics,' Dante said. She looked up. He was wearing a dark suit, silk tie, a long elegant overcoat and looked, no doubt, like the man who'd been destined to run the family business. All it needed was a red cashmere scarf to complete the image. Instead, he had the black one, hand-knitted by her grandmother, draped around his neck. 'One tablet in the morning until they're gone. She's had today's dose.'

'I'll take care of her. You're going to Rome now?'

'I've got a taxi waiting. Will you take the carry basket back to the vet?'

'Of course.'

'You'll need your scarf,' he said.

'No,' she said, her hand on his to stop him as he began to unwind it. 'It's freezing out there and I have others.'

'If you're sure. Thank you.' He reached in his pocket, took out a key and placed it on the kitchen table. 'Here's the spare key to Lisa's place. The lights are on a timer switch and I've set the heating to run continuously on low, but the goldfish will get lonely.'

'I'll take care of him. Go... *Arrivederci! Buon viaggia!*'

He smiled again, touched her cheek lightly with the back of his fingers. '*Arrivederci, cara.* Take care.'

Cara...

It meant nothing. Italians used it all the time. The market traders, the waiters, the customers all called her that.

It was only when she was watching Mamma Cat, purring as her babies rubbed against her, that she realised what he'd said.

The goldfish will get lonely...

There was no more snow but the temperature remained below freezing. While daytime business was brisk, with everyone looking for hot food and drinks to keep them going, Dante was right; once they were home nothing was going to tempt them out again.

Geli worked the early morning shift when there was a rush for espresso and pastry, but finished at nine, leaving the rest of the day to the regular staff, who were short of evening tips. The money would have been useful but she nagged the bank and, with no distractions, she got an awful lot done. She hardly had any time to think about Dante.

Okay, she thought about him when he surprised her with a text to let her know he'd arrived safely and a photograph of a frosty Coliseum to show her that Rome was freezing, too.

Obviously, she replied—it would be rude not to—and

in return sent him a photograph of Mamma Cat, recovered enough to give her kittens a thorough wash.

She couldn't help thinking of how brilliant he'd been about the cat when she dropped off the carry basket and paid the vet's bill using her credit card, despite the receptionist's insistence that she'd send a bill at the end of the month. It was wince-making but there was no way she was letting Dante pay it.

She thought of him later, too, when the vet's nurse called at the café on her way home with a bag containing his scarf, stiff with blood and mud, and was disappointed to discover that she was not going to be able to hand it over in person.

Shame she didn't bother to wash it, Geli thought sourly, but it had simply been an excuse to see Dante. The scarf was ruined.

She gave him the bad news the next day, when she emailed him photographs of the mood boards she'd prepared for three different schemes for his ice cream parlour and colour-wash impressions of what each of them would look like.

The first was a full-on US fifties-style diner, with booths and a jukebox and hot rods. In the second she replaced the booths and paid tribute to Milan with ultra-modern furniture and an artwork motif of sleek Italian cars. For the third she used her own vision of the room. Dark green walls, the mix-and-match furniture painted white and a sparkly red jukebox. She suggested shelf units for the walls, with bright jars of toppings and blown-up details of ice cream sundaes on the walls and, through the open French windows, a glimpse of planters overflowing with flowers. It was the simplest, least expensive and, in her opinion, would be the most adaptable.

He responded instantly.

You're right. Let's go with number three. D.

She smiled, and replied.

You have excellent taste. How are the meetings going? G.

It was only polite to ask.

Slowly. Important men make a point of keeping you waiting so that you'll understand how generous they are in
sparing you five minutes of their valuable time. D.

He didn't mention the scarf.

They're all too busy sending tweets and posting pictures
of themselves doing good works on Facebook to waste
time on real people. Social media is the way to go. G.

And she attached a picture of Lisa's goldfish, peering
at her out of the bowl, to which she added a speech bubble
so that he appeared to be saying, 'Tweet me!'

She went to the Tuesday market and bought more beads
from Livia for a project and looked at some wonderfully
soft cashmere yarn in the same clear bright scarlet as
the scarf that had been ruined. She passed over it and
picked up half a dozen balls in a dark crimson that exactly
matched the colour of her nails.

Dante, clearly bored out of his skin hanging around
waiting to talk to people, sent her a text asking how the cat
was doing. She took a photograph of Mamma Cat looking
particularly Frankensteinish and then she opened a new
page on her Facebook account that she called *A Kindle
of Kittens*.

She posted snippets of the story, pictures of the kittens
and then the one of Mamma Cat. Then she added a speech

bubble to the photograph of Mamma Cat, saying, 'Like me on Facebook' and sent it to Dante with the link.

He immediately 'liked' the page and left a comment.

I'll keep the black one. D.

The black one? Was he making some kind of veiled reference to her? She shook her head and replied.

She's all yours.

The icon on his post was for Café Rosa's Facebook page and when she checked it out she discovered that it was simply a listing of the musicians who would be appearing and the artists who were exhibiting there with some of their work. Nothing personal.

Elle and Sorrel sent her identical texts.

Who is D?

She replied:

He's my landlord and my boss. Why didn't you warn me that it would be freezing here?

She sent Dante a text, asking him how he was sleeping.

I've been making a list, remembering the things I've done, thinking about what I'm going to do the next day. It's not working. D.

That's politics for you. Concentrate on the small pleasures. Every life needs ice cream. G.

And thinking about him was unavoidable when she

curled up on the sofa in the evening with her headphones on as she worked on her Italian and knitted his scarf, her head against a cushion that smelled faintly of the shampoo he used.

Fortunately, there were distractions.

She had called in at a fashion co-operative where local designers displayed high quality one-off pieces, and designs that could be produced in small quantities for boutiques. She wasn't sure if they would accept work from a non-Italian, but she was living and working in Isola and that, apparently, was enough. She'd worn her coat and had photographs of other pieces on her phone and she'd been invited to bring along a finished piece for consideration.

Of course, she'd had to tell Dante and he'd been thrilled for her.

Marco came in every day, still hoping that she'd change her mind about spending the evening with him. He was charming, good-looking and she knew she was mad not to get out for a few hours, try and get Dante out of her head, but he wasn't the man to do it. She wasn't sure if such a man existed.

Dante laughed at a video Angelica had posted on the kittens' Facebook page of one of the kittens chasing a strand of wool and falling asleep mid-pounce. It earned him a stern look from the Minister's secretary. She was right. It wasn't funny.

He could hear Angelica saying, 'Pull it, pull it...' and the rumble of a man's laughter in the background.

Who was pulling the wool? Marco, Nic, Gennaro...?

He told himself that he had no right to care. But he did. He cared a lot.

He'd been cooling his heels in a dozen offices since he'd arrived, been given a dozen empty promises and he'd scarcely noticed. The only thing he'd cared about were the texts from Angelica. The photographs she sent him.

A selfie of her with Livia, and a stack of beads she'd bought. A bowl of porridge lavishly embellished with fruit, honey and cream. Some balls of wool she was using to knit him a scarf to replace the one that had been ruined. He'd seen Nonnina knitting and he knew that every inch of the yarn would have been touched by her as it slid through her fingers...

She hadn't said one word about the kitten-botherer.

He put the phone away and stood up. 'Please give the Minister my apologies,' he said, picking up his laptop bag and heading for the door.

'You're leaving?' she asked, startled. 'But you have an appointment with the Minister.'

'I had an appointment with the Minister over an hour ago and now I have to be somewhere else.'

'But—'

'I'll tweet him.'

He stood on the steps of the Ministry, breathing in the icy air as he pulled on his gloves, wrapped Angelica's scarf around his neck.

He'd spent four days chasing his tail in Rome, waiting for people to see him and getting nowhere. No surprise there. He'd known how it would be and yet he'd come anyway.

Wasting his time.

Running away from what had to be done. Running away from his feelings for Angelica Amery.

On Thursday evening, Geli settled down with her head-phones on, working on her Italian while she added a few more inches to the scarf.

Listen then repeat...

Buongiorno. Desidera?

'Buongiorno. Desidera?'

Buongiorna. Mi dà uno shampoo per capelli normali per piacere.

'Buongiorna. Mi dà uno shampoo per capelli normali per piacere.'

Si, ecco. Abbiamo questo...

Geli heard another sound over the lesson and lifted one ear of the headphones. Someone was at the door. She checked her watch. They'd be clearing up downstairs and this would be Matteo bringing her some little 'leftover' treat.

She switched off her iPod, stuck her needles in the wool and went to open the door and the smile of welcome froze on her face.

It was the same every time—no, not the same; this time it was worse. Or did she mean better? The heart kick, putty knees and a whole load of X-rated symptoms were getting a lot of practice.

'Dante... You're back,' she said stupidly.

'Despite the best efforts of the airline and the weather to keep me in Rome for another night,' he said. 'I waylaid Matteo on his way up here with this,' he went on, indicating the small tray he was holding. Not coming in, despite the fact that she'd stood back to give him room. 'Is there something I should know?'

'Know?' For a moment she didn't understand what he meant. Then the penny dropped. Did he think that she and Matteo...? Shocked that he could believe her so fickle— and just a bit thrilled—make that a whole lot thrilled—that he actually cared—she managed a puzzled frown. 'Didn't you ask him to come up and check that I was okay every night before he went home? Bring me up a little treat? What is it?' she asked, reaching for the cover. 'Chef was making cheesecake—'

'No,' he said, moving it out of her reach.

She looked up. 'It's not cheesecake?'

'It's chocolate truffle tart. And no, I did not ask him to come up here bothering you.'

He did! He thought that she was encouraging Matteo and he was not amused. Considering that he'd made it plain more than once that he wasn't interested—okay, they both knew that he was interested, but he wouldn't, couldn't do anything about it—his attitude was a bit rich, but it still gave her a warm, fuzzy feeling that wasn't helping the knee problem one bit.

'He wasn't bothering me,' she said, leaving him standing on the doorstep. 'On the contrary,' she called back as she headed for the kitchen, leaving him to follow in his own good time. 'I'm assuming there's enough of that tart for two?'

She took a couple of cake forks from the cutlery drawer then, as she heard the tray hit the kitchen table, she stretched up to take two plates from the rack. Before she could reach them, Dante caught her wrist and turned her to face him.

'Was it Matteo pulling the wool?'

She didn't pretend not to know what he was talking about, but met his gaze head-on. 'You didn't have to fly back from Rome to ask me that,' she pointed out, quite rationally, she thought, considering that she was backed against the work surface, that the front of his overcoat was pressed very firmly against her sweater. That his breath was warm against her cheek. That his hand had slid from her wrist and his fingers and hers were somehow entangled... 'You could have just sent a text.'

His fingers tightened over hers. 'What would you have replied?' he demanded, his eyes darkened with an intensity that might have scared her if it hadn't been making her heart sing. He cared...

'I'd have replied that Matteo brings me cake every evening as an excuse to play with the kittens.'

'The kittens?' he repeated, confused. 'Why would anyone even notice the kittens when you're here?'

She leaned into him to hide a smile too wide to fit through a barn door.

'He's besotted with them.'

'The man's a fool.'

'No... He's going to take one, maybe even two of them, when they're old enough to leave their mother.'

'Not the black one.' His face softened as he looked down at her. And this time there was no doubt about his meaning. 'Not Mole.'

'Molly. She's a girl.' Her legs were trembling. 'I told you, Dante. She's all yours.' And then, because she had to say something to break the tension, 'Do you like chocolate tart?'

'I like this.' He took the forks from her, placed them on the work surface behind her, took her face between his hands, brushed his lips over hers. 'I've been thinking about this.'

'This' was a kiss, angled perfectly to capture her mouth. Tender, thoughtful, tasting lips, tongue, nothing hurried or snatched, he bombarded her senses with a flood of heat until, like the city bells on Sunday morning, they were clamouring for attention. Screaming, *Nooooo*...as he drew back a little to look at her.

'I've been thinking about you, Angelica Amery, and all the good things I'm going to do with you.'

Okay, enough with the talking—

She reached for the buttons of his overcoat but he put his hand over hers, stopping her, and she looked up. 'You have too many clothes on.'

'Not for where we're going.'

What? 'I don't—'

'This is date night,' he said. 'I've called for you at your door and I'm going to take you stargazing. We'll also eat, talk and, at some point during the evening, I'll undoubtedly hold your hand.'

'Just my hand?'

'It's our first date. Your rules.'

'No. I was just—'

He touched his finger to her lips to stop her saying that she was just... Actually, she didn't know what she was 'just' doing. Mouthing off that all men saw when they looked at her was an opportunity for sex? A bit hypocritical when the whole idea of old-fashioned commitment terrified the wits out of her.

His hand moved to her cheek. 'It's not just about sex, Angel.'

She swallowed. 'It's not?'

He could read her mind now? She'd thought she had a problem when she'd discovered that her apartment didn't exist, that her money was gone, but this was trouble on a whole new level.

This wasn't about mere stuff. This was about taking the biggest risk imaginable.

'No.' His hand cradled her cheek, his touch warming her to her toes as he looked straight into her eyes. 'I've learned that the hard way. There has to be more if a partnership is going to clear the hurdles that life throws in your way. Survive the knocks.'

'That's a heck of a lot to put on a first date, Dante.'

'I know, but if you don't start out with the highest expectations it's always going to be a compromise. Are you okay with that?'

Was she? He'd been totally honest with her from the beginning and she'd tried to be the same. She hadn't been coy, hadn't tried to hide the way she felt whenever she was within touching distance of him. But this was exposing the soft nerve tissue, the stuff that hurt when you poked it.

'You want the truth?'

'*Parla come magni, cara.* Speak as you eat. I have always told you the truth,' he reminded her.

'I remember,' she said. 'Even when it hurt.'

'Even when it hurt,' he agreed, easing back a fraction, as if preparing for bad news, and the bad news was that she wanted to grab him, hold him close.

'The truth is that it scares the pants off me. The metaphorical pants,' she added quickly, trying to keep this light.

He didn't smile. 'Do you want to tell me why?'

'I've spent my entire life losing people. My father, half of everything I am, was gone before the stick turned blue—unknown, unknowable. No name, no picture, just an empty space.'

'Your mother didn't tell you anything about him?'

She shook her head. 'And when she was there it didn't matter. She filled our lives, Dante, and I never thought about it, about him, but when she died—'

He put his arms around her, drew her close. 'You realised you would never know. That you'd lost not just one but both your parents.'

'Then along came Martin Crayshaw—obviously not his real name—and for a while he was everything a storybook father should be until, having stripped us clean, stolen our lives, he disappeared without so much as goodbye.'

'Did the police ever catch up with him?'

'My grandmother was in a state of nervous collapse and Elle, my oldest sister, was only just eighteen. She was afraid that if the authorities discovered what had happened Sorrel and I would be taken into care.'

'She didn't report it?' She shook her head. 'How is your grandmother now? You are very close, I think.'

'Better. Much better. Great-Uncle Basil's arrival has given her something I never could. He takes wonderful care of her now. They are the dearest of friends.'

'And your sisters fell in love, got married, have families of their own.'

'I'm happy for them. They married wonderful men and I love my nieces and nephews to bits, but it's as if I've been left behind.'

'No, Angel. They haven't left you behind; they've simply moved on to the next stage in their lives.' His lips brushed her hair. 'Relationships change. When my mother made a new life for herself, started a new family, I was so angry...'

'Angry?' she repeated, surprised. 'I can't imagine that.'

'One of the things I put on that list you said I should make was to call her.'

She leaned back a little so that she could see his face. 'Did you?'

'We had a long talk. Cleared away a lot of the dead wood. I've been doing a lot of that.'

'So that there's room for fresh new growth.'

'I knew you'd understand.' He caught her hair between his fingers and pushed it back so that she couldn't hide behind it. 'I told her all about you and your lists. About that moment when I first saw you, the front of your coat plastered with snow and looking exactly like the princess in a fairy tale book she used to read to me when I was little. About Rattino's unscheduled appearance. That made her laugh. She wished she'd been there to see it.'

'Hmm, I suspect it's one of those experiences that improves with the rose-tinted spectacles of time.'

'The sort of thing you tell your grandchildren when they ask how you met.'

Grandchildren? This was their first date...

'And I told her that you were knitting me a scarf to replace the one she sent me at Christmas because it was ruined when we rescued Ratty's mother.'

'Your mother gave you that scarf?'

'Yes…' She saw the moment when he realised what she'd actually thought. 'Did you imagine that I would wear something that Valentina had given me?'

'I… It was a beautiful scarf,' she said.

'Yes, it was.'

'Now I feel really bad. Maybe I could have rescued it if I'd tried harder, but I have to confess that I really enjoyed putting it in the rubbish.'

He roared with laughter. 'My mother said that you sounded like a keeper.'

'She doesn't know me, Dante. You barely know me.'

'It's been a steep learning curve,' he admitted, 'but so far I like everything I've seen.'

'Ditto,' she said, pleased, awkward. 'I'm glad you talked to her.'

'I have you to thank for that,' he said, 'and I'll tell you something—the hardest part was picking up the phone.'

'Are you saying that I need to pick up the metaphorical phone?'

'It's just a date, Angel.'

She shook her head. 'No, it's not,' she said. They both knew it was a lot more than that. 'We're both trailing baggage. We should both probably start with something less intense.'

'I'm doing my best here.'

'It's not working but, given the choice between staying here and knitting a scarf or having you hold my hand while we look at the stars—'

'The stars have it?'

She shook her head. 'You had me at holding hands. The stars are a bonus.'

'In that case, I think we'd better get out of here before my good intentions hit the skids. You need to go and wrap up in something warm. I'll go and put Matteo out of his misery and tell him that he's got overtime babysitting the kittens.'

CHAPTER ELEVEN

'Love is an ice cream sundae with all the marvellous toppings. Sex is the cherry on top.'
—from *Rosie's Little Book of Ice Cream*

THEY WERE BOTH unusually quiet as Dante drove out of the city. He was, presumably, concentrating on the traffic— driving in Italy was not to be taken lightly—while she was absorbed in the change in their relationship. Wondering what had happened in Rome...

Then Geli, sneaking a glance at his profile, lit only by the glow from the dashboard, discovered that Dante was doing the same and practically melted in her seat.

'Where are we going?'

He returned his full attention to the road. 'Does it matter?'

'No. The only thing that matters is that I'm going there with you.'

And in the darkness he reached across and took her hand, holding it lightly until he slowed to turn off the highway and they began to climb into the mountains.

After a while, the lights of a village appeared above them but, before they reached it, he turned off and pulled onto an area that had been levelled as a viewing point.

'Wait...' Dante came round, opened the door and helped

her from the car, keeping her arm in his as they walked to the barrier and looked out over the valley.

There was no moon, but the Milky Way, so thick that it was hard to make out individual stars, silvered the flat dark surface of a lake far below them.

'What lake is that?' she asked. 'I know Como is the nearest but there don't seem to be enough lights.'

'No, that's Largo D'Idro.' He glanced at her. 'It's the highest of the lakes but very small. There are no tourist boats doing the rounds of celebrity villas because there are no celebrities. It's popular for water sports.'

'But not in this weather. There's snow right down to the shore. I thought the lakes had a famously mild climate?'

'Nowhere is mild in February,' he assured her, 'and the lakes have been known to freeze over in severe winters.'

'They don't tell you that in the tourist brochures.'

'Maybe that's because we like to keep it to ourselves. There's something rather magical about sitting in a steaming hot tub when the air temperature is below freezing.'

She gave him a thoughtful look. 'Is that what you have in mind?'

'On our first proper date?' He took her hand and held it. 'You will be escorted to your front door and maybe, if I'm lucky, you'll have enjoyed yourself enough to risk a second one.'

Geli thought that she was more than ready for an improper date; that hot tub sounded like a lot of fun. But she had complained that men never asked women out on dates any more and, while she wasn't totally convinced that he was going to kiss her on the cheek and say goodnight at the door, she would go along with it.

'In that case, if we're going to act like kids, it's time to make snow angels.' She looked around, caught his hand and, tugging him after her, headed towards a gently sloping area of untouched snow. 'The stars will look even better if we're lying down.'

She flung herself down into the snow, laughing as she swept her arms and legs wide to make an angel while Dante looked on.

'If you don't get down here and join in I'm going to feel stupid,' she warned. 'You are also blocking out the stars.'

'I just love watching you.'

Geli stilled.

'What happened to you in Rome, Dante?'

'Nothing happened. Everything happened. For months my head has been filled with the past, the mess we all made of it. While I was in Rome all I thought about was you. How much I enjoyed getting your emails and texts. How much I wished you were there with me.'

'And yet you're standing up there and I'm down here.' She held out her hand. 'I promise you, this is a lot more fun if you join in.'

He took it and then lay beside her in the snow. About to tell him that the magic only happened when you made your angel, she pressed her lips together. He had missed her. Now they were lying together in the snow, looking up at the stars and Dante Vettori was holding her hand. That was all the magic she could handle right now.

'Do you know the constellations?' she asked.

'Some of them…'

They lay there in the snow pointing out the stars they recognised until the cold drove them in search of warmth, food and they drove up to the ski resort where, in a restaurant lively with an après ski crowd, they shared an *antipasti* of grilled vegetables and a *risotto alla pescatora*, rich with prawns, squid and clams.

As they finished their meal with ice cream and espresso, Geli said, 'No meat and nothing to drink. I'm a tough date.'

'I don't drink and drive, I didn't have to have the grilled

vegetables and I would have chosen the risotto even if I'd been on my own. Are you free tomorrow?'

'The dating rules say that I shouldn't be that easy,' she said. 'I'm going to sound desperately sad and needy if I say yes.'

'I'm doing the asking so that makes two of us, but this isn't something we can do next week. I have an invitation from one of the big fashion houses to their pre Fashion Week party. It's tomorrow,' he said, 'or you're going to have to wait until the autumn and hope I'm still on their party list.'

'You're kidding me?' Milan Fashion Week was as big as it got. Invitations to parties thrown by the designers were like gold dust.

'They probably think I'm my father. Dante, Daniele… What are you doing?' he asked.

'Just checking that my chin isn't down there on the floor,' she said. 'Do you think he'll be feeling slighted? Your father?'

'He won't notice. Valentina presents a local evening television show so she gets invited to everything.'

'Oh… I had no idea.'

'Lisa didn't tell you?'

'No. She started to talk about her but I said that you had already told me what happened and she got the message.' But it explained his reluctance to contact local TV about his film. 'Will Valentina be there? With your father?'

'More than likely, but this is not about them. I'm asking you. Would you like to go as my plus one?' And then Dante told her who the invitation was from and she nearly passed out with shock.

Her mouth was moving but nothing was coming out and she fanned herself with one hand while indicating that she'd be with him in a moment with the other. He caught the fanning hand, said, 'I'll take that as a yes.'

'No—'

'No?' He sounded genuinely shocked, as well he might.

'You don't have to put yourself through this for me.'

'She's married to my father, Angel. If he and I are going to have any kind of relationship we have to move on. But you're right. Maybe what I'm asking…' He linked his fingers through hers. 'Will you do this for me?'

'You want me to be your wing man?'

'Above and behind me? No, my angel, I want you beside me all the way.' And he leaned across the table and kissed her.

His lips tasted of coffee and pistachio ice cream and, like every kiss they'd shared, it was all too brief. She'd waited long enough…

'Dante—' He waited. 'You do realise that this isn't actually our first date?'

'It isn't?'

'Don't you remember? When you insisted on taking me to the *commissariato*—'

'I certainly remember that. I hope there wasn't an emergency while you were there because no one would have heard the phone.'

She rolled her eyes. 'No, think… You said, "Is it a date?"'

'And you said yes.'

'Actually, I asked if it was "another" date. Made some stupid comment about going steady. We'd already made a date to sit up late one night and tell one another stories. I think we can quite legitimately count this as a two-in-one. A double date for two.'

'So you're saying—be patient with me, I don't want to get this wrong—that this is our third date?'

She just smiled and he raised a hand in the direction of a passing waiter. *'Il conto…'*

* * *

Dante opened his eyes, saw Angelica's dark hair spread across the pillow, her lovely mouth an invitation to kiss her awake and thought for a moment that he was dreaming.

He kissed her anyway and, like Sleeping Beauty, she opened her eyes, smiled, hooked her hand around his neck and drew him down to her so that she could kiss him back. A morning kiss, new as the dawn, as welcome as the spring.

'Ciao, carissima,' he said, his hand tracing the profile of her body as she turned towards him; the lovely curves he'd explored with such thoroughness during a night in which he'd been reborn. *'Come posse servirvi?'*

She frowned, mouthed the words then, her smile widening into soft laughter, she said, 'Did you really ask how you can serve me?'

'Would you like tea?' he asked, his hand lingering on her thigh. 'Or I could carry you to the shower and get creative with the soap. Or—' a blast of Abba's *Dancing Queen* shattered the silence '—*Dio!* What is that?'

'The alarm on my phone.' She rolled out of bed and he watched her walk, naked, to her bag, find her phone and turn it off. She looked back at him. 'Your service will have to wait, I'm afraid. I have to go to work.'

'Matteo is not expecting you. I told him that you had other plans today.'

'What? You can't do that.' He loved how shocked she was. How committed…

'I'm the boss. I can do what I like.'

'But it's market day. They'll—'

'They'll manage,' he said, peeling himself off the bed, wrapping his arms around her. 'Now, where were we, *mio amore*? Tea, shower—' he nuzzled the lovely curve of her neck '—or is there some other way I can serve you?'

She kissed his neck, ran her hand down his back. 'Why don't we start with the shower and see how it goes from there?'

Geli's hand was shaking as she called Elle. She hadn't the faintest clue what she was going to say to her; she only knew she had to hear that calm voice.

'Sorry, I can't talk right now. Leave a message and I'll call you back when whatever crisis I'm having is sorted.'

A message? Which one would that be? *I'm going to a swanky party thrown by one of the world's most famous fashion designers. I can't stand up because Dante Vettori spent the night melting my bones. I'm in love...*

No, no, no! It had been the most thrilling, tender, perfect sex, outshining anything she could have imagined in her wildest fantasy, but Dante was right, love was more than that.

It was lying together in the snow in a universe so quiet that you could hear a star fall. It was making the toughest phone call in the world in order to find a cat which might already be dead. It was small things, like texts that said nothing except I'm thinking of you.

'Just me,' she said. 'Nothing important, just looking for some big sister advice about what to wear to a bit of a do. Love to everyone. Catch up soon.'

Clothes... Concentrate on clothes.

She was standing in front of her wardrobe when Dante returned from Lisa's flat. 'You were an age. Was there a problem?'

'You could say that. The goldfish was floating on the top of the tank. I've been at the pet shop trying to find a match.'

'Any luck?'

'We found one with similar markings. It's a bit bigger, but with any luck Lisa will put that down to a growth spurt.'

'And if she doesn't?'

'You'll just have to own up.'

'Thanks for that.' She turned back to the wardrobe and the two dresses hanging over the doors. 'Have you heard from her since she arrived?'

'Just a text to let me know that she arrived safely. What are you doing?'

'I'm trying to decide which dress to wear tonight. The black or the burgundy-red.'

'So nothing taxing, then.' She gave him what Elle called 'the look'. 'Obviously, you'll wear the black but you'll look fabulous whatever you wear, *cara*. Meanwhile, I have something important to say. I need you to concentrate.'

Heart in her mouth, she turned to him. 'What is it?'

'It's this. *Posso baciarti, carissima*?'

'Testing my Italian, *carissimo*?' she asked, raising her arms and looping them around his neck. *'Voglio baciare si...'*

His answer was a long slow kiss, followed by an intimate lesson in advanced Italian.

It was the accessories that finally settled the matter of what she would wear. Her black dress had been refashioned from a fine jersey vintage dress that she'd found in a trunk in the attic.

The sleeves had been cut in one with the dress and she had narrowed them below the elbow. The neck was a simple V, cut low, but merely hinting at her breasts and she'd used a series of darts to bring it in at the waist. Worn as it was, it was timelessly elegant. Tonight, she'd cinched it in with an eight-inch-wide basque-style black suede and silver kid belt that was fastened at an angle by a series of small diamanté buckles.

When she was finally satisfied that every detail was perfect, she picked up a tiny silver and black suede clutch and her long black velvet evening coat and went through to the living room.

Dante, looking jaw-droppingly handsome in a tux, was standing in front of the fire, one hand on the mantel, the other holding a glass, his face burnished by the flames as he gazed into some dark abyss. Then, as he lifted the glass, he saw her and it never made it to his mouth.

'Angel…' He put down the glass, crossed to her, took the coat from her, holding onto one of her hands. 'Pretty gloves,' he said, admiring the fingerless black lace mitts she was wearing. 'I want to kiss you but you look so perfect.'

She lifted her hand so that he could kiss her fingers and he took his time about it, kissing each one in turn before turning her hand over and kissing her palm.

'What a gentleman,' she said, laughing, to disguise the fact that she was practically melting on the spot, and tapped her cheek. 'You can't do much damage there.'

He touched his lips to the spot.

'Or there.'

She lifted her chin so that he could kiss her neck, by which time he'd got the idea and continued a trail of soft kisses along the edge of the neckline of her dress. When he reached the lowest part of the V he slid his hand beneath the cloth and pushed it aside, then audibly caught his breath as he realised that she wasn't wearing anything underneath it. *'Mia amore…'*

He settled her silver and jet necklace back into place, carefully removed his hands, stepped back and held out her coat. As she turned and slipped her arms into the sleeves, he said, 'Have you grown?'

She hitched up her skirt a few inches to reveal the slender steel vertiginous heels of her intricately laced black suede boots.

He studied them for a moment, then her belt, then he looked up and smiled. 'I am so going to enjoy undressing you when we get home.'

By the time the limo approached the red carpet, Geli was shaking with nerves. 'All the women will be wearing designer dresses, diamonds,' she said.

'You *are* wearing a designer dress. And every one of those women will wish they were wearing that belt.'

'You think so?'

'Believe me. They'll know that every man in the room will be wishing he was the one unfastening those pretty buckles tonight.'

'Now I'm blushing.'

'Then it's just as well I'll be the only man in the room who knows for sure what you're not wearing tonight.' It was probably as well that the car stopped at that moment. Dante climbed out, offered her his hand, said, 'Big smile, Angel…' and she stepped out of the car to a blaze of flashlights from the army of paparazzi waiting for the celebrities.

The room was like a palace in a very grown-up fairy tale: everything beautiful, everything perfectly arranged, a stage set for exquisitely dressed players who moved in a circle around the legendary central character who was their host, and she watched, fascinated, as the famous— Hollywood stars, supermodels—paid court.

Dante introduced her to some people he knew, she drank a little champagne, ate a little caviar and wished she hadn't. He went to fetch her a glass of water and, as she turned, searching the crowd for a sight of Valentina or his father, she came face to face with the Maestro himself.

'Signora…'

'Maestro. *Piacere... Mi chiamo* Angelica Amery. *Sono Inglese*. My Italian is not good.'

'Welcome, Angelica Amery,' he said, switching to English. 'It's always a pleasure to meet a beautiful woman, especially one with so much courage.'

'Courage?'

'I believe that, including the waitresses, you are the only woman in the room not wearing a dress designed by me. This vogue for vintage clothes will put us all out of business.'

'*Mi dispiace,* Maestro, but I could not afford one of your gowns or even the one I'm wearing for that matter. This belonged to my great-grandmother.'

'She was a woman of great style, as are you, *cara*. And I adore your belt. The asymmetrical slant of the buckles complements the era of the dress so well. Where did you find it?'

'*Grazie*, Maestro. I designed it myself. I was inspired by an Indian bracelet I saw on the Internet.'

'Quite perfect.' He nodded, held out his hand before moving on and when she took it he raised it to his lips. 'Come and see me next month. We will talk about your future.'

'*Grazie...*' But he was already talking to someone else and, when she looked down, she realised that he'd tucked his card under her lace mitten.

He'd given her his card. Asked her to come and see him. He'd said her belt was 'quite perfect'...

She stood for a moment trying to breathe, trying to take in what had just happened and then spun round, searching for Dante so that she could tell him.

Taller than most in the room, he should be easy to spot, even in this crush, and after a moment she spotted his broad shoulders jutting from a small alcove. He had his back to her but, as she took a step in his direction, she saw who he was talking to.

Valentina Vettori was older than she'd realised, older than Dante, but even more beautiful in the flesh than in her photograph despite, or perhaps because, her eyes were brimming with tears.

It was like watching a car crash you were unable to prevent. The way she reached for him, the way he took her into his arms and held her while her tears seeped into the shoulder of his jacket. And all the joy of the last twenty-four hours, the triumph of the evening, turned to ashes in her mouth.

Valentina had been his lover—he'd grieved for her loss for over a year.

He'd only known her for a week.

Look away, she told herself. *Look away now...*

It was a moment of the most intense privacy and no one in the celebrity-hunting crowd had noticed. No one cared but her.

As she dragged her eyes from the scene in the alcove she saw someone else she recognised. Make that no one but her and Daniele Vettori who, glass in hand, was looking around, clearly wondering where his wife had got to.

'Signor Vettori,' she said, walking towards him, hand outstretched. 'I am so glad to meet you. I wanted to thank you for your help the other night.' His smile was puzzled but he turned to look at her. '*Sono* Angelica Amery,' she said. 'The crazy cat lady.'

'Signora Amery... *Piacere*.' He took her hand. 'I did not realise that you were English. You are here with Dante?' He sounded surprised. Looked hopeful.

'I'm a dress designer—in a very small way,' she added. 'Dante thought I might enjoy this.'

'And are you?'

'Very much.' Until two minutes ago she had been on

top of the world. 'Is your wife with you?' she asked as his eyes wandered in search of her. Anything to keep him focused on her.

'She's here somewhere, making up for lost time networking. We were very late. Alberto—our son—wouldn't settle. We have a nanny but Valentina… I'm sorry; you do not want to talk about babies.' He smiled, gave her his full attention. 'Where is my son?'

'He's gone to find me a glass of water. It's rather a crush.'

'Please, take this.' He offered her the glass he was holding. 'My wife is breastfeeding so she's avoiding the champagne.'

'Oh, but—'

His smile deepened and it was so much like his son's that a lump formed in her throat. 'There's a price to pay. You will have to stay and talk to me until Dante returns.'

'That's not an imposition, it's a pleasure.' She took the glass from him, hoping that her hand would not shake as she took a sip.

'Did you meet Dante in England, Signora Amery?'

'Please, everyone calls me Geli.'

Everyone except Dante…

'*Grazie*, Geli. *Mi chiamo*, Daniele.'

'Daniele… And, in answer to your question, no. I came to Isola to work. Dante helped me when I had a problem with my apartment.' She had to chase up the bank. She'd let things slide; there had been no urgency, but now—

'Angelica…' She physically jumped as Dante placed his hand on her shoulder, standing possessively close. He was paler and there was the faintest smear of make-up on the shoulder of his jacket that only someone who knew what to look for would see, but he had remembered her water. 'It appears that I'm redundant here.'

'Not at all.' She took the glass from him and handed it

to his father. 'Daniele merely loaned me this glass until you returned. It was for Valentina but she seems to have disappeared.'

'I saw her a minute ago. I believe she was heading in the direction of the cloakroom.'

'Then I will wait here with you if I may,' Daniele said.

The two men looked at one another for a long intense moment before Dante put out his hand and said something in Italian that Geli did not understand. And then she was holding two glasses as the two men hugged one another.

And she was the one blinking back tears when Valentina found them, linked her arm in Daniele's and said something to her in Italian, speaking far too quickly for her to understand.

'Geli is English, *cara*,' Daniele said, taking the fresh glass from Dante and handing it to her. 'She is the heroine who searched my construction site in the snow and saved the injured cat.'

'*Alora*... Such drama. You are so brave...' Her expression was unreadable and she could have intended anything from genuine admiration—possibly for risking her nails—to veiled sarcasm. '*Come*... How is she? The cat?'

'She is healing fast and contented now that she is with her kittens,' Geli assured her.

'Then all is right with her world.' She looked at Dante and for a long moment it was as if she and Daniele were not there. Then she snapped on a smile and said, '*Dolci...*' before turning to her. 'Sweet... I do not know if you are aware but I present an early evening magazine programme on regional television. We are always looking for light stories. Good news. Maybe we could feature your cat and her kittens? Are they photogenic?'

Geli, astonished and not entirely sure what to make of her invitation, turned to Dante but, getting no help there, said, 'Well, Mamma Cat is a looking a bit like Frankenstein's monster at the moment, shaved patches and stitches, but the kittens more than make up for that.'

'Perfect. Will you do it? Obviously, the programme is in Italian, but I can translate for you or—' Geli waited for her to suggest that Dante came along to translate '—we could film them at home and I can do a voice-over.'

'*Grazie*, Valentina. I'm working on my Italian but it might be kinder to your viewers if you did the talking.' Valentina's smile was strained and, on an impulse, she began telling her about the drama of Rattino's appearance, giving it the full action treatment as she described Lisa's horror, the women leaping on chairs, her diving under the table. By the end of the story they had gained a small audience and everyone was laughing.

'*Bravissima!*' Valentina clapped. 'That! I want that! We'll use subtitles. *I gattini*…where are they now?'

'They're in our apartment,' Dante told her. 'Why don't you come and see them? Come to lunch tomorrow, both of you. I have a gift for Alberto—' his father looked wary rather than pleased '—and I have a project that I'd like to discuss with Valentina.'

'Oh?'

'Angelica is an artist and we're making a film about the need to preserve the heart of Isola.'

'From people like me?'

'It isn't personal, Papà. It was never personal.'

There was another of those long looks, but after a moment his father nodded. They chatted for a few more minutes before Valentina spotted someone she had to talk to and the party broke up in a round of very Italian hugs. Only Geli saw that, while her husband was occupied with her, Valentina took the opportunity to whisper something in Dante's ear, saw his nod of acknowledgement, imperceptible to anyone who wasn't watching closely.

'Would you like to go on somewhere?' Dante asked as they climbed into their car.

'No. Thank you.'

'You can't know how glad I am you said that. Did you have a good time? I saw you talking to our host.'

'Did you? Actually, he was congratulating me on being the only woman present with the courage not to be wearing one of his gowns.'

'Amore...' he exclaimed. 'I never thought. I'm so sorry.'

'Why? It is what it is and when I explained that this dress had belonged to my great-grandmother he forgave me.'

'Are you serious?'

'That my dress is eighty years old or that he forgave me?'

'Madonna, mia! Either...both. Is it really that old?'

'My great-grandmother kept a ledger of her clothes. When she bought them, how much they cost, where she wore them. This one is by Mainbocher, the man who designed the dress Wallis Simpson wore when she married the Duke of Windsor. Great-grandma didn't wear it after that. She disapproved of divorce, disapproved of the abdication...disapproved of pretty much everything, apparently, except beautiful clothes.'

She knew she was talking too much but Dante, it seemed, was disinclined to stop her. Maybe he was interested in vintage fashion...

'We have trunks full of clothes in the attic, not just hers, but my grandmother's too. She was a sixties dolly bird, a contemporary of Twiggy, but that's more Sorrel's era. Lucky for us that Elle had no idea of the value of vintage clothes when she was selling off the family silver to pay the creditors.'

Talking too much and all of them the wrong words.

'The dress is perfect, Angel. You were so busy looking at everyone else that you didn't notice that they were all looking at you.'

He reached across the back seat of the limo to take her hand but she pretended she hadn't noticed, lifting it out of his reach to check the safety of a long jet earring.

'The Maestro admired my belt, too,' she said. 'It's a Dark Angel original.'

'I hope you told him so.'

'I did… He kissed my hand, gave me his card and asked me to go and see him next month. When the shows are over.'

'I think that is what you call a result.'

'Beyond my wildest dreams,' she assured him. And maybe that was it. The jealous gods only let you have one dream at a time… 'And you, Dante? Did you accomplish everything you wanted tonight?'

He sighed, leaned back. 'Everything is not for mortal men,' he said, eerily reflecting her own thoughts, 'but as much as I could have hoped. The fact that you were already talking to my father made it a great deal easier.'

'Did it? You sounded rather cross.'

'No…' He shook his head. 'How did you come to be talking?'

'Oh, the usual way. You know how it is at parties. We were in the same space at the same time. I was looking for you so that I could tell you about meeting the Maestro. He was looking for his wife and about to see her crying into your shoulder so I distracted him by introducing myself as the crazy cat lady.'

'Then I'm not imagining the touch of chill in the air. Congratulations, Angelica. You have not only made a hit with the one man in Milan famously impossible to impress, but appear to have excelled yourself in diplomacy.'

'My sisters would be astonished on both counts,' she

assured him. 'I usually say exactly what I think and hang the consequences.'

'I applaud your restraint but, since we're alone, feel free to share your thoughts with me.'

She closed her eyes. That was it? No explanation, no attempt at justification? No reason for her to forget what she'd seen and…no, she would never forget the tenderness with which he'd held Valentina. She knew how that felt and she wasn't in the mood to share.

'I'm thinking that you took me to the party as an excuse to see Valentina. That, sooner or later, she will leave your father and come back to you and he knows it.' When he still said nothing, made no attempt to deny it, she added, 'And I think that new goldfish will be nervous, all alone in a strange tank. You should keep him company tonight.'

CHAPTER TWELVE

'Eat ice cream for a broken heart. It freezes the heart and numbs the pain.'
—from *Rosie's Little Book of Ice Cream*

DANTE TOLD THE driver to wait, walked Angelica upstairs to the door of his apartment, unlocked it and waited while she walked in, turned to him, blocking the way.

'Angel—'

'Don't... Don't call me that.'

'I just wanted to thank you for everything you did this evening. You were kinder than any of us had a right to expect and we are all in your debt for ever.'

'I didn't do it for you. I did it to spare your father's feelings.'

'I understand, but whatever you think you saw...' He wanted to tell her that what she'd seen was not what she imagined. She was right about Valentina—he had thought that meeting her on neutral ground with hundreds of other people present would be easier for both of them. He had been as wrong about that as Geli was about everything else. Valentina had almost fainted with shock when she'd seen him, had been desperate for reassurance that he wasn't about to blow her life apart.

Now he was the one clinging on, hoping that Angelica would remember that he'd respected her enough to be honest with her about Lisa's motives when he could have gone for the easy lie.

She'd been angry then, too, but not for long. She'd thought things through and accepted that he had been doing what was right.

All he could do was hope that, given time, she would understand that tonight—

'Hello, you're back early.' Matteo, slightly tousled, as if he'd been asleep, appeared from the living room. 'I thought you'd be going on somewhere.'

'It's been a long day,' he said. 'Any problems?'

'No.' He grinned stupidly. 'Actually, I've been talking to my mother. She's at home all day and she'd be really happy to take care of the cats. If it would help?'

Not in a million years. Right now, the only thing anchoring Angelica in his life was the cats and they were going nowhere.

'We'll talk about it tomorrow. Go down and wait in the car. I'll give you a lift home.'

'Thanks. *Ciao*, Geli.' He grabbed his coat from the hook and thundered down the stairs.

When he had gone, Angelica opened her mouth as if to say something, but closed it again. Closed her eyes as if it was too painful to look at him. He felt the shock ripple through her as he cradled her face, wiping away the tears squeezed from beneath her lids with the pads of his thumbs, but she didn't pull away.

'Carissima...' Tears clung to her lashes as she opened her eyes. 'May I offer some words of wisdom from a woman it is my honour, my privilege to know?'

'Please, Dante,' she protested, but she was still there, the door open.

'Cherish the good things that happened to you this evening, hold them close. They do not come often.'

'I know...'

'Make a list of all the things that hurt you so that you won't lie awake turning them over in your head.' Her mouth softened a little as she recognised her own advice returned with interest and, encouraged, he continued, 'Take a bath, not too hot. Sprinkle a little lavender oil on your pillow and then, while you wait for sleep, think of all the good things that you will do tomorrow so that you'll wake happy.'

She swallowed. 'Good things?'

'The early shift in the café, flirting with Marco and all your other admirers.' She shrugged. 'The appointment with your client to finalise the scheme for his ice cream parlour.' She might move out, but she wouldn't walk away from a promise and it would keep her close. Give him hope.

'That's not in my diary.'

'It's in mine. Ten o'clock.'

Another shrug.

'And then lunch with—'

'You expect me to have lunch with you and... With all of you?'

'I believe, in fact I'm certain, that if you will talk to my father about our film he'll be more receptive.'

She frowned. 'Why would he listen to me?'

'Because you are a beautiful woman. My worst moment tonight was seeing you with him, watching him flirting with you. He has Valentina and yet he still cannot help himself.'

'Maybe he's protecting himself,' she said. 'Making an exit plan. Preparing to be left.'

'Something you'd know all about, *cara*?'

'What?' She shook her head. 'What are you talking about?'

'You told me yourself that you're scared to death to risk your heart, always holding something back, protecting yourself from hurt in case you're left behind by those you love. Wearing mourning black in case they die.'

She opened her mouth to protest, but nothing emerged.

'It isn't going to happen. Valentina will stay with him because he gives her everything she ever wanted.'

'Not you.'

'She was the one who left, *cara*. I would never have made her happy and she had the sense to know that. The courage to go after what she wanted.'

'Taking part of you with her. You still love her, Dante. Admit it.'

'You're right. She took something of mine, but love?' He shook his head. 'I was dazzled, infatuated, but in the end it was just sex.'

Enough. He'd said enough. He had to go before he heard himself begging to stay and he took her hand, placed his key in her palm and closed her fingers around it. 'Take this.'

'But it's your key.'

'Now it is yours.' He bent to kiss her cheek and she leaned into him, drawn to him despite everything, and it took every ounce of self-control not to put his arms around her, hold her.

To his infinite regret, she'd seen him hold Valentina and it would be there, between them, until she could trust him, believe that he was hers, body and soul. He could show her in everything he did, but only she could choose to see.

'Dormi bene, mio amore. Sogui dolci.'

Something inside Geli screamed a long desperate *Noooooo!* as Dante turned and headed down the stairs. The hand he'd kissed reached out to him but he did not look back and when she heard him hit the lower flight, she closed the door and leaned back against it, clutching the key he'd given her.

'Now it is yours.' What did that mean?

That he had locked himself out until she invited him in? But this was his apartment… No, wait. This evening, when Valentina had asked him where the cats were, he'd said that they were in 'our apartment'. Not his, but *our* apartment. And Valentina hadn't batted an eyelid.

But she'd cried in his arms. And whispered something in Dante's ear before walking away.

What? What had she said to him? She tried making her lips form the words but it was hopeless.

She gave up, fetched a tub of ice cream from the freezer and ate it while the bath filled. Then she slid beneath the water and, letting its warmth seep into her, she blanked out Dante and his whole wretched family and did as he'd advised, focusing her entire mind on that moment when one of the world's most famous dress designers told her that her belt was 'quite perfect'.

She sprinkled a few drops of lavender oil on her pillow and then lay in bed and wrote down everything she could remember about the evening. What she'd worn down to the last stitch and stone—she should start keeping a clothes journal like her great-grandmother. She wrote how Dante had looked as he'd stood by the fire waiting for her because he was beautiful and she loved him and it was a memory to hold, cherish.

So much for nothing serious, not for keeps but for fun. If it had been that, then what had happened this evening would not have mattered.

So not like her mother…

She wrote everything she could remember about the limousine, about being snapped by the paparazzi as she'd walked the red carpet, the people she'd seen, every word that the Maestro had said to her.

Every word that Dante had said.

'Our' apartment. *'Our'* film…

His certainty that Valentina would not leave his father because she had everything she was looking for. If that was true, why had she been crying into his shoulder? Guilt, remorse…?

What had she whispered in Dante's ear?

It was the last thing she thought before *Dancing Queen* dragged her out of sleep.

Dante arrived on the dot of ten and they had a straight-forward client/designer meeting downstairs in the room that was to be converted into an ice cream parlour, making final decisions about colours, furniture, artwork. They chose the ice cream cabinet and Dante used his laptop to go online and order it. Then he turned it around so that she could see a vintage jukebox he'd found.

'It plays old seventy-eights.'

'Boys' toys,' she muttered disapprovingly. 'It'll cost you a fortune to find records for it. And you won't get anyone later than…'

'Later than…?'

'I don't know. They pre-date my grandmother. Frank Sinatra?'

'That's a good start. See if you can find *Fly Me to the Moon.*'

She rolled her eyes but made a note then reached for her file as he picked it up to give it to her. Their hands met and, as he looked up, she might have forgotten herself, grabbed hold of him—

'I'll organise the decorators,' he said, standing up. 'Will you supervise them?'

'It's part of the job.' She checked her watch. 'If that's all, I have to go and change for lunch.'

The cleaning staff had been in. There were fresh flowers and a soft cat bed had been placed near the freshly lit fire, glowing behind the glass doors, for Mamma Cat and her kittens.

She checked on the cats, changed into her black mini-dress, topped it with the red velvet jacket that Lisa had so admired and wore the laced boots from the night before. Her reflection suggested that it was too much.

It looked as if she was competing. She was at home and she should be more relaxed, informal, allow their guests to shine.

Our apartment...

She changed into narrow dark red velvet trousers and a black silk shirt which she topped with a long, dark red brocade waistcoat and ditched the boots for ballet flats.

Better. But, for the first time in her life, she wished her wardrobe contained at least one pink fluffy sweater. Because although she didn't want Dante to be right, deep down she knew he was.

She picked up his key and slipped it into the pocket of her waistcoat. It was a pledge of some sort. Of his sincerity, his commitment, maybe.

If only she knew what Valentina had whispered to him.

Her phoned beeped and, grateful for anything that would delay the moment when she'd have to go downstairs to the café, she picked it up and discovered a reply to the somewhat sharp message she'd sent to the bank.

Her balance had been restored, along with five hundred pounds for her inconvenience. What? Banks didn't pay up like that unless they were being harassed by consumer programmes. Clearly they'd discovered some monumental error...

She had no excuse to stay now. Only the cats, but Matteo was desperate to give them a home.

She checked the clock. She couldn't put it off any longer. It was time to go, in every sense of the word.

She could hear Dante talking to someone on the phone as she passed his office. The door was slightly ajar; she didn't stop but she couldn't help wondering who he was talking to. That was how it was when you weren't sure. It was how Daniele must feel every day of his life but she couldn't live like that.

She was checking the table that had been set up in the corner when Dante joined her.

'Lunch first and then we'll go upstairs for coffee so that Valentina can meet the cats. Did the basket arrive?'

'Yes. Good thought. They'll look adorable.'

'If they're going to be on television they need more than a cardboard box...' He turned as the door opened and Valentina appeared in a gush of air kisses.

'*Ciao*, Geli. *Ciao*, Dante... Daniele had to park around the back somewhere. He's just coming. Can you get the door for him?'

Dante was calling out to Bruno behind the bar to bring water and menus as he opened the door so he didn't immediately see what was hampering his father.

Then he turned, looked down and saw Valentina's sleeping baby nestled in a softly padded buggy and in that moment Geli understood everything.

Valentina's tears, Daniele's uncertainty, Dante's grief.

He had not been mourning the loss of his love, but the child she had carried, given birth to and then placed in his father's arms.

In the excitement created by the arrival of the baby, the staff crowding around to coo over him, Geli reached out a hand to him and he grasped it so tightly that it hurt while he arranged his face into a smile.

Hours later—actually, it was no more than two but it had felt like a thousand—Geli shut the door behind their visitors and turned to Dante.

'Your father knows, doesn't he?' she said. 'That the baby is yours.'

'He had a fever when I was a child. That's when I first came to stay here with Nonnina. Valentina is his fourth wife but there have been no more children when, as you can see, he loves them…so I imagine there was some damage. I should have told you. I would have told you, but last night—'

'Don't…' She did not want to think about last night. That familiar, horrible sense of loss— 'We have known one another just over a week. Okay, we've probably spent more time together than some couples spend in months, but it's still new. We're still learning about one another. And that is a huge secret to share with anyone.'

'Secrets are poison. Valentina nearly fainted when she saw me last night. She was sure I was there to make trouble, to tell my father that Alberto isn't his child. Blow their lives apart.'

'Are you saying that she doesn't know that he knows?'

'Apparently not. That's when she cried, when I told her. With relief and joy, I think, to realise just how much he loved her.'

'I see.' And remembering the way Valentina had gone straight to her husband, put her arm in his—not a guilty wife returning to her husband's side, but one who knew how much she was loved—she did see.

'You asked me once if I regretted my choice, do you remember?'

'You said it was the wrong question. That I should be asking if you'd make the same decision again.' Could she ask it? Could she live with his answer… 'Would you?'

'The truth?'

Parla come magni, caro.

He smiled as she quoted his words back at him and her heart broke for him. After that first shocked moment he'd been so generous, admiring the baby, holding him, handing him back to his father to put in his buggy for a nap when it must have been tearing his heart out.

'There will always be regret, Angel, but a baby's place

is with his mother and his mother's place is with the man who will make her happy. I can only hope that, should I be given the chance, I'd have the strength, the wisdom, the humanity to make the same decision.'

'You'd do that for them?'

'What should I do? Demand DNA tests? Give the readers of *Celebrità* a scandal to thrill them over the breakfast table? Make his mother the centre of vicious whispers?'

'No.' She shook her head. 'No...'

'I created a trust fund for Alberto when he was born, *cara*. And today, when you took Valentina to your workshop to show her your designs, Papà agreed to sign documents giving me legal access to Alberto, and to name me his guardian in the event of a divorce.'

'Will Valentina agree to that?'

'She knows that he will always be a part of my life,' he said. 'I want you to know that.'

'I treasure your trust. You are a very special man, Dante Vettori.' And to show her confidence, her trust, she took his key from her pocket and offered it to him.

'You are returning my key?'

'No, *caro*, I'm not returning it; I'm giving it to you for safe keeping.'

He took the key, put it in his pocket and then took her hand. 'I've missed you.'

'It was ten hours, Dante,' she said, stepping into his arm. 'But I've missed you, too.'

'Did I tell you that you look lovely today?'

'Make the most of it. I'm going to buy a pink fluffy jumper at the market on Tuesday. And if you don't kiss me right now, I'll wear it on television.'

His kiss was thorough and then, as a demonstration of how seriously he took her threat, he picked her up and carried her through to the bedroom and kissed every single part of her.

Later, when she was lying in his arms, he said, 'Tell me about this pink jumper thing. Is it going to be an ongoing threat? Not that I'm complaining.'

'I'll tell you when you can relax.' She looked up at him. 'Can I ask you a question?'

'Ask away.'

'What did Valentina whisper in your ear last night?'

'You saw?'

'I saw.'

'She said, *"Si prega di essere felice..."* I'd told her that I'd met someone and, having met you, she was urging me to be happy.' He leaned down and kissed her. 'A command that I'm delighted to obey.'

'Uh-oh.'

'Cara?'

'I've had a text from Elle. I knew opening the ice cream parlour at Easter was a mistake. They're all coming to see it.'

'They're flying to Milan to see an ice cream parlour?'

'Professional interest?' she offered.

'Cara...'

'Okay, they're coming to check you out. Sorry, I've tried to be as casual about us as I can be, but the less you say, the more big sisters read between the lines.'

'Is there anything I should know? Topics not to be mentioned?'

'Just be yourself and they'll love you. But I have to find somewhere for them to stay.'

'I'll call Papà and ask if the villa at Lake Como is going to be free.'

'It's not. Valentina told me that they're going to the Lake for Easter. She rang to invite us while you were out. I thought that maybe we could go down on Sunday for the day so that you can spend time with Alberto but...'

'But nothing. There's plenty of room.' He took out his phone. 'Four adults, three children, one baby, right?' She nodded and he made the call. 'They're delighted to have them and we'll stay over until Tuesday. It'll give you plenty of time to catch up with your sisters.'

'Did I ever tell you that I love you?' she said.

'Not since breakfast. Are we done here?'

She looked around at the rich green walls, the huge brilliant print—just the corner of an ice cream sundae with all the focus on a huge, glistening red cherry—the white-painted furniture, vintage jukebox and gleaming ice cream counter waiting to be filled.

Outside in the courtyard, tubs of red and white flowers were overflowing from old stone troughs and she'd threaded tiny white solar-powered fairy lights through the vines that would light up as dusk fell.

'It looks done to me.'

'Then come with me. I have something to show you.'

He took her outside and unlocked the front door of the tall narrow building next door that had, until the owner retired a few weeks ago, been a hardware store.

'More expansion plans?' she asked. 'Only I'm a bit busy.'

She'd been working flat out since the photograph of her talking to the Maestro had appeared in an Italian lifestyle magazine reporting his interest in her belt. Now it seemed everyone wanted one.

He had offered her a job in return for the rights to reproduce it but, flattered as she was, she didn't want to be a nameless designer producing ideas for a designer 'brand'.

She had her own label and was collaborating with a student who could do amazing things with leather to produce variations on her design in gorgeous colours.

She'd also had an order for a dozen of her spider web beaded silk chiffon tops for a Milan boutique.

'I know how busy you are and that you need more space,' he said. 'Welcome to your *atelier*.'

'What? No...'

'No?' Dante repeated. 'You do not think this would make appropriate showroom space for your designs?'

'A showroom...' She spun around, imagining everything painted white, shelves, a display table, one brilliantly coloured piece in the small window. 'You know it's perfect.'

'I'm glad that's settled. There's a room out the back for office and storage and two rooms on the next floor for workshop space. And on the top floor...'

She turned to him, knowing what was coming. She'd told him, that first night in Isola, about her dream. A house with three floors. One for sales, one for work and one to live in.

'There's a little apartment. Just big enough for one?'

'Well, it's a bit bigger than that. I thought we could knock it through.'

She frowned. 'Knock it through? I don't understand. Have you bought this?'

'No. At least not recently. I inherited some money from my maternal grandfather when I turned twenty-one and Nonnina wanted to raise the money to help her son set up in business in Australia. She owned the whole block and it seemed like a good investment, even if part of the deal was that she stayed on, rent-free, until she decided to retire. Papà would buy it in a heartbeat if it was for sale.'

'*Madonna*, Dante, you know how to take the wind out of a girl's sails.'

He shrugged. 'So you're good with that? Extending the apartment? Only we'll need more space when we're married.'

And, while she was struggling to get her chin under

control, he produced a small leather box from his pocket and opened it to reveal a large solitaire diamond.

'Dante, *caro*, my love, are you sure? There's no hurry...'

He did not pretend that he did not understand but said, 'This is different in so many ways from Valentina. We are not just lovers, Angel, we're friends. *Siete la mia aria*... You are the air I breathe. *Voglio stare con te per sempre*... I want to stay with you for ever. *Ti amo.*' And then again in English, so there could be no mistake. 'I love you, *mia amore.* I would leave here and go to the ends of the earth to be with you.'

She dashed away a tear, took the ring from the box and gave it to him, holding out her hand, and as he placed it on her finger she said, '*Siete la mia aria,* Dante. *Voglio stare con te per sempre*... I would live in a cave with you.'

There were two weddings. The first was in Isola early in May. They said their vows in the *municipio*, with Giovanni standing as his best man and his own bride, Lisa, as her very best woman. Afterwards everyone was invited to a party in the communal garden. The feast was lavish but still everyone brought something they had made to add to the table. Geli's family returned to Isola for the occasion, bringing with them her grandmother and Great-Uncle Basil. Nonnina flew with her son from Australia to be with Dante and meet his bride. A fiddler played so that they could dance and later, as dusk fell, a jazz quartet filled the air with smooth, mellow music while the square was lit up with thousands of tiny white fairy lights.

Six weeks later, in midsummer, Geli and Dante repeated their vows in the Orangery at Haughton Manor, just as Geli's sister had done a few years earlier, followed by a picnic in the park with Rosie in attendance to provide all the ice cream anyone could eat. This time her sisters were her

best women, her small nieces her bridesmaids and Great-
Uncle Basil gave her away.

Over the vintage cream slipper satin vintage gown she'd
adapted for both occasions, Geli wore a luscious new belt
made from shocking-pink suede, which made the front
page of *Celebrità* and its English version, *Celebrity*.

An order book for a limited edition of the design was
filled the same day.

* * * * *

HER FIRST-DATE
HONEYMOON

KATRINA CUDMORE

For Ben

See, the middle child isn't always forgotten!

Love, Mum

CHAPTER ONE

'I ADMIRE YOUR TENACITY, *cara*, but I meant it when I said no.'

Matteo Vieri lay down and spread his body behind the woman already warming his bed. His hand curled around her slim waist. The only light in the room came from the corridor, and in the dark shadows, with her head tucked low into the pillow, he struggled to see her in detail. But beneath his fingers he felt her body edge towards him.

Irritation bit into his stomach and refused to let go, but he forced his voice to remain a low playful tease. 'The last woman who crept into my bed wasn't seen for days. Leave now, or I swear you won't see daylight for a very long time.'

He wanted nothing but to sleep. Alone.

Earlier, when she had phoned him while he was en route to Venice, she had told him she was leaving tomorrow for her home city of New York, but she had promised him a night to remember. They had dated intermittently in the past, when their paths had crossed. It had been fun. But recently he had realised that beneath her cool sass lay fantasies of a future together, so he had good-humouredly turned down her offer. Again. But she obviously hadn't listened and now she lay in his bed.

He stifled a curse.

It was past midnight. His bones ached for a shower and the oblivion of sleep.

'*Cara*, it's time for you to leave.'

Beneath the silk of her nightgown her ribcage jerked. His hand stilled.

Something was wrong. Her scent was wrong. The dip of her waist was wrong. The endless curls in her hair, brushing his hand, making him itch with the desire to thread it through his fingers and pull her towards him, were wrong.

His breathing, his heart, his thoughts went on hold. The red traffic lights of confusion waited to switch to the green of clarity.

Her head inched upwards until wide eyes met his: perplexed, scared, startled.

His own disbelief left him speechless.

Caspita! Who was this stranger lying in his bed?

And then he wanted to laugh. Could this week get any worse?

His starved lungs sucked in air. He could barely make out her features, but still a lick of attraction barrelled through him. Her scent—the clean low notes of rose—the enticing warmth of her body, the mass of hair tumbling on the bed sheets made him want to draw her into him. To take solace in her softness, her femininity, from the craziness of his life.

Her mouth opened. And closed. She swallowed a cartoon gulp. Her mouth opened again. Her lips were full, the hint of a deep cupid's bow on the upper lip. A dangerous beauty.

Her body stiffened beside him. Seconds passed. Two strangers. In the most intimate of settings.

A tiny sound of disbelief hiccupped from her throat.

Then, in a shower of rising and falling sheets and blankets, she flung off the bedclothes and darted towards the door.

In one smooth movement he followed her and yanked her back.

Long narrow bones crashed into him, along with a tumble of hair, a scent that left him wanting more.

'Who are you? What do you want?'

Her voice was a husky rasp, heavily accented, sexy, English. A voice he had definitely never heard before.

Attraction kicked again. Strong enough to knock him out of his stupor. His earlier frustration lit up inside him. Bright and fierce.

He pulled her towards the wall and flicked on the bedroom chandelier. She winced, but then hazel eyes settled on his, anger mixing with shock.

She attempted to jerk away but he gripped her slim arm tighter.

A flare of defiance grew in her eyes. 'If you don't let me go I'm going to scream until the entire neighbourhood, all of Venice, is awake.'

A growl of fury leapt from his throat. 'Scream away. My neighbours are used to hearing me entertain.'

A blush erupted on her cheeks. She dipped her head.

Satisfaction twitched on his lips. He lowered his mouth towards her ear. 'Now, tell me, do you make a habit of breaking into homes? Sleeping in strangers' beds?'

Emma Fox knew she should be scared. But instead an anger, a rebellion, surged in her. She was *not* going to be pushed around again. Her heart might be doing a full drama queen routine in her chest, but the pit of her stomach was shouting, *Enough!* Enough of false accusations. Enough of people telling her what to do. Enough of the mess that was her life.

She grabbed the hand clinging to her upper arm and tried to prise his fingers away. 'What on earth are you talking about? I haven't broken in. I was invited to stay here by the *palazzo*'s owner.'

Her captor took a step back to stare down at her, but

his grip grew tighter. For the first time she saw his face. Her heart went silent. Why couldn't he be on the wrong side of handsome? A few blemishes here and there, a little cross-eyed, perhaps. Instead she faced a gulp-inducing, knee-knocking magnificence that stole all her composure.

His golden-brown eyes flared with the incredulous impatience of a man used to getting his way. 'Signorina, that is impossible. *I* own Ca' Divina. This is *my* property.'

He let go of her arm and moved to the door. He slammed it shut and stood guard in front of the large ancient door, arms crossed.

'Now, tell me the truth before I call the *carabinieri*.'

The *carabinieri*. He couldn't. Her stomach tumbled. She had spent a nightmare morning in police custody only yesterday. She couldn't go through *that* again. The disbelieving looks. Then the impatient pity when they'd realised she was nothing but a patsy in the whole debacle.

Fear tap-danced down her spine and she began to shiver. She was wearing only a barely there nightdress and longed to cover up. To walk away from this fully clothed man, armoured in an impeccable dark navy suit and maroon tie, and from the way his eyes were travelling down her body critically. Something about him triggered a memory of seeing him before—but where? Why did he seem familiar?

She backed towards the bed, away from him, and spoke in a rush of words. 'I'm telling the truth. But how do I know who you are—perhaps *you're* the one who has broken into the *palazzo*.'

He threw her an *are you being serious?* look. 'And I've woken you up to have an argument? Not the usual behaviour of a thief, I would expect.'

'No, but—'

He rocked on his heels and inhaled an exasperated breath. 'In my bedside table you'll find a tray of cufflinks with my monogram—MV.'

She opened the top drawer of the lacquered and gilt carved bedside table with trembling fingers. Beside a number of priceless-looking Rolex watches sat a platoon of silver, gold and platinum cufflinks, all bearing the letters MV.

A sinking feeling moved through her body, draining her of all energy. 'I don't understand... I was in a café earlier today and a lady... Signora...'

Her mind became a black hole of forgetfulness. Across from her, her prison guard scowled in disbelief. Flustered, she tried to zone him out. She had to concentrate. What had her saviour's name been?

'Her name was Signora... Signora Ve... Vieri... Yes, that was it—Signora Vieri.'

He unfurled his arms and walked towards her across the antique Oriental rug covering the *terrazzo* floor. A treasure perhaps imported when the Venetian Republic had been the exploration and commercial powerhouse of Europe centuries ago.

His mouth was a thin line of frustration, his already narrow lips tight and unyielding. 'What did this Signora Vieri look like?'

His words were spoken in a low, dangerous rumble and she became unaccountably hot, with flames of heat burning up her insides at the menace in his words and the way he was now standing over her, staring down, as if ready to murder the nearest person.

Her vow to toughen up, to refuse to kowtow to anyone ever again was going to be tested sooner than she had anticipated. She squared her shoulders and looked him right in the eye. Which was a bad idea, because immediately she lost herself in those almond-shaped golden-brown eyes and forgot what she was going to say.

The anger in his eyes turned for the briefest moment

into a flare of appreciation. Her heart swooped up her throat like a songbird.

But then the appreciation flicked to exasperation. 'I don't have all night.'

Toughen up. That was her mission in life now. She had to remember that. She clenched her fists and tossed her head back, ready for battle. 'I have no idea what's going on here but, despite what you obviously think, I have not been involved in anything untoward. Signora Vieri offered me a place to stay. I accepted her offer in good faith.'

He loomed over her, tension bouncing off his huge, formidable body. 'Tell me what she looked like...or is this just a convenient story? Perhaps you'll be more co-operative for the *carabinieri*.'

Alarm shot down through her and exited at her toes, leaving a numb, tingling sensation behind. She began to babble. 'She's in her early fifties...animated, kind, concerned...full of energy. Brown bobbed hair. She has the cutest little dog called Elmo.'

He exhaled another loud breath and walked away.

She spun around to find him standing before the bedroom's marble fireplace. The huge gilt mirror on the mantel reflected his powerful tense shoulders, the glossy thickness of his brown hair.

'My grandmother.'

'*Your grandmother!* She mentioned that her grandson sometimes stays here... I was picturing a toddler. Not a grown man.'

For a few long seconds he stopped and glared at her, leaving her in no doubt that she had said something wrong. What, she had no idea, but the temperature in the room had dropped at least ten degrees.

'*Nonnina* is sixty-seven. And she has a soft spot for waifs and strays. Although this is the first time she has actually brought home a human one.'

'I'm not a waif or a stray!'

'Then what are you doing in my bed?'

Memories of his hand burning through the material of her nightdress, of the shaming stream of pleasure that had flowed through her dreams until she had woken fully taunted her, causing her confusion to intensify.

'Who did you think was in your bed when you climbed in beside me?'

Her question earned her a tight-lipped scowl. 'A friend.'

Unease swept over her at the prospect of that huge, frankly scary-looking lion's head brass knocker on the front door sounding at any moment, and having to explain her presence to another person tonight.

'Are you still expecting her?'

His eyes swept over her lazily. 'No.'

Every inch of her skin tingled. For a moment she gazed longingly towards her suitcase, propped open beside an ornately carved walnut dressing table. She hadn't had the energy to unpack earlier, but had fallen into bed after a much needed shower instead.

She moved towards the suitcase, aware he was following her every move. She grabbed the first jumper from the messy jumble spilling from it and pulled on the thick-knit polo neck. A shiver of comfort and relief ran down her spine; she no longer felt so susceptible to his dangerous gaze.

He moved back across the room towards the door. 'I need to speak to my grandmother.'

'She isn't here.'

He pulled up short. 'What do you mean, she isn't here?'

'She said she had to return home to Puglia. That there was an emergency.'

He shook his head in disgust and twisted away. He rolled his shoulders and then his spine in a quick, impatient movement, the fine wool of his suit jacket rippling in a fluid motion. He moved with the ease of the super-rich. Even his hair—a perfect one-inch length, tapering down in a perfect straight line to hug the tanned strength of his neck—looked as though it had been cut with diamond-encrusted scissors by a barber to the nobility of Europe.

This room—this *palazzo*, this stunning city La Serenissima—all so grand and overwhelming, proud and mysterious, suited him. Whereas *she* felt like an alien amongst the wealth and elegance.

Wealth. Elegance. A grandmother with the surname of Vieri…

Her brain buzzed with the white noise of astonishment while her heart jumped to a *thumpety-thumpety-thump* beat. No wonder he looked familiar.

'You're Matteo Vieri, aren't you?'

The owner of one of the world's largest luxury goods conglomerates.

He unbuttoned his suit jacket and popped a hand into his trouser pocket. 'So you know who I am?' His casual stance belied the sharp tone of his response.

Did he think she had engineered her stay here because of who he was? Engineered being in his bed for his arrival? Did he think she had designs on him romantically? That possibility, if it hadn't been so tragic, would have been laughable.

'I used to work at St Paul's Fashion College in London. One of your companies—VMV—sponsors its graduation show.'

'*Used* to work?'

'I left last week to move to Sydney.'

Well, that had been the plan anyway. Until it had all fallen apart. When was life going to start co-operating with her, instead of throwing her endless grenades of disastrous calamity?

Yet more uncomfortable heat threaded along her veins.

She had slept in *Matteo Vieri's* bed. He was one of Europe's most eligible bachelors. She needed to clarify how all this had happened.

'Your grandmother told me I was welcome to use any room I wanted. I didn't realise this room was yours.' She paused and gestured around the room to the walnut four-poster bed, the pale green silk sofa—all so beautiful, but without a trace of him. 'None of your belongings are on display, no clothes... I had no idea it might be someone's bedroom.'

'When this *palazzo* was built in the fifteenth century not much thought was given to adjoining dressing rooms... my clothes are further down the hallway.' He spoke like a bored tour guide, tired of the same inane tourist questions.

'But your bathroom is full of...' She trailed off, not sure how to say it. It was full of delicious but most definitely girly shampoos and conditioners, bath and shower gels, lavish body lotions...

He gave her a *don't push it* frown. 'I do own those companies.' His lips moved for a nanosecond upwards into the smile of a man remembering good times. 'Those products are there for my dates to use.'

She tugged at the collar of her jumper, feeling way too hot. The image of a naked Matteo Vieri applying one of those shower gels was sending her pulse into the stratosphere.

She went to her suitcase and squashed the lid down, fighting the giddiness rampaging through her limbs, praying it would zip up without its usual fight.

'I'll move to another room.'

He stood over her, casting a dark shadow over her where she crouched. 'I'm afraid that's not an option. You'll have to leave.'

She sprang up, her struggle with the suitcase forgotten. 'But I have nowhere to go! I spent all of today searching for a hotel, but with it being Carnival time there are no rooms available. I've tried everywhere within my budget. Meeting your grandmother…her kind offer of a room was like a miracle.'

'I bet it was—an invitation to stay in a *palazzo* on the Grand Canal in Venice!'

Did he *have* to sound so cynical? 'I appreciate this situation is far from ideal, but I have nowhere else to go. I promise I'll stay out of your way.'

He adjusted the cuffs of his shirt beneath his suit jacket with a stiff, annoyed movement. His cufflinks flashed beneath the light of the crystal chandelier. 'I apologise for my grandmother's behaviour. She shouldn't have given you a room without my authorisation. I have a busy week ahead, with clients from China coming to Venice for Carnival. It does not suit me to have a house guest.'

'Are they staying here?'

'No, but—'

'Honestly—I've tried every hotel in Venice.'

He glared at her, and for a moment she was transported back to her *pointe* classes as an eleven-year-old, when she used to shake with fear about getting on the wrong side of the volatile ballet master.

'Why are you in Venice, Signorina…?' His voice trailed off and he waited for her to speak.

'Fox. Emma Fox. I'm here because…' A lump the size of the top tier of her wedding cake formed in her throat. She gritted her teeth against the tears blurring her vision. 'I was supposed to be here on my honeymoon.'

His stomach did a nosedive. *Dio!* She was about to cry.

Something about the way she was fighting her tears reminded him of his childhood, watching his mother battle her tears. Unable to do anything to stop them. To make life okay for her. Not sure why she was crying in the first place when he was a small boy other than having a vague understanding that she was waiting for his father to come back. The father he'd never known.

And then in later years, when she had accepted that his father was never going to return, her tears had been shed over yet another failed relationship. But he hadn't even tried to comfort her in those years. His own pain had been too great—pain for all the men who had walked out of his life without a fight, father figures, many of whom he had hero-worshipped.

People let you down. It was a lesson he had learned early in life. Along with coming to the realisation that he could only ever rely on himself. Not trust in the empty promises of others.

A loud sniffle brought him back to his present problem. To her lowered head he said, 'On your honeymoon?'

She emitted a cry and bolted for his bathroom.

This time his grandmother had gone too far. To the extent that he was tempted to follow her down to Puglia and give her a piece of his mind, this time not falling for her apologies and pledges to behave. Nor, for that matter, being diverted by plates of her legendary *purcedduzzi*— fried gnocchi with honey.

He understood her compulsion to help the poor and homeless—but to invite a stranger into his *home*!

He knocked at the bathroom door. 'Are you okay?'

'Yes…sorry. I'll be out in a few minutes.'

Her voice went from alto to soprano, and several notes in between. A muffled sob followed. He winced and rubbed at his face with both hands.

He leaned in against the door. 'We both need a drink. Join me downstairs in the lounge when you're ready.'

He hurried down the stairs. Memories chased him. Those nights when he was seven…eight years old, when he would crawl into his mother's bed, hoping he could stop her tears.

In the lounge, he threw open the doors onto the terrace. Venice was blanketed in a light misty fog. Sounds were muffled. He saw the intermittent lights of a launch moving on the water, its engine barely audible. Technically it was spring, but tonight winter still shrouded the city, and the cold, damp air intensified its mysterious beauty.

He spent most of his year travelling between his headquarters in Milan and his offices in New York, London and Paris. Always moving. Never belonging. The nomadic lifestyle of his childhood had followed him into adulthood. He had hated it as a child. Now it suited him. It meant that he could keep a distance from others. Even acquaintances and those he considered friends would never have the opportunity to hurt him, to walk away. *He* was the one in control instead. It was *he* who could choose to walk away now.

Venice was his one true escape. It was why he had no regular staff here in Ca' Divina. He liked the calm, the peace of the building, without sound, without people awaiting his instructions. Here was the one place he could be alone, away from the intensity of his normal routine. Away from the constant expectations and responsibilities of his businesses, his family.

But tonight the calm serenity of both Venice and Ca' Divina were doing little to calm his boiling irritation. The maverick, eccentric, brilliant chief designer for his fashion house Ettore had thrown a hissy fit—no doubt fuelled by alcohol—whilst being interviewed by a Chinese news team last night. He had not only insulted the reporter but also implied that the exclusive department store chain that sold his designs in China was not worthy of doing so.

The exclusive department store chain Matteo was delicately negotiating with over contracts for the extensive expansion of product placement for *all* his brands.

The company quite rightly had not taken kindly to the designer's words, and had seen it as a huge public insult to their honour. This loss of face—known as *mianzi* in China—might have damaged their relationship beyond repair.

The chain's president and his team were arriving in Venice tomorrow evening. He had a lot of apologising to do and reassurances to make to ensure they understood how much he valued and respected them as a partner. It was vital the trip went well. Or else several of his lines would be in serious financial trouble.

He twisted around to the sound of footsteps on the *terrazzo* flooring. The last thing he needed was to have to deal with a stranger's problems.

She reminded him of a Federico Zandomeneghi portrait in Ca' Pesaro, the International Gallery of Modern Art located further along the banks of the Grand Canal. Delicate, elegant features, a cupid's bow mouth, a perfect nose, porcelain skin, long thick brown curls almost to her waist, tucked behind her ears.

Below the cream polo-neck jumper she was now wearing a pair of skinny jeans and tan ankle boots. She'd tugged the neck of the jumper up until it reached her ears. The tears were gone, but despite the resolute set of her mouth she looked worn out.

Almost as worn out as *he* felt.

'What can I get you to drink?'

'A whisky, please.'

He poured her whisky and a brandy for himself into tumblers, trying to ignore how physically aware he was of her. Of her refined accent, her words clipped but softly spoken. Of her long limbs. Of the outline of the tantalising body her nightdress had done little to conceal earlier. Of her utter beauty.

He brought their drinks over to the sofas at the centre of the room and placed one on either side of the coffee table in between them. He sat with his back to the canal.

She perched on the side of the sofa and stared out through the terrace windows with an unseeing gaze, the hands on her lap curled like weapons ready to strike out. Eventually her eyes landed on his, and the sudden flare of vulnerability in them delivered a sucker punch to his gut.

Despite every fibre of his being telling him not to—she might start crying again—he found himself asking, 'Do you want to talk about it?'

She took a sip of her whisky. Depositing the glass back on the table, she reached down to her left ankle and gave it a quick squeeze. Sitting up, she inhaled deeply, her chest rising and falling. A flash of heat coloured her cheeks. The result of the whisky or something else?

'Not particularly.' Her clipped tone was accompanied by a haughty rise of her chin.

'In that case I'll go and make some phone calls to arrange a hotel room for you.'

He was at the door before she spoke.

'My fiancé…I mean my *ex*-fiancé…was arrested early yesterday morning—at four o'clock, to be precise—for embezzlement.'

She tugged at the neck of her jumper. He returned to his seat and she darted a quick glance in his direction. Pride in battle with pain.

'He stole funds from the company he worked for; and also persuaded his family and friends to invest in a property scheme with him. There was no scheme. Instead he used the money to play the stock exchange. He lost it all.'

'And you knew nothing about it?'

She stared at him aghast. 'No!' Then she winced, and the heat in her cheeks noticeably paled. 'Although the police wouldn't believe me at first…' She glanced away. 'I was arrested.'

'Arrested?'

She reached for her glass but stopped halfway and instead edged further back into the sofa. 'Yes, arrested. On what was supposed to be my wedding day.' She gave a disbelieving laugh. 'I was let go eventually, when they realised I was his victim rather than his partner in crime.'

Her eyes challenged his; she must be seeing the doubt in his expression.

'By all means call Camden Police Station in London, if you don't believe me; they will verify my story. I have the number of the investigating officer.'

His instinct told him she was telling the truth, but he wasn't going to admit that. 'It's of no consequence to me.'

That earned him a hurt glance. Remorse prickled along his skin. But why was he feeling guilty? None of this was his doing. What on earth was she doing in Venice anyway?

'Do you think it was wise, coming to Venice? Without a hotel booking? Wouldn't you be better off at home?'

She crossed her legs with an exasperated frown that told him he wasn't getting this. 'I *did* have a hotel booking. Or so my ex told me. But he never transferred the funds so the booking fell through. He also cleared out our joint bank account. Anyway, I don't *have* a home. Or a job. I moved out of my apartment and resigned from the college because my ex was being transferred to Sydney with his work and I was joining him.'

'And your family?'

A flicker of pain crossed her face. But then she sat upright and eyed him coolly. 'I don't have one.'

Despite all the hurts and frustrations of the past, and the fact that he had far from perfect relationships with his emotional and unpredictable mother and grandmother, he could never imagine life without them. What must it be like to have no family? Had she no friends who could take their place?

'Your friends…?'

With her legs crossed, she rotated her left ankle in the air. Agitated. Upset.

'I appreciate your concern, but I'm not going back to London. I have no home to go to. I can't go back... I can't face everyone. I need some time away. After I was released from police custody I checked out of the hotel we'd been staying in...' She paused and bit her lip, drank some whisky, grimaced. 'I ran away.'

'You're a runaway bride?'

Her generous full mouth twisted unhappily. She refused to meet his eye.

'I'm not putting my friends out by sleeping on their sofas. My closest friend Rachel has just had a baby; the last thing she needs right now is a lodger. This is my mess—it's up to me to sort it out. My ex might have stolen everything from me, but he isn't going to stop me from living my life. I've always wanted to see Venice during Carnival. And I fully intend doing so.'

Her mouth gave a little wobble.

'We had organised our wedding for this week so that it coincided with Carnival.'

She was putting up one hell of a fight to keep her tears at bay. He felt completely out of his comfort zone.

'I'll pay for your hotel room by way of compensation for any inconvenience my grandmother's actions may have caused.'

'I don't want your money.'

Old memories churned in his stomach at her resolve. He knew only too well that it masked vulnerability.

He remembered throwing guilt money from Stefano, one of his mother's boyfriends, who had just shoved it into his hands, off the balcony of Stefano's apartment. He had got momentary satisfaction seeing Stefano's shame. It had been short-lived, though, when he and his mother had been forced to sleep in a homeless hostel that night.

He had stayed awake all night, unable to sleep, vowing he would never be in that position again. Vowing to drag his mother out of poverty and to protect her. Even if her behaviour *had* led them to sharing a room with eight strangers. He would be a success. Which meant he would no longer be held hostage by poverty, by the lack of choices, the motives of other people.

It was an ambition he was still chasing. He still needed to leave behind the spectre of hunger, the fear of not being in control, still needed to prove himself, still needed to make sure he protected his family...and now the tens of thousands who worked for him.

He looked at his watch and then back at her. She was blinking rapidly. Unexpected emotion gripped his throat. He forced it away with a deep swallow. 'It's late. We can talk about this in the morning.'

'I can stay?'

The relief in her face hit him like a punch. This woman needed compassion and care. His grandmother should be here, finishing the task she'd started. Not dumping it on *him*. He was too busy. In truth, he didn't know how to help her. He didn't get tangled up in this type of situation. He kept others at arm's length. No one got close. Even his mother and grandmother. And that was not going to change.

'You can stay for tonight. Tomorrow I will organise alternative accommodation for you.'

Half an hour later Emma lay on cool sheets in the bed of another bedroom, her mind on fire, wondering if the past few hours had actually happened.

A knock sounded on the door. She sat up and stared at the door dubiously.

'Emma—it's Matteo.'

Her heart flipped in full operatic diva mode. Did he

have to speak in a voice that sounded as if he was caress-
ing her? And what did he *want*? Had he changed his mind
about her staying?

She cautiously opened the door and drank in the sight
of Matteo, freshly showered, his thick brown hair damp,
wearing nothing but pyjama bottoms. The golden expanse
of his hard sculptured torso instantly left her tongue-tied.
And guilty. And cross. She should be on honeymoon right
now. Not staring at a stranger's body, trying to keep lust-
ful thoughts at bay.

She folded her arms. 'Can I help you?'

Her ice-cool tone did little to melt the amusement in
his eyes.

An eyebrow—a beautiful, thick eyebrow—rose. Without a word he raised his hand and held out a toy polar bear,
barely the size of his palm, grey and threadbare.

'Snowy!' She grabbed the bear and held it to her chest.

'I found it under my pillow.'

'I forgot about him…thank you.'

His head tilted to the side and for a tiny moment he
looked at her with almost affection, but then he looked
back at Snowy with an exasperated shake of his head.
Probably questioning the wisdom of allowing a grown
woman who slept with a diseased-looking toy polar bear
to stay in his home.

He turned away.

She should close the door, to signal that his appearance was of little consequence, but instead she watched
him walk back to his room—and almost swooned when
he ran his hand through his hair, the movement of the
powerful muscles in his back taunting her pledge to give
men a wide berth.

He swung back to her. 'I'm sorry about your wedding.'

A thick wedge of gratitude landed in her chest. She

wanted to say thank you, but her throat was as tight as a twisted rag.

He nodded at her thank-you smile.

Her heart beat slow and hard in her chest.

They stood in silence for far too long.

He seemed as unable to turn away as she was.

Eventually he broke the tension and spoke in a low, rolling tone, '*Buonanotte.*'

Back inside the room, she climbed into bed and tucked Snowy against her. She was fully aware, of course, that the first thing she should do in her bid to toughen up was to banish Snowy from her bed. But when she had been a child, alone and petrified at boarding school, he had brought her comfort. And, rather sadly, over fifteen years on she needed him more than ever before.

So much for Operation Toughen Up. An hour in the company of Matteo Vieri and all her vows and pledges to be resilient and single-minded had melted into a puddle of embarrassing tears and ill-advised attraction.

But tomorrow was going to be different.

It *had* to be.

CHAPTER TWO

THE FOLLOWING DAY, mid-morning sunshine poured into Matteo's office. He stood up from his desk and stretched his back, grimacing at the tightness at the bottom of his spine.

They said bad things came in threes. Well, he had just reached his quota. First, his exasperating but gifted designer had publicly insulted his most valued clients. Then his grandmother had invited a stranger into his home. And now his event co-ordinator for the Chinese clients' trip had gone into early labour.

His designer was already in rehab.

He would have to put in extra hours to ensure the China trip ran perfectly…which meant even less sleep than usual.

And as for Signorina Fox… Well, he had news for her.

He walked down the corridor of the *palazzo*'s first floor, the *piano nobile*, his heels echoing on the heritage *terrazzo* flooring. He hadn't seen or heard from Signorina Fox all morning. He had a sneaking suspicion that she was deliberately staying out of his way in the hope that he might let her stay.

The lounge balcony windows were open. Shouts of laughter and passionate calls tumbled into the room from outside. Stepping into the early springtime sunshine, he came to an abrupt halt.

Crouched over the balcony, her chin resting on her

folded arms Emma was focused on the canal, oblivious to the fact that her short skirt had risen up to give him an uninterrupted view of her legs. Legs encased in thick woollen tights that shouldn't look sexy. But her legs were so long, so toned, that for a brief moment the ludicrous idea of allowing her to stay and act as a distraction from all his worries flitted through his brain.

He coughed noisily.

She popped up and twisted around to look at him. A hand tugged at her red skirt. Over the skirt she was wearing another polo-necked jumper, today in a light-knit navy blue. Her chestnut hair hung over one shoulder in a thick plait.

'I hope you found my note?'

'Thank you—yes…it was a lovely breakfast.'

The exhaustion of last night was gone from beneath her eyes. She gave him a *can we try to act normal?* smile and then gestured to the canal.

'There's the most incredible flotilla sailing up the canal—you must come and see.' Her smile was transformed into a broad beam, matching the excitement in her eyes. She beckoned him over.

He should get back to work. But it seemed churlish to refuse to look. The canal was teeming with boats, and onlookers were crowding the *fondamente*—the canal pathways.

'It's the opening parade of the Carnival,' he explained.

For a few minutes he forgot everything that was wrong in his life as he joined her in watching the parade of gondolas and ceremonial boats sail past. Most of the occupants, in flamboyant seventeenth- and eighteenth-century costume, waved and shouted greetings in response to Emma's enthusiastic waves.

Seeing the contrast between her upbeat mood now and the sobs that had emanated from his bathroom last night twisted his stomach, along with the memory of his grand-mother's words this morning. He had called her with the intention of lambasting her, only to be pulled up short when he'd learned that she had gone home because one of the homeless men she helped had been involved in an accident, and that she had helped Emma because she had found her in a desperate state in a café yesterday.

He pushed away the guilt starting to gnaw a hole in his gut. He had enough problems of his own. Anyway, he didn't do cohabitation. He had never shared his home with anyone. And he wasn't about to start with an emotional runaway bride.

Below them, the regatta started to trail off.

'I have found alternative accommodation for you in the Hotel Leopolda.'

Her smile dropped from her face like a stone sinking in water. 'Hotel Leopolda? The five-star hotel close to St Mark's Square?'

'Yes.'

She stared back at the canal, a small grimace pulling on her mouth. 'I can't afford to stay there.'

'I'll take care of it.'

She stepped away from him before meeting his eye. 'I said it last night—I'm not taking your money.'

'I can appreciate how you feel. If it makes you happier, you can repay me some time in the future.'

'No.' Those hazel eyes sucked him in, dumped a whole load of guilt on his soul and spat him back out again.

'I'll make some calls myself—check the internet again. I'll find somewhere suitable,' she said.

This woman was starting to drive him crazy. He had had to use all his influence to secure her a room. He doubted she would find anywhere by herself.

'I want to resolve this now. My event co-ordinator for the Chinese trip has gone into early labour. I'll be tied up with organising all the final details for the visit for the rest of the day.'

She stepped back towards him, her crossed arms dropping to her sides. Concern flooded her eyes. 'I hope she'll be okay. How many weeks pregnant is she?'

He had no idea. It had been a sizeable bump. Once he had even seen a tiny foot kick hard against the extended bump during a meeting. It had been one of the most incredible things he had ever seen.

That image had haunted him for days afterwards. Catching him unawares in meetings, distracting his concentration. Bringing a hollow sensation to his chest, a tightness to his belly, knowing he would never see the first miraculous stirrings of his own child. Knowing he would never be a father. Knowing he would choose the empty feeling that came with that knowledge over the certain pain of letting someone into his life, of risking his heart in a relationship.

'I'm not sure…eight months?'

Did she *have* to look at him so critically? Suddenly he felt he had to defend himself. 'I asked for flowers to be sent to her.'

'I don't think flowers are allowed in hospitals these days. Anyway, I reckon flowers are the last thing on her mind right now.' She threw him another critical stare before adding, 'I hope she and her baby will be okay.'

Why, all of a sudden, was *he* the villain in all of this? 'Of course I do too. My employees' welfare is of great importance to me. It's why they all receive a comprehensive healthcare package.'

'I'm glad to hear it.' Her tone didn't match her words. Her tone implied he was a close relative of *Wall Street*'s Gordon Gekko.

'About your accommodation…'

'How long are your clients here for?'

Hadn't she heard him? This conversation was supposed to be about her leaving. 'Why do you ask?'

'Have you someone to take over from your event planner?'

A tight dart of pain prodded his lower back. He stretched with a quick movement, but it brought little relief. 'No. My event management team are already stretched, co-ordinating the upcoming spring/summer shows. Most of the team are already in New York, getting ready for the shows there.'

She pulled her lips between her teeth as if in thought. When they popped back out they formed an even fuller pout, had turned a more sensual red than usual. Emphasising their cupid's bow shape. She had a beautiful mouth...

A sudden urge to take her in his arms and taste those lips gripped him. Maybe he was more stressed than he'd realised?

Emma's mind whirled. Could she drum up the courage to suggest *she* take over the event planner's role? Work for Matteo Vieri? Without question it was what every ambitious marketing assistant dreamt of. She should be genuflecting right now in front of this business legend; this marketing genius, instead of deliberately trying to antagonise him. What was *that* about?

A niggling thought told her that not only was she trying in vain to ignore how attracted she was to him—especially when he openly stared at her with interest, as he was doing right now, with particular attention focused on her mouth—but that it would hurt to have another person reject her. Which, rationally, she knew was crazy. They barely knew each other. But even after so many rejections it still hurt when others turned her away.

Working for him would be the kick-start her career needed. Even a week of working with him would open doors for her.

But she was a mess.

She had come to Venice to heal and to get her game plan together. She felt hollow and abused. She was in no position to deliver the best performance of her career.

A mocking voice echoed in her head. *You said you were going to toughen up. Time for action and a lot less talk.*

And having a purpose, being busy, might stop the stream of guilt and sadness that was constantly threatening to break through her defences—defences of shock and numbness, of a determination to tough it out. Being in control, having a structure to her days, was what she needed.

She spoke before she had time to talk herself out of it. *'I'll* do it.'

His gaze moved from her lips to her eyes. Very slowly. So slowly that time seemed to stand still while her cheeks spontaneously combusted.

'You?'

Did he *have* to sound so appalled by her proposal?

'In my role at the fashion college I often helped pull events together—from the graduation show to organising the visits of academics and sponsors. Last year I co-ordinated the visit of some members of a faculty from a Chinese fashion college. I'm in need of a place to stay... you need an event co-ordinator.'

'But you're on holiday.'

'My career is more important. I'll be frank: having the Vieri name on my CV will be priceless.'

He seemed to be considering her proposal. For a moment hope danced before her eyes. But then he cut that hope off at the legs with a single determined shake of that movie-star-meets-roman-emperor head.

'It's not a good idea.'

'Why?'

'This trip is of critical importance to my companies. The delegation is coming to negotiate contracts which would see the large-scale expansion of our product placements in China's most prestigious department stores. Nothing can go wrong.'

For a moment she considered backing down, admitting that she was probably the wrong person for the job. But she had to believe in herself.

'You can brief me on it this morning, and then I'll liaise with the travel agents and hotels involved. I'll also double-check that all the protocols involved with hosting Chinese guests are followed. If there are any issues I will notify you immediately.'

He leaned one hip against the balcony and folded his arms. 'It's not a nine-to-five position. You would need to attend all the scheduled events with me.'

'That's no problem.'

Those brown eyes darkened. 'We will be working closely together.'

'That's fine.'

Liar! Why is your belly dancing with giddiness if that is the case?

'Please understand I never mix business with pleasure.'

Why was he telling her that? Was her attraction to him so obvious?

'Of course. Exactly my sentiments.' She took a deep swallow and forced herself to ask, 'So, can I have the job?'

'Tell me why I should give it to you.'

This would be so much easier if he wasn't so gorgeous—if he wasn't so self-assured, so ice-cool.

'I will work myself to the bone for you because I have so much to prove. To you—but especially to myself.'

He stared at her as though she was a discount store garment made of polyester. It looked as if she would be packing soon. A heavy sensation sat on her chest—embarrassment, disappointment.

'As I'm stuck, I'll let you take on the position—but any mishaps and you're gone.'

His scowl told her he wasn't joking. Her ankle and heart began to throb in unison.

He came a little closer. Studied her for far too long for her comfort.

'You will need to stay here...'

For a moment he paused, and a heavy boom of attraction detonated between them. She fell into the brown sultry depths of his eyes. An empty ache coiled through her. Heat licked against her skin. She pulled the neck of her jumper down, suddenly overheating.

Matteo stepped back, tugged at his cuffs and cleared his throat. 'I will require frequent briefings from you, so you will need to stay here. I'm hosting a reception in the ballroom on Thursday night, which I will want you to co-ordinate and host alongside me.' He flicked his hand towards the *palazzo*. 'If you come with me to my office I'll brief you on the event schedule and then pass you the files.'

Emma walked alongside him, her enflamed skin welcoming the shade of the *palazzo*. But her mind continued to race, asking her what on earth she had just done.

Could she keep her promise that nothing would go wrong? What if she slipped up and he saw even a glimpse of how attracted she was to him? An attraction that was embarrassingly wrong. Humiliatingly wrong. Shamefully wrong. She had been about to marry another man yesterday. What was the *matter* with her?

They walked side by side into the deeper shadows of the *palazzo*, and she felt guilt and sadness closing over her heart.

Later that afternoon, his phone to his ear, Matteo walked into the temporary office Emma had set up for herself in the *palazzo*'s dining room.

Sheets of paper were scattered across the table. He tidied the paper into a bundle. A long navy silk crêpe de Chine scarf dotted with bright red gerbera daisy flowers was tossed across the back of a chair, the ends touching against the *terrazzo* flooring. A bright exclamation against the dark wood. He folded it quickly and hid it from view by placing it on the seat of the dining chair.

His call continued to ring unanswered.

Where *was* she?

He had told her to be back at the *palazzo* by four so that he could take her to see his stores on Calle Larga XXII Marzo. She needed to be familiar with his companies and their products before her interactions with the clients.

Before lunch they had spent two hours running through the visit's itinerary. Two hours during which he had questioned his judgement in agreeing to her taking over the event co-ordinator role.

With her every exclamation of delight over the events planned, with every accidental touch as they worked through the files, with every movement that caused her jumper to pull on her breasts he had become more and more fixated with watching her.

And throughout the morning she had progressively impressed and surprised him with her attention to detail. Impressed him because she had picked up on some timing problems he hadn't spotted. Surprised him because, tidiness-wise, the woman was a disaster.

Obviously timekeeping wasn't a strength either.

The Chinese delegation were arriving in Venice this evening. He had to be at Hotel Cipriani at eight to greet them on their arrival. Emma had travelled over there, at her suggestion, after lunch to meet with the hotel co-ordinator and the interpreter employed for the duration of the visit.

He hit the call button again.

After yet more infuriating rings, she eventually answered.

He didn't wait for her to speak, '*Dove sei?* Where are you?'

'I'm not sure.' There was a hint of panic to her voice. 'After my meetings in Hotel Cipriani I decided I would visit the restaurant booked for the clients later this week on Giudecca. I found the restaurant and spoke to the owner and the chef. But when I left I must have gone in the wrong direction, because I'm totally lost. I can't find my way back to the *vaporetto* stop.'

Now he really *was* regretting his decision to employ her. 'Can't you ask someone to help you?'

'I have! But each time I follow their directions I end up even more lost down another narrow alleyway.'

Dio! 'Can you see a street name anywhere?'

'Hold on…yes, I see one! Calle Ca Rizzo.'

'Stay there. I'll come and get you.'

'There's no need. I'll—'

He hung up before she had time to start arguing with him. It was already past four.

Emma placed her phone back into her padded jacket's pocket, her already racing heart now acting as if it was taking part in the international finals of the one hundred metre sprint. The day had been going so well until she had gone and got lost in this warren of laneways or, as they were called locally, *calli* that made up Giudecca, an island suburb of Venice.

Her meetings in the opulent surroundings of Hotel Cipriani had gone smoothly, all the little extras she'd requested had been accommodated, and she had then made her way to Ristorante Beccherie, excited at the stunning views across the water to St Mark's Square, the Basilica di San Marco and the Campanile clearly visible under the clear blue sky.

After her meeting at the restaurant she hadn't minded getting lost at first. She had been enchanted by the three- and four-storey medieval red-brick houses on deserted narrow alleyways, by the washing hanging between the houses like bunting, the endless footbridges crossing over the maze of canals. The lack of the sounds of the twenty-first century because of the absence of cars.

But as she'd grown increasingly disorientated, her uneasiness had increased. She'd ended up in dead-end alleyways, silent and beautiful courtyards with no obvious signage.

Matteo was annoyed with her. No—scratch that. He'd sounded ballistic. Would he fire her on her first day?

She walked over to the canal that ran diagonally to the start of Calle Ca Rizzo and moved down onto the canal steps. The temperature was dropping and the cold stone bit against her skin.

Matteo was like Venice. Utterly beautiful but completely frustrating. All morning she had tried to remain professional, but she had been constantly distracted.

Distracted by his deep, potent musky scent when he moved closer to her to point something out in the file sitting between them.

Distracted by the perfect fit of his grey trousers on his narrow hips when he stood.

Distracted by the sight of his large hand lying on the table beside her: golden skin, wide palm, smooth knuckles, long, strong fingers tapering off into pale pink nails, all perfectly clipped into smooth ovals. Several times she had lost her concentration to those hands, dreaming about them on her skin, removing her clothes…

She had been glad of an excuse to get away from the *palazzo*, needing some space to pull herself together.

She dropped her head into her hands. What was she *doing*? Why was she having these thoughts? She wasn't interested in men. In any form of relationship. She had a job to do. And falling for the boss was not only out of the question it was beyond stupid. Well, she *hoped* she still had a job to do. Maybe not when he arrived…

Fifteen minutes later she saw him stop on a footbridge further down the canal and stare towards her. His hip-length black wool pea coat was topped with a dark grey woollen hat. The pull of attraction tugged on every cell in her body. His mouth was turned downwards in a *you're in big trouble* scowl.

She jumped up and tried to match his stride in her direction, but her legs were too wobbly so she careened her way along the canal bank, probably looking as if she had recently consumed a considerable amount of Chianti.

When they met her words of apology became lost. His hat hugged his skull, emphasising the intensity of his golden-brown eyes framed by thick black eyelashes, the beauty of his honey-coloured skin, the proud straight nose, the no-nonsense mouth softened by the cleft in his chin.

That gorgeous mouth hardened. 'We are late for our appointments.'

Did that mean he wasn't going to fire her?

Without another word he walked away and she followed alongside him, over countless bridges and through a maze of *calli*. They passed few people, and in the tight confines of the laneways he seemed taller and more powerful than she remembered.

She gave a quick summary of her meetings, updating him on any changes. Hoping his mood might improve. He made no comment but gave an occasional nod. At least he was listening.

Eventually they arrived at the broad reach of Canale

della Giudecca and he led her to a sleek, highly polished wooden motor boat moored at a landing stage.

After untying the two mooring ropes he held the stern tight against the wooden stage. He held out his hand to her. 'You need to climb aboard.'

She hesitated for a moment, suddenly wary of touching him. But, with the boat swaying in the choppy waters, she decided she'd risk holding his hand over the chagrin of being crushed against the landing stage.

His hand encased hers, and his powerful strength guided her on board. For a crazy few seconds she was engulfed by the sensation that she would always be safe with him in her life.

With practised ease Matteo pulled the boat away from the stage and was soon heading across the canal towards St Mark's Square.

'I'm sorry I got lost. I didn't mean to inconvenience you.'

He gave that ubiquitous continental shrug that might mean he accepted her apology with some reservations or was so irritated by her that he couldn't speak.

At first she thought he was going back up the Grand Canal to Ca' Divina, but just west of St Mark's Square he turned right and slowly motored up a smaller canal. The canal was busy with gondolas, the majority of their passengers embracing and kissing couples.

She plucked her phone out of her pocket and pressed some buttons mindlessly. She had thought she wouldn't mind seeing couples together, enjoying this city of romance. Boy, had she been wrong.

A heavy pain constricted her chest.

She was supposed to be here with her husband. Not with a man who was clearly irritated with her. Not with a man who in truth she was more attracted to than she had ever been to her fiancé.

That truth was shaming.

That truth was bewildering.

'As I explained this morning, five of my companies have a presence here on Calle Larga.'

Matteo came to a stop outside the type of store Emma would window shop at when walking along Bond Street in London but would never dare to enter, knowing her monthly salary wouldn't even buy her a set of barely there but, oh, so gorgeous underwear.

He pointed along the bustling street. 'Verde for handbags, Marco for shoes, Osare is the label for our younger urban clients… Gioiello stocks daywear, and…' Gesturing to the store behind them, he added, 'And VMV for the discerning.'

Was he aware of the constant looks of appreciation he received from passers-by? How within the VMV store a bevy of model-like assistants were flapping their arms in excitement at his imminent entrance?

'I had hoped to take you into each store so that you could familiarise yourself with our product range.' He threw her a reproachful frown. 'But that will not be possible now. We only have time for your fittings.'

With that he turned, and the door of the store was magically opened by a stealthy doorman Emma hadn't seen lurking behind the glass pane.

Matteo gestured for her to enter first.

She took a step closer to him and in a low voice asked, 'What do you mean, "fittings"?'

'You will need dresses and gowns for the various events you will be accompanying me to during the week.'

'I have my own clothes.'

With a raised critical eyebrow he ran his gaze down over her body. Okay, so her black padded jacket and red skirt mightn't be the most glamorous, but she did own some nice clothes.

'I mean I have suitable dresses back at the *palazzo*.'

He stepped closer, his huge body dwarfing hers. His head dipped down and he glared into her eyes. 'I don't have time for this. Let me be clear. You are representing my companies this week. You have to wear clothing from the lines. It's not negotiable. If you don't like it then I'm happy for you to leave.'

Emma gave a quick nod and, with dread exploding in her stomach like fast-rising dough, stepped inside the store and sank into plush carpet. She opened up her padded jacket and yanked at the collar of her jumper. She was burning up. Not only from the heat of the store but from the unfriendly gazes being thrown in her direction by the models.

Matteo walked through the store, pointing out garments which were immediately whisked away to the rear of the store.

'*Bene.* I've selected the gowns which I think will suit you.' He exchanged some rapid words with the woman who had accompanied him in his selection of dresses. 'Andreina will help you try them on.'

Emma smiled warily at the six foot ash blonde diva standing before her. In return she received a cool blue stare. Boy, was she glad she had been waxed to within an inch of her life in preparation for her wedding.

The fitting room was like nothing she had ever seen. A bottle of Prosecco on ice sat on an antique side table, with velvet grey chairs at either side. The floor was tiled in marble, and giant gilt-edged mirrors filled three walls.

She looked at the row of dresses awaiting her. And then at Andreina, who was staring down at her ankle boots, her forehead pinched in obvious disbelief at the water stains on the suede. Yeah, well, maybe Andreina should try walking from Camden Police Station to Highgate in icy slush.

Her stomach lurched. She felt like a gauche fourteen-year-old again, facing her mother's critical stare. Forced to wear only what her mother approved of.

Time for Operation Toughen Up again.

She propelled Andreina by the elbow towards the door. 'I'll call you if I need any help.' She closed the door on a stream of Italian protest, adrenaline pumping.

She approached the dresses warily. She would get this over and done with as quickly as possible. She stripped off her clothes and grabbed the first dress to hand. Her stomach lurched again. She pulled the silk bodice over her head, felt layer upon layer of fine tulle falling from her waist down to the floor. She twisted her arms around to her back in an attempt to tie the bodice but it was hopeless. She needed help.

She fought against the tears stinging her eyes. She couldn't bear the feel of the material on her skin.

A knock sounded on the door. She ignored it.

'Emma, what are you doing?'

Matteo.

She called out, 'None of them suit. I'll just have to wear my own clothes.'

The door swung open.

'For crying out loud, Matteo, I could have been undressed!'

He crossed the room towards her, his eyes darkening. 'I see near-naked models backstage at fashion shows all the time.'

'Well, I'm *not* a model, am I?'

His mouth pursed, and then he asked with irritation, 'Why are you upset?'

'I'm not.'

He threw her an exasperated look. 'That dress is perfect for you—what do you mean, it doesn't suit? Look in the mirror and see for yourself.'

She turned her back on the mirrors, refusing to look, unable to speak.

He came closer, and she gave a yelp when she felt his fingers on the back of the bodice, tying the tiny fastenings.

'Please don't.'

He ignored her protest and continued to work his way down the bodice. Her spine arched beneath his touch as startling desire mixed with the upset dragging at her throat.

At first his movements were fast, but then he slowed, as though he too was weakened by the tension in the room— the tension of bodies hot and bothered, wanting more, wanting satisfaction.

Finished, he settled one hand on her waist while the other touched the exposed skin of her back above the strapless bodice.

'*Cosa c'e'*? What's the matter?'

She couldn't answer. She longed to pull on her skirt and jumper again. To cover every inch of herself. To not feel so exposed. So vulnerable. So aware of him.

'Look into the mirror, Emma. See how beautiful you are. I wasn't comparing you to models.'

She could not help but laugh. 'God, it's not *that*…it's just.'

His hands twisted her around until she was staring at herself in the mirror.

Sumptuous silk on brittle bones.

She spun back to him, her eyes briefly meeting his before looking away. 'I'm sorry…it's just these dresses remind me of my wedding dress.'

CHAPTER THREE

How COULD HE have been so stupid? Stupid to have agreed to let her work for him. Stupid not to have foreseen how these dresses might remind her of her wedding. Stupid to feel a responsibility towards this stranger. It was all so illogical. He barely knew her. He had too many other problems, responsibilities, in his life. But something about this woman had him wanting to protect her.

His hand moved to touch her, to lift her chin so that he could gaze into her eyes. To offer her some comfort. But he stopped himself in time. She was an employee. She was a runaway bride just burnt in love. He had to keep away from her.

'I will ask Andreina to help you undress. You do not need to try on any more.'

'No. It's okay. I'm sorry…this wasn't supposed to happen.'

He needed to get away. Away from the close confines of this dressing room. Away from how stunningly beautiful she looked in the gown, pale skin against ivory and purple silk. Away from the pain in her eyes he didn't know how to cope with, didn't know how to ease.

'I'll get Andreina.'

Her hand shot out and her fingers encased his wrist. She gave it a tug to halt him. 'Not Andreina. Please will *you* help me untie the bodice?'

Why was she so adamant about Andreina?

He untied the clasps of the bodice, saw her shoulder blades contract into a shrug above the bodice.

'All the dresses are stunning. I would be very proud to wear them. I just need to get used to the idea.'

Her voice shook just like her body.

More than ever he needed to get away.

'Let's talk about it outside.'

He walked out of the fitting room, wanting to get away.

Wanting to go back and take her into his arms.

Five minutes later she joined him outside the store.

Instead of guiding her back to his boat, he led her towards Campo di San Moisè. At the footbridge that led to the square and the baroque façade of Chiesa di San Moisè he found what he was looking for—a street vendor selling *frittelle*, the Venetian-style doughnuts only available during Carnival. He ordered a mixed cone.

They stopped at the centre of the footbridge and he offered Emma a *frittella* before biting into a *frittella veneziana*. The raisins and pine nuts mixed into the dough were the sugar hit he badly needed.

Emma bit into her *frittella crema pasticcera*, filled with thick custard cream, and gave a little squeal. The custard escaped from the doughnut and dripped down her chin.

Desire, thick and desperate, powered through his body.

They stood in silence, eating the *frittelle*, and he wanted nothing more than to kiss away the grains of sugar glittering on her lips.

The deep upset in her eyes was easing.

He needed to get this over and done with.

'This isn't going to work. I should never have agreed to it.'

She touched her fingers to her mouth and brushed the granules away, heat turning her pale cheeks a hot pink.

'I'm really embarrassed…about getting lost and about what happened in the store. It was unprofessional of me. I promise it won't happen again.'

'You need time to recover from what you have gone through; you shouldn't be working.'

She drank in his words with consternation in her eyes. 'But I need to work—I want to work.'

Why couldn't she see that he was doing her a favour? That this attraction between them was perilous.

'Why?'

She crumpled the empty *frittella* cone in her hands. 'Because I need the money. Because I want to focus on my career and forget the past year.'

Her jaw arced sideways, as if she were easing a painful tension in her jawline.

'He really hurt you, didn't he?'

Her thick dark eyelashes blinked rapidly, her mouth tensing. She angled away from him to face the canal.

She turned back before she spoke. 'Because of his lies and deception, yes. Because of how he hurt other people.'

How had she not known what he was like? Why had she allowed herself to get hurt like this?

Anger swept through him. Together with the recognition that everything she was going through represented every reason why he would never marry, never give his heart and trust to another person. People always let you down, ultimately.

He had trusted, loved, hero-worshipped Francesco, Marco, Simone, Arnaud, Stefano… All his mother's boyfriends. And they had all walked away from him. Showing just how little significance he'd held in their lives. Blood, family—that was all you could trust in. Nobody else.

'Why were you marrying him?'

She jammed her left heel against the bottom of the bridge rail and rotated her foot. 'You mean why didn't I realise what he was really like? I met him last summer. It was a whirlwind romance. We got engaged after four months. He was charming and outgoing. He seemed to care for me a lot. He worked crazy hours and sometimes he didn't turn up for dates... He always had a plausible excuse and I'd eventually forgive him. When we were together he was kind, if a little distracted...but I never saw the other side to him—the lying, the fraud.'

'Four months isn't a long time to get to know one another.'

Behind them a group of tourists walked by, their guide speaking loudly. Suddenly they all laughed in unison. The guide looked pleased with his joke.

Emma looked at them, taken aback. The tips of her ears were pink from the cold. For a moment he considered giving her his hat. Why did he keep forgetting she was his employee? Was it because they had already lain together in a bed? Even if it had been only for a few crazy minutes of misunderstanding?

She went to speak, but stopped. Her mouth quivered and she looked at him uncertainly. Her chest rose on a deep inhalation. 'I wanted a family of my own...to belong.'

She spoke with such loneliness.

He stamped his feet on the ground. The cold was already stiffening his back. 'Did you love him?'

He had asked the question before he had thought it through. It was none of his business. But he had to know.

Hazel eyes filled with confusion met his for a moment before they fled away. 'Can we not talk about this?'

She was right. But a need to know drove him on to say, 'You must have loved him if you were going to marry him.'

She touched her long slim fingers against her temple and circled them there for a few seconds. The faint impression of a ring recently removed was still there, on the skin of her ring finger. Her eyes scrunched shut. 'I'm not certain of anything any more... Maybe.'

'And what if you had married him but then woke up one morning certain you didn't love him—would you have left?'

She looked at him in horror. 'No. *No.* Absolutely not.'

'Why so certain?'

'I wouldn't just walk away. I take my commitments, my pledges seriously. I don't walk away when things get difficult. Turn my back on someone when things go wrong. I do everything to fix it, to accept where we are.' She threw her head back and looked at him fiercely, her nostrils flaring. 'And, before you say anything, I draw a line at criminality. At months and years of lies and deception. Yes, I walked away from my ex—but I could not stay with a man who had so wilfully hurt so many people.'

She inhaled a breath and her jaw worked. Anger fired in her eyes, and she lobbed a grenade of a question in his direction. 'How about *you*—do you ever want to marry? Have your own family?'

Her grenade exploded in his chest. His stomach clenched at the emotional damage of her question. 'It's not for me— my job, my responsibilities mean I wouldn't be a good husband, a good father. I would be absent too much.'

She considered him for a moment, as though trying to decide if he was a con man too. Slowly she nodded, the anger in her eyes receding. 'That's honourable. Others wouldn't even think to stop and consider whether they would be a good husband and father.'

'There's enough hurt children in this world... I don't want to add to them.'

For a moment he thought he had gone too far. She looked at him questioningly.

But then she stood upright and asked, 'Can I have another chance? I promise no more tears or drama. I would be honoured to wear those dresses. I'll go back and try them on now.'

Back to business. He should end it now.

'Emma, the future of tens of thousands of my employees rest on this trip going smoothly.'

She nodded with a dignified grace, her eyes holding a sombre pride. 'I know. And I respect and understand that. If you firmly believe I'm not right for this position I will walk away.'

Dio! She was good at negotiating.

He checked his watch. 'Lucky for you, I don't have time to argue. I want and need from you complete focus on this client trip. Nothing else. The dresses will all suit you— I'm sure of it. I will have them delivered tomorrow. Now, let's go. I need to get home and change.'

The following evening Emma waited for Matteo out on the terrace, goosebumps of anticipation breaking on her skin. She was accompanying Matteo Vieri to the Venetian opera house, La Fenice. To see Verdi's *La Traviata*. In the opera house in which it had first been performed.

She pulled the belt of her wool-and-angora-blend navy coat tighter. The VMV store had delivered it that morning, along with all the other clothes Matteo had selected yesterday.

The past twenty-four hours had passed without incident. No tears on her part. To the clients she presented a sunny face. At times she had even fooled herself into thinking she was coping. But in the quiet moments, when she hadn't been busy, it had all hit her like a *vaporetto* colliding with a gondola.

She still questioned how she had been so blind to her ex's deceit. And any thoughts of the future left her with heart palpitations. And then there was the constant anxiety that she was going to mess up with the clients, with Matteo.

He seemed to be winning over his Chinese clients with a combination of deep respect and vigilant hosting.

She had accompanied the spouses to Murano Island this morning, to view the world-famous glass manufacturing, along with an interpreter and a tour guide, while Matteo and his clients held business meetings. And in the afternoon the entire group had toured the city by gondola.

As Matteo's designated partner, she had accompanied him in the same gondola as the president of the department store chain, Mr Xue, and his wife. It had been oddly intimate, sitting next to him as they had passed under the Rialto Bridge and later viewed the stunning architecture, mosaics and carvings of Basilica di San Marco and the Doge's Palace. He was professorial in his knowledge and passion about both buildings and the history of Venice in general. No wonder he was so successful, with what appeared to be a photographic memory and a charming persona.

Only with her did the charm fade. When they were alone he was quiet, and she could not help but feel he was keeping his distance from her. Even now she had a strong hunch that he was waiting until the last minute to leave his office for their journey to La Fenice.

She would do anything to take back her behaviour yesterday in the VMV store. She had clearly made him very uncomfortable and it had been totally unprofessional.

Every now and again over the past twenty-four hours she had caught him looking in her direction. He would always look away, but not before a blaze of attraction had surged between them.

'My boat is waiting downstairs for us.'

She turned to find him standing at the terrace doors. 'I'm ready.'

She swallowed the other words that were about to shoot out of her mouth. *You look incredible.* Which was the truth.

His dark grey suit jacket skimmed the wide span of his shoulders, and the tailored trousers emphasised the long length of his legs. He shrugged on a long black wool coat, followed by a black wool hat.

As she neared him he handed her a royal blue hat. 'It's cold tonight. You will need to wear some protection.'

The thin-knit hat, the same colour as the appliqué dashes on her navy cocktail dress, had a crystal flower sewn onto it.

Would her heart *please* stop pounding? It was just a practical gesture—nothing else.

'Let me put it on for you. Otherwise your hair might fall down.'

He had to be joking!

But, alas, no. He took the hat from her and delicately pulled it over her hair, which she had coiled up into a tight bun. It was a style she rarely used, for it brought back too many memories of her life as a ballerina. But tonight it had felt apt—not just because it suited the dress but because she needed its severity against how vulnerable she felt about her wedding imploding, the constant stress of worrying if she was doing her job effectively…and her silly, annoying, futile attraction to her boss.

His fingers stroked briefly against the exposed skin of her neck. Her insides melted. He was standing much too close. His scent, his broad chest were too close. His open coat touching against her…too close.

She stepped back. No weakness. Just toughness and protecting herself. That was all that mattered now.

In the darkened theatre, the lovers Violetta and Alfredo begged each other for forgiveness for all the hurt they had caused each other in the past. Their voices soared, their pain and passion for one another holding the crowd transfixed. Alfredo believed that they had a future together, not realising how ill Violetta was…

Matteo could hardly breathe. In his private box, the president of the board, Mr Xue, and his wife were to his right, closest to the stage. Emma was to his left. Because of the way the boxes were angled towards the stage he couldn't see her without turning around. He wanted to turn. He wanted to see if she was okay.

All evening she had done everything possible to make his clients welcome and comfortable. Had been attentive to them at each of the two intervals. But something was wrong. Her body beneath the stunning pencil-fit dark navy dress with dashes of royal blue was too stiff. Her hair, tied up in an elegant bun that matched the knee-length, cap-sleeved gentle decorum of her dress, exposed the tension in her rigid neck.

Violetta fell to the floor. Lifeless.

Behind Mr Xue somebody sniffled.

He had to check.

Her eyes were on the stage. The endless gilt private boxes of La Fenice cascaded behind her. She swallowed hard but did not look in his direction. She was aware of him. He had no doubt about that. Her refusal to meet his eyes sent hot frustration zipping through his muscles. His hands and feet clenched, he shifted in his seat.

The cast moved forward on the stage to take their bows. The crowd stood and shouted their approval. He needed to focus on his clients. But all he was aware of was the ex-asperatingly beautiful woman next to him.

A woman whose slender waist, small full breasts, high firm bottom and long legs left him with distracted concentration, with a hollow feeling in his stomach, with a desperate compulsion to hold her, kiss her, taste her.

She was an employee. A woman recently heartbroken in love. A runaway bride.

He didn't need any further reasons to stay away from her. If only his libido would receive that message.

With his clients and their tour guide and interpreter safely aboard the private launch, Matteo watched their boat turning in the water towards the direction of the Hotel Cipriani.

Beside him, Emma quickly yanked the clips from her hair. Thick curls tumbled down her back. Memories of her hair fanned on his pillow the night he'd found her in his bed sent a shock of desire through him. She pulled on her woollen hat, giving him a surreptitious look. The uncomfortable suspicion that she was trying to avoid his help in putting it on set his teeth on edge. He wasn't used to women pushing him away.

Deliberately, he moved closer. Emma gazed up. Startled. But she didn't look away. Her cheeks grew flushed and her eyes darkened, making something explode in his stomach. He adjusted her hat, pulling it down further over her head. And as he held her gaze he ran his fingers down the long length of her hair. He was playing with fire but he didn't care.

He studied her lips in a slow, deliberate drag of his eyes across their plump softness.

Her lips parted and she gave a low, shaky exhalation.

His pulse throbbed at the base of his neck, urging him to taste her, to answer the primitive call aching in his gut, to possess her. To grab her and end this irrational hold she had over him—this foolish, reckless attraction that burned brightly between them.

She stepped back unsteadily. She tugged at the collar of her coat with nervous fingers.

She cleared her throat. 'How are the meetings going?'

He too stepped back. Shook his head, trying to silence the heavy insistent beat of his pulse.

The meetings. He shook his head again. Trying to focus.

The meetings. They were going slowly. Which was to be expected. But that did not stop it from being exasperating. All his work over the past few years had been jeopardised by his troubled designer.

The fog of desire slowly lifting, he cleared his own throat. 'Thanks to my designer, I'm having to spend time rebuilding our relationship, re-establishing our respect towards them. They value a long-term relationship rather than a specific deal, and that can't be rushed.'

'What are you going to do about the designer? Will you need to replace him?'

'Trust me, I'm tempted to, and it's what my board would like me to do. But I'm not going to. He has been going through a tough time recently, due to some personal problems. He needs support.'

She gave him a smile that slipped like a pulse of pleasure into his bloodstream. 'Your grandmother isn't the only one with a kind heart.'

'I try to protect my employees, my family...' He paused and swallowed against the sudden kick his heart aimed against his ribs. 'Patrizia—your predecessor—gave birth to a baby boy yesterday afternoon.'

A trace of longing pulled at the corners of her smile. 'That's wonderful news.'

He remembered her words about wanting a family.

Suddenly he wanted to have this night over.

'My boat is waiting for us.'

She gave him a nervous glance before gesturing back towards the city. 'I was thinking of walking back... I haven't seen Venice at night yet.' She took a few steps towards the city. 'I'll see you in the morning.'

She was pushing him away. Annoyance lashed across his skin.

'I'll walk with you.'

His suspicion that she was trying to get away was confirmed by her swift response.

'No! No, I'll walk by myself.'

'Do you know the way?'

'Not really... But I'm sure I'll be fine.'

He threw her an unconvinced look. 'I don't want to have to come and find you in the middle of the night if you get lost, like you did on Giudecca.'

She winced at that. 'I suppose...'

He led her in the direction of Piazza San Marco.

They walked in tense silence.

On the narrow Calle Delle Veste, she darted an uncertain look at him before asking, 'Did you grow up in Venice?'

How he wished he *had* grown up in one single place.

'We lived here for a little while. Originally we were from Puglia, in the South. We moved around during my childhood, here in Italy but also in France and Spain.'

'Because of your parents' work?'

Not so much work as where his mother's latest boyfriend had lived. 'There was only my mother and me. Sometimes my grandmother too.'

'So, like me, you had no brothers or sisters.' She said it with a wistfulness that told him she too had dreamed of having some when she was younger. Some allies in life. Someone to talk to.

But then, would he *really* have wanted another child to endure the constant uncertainty of his childhood? The stomach-crunching walk to the door each day after school, wondering if today was the day they were going to pack and leave. Or to be thrown out. The constant fear in the pit of his stomach that his life was going to change again—a new town, a new school, a new man in their lives, but the same isolation, the same insecurity.

They turned into Calle Larga. He pushed away those

memories. Only then did he notice how she was struggling to walk.

He slowed down. 'You're limping—are you sure you're okay to walk?'

She waved away his concern with a toss of her hand. 'I'm fine. It's just an old injury that flares up every now and again.'

He slowed his pace even more, unconvinced by her answer. He held out his arm. 'Take my arm.'

She glanced at his arm as though he was offering her something illegal. She bit her lip. But then with a shaky smile she placed her hand on his arm, her elbow tucked beneath his, lightly touching his side.

They walked along the empty *calle*, with Emma slowly placing more weight on his arm. Their steps, at first out of sync, quickly matched each other, and his body hummed, firing with protectiveness for the beautiful, guarded, troubling woman at his side.

Her hand relaxing even more on his arm, she asked, 'Did you mind moving around when you were a child?'

'I hated it.'

Her eyes snapped up to consider him. 'Really?'

'I was always the new boy at school. Sometimes the other children reacted well—I was a novelty. Most of the time, though, I was nothing but a new target.'

She grimaced, her quick shudder rippling against the side of his body. 'You sound as if you were as unhappy in school as I was.'

'What do you mean?'

'I was at ballet boarding school from the age of ten. I adored the ballet—most of the time—but I was lonely.'

'You missed your parents?'

'Yes...sometimes. But I eventually got used to it.'

He knew there was more to it than that, but seeing the

closed expression on her face he guessed she didn't want to talk about it.

He decided to change the topic. 'Do you dance now?'

He had hoped to move to neutral territory with his question. But by the crestfallen expression on her face and the way she pulled away from him to walk on her own, without his help, he could see it had obviously backfired.

'No. I haven't danced in years.'

'Why?'

He almost preferred the tears of other times to the stony expression on her face now. Tight, pale lips. The off-kilter edge of upset in her jaw.

He thought she wasn't going to answer, but eventually she said, 'I broke my ankle when I was nineteen. I ended up having to have plates inserted, it was smashed so badly.'

It seemed to have taken a huge effort for her to tell him that much. He should ask no more questions. Leave her be. But he wanted to understand.

'Did it happen whilst you were dancing?'

'Unfortunately not—or maybe fortunately. I was out one night and slipped on wet steps.'

They were once again reaching Campo di San Moisè. The tiny square was empty, and the exuberant exterior of San Moisè church, with its dramatic carved stone, stood like a giant wedding cake awaiting its bride and groom. A lone gondolier floated on the canal below the bridge, his night light briefly flickering over his passengers—a couple entwined. He and Emma stopped at the centre of the bridge and looked down into the water.

Emotion welled in his chest. He wanted to reach out to her. Why, he had no idea. 'Your limping tonight…is that because of the accident?'

Her eyes fixed on the passing boat, she gave a knee-jerk shrug. The shrug of someone who had been pretending for too long. Her hands clasped and tightened the belt of her coat around her narrow waist. She stood on one foot. Flicked the other forward and back.

'Yes, sometimes it acts up. Bad weather or stress seem to particularly aggravate it. The past few days—being questioned by the police, having to call my ex's parents... tell them that the wedding was off—has made it ache like never before.'

She spoke with a hard edge, trying to box off her dismay.

'The past few days have been very difficult for you. I admire how determined you are to move on.'

A sad smile broke on her mouth and her eyes dissolved into soft gratitude. 'Thank you.'

'You were upset tonight.'

Her hand flew to her mouth. 'The clients didn't see, did they? I tried not to...' Her voice trailed off.

'No, they didn't see.'

'But *you* did.'

'I pick up on these things faster than others.'

Which was partially the truth. He had spent his childhood attuned at all times to his mother's mood. Now it was a honed skill that was a powerful tool in the boardroom. But he was especially attuned to Emma. None of his guests tonight would have guessed something was wrong, but he had seen...and felt...the very subtle signs as if they shared a special language all of their own.

Which made no sense. And was deeply, annoyingly, frustratingly unsettling.

'Ballet was my life—'

Her voice cracked and she shut her eyes. When she opened them again they pleaded with him to understand.

'It was everything I'd dreamed of. I was on track to a solo position in the Greater Manchester Metropolitan City Ballet. And suddenly it was all over.'

'You still miss it?'

She gave a hurt laugh, as if she still couldn't believe the awful trick life had played on her.

'Hugely. Tonight…tonight was my first time being inside a theatre since my accident. Over the years I couldn't face being reminded of what I was missing…the thrill as you wait in the wings…the elation at the end of a show. I thought I had come to terms with it, but tonight it was such a beautiful production, such a heartbreaking story… I wished I could have been up there on the stage too.'

'If you miss it so much couldn't you teach, or do something else in the ballet world?'

She touched her hand to her forehead and winced. As if that thought alone caused a headache. 'No, it'd be too hard. I can't go back to it.'

Eyes that knew the pain of loss held his.

Something sharp stabbed his chest.

'Do you dance at *all*?'

She shook her head, looked away. 'I haven't danced since I had my accident, seven years ago.'

'In time you may go back to it—don't totally discount it. From how you describe it, I know it was an important part of your life.'

Her mouth tightened and she blinked hard.

He should suggest they move on.

But he wanted to hold her.

Wanted to see her smile.

Wanted to make things okay for her.

'Will you dance with me now?'

She gazed at him as though he had asked her to scale the outside of the *campanile* in Piazza San Marco. 'Dance with you? Here?'

Okay, so it wasn't something most bosses would suggest to an employee. But then most bosses didn't first encounter an employee by finding them lying in their bed. After that, their relationship was never going to be normal.

'We shared *frittelle* here—why not a dance?'

She looked about her. Taking in where they were properly for the first time. 'I thought the buildings looked familiar.'

He held out his hand to her. 'Well…?'

His hand hung in the air. Long tanned fingers.

Her stomach went into free fall.

She wanted to move towards him.

In that moment his hand seemed like a beacon of escape from reality, if only for a fleeting few minutes.

Boom-boom-boom. Her heart shot up to the base of her throat. Clogging her airways.

But what of her resolution to stay away from men? This attraction was nothing more than a manifestation of her loneliness, her vulnerability. The ultimate rebound fantasy.

But it was all so tempting.

She could lose herself in this intoxicating chemistry between them. Forget about everything that was wrong in her life.

Her hand rose up as though independent of her. Tired of her dithering. Her body was intent on making the decision for her, ignoring all the arguments in her brain.

A sexy, satisfied supernova smile broke on his mouth. He tugged her forward slowly, in no rush. His other hand landed lightly on her waist.

Her hand, her arm, her breast, her neck, her belly and then the entirety of her body was blasted with heat, the surge of something unique.

He began to sway and move them around in circles.

He hummed a low tune.

The tremors in her body lessened.

And then laughter bubbled in her throat and escaped into the chilly night air. She laughed at the craziness of the whole situation. Her. Dancing. With Matteo Vieri. In a deserted square in the most romantic city in the world. And the most surprising, crazy part of it all: he had a deep, beautiful singing voice.

He looked down at her with affectionate amusement.

Their eyes locked. The world slowed down.

They moved closer.

His mouth came close to her ear.

His deep humming moved through her body like a caress.

A hot sensual river seeped through her.

She stepped even closer.

Their bodies met.

She closed her eyes. Light-headed against his scent of powerful musk. At the sensation of being held by him. At their feet moving in unison.

She was *dancing*!

Elation and heartbreak constricted her chest.

Tucked into his side, she felt his hard chest pressed against her breast, his hip against hers.

Want tugged at her core. Leaving her weak-limbed.

She shifted in his arms, her hardened nipples grazing against the press of his chest.

She gave a low gasp.

He moved away from her ear.

She looked up.

His eyes had darkened.

With the same heavy desire she was sure shadowed her own.

His head lowered again. Towards hers. Everything inside her went quiet. His lips hovered over hers. She couldn't keep her eyes open.

His breath, with an intoxicating hint of the brandy he had drunk during the interval, feathered over her skin.

Her lips parted. Felt heavy.

His lips moved against hers softly.

Her mind spun.

With a groan he pulled her closer.

And then she was lost to the warm, masculine sensation of his mouth, to the pressure of his hand on her back, the hardness of his body pushed against hers.

CHAPTER FOUR

WHAT WAS SHE DOING?

Emma pulled away. Breathless. Panic pushing her heart hard. It pounded and crashed in her chest. Physically wounding her.

She was kissing a man. Days after her wedding—her life—had crashed and burned. She was kissing her boss.

For a brief second Matteo looked at her in confusion.

'I'm sorry…that shouldn't have happened,' she said unsteadily.

His eyes hardened and his mouth settled into a tight line of annoyance. He gave a curt nod. 'It's getting late. We should go.'

For a moment she looked at him, at a loss. Wanting more. What, she wasn't sure. But not this awkward, tense, angry, frustrated wall that now stood between them.

They turned and walked through the ancient floating city, the clip of their footsteps mocking the silence between them.

Her body was distracted, acutely aware, on high alert to the power and strength, the primitive masculine draw of the man walking beside her.

Embarrassment and guilt ate up any words that tumbled through her brain.

Two days later Emma stared at the event plan for the reception to be held in Ca' Divina that night and marvelled at the neatness of the spreadsheet cells. All so orderly and straightforward. And nothing like the chaos that had ascended on the *palazzo* since early that morning.

She ticked off the box for reconfirming the private launches that would transport the guests to Ca' Divina.

If only she was able to place a satisfying, tension-releasing tick in all the other empty boxes winking up at her, taunting her with their blankness. The caterers, the audio-visual team, lighting and florists were still setting up. They were supposed to have finished over an hour ago.

In her stomach anxiety popped like popcorn kernels. She pushed her hand sharply against her belly. A warning not to give in to her own self-doubts. She had this under control. The reception *would* be a success. Matteo's clients, his A-list celebrity guests and all the local dignitaries would be suitably impressed. Matteo would be impressed.

And maybe then the awful tension that had sprung up between them since they had danced and kissed in San Moisè Square would ease. It was a tension that had seen them talking to one another uneasily, maintaining a ridiculous physical space at all times when they were in the same room, as if standing too close might be dangerous.

Something huge, awkward and unsaid was dangling between them.

Dancing with him had been wondrous, but his strength and care had made her feel even more vulnerable, more susceptible to him.

Raised voices down on the landing stage had her standing up from where she had been working at the dining table out on the terrace and walking to the balustrade.

Matteo was home.

An hour earlier than she'd expected.

He was exchanging terse words with one of the lighting electricians whilst gesturing furiously at some electrical cables lying along the landing stage.

She grabbed her file and ran through the terrace doors,

out into the huge central room filled with stunning frescos that she had learned from Matteo was called a *portego*, and down the wide marble stairs that led to the water gate.

Head down, Matteo charged up towards her. They met halfway.

Anxiety and attraction mixed explosively in her heart, which was about to *jeté* right out of her chest.

Stern brown eyes flaring with coppery tints flicked over her. '*E'tutto pronto per sta sera?* Is everything ready for tonight?'

Her professional smile wavered. And she wanted to weep. Because she wanted nothing more than to step closer. Lay her hand on his arm. Touch the wool of his coat.

Did *he* suffer any of this intense chemistry that made her feel constantly faint?

Did *he* think of their kiss?

Did *he* want, like she did, to have the world sing and shine and sizzle again?

Did *he* spend hours driving himself crazy, thinking about it…and then spend the rest of the day berating himself for thinking such crazy, impossible, self-destructive thoughts?

Probably not.

She clasped the file even tighter in her hand, her nails— French-polished for the wedding—digging into the soft cardboard. 'Everything is on track to be ready…the set-up is just taking a little longer than planned.'

With an impatient sigh he turned away and climbed the stairs at a jog.

She ran after him, cursing the twinge in her ankle.

He stopped at the first room he came to—the cosy and inviting writing room.

Inside, the staff hired to act as cloakroom attendants were still packing the gift boxes that would be given to each guest on departure. They had set up an impressive production line on top of a matching pair of painted cre-denzas. Skincare products, perfumes and designer sun-glasses—all from Matteo's lines—were being placed into exquisite ballet-slipper-pink boxes printed with hundreds of tiny gold VMV logos.

With a shake of his head Matteo turned away.

In the *portego*, he stopped and looked critically at the florists, who were finishing off a huge globe centrepiece filled with pretty roses the same pink as the gift boxes—the signature colour of VMV.

'Isn't it beautiful?'

He didn't respond, but stared critically at the endless cuttings and the florists' paraphernalia on the floor, need-ing to be tidied away.

In the ballroom he stalked about the double-height room like a matador awaiting the release of the bull. He glared at the audio-visual technician, still setting up, and then rearranged some of the gilded furniture which had been moved to the corners of the room to allow the guests to circulate easily.

Emma bit back on her impulse to ask him to stop, to inform him that she had arranged the furniture in such a pattern deliberately. Instead she said, 'The catering man-ager and I will be briefing the waiting staff in five min-utes. The head of security will be here soon with his team. I will also have a briefing meeting with him.'

Matteo made no comment, but strode out onto the ter-race. Emma guessed she was expected to follow.

When she came alongside him he stabbed a finger down towards the water. 'Why is there no red carpet on the land-ing stage?'

She flicked open her folder. Nobody had said anything about a red carpet. Had she missed it in the schedule? Fran-tically she scanned the document.

'I didn't know there was supposed to be one. Shouldn't

it be pink, anyway? To keep it in line with the pink VMV theme of the evening?'

He looked at her with a puzzled frown for a second. Then he said, in a slow *I'm trying to control my temper here* voice, 'Just sort it out.'

He turned and stabbed his finger at the terrace table.

'And sort out that mess on the table.'

'Of course.'

'Do you *always* work in such chaos?'

Okay, so she had left some files and paperwork on the table when she had rushed to meet him. But nothing that warranted such a damning tone. Why was he trying to pick a fight with her?

'Is everything okay?'

For a brief second he looked taken aback by her question, but then that hard Roman emperor jawline tensed. 'Why shouldn't it be?' He didn't wait for her to answer but instead demanded, 'Is the photographer here?'

Why did he have to home in on everything that was going wrong with the plan? 'His flight was delayed. He'll be here in the next hour.'

He walked away from her, but turned at the terrace door. 'I'll be in my office. Send the head of security in to me when he arrives. *I'll* manage his briefing. The same with the photographer.'

Unease prickled at the top of her spine. She rolled her head, but a million tiny pinpricks of pressure persisted. Why was he trying to take over her responsibilities?

'There's no need. I have everything under control.'

He yanked off his outer coat and tossed it under his arm. His light grey suit jacket was open and it flared back to give her a glimpse of his powerful torso, flat stomach, narrow hips. Hips that had crushed against her two nights ago.

Desire spun within her—coiling, whipping, hollowing out her insides.

Her hips, her skin, her mouth suddenly wanted him. Wanted his strength. Wanted the undoing effect of his scent. Wanted the feverish pull of his dazzling fingers trailing across her skin.

His expression hardened. 'But that's the problem. You clearly haven't. The *palazzo* is a mess. Nothing is ready. I'm disappointed. I expected better.'

His words sliced through her.

Through her crazy physical draw to him.

Through her pride.

Through all the promises she had made to herself that she was going to be tough, that she was going to stand up for herself.

'The *palazzo* will be ready. Within the next hour. The guests aren't arriving for another three hours.'

She tilted her head and, despite her mouth feeling like two rigid lines frozen in place, dug out a smile.

'I think you should have belief in me and the rest of the crew.'

Her short-lived smile collapsed, and she didn't care that it was replaced with a scowl.

He tossed his coat onto his other arm and stepped back out onto the terrace. His eyes were dark, dark, dark, as if his every feeling towards her had sucked any light out of them.

'You have to earn my belief first, and so far you're not doing a very good job.'

The corridor down to his office was blocked by two waiters carrying a long wooden table in the direction of the lounge. A lightning glare sent them scurrying away. In his haste, the waiter at the back drove a table leg into the calf of the waiter carrying the table at the front. The waiter grimaced hard, but avoided looking in Matteo's direction. Keen to get away.

A shade of guilt accompanied Matteo into his office. He flung open his laptop. Impatience clung to him. Did it *always* take so long for the laptop to power up?

His clients were stalling. The contracts should have been signed today. For the first time ever he was unable to read his clients, to assess what their negotiation tactics were. Were they still unsure about the relationship? Unsure about the trust and respect between them? Or were they looking to gain an advantage in the contract negotiations?

It felt as though his negotiation instincts had been knocked off course. Nothing had been the same since Tuesday night. When he had danced with Emma. Had held her slight frame in his arms. Had kissed her soft mouth. When nothing had ever felt so right. When in truth it was all wrong.

She had pulled away.

Rightly so.

But that didn't mean it hadn't stung. She had looked aghast. Even now his ego felt affronted by her horror.

He hated how attracted he was to her. How he constantly thought about her. The eternal distraction of her.

He should have been the one to pull away. She was an employee. Living in his home. A bruised runaway bride, no doubt messed up and confused. He hadn't acted honourably. That was what stung the most.

Finally the email icon popped up on his laptop.

He leaned forward in his chair and clicked on a New York Fashion Week update from the head of PR with VMV.

A hot dart of pain stung the base of his spine. He closed his eyes. *Dio!*

Tonight *had* to go smoothly. Thousands of his employees were depending on him. This business was his life, his everything. What would he be without it?

Tonight he was about to reveal his final bargaining chip to secure the deal with his clients. A promise that the globe's hottest celebrity couple, Hollywood stars Sadie

Banks and Johnny North, would open his collections at the Chinese clients' flagship stores in Hong Kong and Beijing.

Sadie and he had dated years ago, and had kept in contact for business purposes. She and Johnny were both going to attend the reception tonight. Their first appearance since their surprise marriage a fortnight ago, conducted in complete secrecy with only immediate family and friends in attendance. Sadie had worn a VMV gown.

Denied shots of the wedding, the media and public would be clamouring for a photo. Which, of course, would be taken with the president of China's most prestigious department store chain standing in between them.

The reception needed to be relaxed, slick, effortless. Everything it currently wasn't.

A knock sounded on his door. Before he had the opportunity to respond Emma entered and introduced a short, intent-looking man. The head of security.

Matteo gestured for the man to sit. Emma sat next to him, across the desk from Matteo.

Her hair was tied back in a ponytail, and she wore a white blouse with thin aqua-blue strips, a wide bow on the high collar. Beneath: dark navy tailored trousers. Her only obvious make-up was a deep red lipstick on her generous cupid's bow lips. Desire hit him hard. For a moment he could only stare at her. His fingers itching to undo each tiny pearl button running down the front of her blouse.

She was the cause of his negotiating instincts being off course. *She* was to blame. She had asked him earlier to believe in her. He had learned a long time ago not to trust in anyone but himself. That was not going to change any time soon—especially with a woman who had such a disturbingly bewitching effect on him.

Frustration wrapped around his throat. 'Emma, I will handle this.'

Ignoring him, she twisted to face the head of security, flinging her head back defiantly. She delivered a killer smile to the man, whose focused demeanour crumbled into a smitten gaze.

She passed him a file. 'This is an updated list of guests. Prince Henri is no longer able to attend.'

Matteo sat back in his chair as Emma continued to brief the security head. Anger fused with his earlier desire. Tension leached into his muscles. He forced himself to maintain restraint. Until he got her alone.

He couldn't fault her performance. She provided the head of security with every key piece of information he needed and easily answered all his questions.

But he *could* fault her insubordination. Her intrusion into his life. He *could* fault his own absurdity in feeling things for this woman that had him unable to concentrate in meetings. That had him craving the opportunity to spend time with her, to talk with her, to touch her, to taste the exhilarating heat of her mouth again.

Ten minutes later the meeting was wrapped up. The head of security provided Matteo with reassurances that, together with assistance from the local *carabinieri*, his team would be able to handle any potential security issues.

Emma walked to the office door with the security head. She offered Matteo a brief nod. Throughout the meeting she had held his gaze resolutely whenever he'd addressed her. He had deliberately pinned her with a furious stare. Wanting to see contrition in her eyes. Contrition for not obeying his orders. Contrition for turning his life upside down from the moment he'd found her lying in his bed.

'Emma, please wait.'

She stood by the open door as the security head walked away.

Music floated on the air. The string quartet rehearsing in the lounge.

For a moment he couldn't speak—couldn't break away from the powerful beauty of her hazel eyes. The soft, tender, romantic music wrapped around his heart—and then frustration hurled through him again. He gritted his teeth against his own insanity.

'Close the door.'

She did as he asked, but stayed at the now closed door, her shoulder hugging the edge of the door frame.

'I said that *I* would handle the briefing with the security head.'

Her body gave a start at the anger in his voice but then she stood upright, tilting her head back to gaze at him. 'It's okay. I was free and I had the most up-to-date guest list.'

'No. It *isn't* okay. I said that I didn't need you.'

Perspiration was breaking out on Emma's skin.

Her heart was banging a slow booming beat in her chest while the soulful melodies of Shostakovich's 'Romance Theme from The Gadfly' continued to seep under the closed door. Adding to her sense of foreboding.

She had guessed that Matteo wouldn't be happy with her leading the briefing. But she hadn't bargained on the alarming fury in his eyes. The dangerous coiled energy pulsating from his every pore.

Logic and her heart teamed up to beg her not to speak. Not to ask the one question boiling in her stomach.

But her new-found reckless defiance didn't heed them. 'Are you like this with *all* your employees?'

Her heart thundered in disbelief that she said those words out loud. She took small consolation from the fact that she hadn't also asked if it was only with her that he acted so harshly. *Because of their kiss.* Did he regret it so much? Was he determined to push her away?

'When I need to be.'

'Matteo.' Her throat tightened even at saying his name.

Regret punched her gut. But then anger overtook her. Anger that she was so drawn to this man. Anger that all her pledges to toughen up, to protect herself, had been nothing but empty promises.

She stepped away from the door. 'You employed me to do a job. Please let me do it.'

'Are you always this obstinate?'

'No. And unfortunately I have paid dearly as a result.'

'Meaning?'

'I allowed my ex to convince me that a short engagement was the right thing, when in truth I wanted more time. I allowed my mother and father to push me, to control every part of my life.'

She paused, emotion caught in her throat. She wanted to turn around and walk out of his office. Away from the hardness in his eyes. She didn't know where her throat ended and her heart began. Both were aching...a continuous fault line in her chest.

'I should have pushed for what I wanted and maybe then they would have had more respect for me.'

He folded his arms. His jaw tightened.

He looked down at his desk.

He unfolded his arms.

He pressed the metal of one cufflink. And then the other.

He prodded some paperwork.

He looked back up, his gaze trailing over the wall behind her, inhaled deeply.

He looked at her briefly and then gestured to the chair where she had earlier been seated. 'Sit down.' He stopped and exhaled a lungful of irritation. 'Sorry, *please* sit down.'

The second time around his voice was more conciliatory. Less harsh. Almost like the voice of the Matteo who had taken her in his arms the other night.

She sat, but kept her mask of imperturbability firmly on. She held his gaze, refusing to acknowledge the horrible vulnerability stirring in her stomach.

'I do respect you.'

She raised a single eyebrow.

He continued. 'Tonight *has* to go well. The clients are refusing to sign. Tonight I have to persuade them to do so. I expect that when they meet Sadie Banks, who is a brand ambassador for VMV, they will fully appreciate the mutual benefits of our alliance.'

Fresh unease grabbed hold of her stomach at the thought of all the sophisticated guests attending the reception. What on earth was she going to speak to them about?

'What role do you want me to play tonight at the reception?'

He drew a hand across his face, his long fingers brushing against his lips. Tired. Puzzled. Weary. 'You're my co-host, as with all the other events. Why would it be any different?'

The vulnerability chilling her bones, setting her on edge, had her speaking out, needing to understand where she stood with him. 'After Tuesday night I wasn't sure.'

He shifted in his seat. 'That obviously was a mistake.'

A mistake?

She knew it was. But hearing him say it in such a cold, dispassionate tone was like a slap.

'Yes, it was.' She gave him a polite smile, despite the anger propelling through her, making her want to snarl instead. 'I think they call it a rebound kiss.'

His jaw worked. And then a cruel smile crept onto his mouth. '*Cara*, we both know that was a lot more than a rebound kiss.'

His voice, dangerous but laced with sexy appeal had her shooting out of her chair. 'I must go and check if the photographer has arrived.'

* * *

Matteo gave a low curse. He felt as though his stomach had sunk down to the bottom of the canal.

He slammed shut the lid of his laptop. What was the matter with him? Why was he playing mind games with her?

He called to her retreating back. 'Being with anyone is a bad idea for you right now...especially someone like me.'

She twisted around. 'Like you?'

'I date women, Emma, but I'm not interested in anything serious. My longest relationship lasted less than six months. I have never even lived with a woman. I'm not interested in the emotions and demands of a relationship.'

Her mouth pursed indignantly. 'Do you *really* think that I want to be in a relationship? After everything I've gone through? I want to be on my own, to be independent, create my own life. I'm not trusting a man again for as long as I live.'

'But you said the other day you wanted a family.'

'Well, I can't have one now, can I?'

The thought of her with another man stuck in his throat like a bite-size canapé, but he forced himself to say, 'Not all men are like your ex. In time you'll meet someone else.'

She threw her eyes heavenwards, as though he was trying her patience. 'I'm not interested.'

Somewhere deep within him longing stirred. His stomach clenched at the way it grabbed his heart. Without thinking he said, 'Give yourself time. I can see you with lots of *bambini*.'

'I really don't think so.' She spoke with a dispassionate tone but her eyes told the truth of her vulnerability.

A vulnerability that was uncomfortably familiar.

He knew he should shut down this conversation. That he was single-handedly pulling them both into dangerous territory. But something inside him needed to know.

Needed to know if it had hurt her as much as it had him to be rejected.

'On that first night you said you have no family. What did you mean?'

She considered him for a moment and then said starkly, 'When I was no longer able to dance my parents made it clear that they no longer wanted me in their lives.'

'Why?'

'Because they blamed me for ruining everything.'

'Ruining what?'

'Their dreams of having a daughter who was a world-famous ballet star. I told them time and time again that that had never been going to happen, even if I hadn't got injured. I was a good ballet dancer, but I was never going to make it onto the world stage... They persisted in thinking otherwise.'

'And just because you couldn't dance they pushed you away?'

She gave a dispassionate shrug. 'Yes, and it's understandable. They spent years supporting me financially. They both worked two jobs to put me through ballet school. They had no life other than ballet—the endless rehearsals and auditions, travelling to see me perform. Supervising me stretching in the evenings. Repairing my kit. They sacrificed everything. And I let them down.'

'It was an accident.'

'I know. But to them it was the end of the world.'

Defiant hazel eyes held his, but her voice and her lips, too tightly marshalled, told another story. One of pain and bewilderment.

And Matteo realised he had never felt so undone.

In the past he had always effortlessly moved women in and out of his life with words full of charm and regret. But for some reason he wanted to help Emma. Even knowing that to do so would be dangerous, that he should be keeping his distance, not becoming desperate to know her better, to wipe away the fear and anxiety that were now flooding her eyes.

'But your parents, the accident, your wedding…none of what went wrong is your fault. You're so matter-of-fact about it all. Aren't you angry?'

'Matteo, you're my boss. Why are we talking about this? What does it matter?'

'Just because I'm your boss doesn't mean that I can't be human.'

She arched an eyebrow at that.

He touched the platinum of his cufflinks. Cleared his throat and said, 'Life has been pretty unfair to you recently.'

'I can cope on my own.'

Her defiant tone had him demanding, 'So is that why you are staying here?'

She didn't answer—just looked away, her mouth twisting unhappily.

'Can you reconnect with your parents? Is that an option?'

She leaned back against the wall beside the door with a tired exhalation. 'No. After my accident I thought that maybe with time they would adjust. Accept what had happened. I'd send cards for their birthdays, for Christmas, but they would just send them back unopened.'

'Why were they so unforgiving? It was an *accident*.'

Her eyes moved upwards to the eighteenth-century frescoed ceiling, a blush the same colour as her lipstick appearing on her cheeks. 'Because I had had a glass of wine the night I fell down the steps at the nightclub I was in. They chose to believe that I was drunk. When I wasn't. They blamed me for going out. For choosing to spend time with my friends rather than focusing exclusively on my ballet.'

How could they have turned her away? Their own flesh and blood.

'They should have put you first—your happiness. That should be every parent's priority. What about your friends? Were they able to help?'

'My friends back then were supportive at first...' Her hand moved up and drifted across her neck, her fingers tapping against her skin. 'But they were all in the ballet world. I drifted away from them eventually. It was too hard for everyone. I could see their guilt when they spoke about ballet in front of me...'

For the first time since she had entered his office she looked at him with total honesty, no artificial mask of hardness.

'And it tore me apart.'

Her sadness filled the room with the stinging effect of invisible tear gas.

His throat stung...his chest felt heavy.

He suddenly wished he had been there for her. Had known her when she was nineteen. Had known her even earlier. Had been able to protect her from life's unfairness.

She closed her eyes for a few seconds, her face tightening into a wince. 'I just wish I'd stood up to my parents, to my ex.'

'What do you mean?'

Instead of answering she glanced uncertainly towards the chair where she had earlier been seated. She edged back towards it and sat. Her eyes fixed on to a point over his shoulder, she said, 'I had a very intense relationship with my parents. I was an only child. There was a lot of expectation. I always wanted to please them. But even when I was selected at a competition or an audition, and I looked out at them in the audience...I knew that on the way home they would only talk about the next audition, how to get me to the next level. The extra classes they would organise. The money they were saving to send me to ballet school.'

'That was a lot of pressure for a child.'

'I guess… I loved dancing so much…but it was lonely. I was never allowed to spend time with my friends. When the neighbourhood children knocked on the door for me to come out and play my mother would refuse to let me go. I thought ballet boarding school would change all that… and it did eventually—I made some good friends—but for the first few years I was homesick.'

She tilted forward in her chair and squeezed both knees with her hands. Tight. Memories were causing a line of tension to dissect her forehead.

'At some auditions my mum used to be really nasty about the girls she saw as my rivals. People would overhear—it was horrible. I tried to get her to stop but she wouldn't… It was so embarrassing. And unfair. The other girls thought that I was the same as her; it took a long time before they realised I wasn't. I never stood up to my parents because I was frightened that they would take away what I loved so much. My ballet lessons. The funding for the ballet school.'

She looked down towards her feet. Not looking up, she gave a shrug while her body tilted ever so slightly forward and back, propelled by the movement of her feet.

'Being on stage was magical. In the rehearsals, in ballet class, I would lose myself to the beauty of the movements. Even when I was injured and struggling, ballet gave me life. Happiness.' She looked up suddenly, her eyes sparking with anger. 'But if I had been brave enough to get past my fear of upsetting my parents—been tougher and pushed for what I wanted—told them that I didn't want them controlling every aspect of my life—maybe they would have backed off, become less obsessed. Not have been so devastated when it all came to a crashing end.'

'You can't blame yourself for their reaction to the accident.'

She gave a *you don't understand* sigh. 'It was the same with my ex. Maybe if I'd said no to him, that I wanted a longer engagement… So many people wouldn't be hurt. Now his poor parents have not only his embezzlement to deal with but also the embarrassment of the wedding being called off on the day of the ceremony. They had invited over a hundred of their friends. They're lovely people… His mum was so happy about us marrying. They were both so proud of him.'

'You're not to blame.'

'But what about my behaviour? I didn't rock the boat, say no, stand up to my parents, because I wanted to stay in ballet. I didn't tell my ex that I didn't want a rushed wedding because I wanted a family of my own so badly. I was so damn *passive* in it all. I refused to listen to my own doubts about marrying him. Was I putting my own happiness in front of what was right for my parents? For my ex? Was I complicit in things going so badly wrong? I should have been stronger, tougher.'

CHAPTER FIVE

MATTEO SPRANG FROM his chair, hating to hear her blame herself. 'You had the right to want those things. A career in ballet and...'

Pain shot from his spine down into his glutes.

He lowered his head and gave a low curse.

'And a family.'

His heart began to pound unaccountably and he found it difficult to speak.

'Nobody would blame you for wanting those things.'

He turned away from her cool shrug to look out of the window.

Soft, decadent Botticelli clouds hung over the red-tiled rooftops and the endless church domes and *campaniles* of Venice, pausing at the will of the unpredictable breeze to dance before the sun.

He had long ago accepted he would never have a family of his own. He never wanted to have his heart ripped in two ever again. Why, then, did it sadden and disturb him so much to talk about family with Emma?

'It doesn't matter anyway. It's all in the past.'

He turned around at her words. The clipped, clear tone was not really her voice.

'Now I just want to focus on my future, on being truly independent. I'm tired of being answerable to others. I

want a career I can be proud of. And I'm going to fight
for it.'

'By fighting me?'

'Not fighting you. Standing up to you. Because I'm
good at my job, Matteo. And I want to be a new me. More
independent... I want to be hard-headed and resilient.'

'I'm no pushover.'

'Good.' She stood and walked to the door. 'And now
that we understand one another, the first thing I'm going
to do is show you some Pilates stretches for your back.'

Puzzled, he said, 'My back?'

She cast a critical gaze over him. 'It's obviously hurting you. What caused it?'

'I was sailing last summer, and after I'd winched in a
sail in heavy seas it felt a little tighter...it's been bothering me ever since.'

'What has your doctor said about it?'

'Nothing. I haven't had the time to visit him.'

She shook her head, disappointed in him.

He stood a little straighter. He took care of himself
physically. He didn't need Pilates. 'Thanks for the offer,
but I have business to take care of.'

She threw him a challenging gaze. 'Now, let's not have
a stand-off over this. You've said that tonight is important
to you. I know how energy-sapping pain is. Let me show
you some exercises that might ease yours. Less pain will
allow you to enjoy tonight more and concentrate better.'

She didn't wait for his answer, but spoke as she walked
towards the door. 'There isn't enough room in here. Follow me upstairs. The floor space in one of the bedrooms
will be perfect.'

A little while later, lying on an antique rug in the *sala
azzurra*—the blue bedroom—staring up at the Virgin-
blue ceiling, Matteo couldn't decide if he had lost his

mind or whether it was rather enjoyable to be lying beside Emma. Pretending to listen to her instructions when in truth his concentration was shot to pieces because she kept touching him.

So much for keeping her at arm's length.

'Now that you have your chin, shoulder blades, arms, pelvis and feet correctly positioned, we will start with a basic move: the leg slide.'

Sitting up beside him, while he remained lying on the floor, with his legs bent, she moved her hands once again onto his hips and applied a gentle pressure. He swallowed a groan.

'Remember to keep a neutral pelvis position.'

Dio! Had she *any* idea what it was like to have her so close? To have her fingers touching him?

'Now, on an inhale slide your right leg out until it's fully extended, and on an exhale pull it back into position.'

He did as she said.

She lay down next to him. 'Good—now do the same with the left leg.'

He followed her count for drawing alternate legs in and out. Next he drew alternate arms back to reach behind him, with Emma all the time telling him to focus, to maintain a neutral position. To breathe.

This was a workout his *nonnina* would enjoy.

'Are you sure that these exercises are of use?'

'Absolutely. They're a major part of any dancer's life and I still practise Pilates every day. It strengthens your core and it's vital in recovery from injury. These exercises are hugely beneficial to people with back pain.'

They finished the arm extensions and Emma sat up. 'The exercises will help, but you need to visit your doctor too.'

'I will after this week.'

'You *could* say it with a little more conviction.'

'I'm busy.'

She tucked her feet underneath her bottom, her crossed legs folding easily into a yoga position. She leaned towards him. 'Being stressed is a major cause of back problems.'

'I'm not stressed.'

She folded her arms and gave him a *who are you trying to kid?* look. 'Stress always aggravates my ankle. Why is the China deal so important to you?'

He shuffled on the ground, suddenly uncomfortable lying in such a vulnerable position. 'Can we just focus on the exercises, please…? The photographer will be here soon.'

She studied him for a moment, but then with a shrug said, 'Fine—let's move on to the bridge exercise.'

She instructed him on the movements needed with her hand touching his stomach. The gentle weight burnt through the cotton of his shirt. Her little finger rested on the silver buckle of his belt.

Dio!

'Remember to keep your pelvis neutral. And *breathe.* You're not breathing!'

What did she expect? He was having to lie there pretending that his body *wasn't* a heat-seeking missile about to launch. Having to fight every instinct that was yelling at him to intercept those torturous touches and pull her down on top of him and kiss her for the next fortnight.

Why hadn't he just said that this wasn't working earlier in his office? That having her live here in Ca' Divina was akin to torture? Knowing that she was lying in her bed at night, only a few doors away… A thought that had kept him awake, pacing the terrace into the early hours every night.

He was even more out of control than Ettore's head designer.

Her hand pressed a little more firmly. 'Now, one verte-bra at a time, sink your spine down to the ground.'

He needed to speak. To distract himself.

'I need the Chinese clients to sign because many of our other major markets are contracting due to recessions and political instability.'

She lay down beside him once again and silently indi-cated that he should follow her lead in pulling his left leg in towards his body and then his right leg. She hugged her own legs with a graceful flexibility.

He gazed back up at the ceiling. She would never dance in a ballet again. How incredible it would have been to see her dance.

Without looking, he knew she was staring directly at him. His heart slowed as beautiful dread moved through him.

Why was she getting to him so much? Why did he feel such a thumping connection with her?

His gaze blended with hers. And despite himself he smiled at her. Wanting to reach out.

Rosy-cheeked, she smiled back. That smile touched something inside him every time she punched him with it. And then her gaze whooshed away. As if she had been caught unawares.

The door to the bedroom was slightly ajar. From down-stairs he could hear the quartet rehearsing. The sound of raised voices. But it felt as though they were alone in a co-coon of connectedness. Of understanding. With the early spring sun warming the room.

Her hands were clasped together on her stomach, as if in prayer. Her lips worked for a while before she spoke. 'What might happen if they don't sign?'

Just like that the peace of a few moments ago was shat-tered. His fear for the business fused with his fear about what was happening between them.

'Worst-case scenario: I'll have to shut down some operations. Consolidate. Which will put people out of work.'

'That upsets you?'

He had been about to stand up. He needed to walk out the tension in his body. Move away from the power she exerted over him. But her question, so quietly asked, so full of softly spoken understanding, had him looking back into eyes that practically swallowed him up with empathy.

'I set up my factories in areas with significant unemployment and poverty. People will struggle to find alternative employment. I put years of training into giving them the skills required. They depend on me.'

'You gave them skills—skills they can bring to other employers.'

'Yes, but there *aren't* employers in those areas.'

'But having so many skilled workers might attract new employers into the area. Maybe some of your staff will go on and set up their own companies. Whatever happens, it doesn't have to be the end. There's always another solution.'

Taken aback by her arguments, by the fact that she was challenging him, he considered them for a moment in silence. And quickly dismissed them. She didn't understand his level of responsibility to so many people. Already irritated, he felt a spark of annoyance as a truth he had been ignoring flamed into life when he thought further about her words.

'Am I the solution to *your* current situation?'

She stared at him, her mouth silently opening and closing. 'Are you asking me if I'm using you?'

'*Are* you?' he shot back, vocalising the hurt and frustration coiling in his body.

She looked away and stared up at the ceiling. 'What have I done to make you think that?'

Her voice was low, resigned. The voice of someone

who wasn't surprised by his unfair question. The voice of someone who was used to being disappointed by others.

Guilt tore through him. 'I'm sorry.'

'Do you want me to leave?'

Above him, the Murano glass of the bedroom chandelier swayed slightly as a breeze blew through the ajar door.

He should say yes.

He shouldn't be lying here with her, distracted from his responsibilities.

He shouldn't be feeling so attracted—*Dio*, so innately connected—to a woman who had been so recently hurt.

But all those shouldn'ts failed to cancel out his desire to spend time with her. 'I want you to stay.'

She nodded to this. And then her entire body gave a shudder.

She was shaking off his earlier words.

Shaking *him* off.

He sat up. Needing to put this right.

She looked at him warily.

'I'm cautious about who I let into my life.'

At first she nodded, but then she sat up too. Her head bent, she ran her fingers over the blue and ivory motifs on the rug. 'I can understand why... I would be too, in your position.'

She looked at him with solemn eyes, filing away another piece of information on him. And then a small smile broke on her mouth.

It grew even wider.

She gave a giggle which danced into his heart.

She toppled sideways, reaching out a hand to the rug to steady herself.

Vibrant. Elegant. Fairy-tale pretty.

'Finding me in your bed must have been a huge shock!'

He found himself grinning alongside her. 'It was a most unusual homecoming present.'

She tilted towards him, amusement lighting up her face.
'I've never seen myself as a *present*.'

Her voice was light, playful, teasing.

'A beautiful, distracting present to keep me sane this
week.'

Why was he talking to her like this? Why did he have
an unstoppable urge to flirt with her? To see her smile
and laugh.

'I'm glad I have my uses.'

They sat and smiled at each other.

Foolishly, light-heartedly, soul-enhancingly.

Life buzzed in his veins.

A door closed downstairs.

His fingers tingled with the urge to reach out, to place
his hand on her bent knee, to connect physically with her.

To untie the bow at the neck of her blouse…to curl her
hair between his fingers.

To kiss her. To have some fun. To know her better.

Her smile slowly faded. And was eclipsed by eyes full
of questions and longing.

The same longing that was banging in his chest.

Longing which filled the cavity of space that separated
them.

He needed to get them back on solid ground. To es-
tablish the nature of their relationship. To stop flirting
with her.

'You know, my back *does* feel better. But we need to
go downstairs… You should be supervising.'

It took a few seconds for the giddiness in her belly to dissolve and for reality to take its place. He was her boss. She
had to protect herself. Stop allowing her physical attraction to him overrule all logic.

He had taken off his jacket when they had come upstairs and draped it on the back of a chair. He had also re-

luctantly removed his tie and shoes, at her suggestion. He sat before her, his legs bent and crossed, almost matching her lotus position. She was desperately trying not to stare at the powerful strength of his thighs, the captivating narrowness of his hips, the broadness of his chest beneath his white shirt. He dominated the room.

A question was twisting and twisting in her airway, being driven upwards by the unease flapping in her stomach like a hundred butterflies trying to escape.

'Is this going to work?'

The soft espresso warmth of his gaze moved to the coolness of coffee *gelato*.

'It can work if we are both clear that this is a *business* relationship. Two colleagues working together for another few days.'

She wanted to ask what would happen at the end of the week. Would they ever see each other again?

But how on earth was that going to work? A billionaire retail legend and a marketing assistant...a runaway bride.

He studied her, waiting for her to speak.

And the puzzle in her brain as to how they could possibly be just colleagues was constantly jumbled by her glances at him. Thick dark eyebrows were drawn in, there was an evening shadow on his golden jawline, his wide mouth set in neutral...all waiting, waiting, waiting. Waiting for her to speak. But all she could think of was how much she wanted to run her fingertip across that jawline, down his powerful neck, along the topography of his shoulders.

The chemistry between them was about to burn her up. She had never before met a man who literally took her breath away with his looks alone.

Maybe they *could* be colleagues for this week. And in years to come she would look back on the week she'd spent in Venice with this most beautiful man with hope-fully fond memories. And her heart intact.

Being his colleague and having the professional friend-ship that entailed she could just about handle.

Anything more would be devastating.

So it was time she put her 'colleague' mask on and ig-nored the way her body was screaming out for him like a truculent toddler in the sweet aisle of a supermarket.

'Colleagues need to be honest with one another—do you agree?'

Cautiously he answered, 'It depends…'

She shot him a challenging look. 'I've told you about my parents, my past…things I have never spoken about before.'

His eyes narrowed suspiciously. 'Okay…what's your point?'

'I have a question. When you've accomplished so much, why are you so tough on yourself? I've seen the light on in your office late into the night. You work so hard. Why are you so driven? So worried about the future?'

He rested a hand behind him on the rug and leaned back, considering her question. His silver belt buckle winked up at her. *Remember me? Remember how it felt to touch the hard muscles of this stomach?* No unengaged abdominal muscles there. Just firm muscles layered below hot skin.

Her eyes darted up to where he had undone his top but-ton. Golden skin called to her. She inhaled a deep breath, her insides collapsing into a puddle of desire.

'Because I have people dependent on me—my employ-ees, my family. I have responsibilities that *demand* that I worry, take nothing for granted. Anticipate the worst.'

His words and his serious tone pulled her out of her vi-sual voyage of discovery. Immediately she felt guilty. What type of colleague was she? To be distracted by the super-ficial when he was telling her something so important?

'That's a whole load of responsibility for one man to carry.'

His eyes held hers and whipped open her soul. Even before he spoke her heart began to thump in anticipation.

'I grew up in poverty. I know how awful it is.'

His tone was bleak. His eyes held hers for a moment, memories haunting him, punching her in the stomach.

He continued, 'I can't be responsible for putting my employees back into a situation where they are struggling on a daily basis to eat, to pay their bills. To see no future for themselves or their children. Having no choices in life. The shame and feelings of worthlessness.'

'You have strong memories of those days…of your childhood?'

'Yes.'

Things were starting to make sense now…his grandmother's kindness. 'Your grandmother taking me in…she feels responsible too?'

He nodded grimly. 'She's involved with a number of organisations for the homeless.'

Her heart tumbled to see the way he was trying to act detached, his stoic expression, the matter-of-fact way he spoke. When the tight lines at the corner of his eyes told another story.

'Were *you* homeless?'

He studied the rug for a few seconds, his arms folded in front of his chest. His head rose and he stared at her, with his jaw set in *don't pity me* tightness.

'For a few days, yes. My mother, grandmother and I had all moved from Puglia to Milan. We were staying with my mother's then boyfriend. They had a row. He threw us out. We had no money and nowhere to go.'

'How old were you?'

'Fourteen.'

What must it have been like to be a young teenage boy, facing living on the streets?

'Were you scared?'

'We slept for four nights in a doorway in a back alley. It was daunting...but the worst thing was the humiliation. I swore then that I would never allow it to happen again—that I would always protect my family from such embarrassment.'

'That's what drives you? The reason you put such pressure on yourself?'

'Yes.'

'But you need to accept what you have accomplished too, Matteo. Believe that if you did it once you can do it again. What's the point of everything you've achieved if you can get no happiness, no sense of reward from it?'

'That isn't of importance.'

'That you are happy? Satisfied? Why not?'

'If I'm satisfied I'll stop being so driven. And that's dangerous.'

'But you need both—to have drive and also to be happy.'

He shook his head vehemently, not prepared even to consider her arguments. 'I can't be complacent. Not in this industry.'

'Of course—I accept that. But maybe you need to accept what you've achieved—and most importantly believe that you *will* deal with whatever the future brings. Don't let the fear of poverty, of homelessness control you. They are only fears, thoughts... They're not a reality now. You've proved yourself, Matteo. By everything you have achieved. You need to believe that you can do the same again if necessary.'

His eyes narrowed, their coffee *gelato* now frozen rock-hard. 'Do *you* believe in yourself?'

She hated the way he had turned this back on her. But

maybe, if she was honest with him, he might see that there was some merit in what she was saying.

'Probably not enough.'

She paused and realised that the burden of guilt she had been carrying around—about her parents, her accident, her wedding—felt a little lighter now that she had spoken about them and Matteo's insistence that she wasn't to blame.

'But you know what? Each time I've been knocked down I've come back... When my career in ballet was snapped away from me... My wedding. Other paths have opened up to me.'

He looked so burdened by the responsibilities he was carrying, she wanted to ease his tension, to see him smile again.

So with a cheeky grin she added, 'I even got to meet *you*—which has to be some consolation.'

The hard lines of his face dissolved into a charismatic smile—shining eyes and gorgeous white teeth. 'Whoa! Careful or I might get a big head.'

Trying not to swoon, she tried to adopt a cool-girl pose of easy nonchalance. 'Of all the men I have met, you are the one person who deserves to have a massive ego. But you don't.'

His head dipped. Was it her imagination or did his cheeks colour ever so slightly? Crikey, this guy *really* knew how to get to a girl.

When he looked back up he cleared his throat, his expression telling her little of what he was thinking.

'I take nothing for granted.'

'Which is good...but maybe you should start enjoying what you have—even a little bit.'

He leaned towards her and those brown eyes were alight with mischief. 'I'm lying here on the floor with you when I have an important reception to host in less than two hours. Is that a good enough start for you?'

That expression about cutting off a limb in order to get something… Well, right now she understood it perfectly. Because every atom in her body was crying out to lean in towards him, to touch the smooth golden skin of his cheek, to touch her lips to his.

The friendship of a colleague.

She had to remember that was all she could—should—hope for.

With a man who set her alight with a single look.

A man who through his power, strength and empathy made her feel like a real-life Odette from *Swan Lake*.

CHAPTER SIX

EMMA STABBED THE 'send' button on her text message, clasped her phone tight in her fist and went and stood by her open bedroom door. She peeked down the frescoed corridor. It was empty. She stepped back into her room, quickly patting the loose curls of her pinned up hair, testing its stability.

Please, please let him read my message. And soon.

The first guests were due to arrive any moment now. She dashed across the room to the windows overlooking the Grand Canal.

A powerful motor boat was already approaching Ca' Divina's landing stage. The lights of other intimidatingly expensive boats were following in its wake.

She stepped a little closer to the window, the better to peer through the ripples of the antique glass. The scene below was illuminated by the discreet low lights on the landing stage. And just then the person waiting to disembark looked up at her.

Sebastian King! The world-famous composer.

She had seen his name on the guest list. But seeing him in reality was a whole different matter.

And now he was staring up at her, clearly amused.

She leapt away from the window. Her pounding heart was sending flames of heat onto her cheeks.

'Guests are already arriving. Why aren't you ready?'

She spun around, her heart slipping into a wild allegro beat.

Dressed in a dark midnight-blue suit, a light blue shirt and a navy and silver tie, Matteo did a pretty good job of filling the extrawide doorway.

She swung away from him and reached behind her to point a finger at the cause of her delay. 'I can't fasten the back of my dress. That's why I texted you. I need your help.'

She turned back in time to see his mouth tighten as he moved towards her and then she looked away. Back out to the lights shining from the delicately carved windows of the Gothic *palazzo* across the canal.

His scent wrapped around her. Musk with a hint of vanilla.

She dragged in a deep breath against the quiver in her belly.

He worked in silence, his fingers tracing against the top of her spine. She held herself rigid, determined not to let the threatening shivers escape. But as his fingers moved across her bare skin she instinctively arched her back. Feeling totally exposed.

Her full-length gown had a wide cut-out section at the back, all the way down to her waist, exposing most of her spine. A gold chain was sewn into one border of the barely there side panels, and she needed Matteo to secure it to the gold clasp sewn onto the other side panel. With the gold chain unsecured she was in danger of the whole dress slipping off. Which, considering she was unable to wear a bra with this dress, was definitely not a good idea. Especially with a papal representative attending tonight.

'I expected you downstairs ten minutes ago.'

His voice, a sensual caress even when he was admonishing her, was so suggestive of carnal pleasures it left her rubber-boned.

She swallowed against the shimmers of desire skipping along her skin.

'The mixologist didn't arrive. I had to organise a replacement.'

Those strong hands twisted her around. A flicker of amusement sent golden sparkles radiating through his brown eyes.

'I like a martini with lemon peel.' Then the amusement in his eyes died and he inhaled a deep breath that spoke of hidden unease beneath his cool exterior. '*Andiamo.* Let's go.'

'I have to do my make-up.'

'You don't have time.'

He had to be kidding!

'I can't meet your guests with no make-up on.'

'Yes, you can.' His eyes travelled over her face, quietly devouring her. '*Sei bellissima.* You look beautiful.'

There was a low, seductive note to his voice and she suddenly felt light-headed.

'You don't need make-up. Your skin is perfect.'

His hand moved to take her elbow, and although her bones now felt like melting rubber she jumped out of his way and wobbled over to the dressing table. There she grabbed her favourite scarlet lipstick and quickly applied it, a swirling vortex of panic and desire spinning inside her as she tried to ignore Matteo's dark and dangerous reflection in the mirror glass.

She twisted back and ran to the stairs.

On the first step Matteo joined her and held his hand to her elbow, steadying her progress as she tottered down on much too high gold sandals that she would never have dared buy herself.

He pulled her to a stop halfway down and pointed at her feet unhappily. 'Those sandals are much too high for you. I asked for them to be delivered before I knew about your ankle.'

She took her arm from his continuing grip and placed her hand on his elbow instead. With a little push she urged him forward. 'They're fine, honestly. Let's go.'

She couldn't let him see how nervous she was about co-hosting the reception with him. How, now that it was an imminent reality, her self-confidence had fallen through the floor. She was a runaway bride, duped by her ex, rejected by her parents. A failed ballerina. How on earth was she supposed to entertain some of the world's highest achievers? She was about to let Matteo down. Let herself down.

They made it to the *portego* just as Sebastian King climbed the final steps of the stairs leading up from the landing stage.

Matteo and he embraced, with a lot of clapping each other on the back.

'Sebastian, let me introduce you to Emma Fox.'

Sebastian King was a big bear of a man, with a ruddy complexion, an easy smile and a tight crew cut that left only a light covering of grey stubble on his head. He took her hand, and then yanked her in for a hug.

'Was it you I saw staring out at me from the window?'

She gave him a non-committal smile and dared a quick look in Matteo's direction. He gave her a *what were you doing?* frown.

Time to move the conversation on.

'I'm so excited to meet you. I saw you perform at The Lowry in Salford with my school. I was only twelve but I have such wonderful memories. I'm a huge fan.'

Sebastian gave a loud chuckle. 'Delighted to hear it, my dear. Been to see any of my recent work?'

She could feel herself pale. 'I'm afraid not. But I hope to.'

It was Sebastian's turn to look unimpressed. He twisted

away. 'What direction is the bar?' His tone said that he needed a drink. *Now*. And some decent company.

She was about to apologise to Matteo for her less than auspicious start, but pulled back her words. Apologising would only add to her humiliation and her sense of not belonging here. Of being out of her depth. So instead she smiled warmly at a group of glittering guests coming towards them, her insides filling with dread.

She had nothing in common with any of these people. What was she going to say to them all? And what if something went wrong with the reception? Would she cope? Would Matteo forgive her?

The next half an hour passed in a whirl. She shook hands and smiled. Nodded as Matteo spoke to his guests, more often than not in rapid Italian, only understanding the occasional word. So much for the *Beginners' Italian* podcast she had listened to religiously every morning on the way to work, daydreaming of effortlessly ordering a *bellini* in Harry's Bar.

It had been arranged that the Chinese delegation would be the last guests to arrive—a silent signal of their importance and status. But as they began to ascend the stairs, stopping to point and gaze at the frescos and gilt-adorned walls and high ceilings, Matteo lowered his head and said in a low, urgent voice, 'Sadie and Johnny haven't arrived yet. I need to call her. Take the delegation through to the ballroom once I have greeted them. Introduce them to the other guests.'

Her stomach thumped to the floor. And her heart followed soon after. Apart from the famous faces, she wouldn't remember who was who.

She leaned closer to him, panic pumping through her body. Totally out of her depth. '*I'll* call Sadie. You go with Mr Xue and the rest of the delegation.'

He pulled back and gave her a curious look. 'But I have

her private number—you don't. Is everything okay? You seem—'

She jumped in, not wanting to hear any more. She needed to pretend she was fine. She had asked for this job. She owed it to Matteo to deliver. 'Everything's fine. I just thought you would prefer to accompany Mr Xue into the ballroom, but I would be delighted to.'

He threw her another curious look. He obviously wasn't buying her breezy tone.

She led the delegation away and entered the ballroom with her heart doing a Viennese waltz. Her mind went blank when she was confronted by a sea of faces.

What did the President of the Region of Veneto and his wife look like again?

She needed to think. Get her act together. She was the one who'd promised Matteo that she was more than able for this role.

She called the translator to her side. 'Elena, I would like to introduce the group to the President of Veneto. Can you direct us towards him? And then will you please stay and translate? I will bring other guests over and introduce them to the delegation.'

For the next ten minutes she moved through the room with a coolness she definitely wasn't feeling, approaching other guests and inviting them to meet with the Chinese delegation. Each time she brought them forward she prayed she had got their names and titles right.

After what felt like several lifetimes of tight, terrified smiles and introductions, Emma gave a massive sigh of relief when she turned to find Matteo entering the room with Sadie Banks and Johnny North at his side. A shiver of recognition and excitement ran through the room.

Johnny North—her teenage crush.

Even more handsome and laid-back sexy in real life. Taller than she'd thought.

She stared at him, and second by second felt her teenage dreams fizzle away.

She gave a huff of disbelief.

Just like that her teenage crush had disappeared in a puff of smoke.

All thanks to Matteo.

He was her secret crush now.

A crush who was staring at her with a dark scowl.

She tried to wipe the starstruck expression off her face and gave him a quick, professional *I have everything under control* smile.

His shoulder twitched, but he turned away to speak to Sadie and then Johnny. Together they moved through the room. They spoke to the other guests with smiles and laughs as they walked but did not stop until they'd reached the Chinese delegation.

No longer needed, Emma slipped away to check on the rest of the *palazzo*. Glad to escape. Glad to be busy and to put a lid on how vulnerable she felt tonight.

First she checked in with the head of security. Then, in the lounge, she paused to watch the replacement mixologist tossing bottles of spirits and assorted fruit in the air, egged on by the crowd surrounding him, who were dancing to the beat of the music being played by the DJ in the corner.

Waiters were discreetly mingling amongst the guests with trays of Prosecco and the exquisite canapés she had tasted with the chef earlier, when she had given her approval for them to be served. Langoustine tails, gnocchi *fritti*, parmesan and poppyseed lollipops.

A magician dressed in eighteenth-century costume passed through the crowd performing tricks, adding to the carnival atmosphere.

Coming out from the lounge into the *portego*, she gave a brief smile to Matteo. He and Mr Xue were having their photo taken with Sadie and Johnny in front of a fresco showing Odysseus's ship in turbulent waters.

She walked away, but her spine tingled with the uncomfortable certainty that a set of unhappy, much too observant brown eyes were boring into her back.

She worked her way through the ballroom, checking that everything was going to plan. The string quartet were playing beautifully, at the perfect volume, the lighting was subtle, and the guests all had food and drink at hand.

Heading in the direction of the kitchen, to check in with the chef, she gave a small yelp when Matteo came up beside her and with a hand to her bare back silently guided her in the direction of his office.

Inside, he did not turn on the light.

He stepped close to her. 'Is everything okay?'

In the dark room he seemed even bigger than usual, his body acting like a magnet, drawing her in towards him against her will. She longed to place her hand on his waist, beneath his open jacket, against the cotton of his shirt, to feel the reassurance of his strength, of the tight muscles she had felt earlier when showing him the Pilates stretches.

She stepped away from him towards the faint outline of his desk. 'Yes, of course.'

'I want you to circulate amongst the guests and try to look like you are *enjoying* yourself.' He said the second half of the sentence in a tone of mild exasperation.

'I need to check that everything is running smoothly.'

'Yes, but as my co-host you need to relax... *Dio*, Emma, I don't want to have to worry about you tonight.'

Embarrassed heat licked against her skin. She gave silent praise that they were standing in the near dark. Her throat thick with disappointment that she was failing, she asked, in a much too high-pitched voice, 'What do you mean, worry about me?'

'You should be having fun—not looking as though this is hard work.'

'But it *is* work. I want to do it properly.' On the cusp of blurting out how overwhelmed she felt, she drew back from it and said in a self-mocking tone, 'I just don't know what to chat to the guests about… I can hardly speak to a Nobel Laureate about the weather, can I?'

'No, but you can enquire if he's enjoying Venice. Introduce him to some other guests. I need you to host alongside me.'

He spoke in a gentle voice, as if he was willing her to relax. To enjoy the night. He should be cross with her—angry, even. He didn't have the time to be taking her aside and encouraging her like a naïve intern.

Tears welled at the back of her eyes.

She swallowed hard. Pushed them away.

'Okay, I'll relax… It's just that I don't want to let you down tonight. I know how important this reception is to you.'

He stepped closer. He held her gaze.

'You're not letting me down.'

His voice was low, deep, sincere. Her heart did a *grand jeté* across her chest.

She opened her mouth to speak but no words came.

His hand moved up as though to touch her, but then dropped back to his side. 'I have to go.'

She nodded and he turned and left the room.

For a few minutes she leaned against the office wall, trying to compose herself.

Inhaling deep breaths.

Cracking her knuckles. That was something she hadn't done since she was a teenager. Hadn't done since the ballet master had rapped her on them for doing so.

Despite every logical warning her brain was yelling down to her heart, she had to face up to a certain fact: she was falling for Matteo. Physically…and perhaps emotionally. A psychologist would have a field day with her. No doubt the words 'rebound' and 'poor decision-making' would feature. These feelings were pointless. She did not *want* another relationship. Not that she supposed Matteo had any interest in her anyway, beyond physical attraction.

Her conversation with him earlier in the day came back to her…his insistence that she wasn't to blame for her past…his belief in her.

She pushed away from the wall. She had to stop her negative thoughts. Stop feeling so self-conscious and unsure. She was here to do a job.

She walked into the ballroom, full of great intentions. And straight into Johnny North. He gave her the smile that had stared back at her from her bedside locker throughout her boarding school years. That *come and rebel with me* smile. That had been her teenage desire. To rebel against the restrictions of boarding school, her parents' expectations.

A rush of excitement fizzed through her. It wasn't too late. She could still rebel, walk away from all her insecurities. Be tough and carefree. Forget the past and move with confidence into the future.

She held out her hand to him. 'Emma Fox.'

He shook her hand and asked in his American drawl, 'So, what brings you to Venice, Emma Fox?'

'I'm on the run.'

He gave her a grin of approval. 'You're my type of girl.'

Matteo tried to pay attention to the conversation between Mr Xue and Sebastian King about a concert Sebastian had conducted at the Beijing National Centre for the Performing Arts last year. But his attention was continually diverted across the room, to where Johnny North was holding court with a rapt audience of one. Emma. Pink-cheeked and dazzlingly radiant. Her porcelain skin glowing against the poppy-red colour of her dress.

Porcelain skin that was so soft it had sent juggernauts of lust powering through him earlier, when he had touched her bare back whilst fastening her dress.

He had longed to touch his lips against that skin…from the top of her long, elegant ballerina neck all the way down her spine.

Stopping to inhale her delicate rose scent.

Despite the saga of Sadie being late and needing to focus on the final subtle negotiations with Mr Xue, he had been seconds away from pulling her into his arms and kissing her soft mouth in the darkness and the seductive silence of his office.

Irritation twisted in his chest and he clenched his teeth. Okay, so she was mingling with the guests now, as he had asked, instead of dashing about the *palazzo*, clearly uncomfortable. But did she *have* to pick the most handsome guy in the room to chat to? And did she *have* to look so enthralled with him? And why wasn't she moving on? Talking to other guests? Talking to *him* instead of Johnny North.

He excused himself from his present company and made his way over to Emma and Johnny. Johnny had one shoulder touching against the frescoed wall of the ballroom. Matteo gave him a lethal stare and without batting an eyelid Johnny moved away from the wall. Matteo stood next to Emma and placed a hand on her lower back. Sometimes men didn't need any words.

Nearby, Sadie left the company of a group of national politicians, cross-party differences forgotten in their collective star-struck veneration as Sadie flashed them her trademark traffic-stopping smile, and swept towards them to plant a kiss on Johnny's cheek. He pulled her tighter towards him and whispered something into her ear. Sadie giggled and gave him a playful push.

As one they looked up, love and happiness radiating from their every pore.

Beside him, Emma tensed.

Sadie moved forward and extended her hand. 'Hi, I'm Sadie... Sadie North.' She laughed and gestured helplessly. 'I'm still getting used to saying my married name.'

Emma smiled, but lines of tension pulled at the corners of her eyes.

'Are you from Venice, Emma, or are you visiting too?'

'She's running away, apparently,' Johnny said, with a wink in Emma's direction.

Sadie clapped her hands in delight. 'Really? How exciting! I couldn't think of anywhere more awesome to run to. Right? Isn't Venice seriously incredible? Gosh, so many times in the past I was tempted to run away. Especially from some of the directors I have had to work with! Not to mention some of the disastrous relationships I've had.'

Sadie paused and, looking in Matteo's direction, gave a light laugh.

'Not counting *you*, Matteo, you were one of the good ones.'

Beside him he could feel Emma stiffen even more. Sadie had no filter. Maybe that was what made her such an acclaimed actor. She was open and candid and most of the time she got away with it, because people found her directness and fun personality refreshing. But tonight, on the high of new love, she was oblivious to the signals Emma was giving that this conversation was making her uncomfortable.

But perhaps it was just he who could read Emma? Maybe others wouldn't see the subtle signals. It was a thought way too disturbing to spend time pondering on.

Sadie's hand moved onto Johnny's chest. 'But now I no longer want to run.'

The honeymooning couple shared an intense and private look.

Emma flinched.

His stomach dipped with sharp regret.

For Emma. For himself.

What Sadie and Johnny shared they would never have.

Sadie twisted back to them, her eyes shining with the wonder only those newly in love and small children could conjure. 'Isn't Venice so cool? The buildings, the food, the canals, the Carnival…it's all so beautiful. It's just perfect for a honeymoon.' She turned to Johnny, who was looking down at her with fond amusement. 'I want to come back here for each of our anniversaries.'

Emma's body gave up a hard tremor that vibrated against his hand. She was staring at Sadie and Johnny with a haunted expression. Shame and guilt ripped through him.

He needed to get her away from here. He should have anticipated this.

But before he could speak Sadie said, 'Matteo, you never told me about Emma. How long have you been together?'

He forced himself to give a casual shrug. 'We're just colleagues.'

'Ah. That's a shame. You're cute together.'

He gave a tight smile. 'We had better circulate.'

Then, to his horror, he realised that there were tears in Emma's eyes.

He was about to suggest that they step out onto the terrace for a moment when Elena the interpreter approached.

'I'm sorry to interrupt, Signor Vieri, but Mr Xue has asked to meet with you in private.'

It could only mean one thing. Mr Xue was ready to sign the contracts. His instinct that the deal would be finalised on the news that Sadie and Johnny would open the collection had been right.

He should get those contracts signed now. He had copies ready and waiting in his office.

But what about Emma? Could he leave her in this vulnerable state?

Should he talk to her, reassure her, and let Mr Xue wait?

It should be no contest.

His business, or this woman he had only known for a matter of days.

He leaned down towards Emma and said, 'I'll be back in a little while.'

He gave a swift nod to Sadie and Johnny before walking towards Mr Xue, Elena following.

Alone with Sadie and Johnny, Emma looked at the honeymooning couple, who were now playfully teasing each other, oblivious to her. Oblivious to the entire room.

For the first time since the police had knocked at her door in the middle of the night she felt her heart shatter. The shock and disbelief were finally giving way to the reality of everything she had lost. All those fantasies she'd had of a beautiful wedding day. A romantic honeymoon. Of finding her own family.

Her heart shattered because she and her ex had never had the love, the fun, the chemistry that was between Sadie and Johnny.

Her heart shattered out of happiness for the couple before her. Touched by the magic playing between them. Touched by the glow lighting up their eyes. Touched by the heartbreaking happiness pulsating from them both.

Her heart shattered because Matteo hadn't realised just how hard it was for her to witness a couple on honeymoon, to hear Sadie talk so exuberantly about her time in Venice.

Or maybe he had realised and had still opted to go and speak to Mr Xue.

And who could blame him with so much at stake?

He'd made the right decision.

But that didn't stop the hurt. Didn't stop the loneliness creeping along her veins. The reality that she was alone in this world. The horrible hollowness in her soul.

We're just colleagues.

His words to Sadie gathered around her shattered heart like barbed wire.

She shouldn't want anything else but the friendship of a colleague. But the chemistry between them was so intense, so personal, it was hard to keep it at bay.

And now everything was mixed up. People thought she was here as Matteo's partner. Nobody had realised she was the event co-ordinator. Had she compromised her professional standing?

She distractedly said goodbye in Sadie and Johnny's direction, but they were so taken up in each other she wasn't sure if they even noticed her walk away.

She moved about the *palazzo*, trying to focus on managing the reception. She forced herself to stop and talk briefly to some of the guests, but she felt too vulnerable. Too confused.

Was her attraction to Matteo just a way of not facing the pain of her wedding imploding? A distraction from guilt and sadness and her fears for the future? Was she hoping he'd save her instead of saving herself?

Back inside the ballroom, the quartet had been replaced by a jazz band with a soulful lead singer who reminded Emma of Ella Fitzgerald. Couples were out on the dance floor, dancing to a slow number.

'*Vuoi ballare?* Do you want to dance?'

She arched her neck away, a long shiver of awareness darting down her spine at Matteo's question, breathed against her ear from behind…a slow, sensual caress on her exposed neck.

He didn't wait for her to answer. Instead he took her hand and led her out onto the dance floor.

He held her close to him and they moved to the slow rhythm of the music.

She tried to resist him, her body rigid as she stared at the fine navy wool of his jacket.

He pulled her closer, whispered in a teasing, sexy tone, 'Relax, I don't bite…unless provoked.'

Immediately she felt undone.

His hand resting on her hip sent waves of desire to the centre of her body. She yearned for his thumb to stroke the delicate skin around her hip bone.

Standing so close to him, surrounded by his raw potency, one hand resting on his broad shoulder, her other hand lost in his grasp, she felt her heart double over, craving intimacy and closeness with him.

She stared at the broad silver and navy diagonal lines of his tie. Wanting to move even closer to him. Knowing she should move away. Protect herself. Be nothing more than his employee. Be a strong and independent woman who thought of nothing but her career. Who didn't fall for false fantasies.

She dared a quick glance up into those golden-brown eyes which stared back at her with open concern.

That concern could either undo her or reinforce her resolve to be distant from him. She chose the latter. 'I thought you had a meeting with Mr Xue?'

'I've organised for us to meet tomorrow morning instead.'

Confused, she asked, 'I assumed he wanted to meet about signing the contracts—are they still holding out?'

'No, just now Mr Xue confirmed that he wants to sign. There are some small outstanding issues that still need to be resolved, but they won't be a problem. I decided that we should wait until tomorrow to address those.'

Why hadn't he wanted to sign tonight? She knew how important those contracts were to him. A horrible thought occurred to her.

'Were you worried about leaving the party…? If you'd had another co-host would you have taken the time to sign the contracts tonight?'

He held her gaze, his expression sombre. 'I should have realised meeting Sadie and Johnny would be difficult for you.'

'No… Yes… But that was no reason to put off the signing.'

'It can wait.'

'But why, when it's so important to you?'

His mouth thinned. 'You're an employee and I put you in a difficult situation. I take the welfare of all my employees seriously. I could see that you needed my support.'

This wasn't what she wanted. She didn't want to need him. Or anyone else. She wanted, *needed* to stand on her own two feet. To be independent.

'I can manage by myself. I don't need you.'

Those brown eyes held hers with an assured certainty. His mouth was a serious line.

'Yes, you do.'

CHAPTER SEVEN

STANDING BESIDE MATTEO on Ca' Divina's landing stage, Emma waved goodbye to the last of the guests before curling her arms tight against her waist. Warming herself. Fending off the pinpricks of awareness that she was alone once again with Matteo. Not quite certain how she felt about that.

It was gone one in the morning. Most of the other guests had left two hours ago. But the remaining group—associates of Matteo—had stayed and chatted around the outside terrace table, wrapped up in coats and blankets, warmed by outside heaters and *grappa*, snug against the cold February air, while the staff had tidied up inside.

Matteo had insisted that everyone speak in English, so that Emma was included in the conversation. He had kept her by his side all evening, his hand resting on her back, guiding her as they moved amongst the guests. It was a hand that was way too comforting. A hand that had at times fooled her into feeling that she had found someone who would care for her; protect her—before her brain kicked in and told her that she was a fool.

It was all nothing more than a rebound fantasy. She was projecting onto Matteo her need for security. Her fears for the future. All the uncertainties facing her. Where would she live? How long before she got a job? Before her meagre savings ran out?

And that wasn't fair on him. Or herself.

He was her boss—a colleague.

Nothing else.

He didn't want a relationship.

The lights and the noise of the engine on the launch taking the guests away faded across the water. The only sound that remained was the lap of water against the walls of the *palazzo* and the landing stage.

'I'm sorry about Sadie; I should have realised that meeting someone on honeymoon would be upsetting for you.'

He spoke slowly, as though needing her to understand the sincerity of his words.

She bunched her hands in the pockets of her wool coat, felt the soft material grating against the tension in her fists. She needed to keep this conversation professional. Keep her guard up against his employer's concern. Against how physically aware she was of him.

'I didn't need you to cancel the meeting with Mr Xue.'

He pointed towards the *palazzo*, gesturing for them to head back inside. 'You were upset. I couldn't leave you… especially when I could have prevented it.'

The red carpet, hastily organised via a business contact of the caterers, still remained on the wooden landing stage, soaking up the sound of their footsteps.

'But why delay signing the contract?'

Matteo held open one of the heavy wood-panelled double front doors for her, and then busied himself shutting and securing it once they were both inside. When finished he turned and regarded her with a look she couldn't quite decipher.

The hired staff had left prior to the departure of the last of the guests. Matteo now locking the two of them into the *palazzo*, all alone, suddenly felt very intimate. Very personal.

He took off his coat, dipping his head down. When he

looked up his jaw worked for a few seconds, as if he were fighting something inside himself.

'You said today that I need to believe I can deal with whatever life throws at me. You're right.'

He paused for a short breath, but then continued on at a fast pace. Sounding as though he needed to say all this now or never.

'I need to stop worrying about the future; it's too draining. For as long as I can remember I've felt a huge burden of responsibility. It's still there, but I need to get things into perspective and know what my priorities should be.'

'You didn't need to delay the meeting because of me… or insist I stay with you all night. I'm an employee… I don't expect any of that from you.'

Her voice echoed off the high ceilings of the entrance hall. Sharp and petulant.

He walked to the stairs and waited on the bottom step for her to follow. A new tension pulled on his mouth. When she'd joined him he pointed down at her sandals.

'Take them off.'

Taken aback, she stared down at her feet blankly. And then, not quite knowing why, she set her mouth into a fierce scowl. 'No.'

He glared at her, his eyes dark with anger…and passion.

A current of desire whooshed through the air.

He flung his coat onto the balustrade. It slid for a second before coming to a stop beside one of the carved figures of a young woman holding a light aloft that topped both of the stairs' newel posts.

He placed his hands on his hips.

She gave him a *don't you dare* stare.

Which only seemed to embolden him.

In one quick movement he was beside her. Then he was walking up the stairs with her in his arms.

She wanted to demand to know what he thought he was

playing at. But she wouldn't give him the satisfaction of showing she cared enough to ask.

Crushed against the hard heat of his chest, the muscles of his forearm tense beneath her back, she felt long fingers clasp around her outer thigh. She refused to look up at him. Flames of desire burned in her belly.

He dropped her at the top of the stairs and gave her a stare of utter exasperation. 'I could see that you needed support tonight. Why are you blaming me for wanting to be there for you?'

Her confusion boiled and simmered inside her, along with frustration. Because she damn well wanted him to kiss her right now. To feel his body pushed against hers.

'You're my boss!'

He threw his hands upwards at her shouted words, but something in his eyes—a tiny hesitation before he spoke— told her that he too had his doubts about what was happening between them.

'So? Can't a boss care?'

No. Not when there's fire between you.

She rubbed her hand against the tightness in her temple 'It's all getting too confusing.'

He didn't speak, and in the unsettling silence she pretended a sudden fascination with Odysseus's ship on the wall behind his shoulder.

'I'm fond of you, Emma. I want to help.'

His low-spoken words curled around her. Like a tight fist around her heart.

She wanted to tell him that she was afraid. Afraid of falling for him. Afraid of how intensely she liked him already. Afraid of how attracted she was to him.

With a helpless questioning show of her palms, she gave him a truth she could hide behind. 'Why help…when I'm more of a burden to you than anything else?'

'No.'

He moved closer. His eyes dared her to look away, to deny what he was saying.

'I like spending time with you. I like how you stand up to me. Your sense of humour. Your enthusiasm.'

She couldn't listen to this. She had to ignore his words and how badly her heart wanted to believe him.

She shook her head and gave him a teasing frown. Pretended that it was all rather amusing. 'Really? I spend more time in tears than anything else.'

'You found out on your wedding day that the man you were about to marry was corrupt—of *course* you're in tears.'

Hearing his blunt words killed the pretence. And in the face of his soft, searching eyes which refused to look away, the truth bubbled out of her.

'I don't know what I want any longer.'

Embarrassed by her admission, she moved away and walked over to the window overlooking the canal on the opposite side of the room.

So much for being tough.

How did Matteo manage to get to her every time they spoke?

How did he manage to cut through every pretence?

Why did she feel protected yet in deep danger whenever she was with him?

When Matteo eventually joined her they both stared out of the floor-to-ceiling picture window to the lights of Venice. In a low, matter-of-fact voice, he said, 'I have to leave on Sunday for New York Fashion Week. We have two more days together.'

His eyes swept over her face, waiting for a response. She looked at him blankly, feeling numb at his words. Two days. That was all.

His chest rose heavily as he inhaled a deep breath. 'Mr Xue and his team are travelling to Verona tomorrow after our early-morning meeting. I would like to spend the rest of the day with you—show you Venice.' His mouth curled downwards and he shrugged. 'But it's up to you.'

She needed to understand why he was being so kind to her. What did he want? What could she possibly give him?

'Why are you doing this?'

His eyes narrowed, impatience flaring. 'Why did you spend time showing me those Pilates moves today?'

She didn't have to think about her answer.

'Because I wanted to help you.'

But she stopped herself before she could add, *And I wanted to spend time with you, connect with you. Touch you.*

A reluctant smile grew on his mouth. But his eyes stayed startlingly sober. 'Just as I want to help *you.*'

She closed her eyes for a moment. What was she going to do?

She was still unsure when she opened them again. But seeing him silhouetted against the backdrop of Venice, his face set hard with pride, his eyes burning bright with the strength of his commanding but compassionate personality, she knew he would only ask once. If she said no, the next two days would be nothing more than a business formality.

'I would like to see Venice with you.'

She had tried to speak in a dispassionate voice, but it came out in a rushed whisper.

He nodded, not giving any other reaction, and she spun away, gabbling, 'I'll see you in the morning…'

She was almost at the stairs when he called out, 'You'll need help undoing your dress.'

Her heart and stomach collided midway in her body, and then sickeningly ricocheted back to where they belonged.

She rolled her shoulders before walking towards him,

telling herself just to get it over and done with. He was a colleague. Undoing her dress. Nothing more.

She slipped off her coat and turned her back to him.

His hand touched against her skin.

She jerked away.

Desire—strong, excruciating, wonderful—streamed through her, pooling in her core. Exquisite pressure.

He made no comment, but stepped closer.

His fingertips grazed her skin again. She dipped her head against the fresh wave of need which engulfed her, leaving her afraid to breathe.

The unclasped chain fell downwards, its heavy cool weight swinging like a pendulum against her bare skin.

She should move away. But she stood there and wrapped her hands around her waist. Vulnerable. Exposed. Electrified.

His hand touched the top of her spine. And then, inch by inch, ran down her back to her waist. A definite, deliberate movement. The movement of a man wanting to possess.

Her body gave another intense shiver.

His lips briefly skimmed the top of her shoulder blade.

For a moment she stood there, hoping he would go further. But then she understood. There would be nothing more. Tonight.

She walked away from him, each step an effort. Walked away from the one place where she belonged.

The following morning Matteo left the Hotel Cipriani with a burning sense of having been robbed.

The Chinese deal had been signed.

He felt relieved. But nothing else.

None of the sense of accomplishment that usually came with such a major deal. None of the pleasure that he'd taken yet another step up on the ladder of life, away from the lower rungs that led to the crypts of poverty.

He should be happier.

He manoeuvred his boat around the busy traffic on the Grand Canal, irritation and tiredness destroying any hope of him revelling in his success in the beauty of the Old Lady of the Lagoon on a blue-sky spring morning.

He had woken early, doubts whispering in his ear.

What had he done? Why the hell hadn't he signed the deal last night, when Mr Xue had been ready to do so? What if Mr Xue had changed his mind overnight? Just what had he sacrificed for a woman he'd only known for a handful of days?

Last night at the reception it had felt so right to want to be with her. To want to protect her. To actually *do* something about her resonating words earlier, telling him that he must believe, trust that he could handle whatever life threw at him. That he couldn't allow his fear of poverty, of failing others, to control him.

But in the darkness none of that had seemed so obvious, so right.

He couldn't go back to Ca' Divina yet. Even though he wanted to see her. Wanted to hear her voice. Wanted the calm that formed in his stomach every time he was with her.

The unfathomable sense of belonging that settled on his heart when he was with her.

He needed to clear his head.

At Ca' Foscari he swung the boat towards Campo Santa Margherita in the *sestiere* of Dorsoduro.

As ever, the picturesque square was a serene refuge. Locals were enjoying an early coffee at the cafés lining the square, buying bread at the bakery reputed to be the best in Venice, others were buying fish and vegetables at the market stalls.

Usually he would order an espresso at the bar and drink

it quickly. Always pressed for time. Today he sat out at one of the pavement tables with his espresso.

Dog walkers, grandparents holding the hands of unsteady toddlers, students from the local university—all ambled through the square. Happy to enjoy the start of another Carnival day.

When had he last sat and watched others go by?

Had he ever?

Emma.

She was changing everything.

With her he felt a connection, a bond that was familiar, comforting, yet exhilarating. A physical attraction that was tearing him apart. But there was also her intelligence, her sense of fun. Her vulnerability.

Her pride, her resilience, her strength.

She had lost her career, her family, and had battled to rebuild her life. And now she was determined to rebuild it once again, in the face of yet another abysmal setback.

Yesterday, when she had shown him the Pilates moves, she had done so with such serious intent that he'd known it was important to her to see him better. She cared for him. He could see it in her eyes. In the way her body rocked towards him.

He drained his cup and stared up at the fifteenth-century carving set high up in the building. Santa Margherita and the dragon who had tried to consume her.

His heart suddenly lurched and began to free-fall.

His mind buzzed.

He fought the realisation forming there. Tried to put a stake in the heart of that thought. But it fought back. Ready to consume him.

He was falling in love with Emma.

Was that possible?

The dragon was open-mouthed. Ready to attack again.

This wasn't what he wanted.

This was his worst nightmare.

To fall in love.

He had seen how love had destroyed his mother. Had destroyed his childhood.

This was the last thing he'd ever wanted.

To fall in love with a woman who couldn't, *wouldn't* love him back.

How many times had she said she didn't want to be in love?

She reminded him of himself. Of how definite he'd been about not wanting love.

Until she'd came along.

He was falling in love with the one woman he couldn't have.

This couldn't be happening.

This was why he had always sworn he would never love.

He had stopped believing in love when he was a teenager. Knowing that ultimately it would destroy you.

He felt sick.

He had to pull back.

He had to detach himself from her.

But he couldn't walk away. Not yet.

He wanted the next few days. He wanted to be with her. Two days. No more.

The scheming crocodile loitered behind the little boy who was happily fishing, oblivious to the danger he was in. The children standing in a corner of Campo San Polo, enraptured by the puppet show, shouted and screamed for the little boy to run away.

Their shouts were deafening, and Emma playfully grimaced in the direction of Matteo. But he didn't notice her. In fact for the past half an hour, since they had left Ca' Divina, he had been distant. Distracted.

A vine of anxiety wrapped itself around her left ankle—

not quite hurting, but tight enough to warn her what was to come if she didn't shake off her uneasiness.

What was the matter?

Was he already regretting his decision to spend the day with her?

The sun slanted off his face, highlighting his golden skin. His thick dark eyelashes only occasionally flickered, as though he was in a trance. His mouth was a constant thin line.

Nervous attraction zinged through her veins. She clenched her hand against the temptation to reach out. To touch his cheek. To whisper, *Is everything okay?* To have him smile again.

This morning she had lain in bed, her body twisted towards the bedroom window and the majestic pale pastel buildings and faded red-tiled rooftops beyond. Knowing she had two choices.

Give in to her fear that she would be hurt and walk away now. Away from this too intense, too soon, too confusing relationship.

Or embrace these two remaining days. Two days that could give her a lifetime of happy memories.

But for that to happen she *had* to remember their relationship was boss and employee—colleagues at best. Nothing more.

She moved closer to him and rested her hand on his arm. He looked down at her with a frown, as if he was unsure of everything about her. For a moment awkwardness, suspicion, doubt passed between them.

The twisting sack in her chest tightened. He had changed his mind.

His eyes held hers but then flew away. As if he didn't want to look there.

She was about to make a joke—anything to lighten the tension between them—when she stopped herself. She was doing it again. Being passive. Afraid to rock the boat. Afraid that Matteo might reject her. Afraid that if she spoke her mind he might be angry, dismissive, provoked. Everything she had spent her childhood trying to prevent.

Her stomach lurched and her throat suddenly felt like nothing more than a thin straw through which she had to speak.

It would be so much easier to smile. To jolly him along. Not to have to face the reason why he now didn't want to be here with her.

The spacious square reverberated to the sound of voices. Friends chatting loudly outside pavement cafés. Children chasing around the fountain. Others giggling and whooping on the temporary ice rink. The sounds echoed off the surrounding tall historic buildings.

Sounds which made the silence between them as they walked through the square even more pronounced.

She cleared her throat. 'We can go home if you like.' Her trepidation was hidden behind her sharp, snappy, defensive tone.

He looked at her impassively, as if quietly contemplating her offer. No quick denial, as she had secretly hoped.

'Do you want to?'

No! He wasn't turning this back on her.

She was about to tell him so when her phone began to ring. She flung open her handbag, leaving the two handles hanging from her forearm, and began to rummage through it. Where was it? She could hear it, but for the life of her she couldn't find it.

With a huff, she moved to the window of a nearby antique shop, dominated by the huge gilt frame of a dark religious artwork, and balanced her bag on the stone window ledge as she continued her search. Eventually she found it—under a pile of paperwork.

It was the tour guide, calling from Verona to give her an update on how the Chinese delegation was faring.

She spoke to the guide with her back deliberately towards Matteo, but in the window's reflection she could see that he was staring at her, his arms folded impatiently.

Dressed in a grey wool overcoat, open at the collar to reveal a light blue shirt and a navy pullover, his broad frame loomed large in the window reflection. Dark and menacing. And unfairly gorgeous.

Her anger, her defensiveness, was sinking as fast as it had risen.

When she turned back to him she had reverted to her professional mode. 'That was the tour guide. The group have booked in to their hotel and are about to tour the city. I've confirmed that they need to be back in Venice at five tomorrow, as the ball is starting at eight.'

Tomorrow evening Matteo was hosting the delegation at one of the Carnival's masked balls. She would be Matteo's partner again.

It would be their last event together.

The morning after he would be leaving for New York.

They might never see each other again.

That thought had her inhaling a deep breath against the loneliness that sideswiped her.

The vine clinging to her ankle tightened.

She opened her handbag and threw her phone back into its depths.

Matteo stared in after it. 'I'm surprised that you were able to find your phone in the first place...' He paused and grimaced, as if he was looking into the bowels of hell. 'In *there*.'

Did he have to sound so appalled?

'A woman's handbag is her business. Nobody else's.'

He tucked his arms into a tighter fold across his chest. And shot her an unimpressed eyebrow-raise.

She was about to ignore him. But then the new Emma stepped forward. The Emma who had got on the plane at Heathrow, determined to have her week in Venice. The Emma who'd sworn she would be tough and take no nonsense from anyone again.

Well, she was going straight to the top in giving someone a piece of her mind: Matteo Vieri, the Italian god of fashion.

Her jaw jutted out.

Her shoulder blades were so rigid she reckoned they would easily slice someone in two.

'I had a childhood of not being able to have a hair out of place, in a sterile home that smelt of bleach. That's to blame for my preference for messiness. What about you…? What's made *you* so proper…so strait-laced?'

So the legendary Matteo Vieri *could* do astonishment.

His mouth dropped open for a couple of seconds. And then it slammed shut.

His hands landed on his hips 'Strait-laced?'

'Yes…nothing is ever out of place in Ca' Divina. You are always immaculately groomed. Cufflinks always perfectly aligned, your hair always looking like you're on a fashion shoot. Do you *ever* look messy?'

His expression shifted from narked to nonchalant, as did his tone. 'I own several luxury goods companies. It's my duty to look good. I'm representing my businesses.'

True. But that didn't mean he didn't have down time. Time when he relaxed.

'Do you even *own* a pair of jeans? A tee shirt?'

He gestured to a street that ran beside the church of San Polo, indicating that they start walking again.

The street quickly narrowed to a laneway that could barely accommodate them both walking side by side. She tucked her handbag closer. Worried that in the tight confines she would bump into him. Worried that she might not be able to move away if she did.

'I own…a pair of jeans.'

His deadpan voice held a poorly disguised hint of humour.

A smile broke on her mouth. 'One! Most men I know own at least a dozen.'

His mouth twisted but his eyes were alight with humour. 'Well, I'm *not* most men, am I?'

Despite the shadows of the narrow alleyway, the day suddenly felt bright. Hopeful.

She gave him a cheeky smile. 'No. You're certainly not.'

He smiled back. The doubts, the unease of earlier erased.

They crossed over a canal and he led her down another side alleyway. 'We need to buy you a mask for the ball tomorrow night. There's an atelier down here, close to Campo San Rocco.'

Along the alleyway they passed two boys kicking a soccer ball against a wall, the dull thud in competition with their lively lyrical chatter.

'I liked your friends last night.'

Mischief sparked in his eyes. 'You sound surprised.'

Her mouth twitched. She cleared her throat. 'They're different to you—more laid-back.'

He slowed down as they approached a shop window adorned with masks. Some were stark and frightening, with long, exaggerated pointed noses—the masks of death and plague. Others were ornate and elegant, wisps of beauty and intrigue.

He caught her teasing tone and threw it back to her with an amused shrug. 'I guess…'

He rolled his shoulders and his eyes grew serious.

'Last night I remembered what you said yesterday about trying to enjoy life more, not worrying about the future.'

He gave her a small smile. 'I think you might be right, so I've decided I want to spend time with my friends. In the past I wouldn't have asked them to stay, wanting to catch up with work instead.' He paused and a brief storm of doubt passed over his expression. Quickly it cleared to calm certainty. 'I also wanted them to meet you.'

Not even trying to pretend that she wasn't shocked by what he'd said, she asked, 'Why?'

'You mean a lot to me.'

What did he mean by that?

She opened her mouth to ask, but clamped it shut again. She didn't want to hear his answer.

She wasn't ready for any of this.

So she laughed and said, 'You could have fooled me! All morning you've been acting as though you don't want to be here.'

For a moment he looked as if he was going to argue. His eyes swept over her. Her heart pleaded with him not to. Something even deeper within her pleaded with him to tell her that he felt what she did too.

He tugged at the bottom of his coat sleeves, a rueful grin transforming his expression to one of playful teasing. 'I didn't get enough sleep last night, and I woke early. Can we start again?'

'Do I hear the hint of an apology in there?'

'Yes. I'm sorry.' His smile grew even wider, a sexy challenge now sparkling in his eyes. 'Now, I think it's about time you and I had a little fun.'

CHAPTER EIGHT

AN HOUR LATER, close to Campo San Giacomo dell'Orio, in the *sestiere* of Santa Croce, they paused for lunch at one of Matteo's favourite restaurants in Venice—Alloro. The tiny restaurant, located on the banks of a narrow canal, had a dark wooden interior infused with over a century's worth of cooking aromas: garlic and rosemary, the earthiness of truffle, the hit-you-at-the-back-of-the-throat power of Asiago d'Allevo cheese.

Emma, bright-cheeked from the sharp February air, handed the blue and purple striped box containing her mask for tomorrow night's ball and her navy woollen coat to the maître d', who then showed them to their table overlooking the canal.

Their knees clashed as they settled into the small table, and for a few brief seconds a blast of heat fired between them. Deep longing. Two souls in need.

Emma was the first to look away. Her hands moved quickly to tuck a loose curl behind her ear before she straightened first her knife and then her fork on the starched white linen tablecloth.

He poured them both some water, his gut twisting.

So much for staying detached, unaffected by the realisation that he was falling for her. He had spent most of the morning quarrelsome and argumentative, frustrated with every feeling he had for her.

But the truth of his attraction to her had been determined to leak out. His willpower had proved useless against the continual adrenaline rush of physical chemistry and the emotional connection of being with her. Hope and pleasure were strong-arming fear and resistance.

In the designer's studio she had tried on various styles of masks, at first carefully watching for his reaction.

But then something dark and sensual had whipped between them.

Her eyes had toyed with him from behind the masks. Dancing hazel eyes that could be his undoing.

They had grown bolder and bolder in their teasing and flirting.

Casual touches had skittered across his skin, jolts of pure pleasure.

Smiles had spoken of heart-pounding delicious desire.

For the first time ever he wasn't listening to his own cool logic. The logic that was telling him to walk away. That this was uncharted territory he shouldn't be meddling in. That to have had his heart broken as a child was one thing. To have it broken as an adult would be a whole different matter.

Opposite him, Emma stared at the lunch menu with a frown, her lips silently shaping the words she was reading.

'Would you like some help deciding?'

She shook her head without looking up, her expression fierce. 'No, thank you.'

He smiled to himself. Another piece of his heart was falling for this determined woman.

The waiter returned with a glass of Prosecco for Emma and white wine for him, as he had ordered.

On a deep breath Emma placed her food order in faltering Italian.

The waiter advised her, also in Italian, that her risotto

would take thirty minutes to prepare. She blushed and looked at the waiter clearly confused.

Matteo translated for her, trying not to smile.

She nodded that it was okay, giving the waiter a faint smile.

When the waiter left, he lifted his glass. 'To new friends.'

Emma touched her glass to his and then gave a quick shoulder-roll. She drew in a deep breath. *'Ai nuovi amici.'*

'I'm impressed.'

'No, my pronunciation is terrible. I tried to learn some Italian before the wed—'

Her eyes swept away from his.

At first she grimaced. Then a haunting sadness settled over her features. Remembering the past was physically hurting her.

He shifted in his seat, his heels digging into the parquet floor.

Top notes of disgust and anger filled his nostrils to think of her ex, but deep in his belly the only note was one of jealousy.

She had almost married another man.

What if he had seen her out on the streets of Venice with her new husband?

Would the rage of attraction he had felt for her the first time they'd met still have been the same even though she was in the arms of another man?

Would he have walked away with a sense of loss?

With feelings he couldn't process for a woman he had merely passed in the street?

But would he have been better off if he *had* only seen her from a distance?

Would he have been better off never even setting eyes on her?

He lanced those uncomfortable, troubling thoughts with

a question that drew him back to the reality of their situation.

'What are your plans for the future?'

Emma tugged at the neck of her cream polo-neck jumper. The same jumper she had worn the first night they had met.

'I'm going back to London.'

'To your old job?'

Her hand rubbed against her neck and then patted upwards to the base of her ponytail, her fingers attempting to smooth down the renegade curls that insisted on breaking free from the confines of her elastic band.

'No. I want to start afresh. I've enjoyed this week, so I've decided that I want to work in event management full-time.'

'You've done an excellent job for me. I'm sure you'll be very successful.'

She rested an arm on the table, a shoulder and an eyebrow rising simultaneously in challenge. 'I wouldn't go so far as saying *excellent*.'

'You're intelligent, flexible, personable and warm…and most of the time you're organised. You have all the traits needed to be a successful event manager.'

A deep blush erupted from the depths of her jumper, spewing upwards. She angled herself away from him, a hand hiding the lower half of her face. Pride and embarrassment vied for dominance in her gaze.

Ultimately neither won. Instead she batted away his words with a smile that was too fleeting, too nervous, too forced.

'And what's in the future for Matteo Vieri? World domination?'

She didn't trust him.

She didn't trust what he said.

He gritted his teeth and tried to ignore the sharp tap of

her distrust that was prodding against his heart like the tip of a sword.

Threatening to stab him.

He slowly twisted the circular base of his wine glass on the linen cloth. Disquiet rolled in his stomach. *He needed to protect himself.*

'It's going to be a busy year. I have all the upcoming Fashion Weeks, I'm looking to expand aggressively into South America and I'm in the midst of a major renovation of my villa on Lake Garda.'

She nodded. And nodded again.

She yanked once more at the neck of her jumper. Beneath it her throat worked. Her pale toffee-mixed-with-peppermint eyes held his, but with a hesitancy, a sadness that sent that emotional sword she wielded straight through his raging heart.

'We're both going to be busy.'

Yes. Living separate lives.

The waiter arrived with their antipasti: asparagus and quail eggs for Emma, *carpaccio* for him.

He lifted his knife and fork, tasted his food and lowered his cutlery again.

Too distracted to eat.

The urge to connect with her, to reach out, detonated within him.

Without any thought he heard himself blurt out, 'When I was a child I lived close to here for a few years.'

Why had he told her that?

She too lowered her cutlery, her antipasto barely touched. 'What do you remember?'

Tension pinged like electric shocks in the small of his back. He moved forward in his chair and rested both arms on the table, stretching his spine. 'The apartment was on the third floor. I could see the Frari Campanile clearly from my bedroom window. At night, I used to pretend that...'

The words that had been spilling out of him dried up in an instant.

He had never spoken to anyone about his childhood before now.

He needed to stop.

'Pretend what?'

He didn't answer her question. Instead he stared down at the brilliant whiteness of the tablecloth, the loneliness of those years engulfing him.

Itchy, suffocating heat blasted his insides.

Her knees bumped against his. Her hands landed on his. Long, slim, pale hands that sat lightly against his skin. Not cloying or overpowering.

Just there.

His heart decelerated.

He closed his eyes.

Eventually he spoke. Needing to tell her. 'I used to pretend that my father watched me from the Frari Campanile. That he had come…that he had found me.'

'Found you…what do you mean?'

Her voice was gentle. Her eyes, when he looked up, were calm and accepting, inviting him to tell her all about himself. Inviting him into her life. Inviting him to trust in her.

Maybe if he showed that he trusted her she would learn to trust in him.

But at what cost?

Time slowed down. Around them people chatted. A gondola with no passengers on board passed outside their window. Was the gondolier going home to his family? To his wife and children?

'I never knew…' He paused, unable to finish the sentence, unable to say the words *my father*.

'But you wanted to?'

'Up until I was nine years old I believed he would one day come and live with us. My mother said that he would.'

'But he didn't?'

'No. My mother told me when I was nine that she had met a man and we moved into his apartment in Rome. I kept asking her… What about my father? How would he find us now that we had moved? She told me that he would never come. That he didn't even know that I existed…and she had no way of letting him know.'

'Who *is* your father?'

A tight cord wrapped around his throat. He struggled to swallow. 'Apart from his name…Paul…I don't know.'

Her fingers curled a fraction more tightly on his hands.

Her cool skin was a balm to the heat burning in his stomach.

'My mother was eighteen when they met. He was an American student, travelling through Europe. He and my mother met at a music festival in Rome. They spent the weekend together. It was only after he had left that my mother realised that she was pregnant.'

'Did she try to find him?'

'She knew his first name—Paul—but couldn't remember his last name. She hadn't thought it was important. They were teenagers having fun.'

'It must have been tough for your mum, bringing you up alone.'

'We didn't have a lot of money. Her work was precarious. She worked as a model; but never got the big-earning jobs. My grandmother lived with us too, on and off.'

Memories collided in his stomach. He sucked in some air at the punches they delivered. The constant worry of not having money. His mother's mood swings. The sobs coming from behind the bathroom door at night. Her red-rimmed eyes clashing with her cheery smile when she walked from the bathroom in a cloud of steam. Pretending, burying, denying.

Those memories pushed upwards, heavy in his chest, spewing from his throat.

'When I was younger she never dated. Now I know she was hoping that my father would return. That by some miracle he would find her. On the tenth anniversary of them meeting she even went to the concert venue. Hoping he'd be there. She told me all this when I was older. All night she stood outside. Hoping. But he never came. After that she gave up hoping and started dating other men. She ping-ponged from one relationship to another. Within weeks of her meeting a new boyfriend we would move in with him. We even moved countries so that she could be with them. Invariably she would either end the relationship or behave so appallingly that her boyfriend would end it.'

He took a gulp of his wine.

'When I was sixteen she broke it off with a man who was perfect for her, who loved her. She would have had a good life with him. I knew she was fond of him so I was angry, frustrated. We had a massive argument which ended in her admitting that she had never got over losing my father. She claims that she fell in love with him the moment she first saw him, queuing ahead of her at the entrance to the concert, but didn't realise it until after he had left. She says that she's still in love with him.'

The waiter came once again and glanced at their table, clearly confused as to why their plates were still practically untouched.

Matteo asked him to take them away.

When the waiter had gone, Emma gave him a wide-eyed look of disbelief. 'She's still in love with him? Even though they only spent a weekend together?'

He couldn't blame her for her incredulous tone. 'I know. I told her she was living a fantasy. She disagreed. But ever since that night when we argued she hasn't dated again. She says that she now realises she was always trying to replicate her love for my father with other men. And that it will never work because her heart is still with my father.'

'That's so sad. For her and you.' Her tone was sombre, sincere.

He shrugged. 'These things happen. She was a good mother in most respects... She looked so young that when I was a boy people assumed she was my older sister. That my grandmother was my mother.'

'Did you mind that people thought that?'

He *had* minded. A lot. Not only had he not known his father but people had constantly assumed the wrong person was his mother.

'It didn't help that we constantly moved, and my mother stood out compared to the other mothers. She was so much younger. She never managed to become part of a community. It always felt like we were on the outside.'

'I'm sorry.'

'I'm not. It taught me that I needed to be self-reliant. It gave me a determination to succeed.'

'And you *have* succeeded.'

Had he? Until this week he had thought he had. But now all those certainties about what he wanted in life were crumbling.

'Perhaps.'

'I'm sorry you never got to know your dad, Matteo. For your mum to love him so much still he must be a special person. And I'm sorry your childhood was so disruptive as a result...it's all really sad.'

He drew back into his own chair.

It *was* sad.

He had never thought of it like that before.

Instead he had shut himself down. He had lived only for protecting himself against poverty, against allowing others to hurt him again. Had he been living in an emotional vacuum all that time?

Emma was waiting for him to respond. He could not meet her eye.

He tugged at his shirt-cuffs. 'I got used to it. Lots of children grow up in one-parent homes.'

'Yes…but it sounds like your mum was always searching for happiness. That must have had an impact on you.'

He closed his eyes for a moment. But the darkness did nothing to assail the memories of the summer when he'd turned twelve.

Francesco.

In the corridor outside his Turin apartment. Begging his mother not to leave. Clinging to him. Feeling Francesco's arms so tight around his torso that he couldn't breathe.

Francesco begging his mother not to take him away. Not the boy he considered his own son.

Panic had gripped him.

He'd been terrified that she would take him away. Equally terrified that she might leave without him.

Now his throat felt raw with emotion. A separate entity from the rest of his body. As if all his emotions were concentrated there.

He wanted this conversation to end.

Now.

It had gone too far.

He didn't want to talk about his past any longer.

'I guess.'

The only indication that Emma wasn't convinced by his answer was an almost imperceptible narrowing of her eyes before she asked, 'Are you close to your mum now?'

Their argument when he was sixteen had left them both raw and bruised, but in the years since they had formed a truce. A truce based on burying the past. Ignoring past hurts. It had worked for them. Hadn't it?

'Yes. And with *Nonnina*—my grandmother…'

Glad of a way to break the heavy emotion bouncing between them, he smiled and added, 'Even if she *does* bring home waifs and strays.'

Her eyes duelled with his for a few seconds. A smile of tenderness lightly lifted her full lips. But then it faded. 'You're lucky to have them.'

Her words were spoken with a gentle wistfulness.

It pulled him up short.

Despite all their faults—his mother's tempestuous nature, his grandmother's anger on behalf of the poor that so often got her into trouble with the authorities—he *was* lucky to have them in his life. He had never stopped to appreciate just how much before now.

'Yes, I guess I *am* lucky,' he said.

He had family.

Emma had none.

A wave of protectiveness towards her swept through him. What was the future going to bring her? Who would look out for her? Who was going to be in her corner, fighting for her, supporting her, cheering her on?

Who was going to ask the hard questions? Challenge her?

'Will you go back to ballet?'

Emma's fingers trailed lightly against the rosemary growing in a small green metal pot to the side of their table. She prodded the pot with a finger until it tilted.

Why on earth was he asking her about ballet? Hearing him speak about his childhood had brought a feeling of closeness and understanding between them. She didn't want it to end. Talking about ballet was the last thing she wanted to do.

'Where does your mum live now?'

'In Puglia. What about you going back to ballet?'

He wasn't going to let it go. The challenge in his eyes told her so. Why was it so difficult to answer his question?

Was it because of the intimacy that had been growing all morning? Their earlier argument? Their laughter in the mask studio? Matteo opening up just now about his past? The connection, closeness, *confidence* of his admissions? The fact that he trusted her enough to share his past?

It was thrilling, yet terrifying. Could she ever again trust a man enough to reveal what was in her heart?

For a few seconds she hesitated on the brink of telling him everything—how she was terrified of dreaming again. Scared to dare risking her heart to ballet, to a man. Her fear of it all going wrong yet again.

'Go back to ballet? Why should I? It's in my past.'

Much too intelligent soft brown eyes held hers. 'It doesn't have to be.'

Her gaze shifted to the elegant middle-aged couple at the next table, who were leaving amidst much chatter and laughter. The woman was searching under the table for forgotten items. The man was patting his pockets. Mentally checking his belongings.

'I want it to be in my past.'

'Why?'

His quietly spoken question crept through the cage of fear engulfing her heart, and the tender expression in his eyes released—just a little—the burden of failure clogging her throat.

'Because it hurts too much to think about what I lost.'

'But you could create a new future in ballet through teaching, Pilates instruction, choreography... Maybe you can find something even better than you had ever hoped for.'

'And what if I don't? What if it only brings up bad memories or I fail again?'

'You have to take risks in life, otherwise it will be a life half lived.'

He was wrong. Risks...daring to dream...led to bitter

disappointment, despair. She would prefer to live a life of caution, knowing just how cruel life could be, rather than have every hope wiped out again in the blink of an eye— in the seconds it took to fall down some stairs, the seconds it took for a policeman to rap at your door.

'I want to focus on my career.'

'You can have more than your career.'

'Seriously? *You*, Mr Workaholic, are telling *me* that?'

'Nobody said I was perfect.'

From where she was sitting he seemed pretty perfect to her. His open-necked blue shirt hinted at the golden-skinned muscular chest beneath, and long, elegant fingers were toying with his glass...toying with her heart.

'So are you saying that *you* might open up your life to other things?'

Matteo rocked back in his chair, answering her question with a brief shrug.

Irked by his nonchalance, feeling a desire to provoke him, she asked, 'How about a relationship?'

He leaned forward in his chair, his hand once again twisting and twisting the stem of his glass. 'Maybe, if... *Dio*, I don't know.'

He threw himself back into his chair. Raised a hand in the air in exasperation.

Outside, the sun disappeared behind a white puffball cloud. The shaft of light that had been highlighting the chestnut depths of his hair, the golden tone of his skin, disappeared.

The chatter of the other diners dimmed in her ears. Her heartbeat drummed against her chest.

'She'll be a lucky person.'

His eyes searched hers. 'Will she?'

She bit down on her impulse to laugh, to tease him. To ask him glibly why *any* woman wouldn't feel lucky to be the partner of a gorgeous, intelligent, kind man.

But to do so would be a disservice.

He deserved more from her. He deserved the truth. Not some superficial answer.

She shuffled forward in her chair, leaned towards him.

Her eyes locked with his and her heart was now in her throat, her tummy coiling tighter and tighter.

'Only if you open your heart to her.'

Her answer came out in a whisper.

He blinked as he took in her words. And then his gaze became one of tender intensity.

He was looking at her in a way that no man had ever stared at her. As though she was the only person alive, ever to have existed.

Her heart sank back down into her chest and exploded into a million droplets of pleasure, of wistfulness, of emotional desire for the man sitting opposite her.

The waiter appeared at her side, a large white circular porcelain plate in each hand. She jumped in alarm. For a moment she had forgotten where she was.

When the waiter had left, she dubiously prodded her risotto with her fork. It was ink-black in colour.

Not what she had expected.

She glanced over to Matteo.

'Your first time having black cuttlefish risotto?' he asked with a teasing grin.

'It's so strange-looking—not exactly appetising.'

'Try it—it's delicious.'

'It looks like something spewed up by a volcano.'

He shook his head, laughing. 'Trust me...try it.'

She picked up some grains with her fork. Stared at it for a while and then tentatively popped it in her mouth. Salt. The taste of the sea. Garlic. She tried another forkful. And then another. She lowered her fork with a sigh.

'Oh, wow. That's *so* good. I'll have to add it to my list of favourite Italian food.'

'You like Italian food?'

She took another forkful and answered his grin with her own smile. 'I *adore* Italian food.'

He spiralled some of the spaghetti from his soft-shelled crab, langoustines and tomato sauce dish before saying, 'You'll have to come back and visit again some time.'

He spoke as though his invitation was sincere. As though he actually believed it would be possible.

She hid her confusion behind a teasing smile. 'Maybe. Although it's much more likely that the next time we meet I'll be at the end of a walkie-talkie while you are swanning around some glitzy event in London.'

His eyes twinkled. 'I'll make sure to wave to you.'

She gave a sigh and shook her head. 'We're really from different worlds.'

'No. Same world. Same problems and doubts.'

Hardly. He was rich and successful. She was a runaway bride without a job or a home. But now was not the time to point those facts out. Now was about forgetting about the past *and* the future.

'If I'm in a good mood I'll make sure to send you over a martini with lemon peel instead of champagne.'

He paused in twirling his pasta. 'You remembered?'

Her heart danced with pleasure at being the focus of his smile. 'Of course.'

He reached over and stole some of her risotto. 'And I'll tell the host just how incredible his event co-coordinator is.'

She playfully pulled her plate out of his reach. 'Make sure to add that I'm deserving of a bonus.'

As they ate the rest of their meal they spoke about food. Matteo grew increasingly appalled on hearing Emma's description of her boarding school fare.

As the waiter cleared away their main course Matteo said, 'Tinned sausages, gravy and potatoes…? It sounds horrible.'

Emma gave a shudder. 'Trust me, it tasted even worse.'

Matteo frowned hard, as though her boarding school's food was an affront to all humanity. When the waiter had left, he said, 'I will cook for you some day...to make up for all that terrible food.'

At first they smiled, both enjoying the teasing. But then their smiles faded. And Emma felt her cheeks grow hot. Her entire body, in fact.

His eyes darkened.

Silence pulsated between them.

He leaned towards her.

Her heart wobbled and quivered and pinched in her chest.

Serious, intent, masculine eyes devoured her, travelling down over her mouth, her throat, lingering on the pull of her jumper over her breasts.

'I have a surprise I want to show you.'

Her stomach tumbled at the low, sensual timbre of his voice.

She nodded.

Followed him on giddy legs when he stood.

Outside, she didn't object when he reached for her hand. His touch sent her heart careening around her body. The ever-growing ache in her body was physically hurting now.

Ten minutes later she found herself at the rear street entrance to Ca' Divina.

Puzzled, she asked, 'What about my surprise?'

Opening the door, Matteo unbuttoned his coat and gave her a mischievous smile. 'A little patience, please.'

Emma paused at the door, thrown by how much she wanted to be here. In Ca' Divina. Alone with him.

Inside, she followed him up to the second floor. At the end of the corridor, past all the bedrooms, Matteo pressed firmly against the pale-blue-painted wall. A hidden door popped open. Emma gave a gasp of surprise.

Behind the door was a staircase, a skylight high above it filling the wood-panelled stairway with warm light. Dense, peaceful air filled the enclosed space.

At the top of the stairs he opened a dark wood-panelled door and led her out onto a flat red-brick roof terrace. Large bay trees in pots were dotted around the vast space; all-weather outdoor furniture stood at the centre.

She moved about the terrace, her hand lifting silently, a huge beam of excitement on her face. Pointing to St Mark's Basilica, Campanile San Giorgio Maggiore in the south, the Rialto Bridge to the east, the utter beauty of the Grand Canal below.

She left out a happy, thrilled laugh. 'This is so *incredible*.'

Matteo leaned against the stone balustrade overlooking the canal. Watching her. Amused. 'I told you to trust me.'

She was feeling decidedly giddy. Especially with the way he was looking at her. Interested. More than interested. With a definite spark.

She gave him a cheeky smile. 'So you did.'

He gestured to her to come over to where he was standing. A quick, flirting curl of his index finger. There was a lazy, sexy smile on his lips. Something dark and dangerous sparking in his eyes.

Adrenaline zipped through her.

She went and stood beside him. Convinced he must be able to sense the buzz vibrating through her body.

He turned and pointed to the south. 'Do you see the red-brick *campanile* to the east?' She nodded and he continued, 'The *palazzo* next to it is where, according to legend, Casanova once lived.'

His voice was low, knee-wobblingly sexy. He was flirting with her.

Her heart thrashed against her breastbone. A light, swirling ache went through her. She inhaled deeply, her lungs fighting her juddering heart.

'Casanova…the gambler…' she paused and looked him in the eye, trying to ignore the heat firing in her cheeks '…the famous lover.'

He edged a little closer to her. Inches separated them as they stood against the balustrade. A light breeze fanned her burning cheeks.

'Apparently he once held a lover imprisoned there when he didn't want her to leave.'

Her entire body tingled. In a croaky voice she said, 'He was a renowned lover…maybe she didn't mind.'

She stared into heated, dangerous, intent eyes.

His hand reached out and grabbed the belt of her coat. He pulled her towards him.

A dangerous smile broke on his mouth. 'I wonder how many nights he kept her there, imprisoned in his bed?'

Every bone in her body melted. 'I suppose until he was satisfied…'

His head moved down towards hers.

Musk and vanilla…his heat grew stronger. Set her heart to a different beat.

His mouth hovered over hers.

He breathed out, his warm breath playing on her skin.

For a lifetime they remained inches apart, their bodies pulsating, time suspended.

He pulled her in even closer to the hardness of his body. 'I can't stand this any longer.'

His deep voice, impassioned with need, spun like magic thread around her, pulling her closer and closer.

In a sigh, she breathed, 'Me too.'

His hand captured her cheek. A thumb stroked the sensitive skin beneath her ear. '*Voglio fare l'amore con te.* I want to make love with you.' His grip tightened. 'I want to take you to my bed. *Now*.'

She closed her eyes, moved her head so that her lips grazed against his palm 'I want that too.'

He drew back an inch, blinked hard. 'What about the future?'

She shook her head an inch to the right. To the left. Desire had left her too weak to move with any more effort. 'We don't have one…but we *do* have now.'

'And that's enough?'

She hesitated. Her physical need for him was making her dizzy. The core of her body was shouting out for him. Silencing her heart, which wanted to know what she was playing at.

He opened her coat, pushed up her jumper.

On a gasp she breathed out. 'It has to be.'

CHAPTER NINE

AT LUNCHTIME THE following day Emma paused at Matteo's office door. Her mouth dried as she drank in the broad width of his shoulders beneath his dark blue shirt, the fact that his hair was still dishevelled from when she had run her hands through it earlier.

But in the pit of her stomach unease stirred.

She pushed it away. Disquiet, doubts, disbelief—they could come tomorrow.

When he was gone.

Sadness and regrets were for the future.

Not now.

She knocked lightly on the office door. 'Hi, I'm back.'

Matteo leaned away from his desk, a hand running through his hair, smoothing it down. A sexy smile grew on his gorgeous mouth, competing for her attention with the fondness shining in his eyes.

He nodded towards the shopping bags she was carrying. 'You found what you needed?'

She walked further into the room and dropped the bags to the floor. Her hand touched against the soft brown leather of the tub chair in front of his desk.

'Eventually. Thanks to a lot of pointing and hand gestures. Although at one point it looked a distinct possibility that we were about to have a fish that resembled a deflated soccer ball rather than mussels for lunch.'

His laughter tripped along her veins. Her fingers squeezed the soft leather of the chair. For a moment it felt as if gravity didn't apply to her. Dizzying memories came of their heads colliding in bed last night and Matteo pretending to be concussed. She had tested that pretence by slowly kissing him, until he had groaned in capitulation and tossed her onto her back.

She should go and make lunch. Her forfeit for being the first to beg in a game this morning.

His laughter died. And now his intense gaze wrapped her in a bubble of glorious hope.

'I missed you.'

She looked away. Unable to cope with the sincerity in his eyes. 'I doubt that—you were engrossed in your work just now.'

With a playful grin Matteo stood and walked towards her.

Anticipation tickled her insides. She was not going to blush. Or think about what he had done to her body last night. How she had moaned as his mouth had travelled down her body, staying far too long at her breasts.

He stood over her, his grin now plain sexy, thanks to the heat in his eyes. His scent rocketed through her senses, leaving her temporarily stunned and having to fight the temptation to close her eyes, sigh, lean into him.

'You're determined not to believe a word I say, aren't you?'

She had to brazen it out. Not give any hint that last night had changed anything. Pretend that it *hadn't* left her wanting to crawl right into his skin and know him better than anyone else in this world.

'As I've told you already, it's the new me...tough, independent.'

He sat on the corner of his desk, his long legs in exquisite navy wool trousers spread out before her. Earlier, before she had left for the market, he had kissed her in the kitchen as they'd tidied up after a late breakfast. His hips had moulded against hers, which had been pushed against a kitchen cabinet, and her fingers had marvelled at the smooth texture of the fabric of his trousers and the strength of the muscle and hardness beneath.

'How about we put that alleged toughness to the test?'

There was a dangerous glint in his eye.

She pointed to the grocery bags on the floor. 'What about lunch?'

He gave her a *you're not so tough now, are you?* grin and beckoned her forward with the curl of a finger. 'Come here.'

His command was spoken in a low, husky voice. His smile had disappeared. His eyes devoured her. Her heart thumped and pounded and ricocheted around her chest. Desire left her faint with the craving to be in his arms again.

She stopped two paces away.

When he didn't react, she edged a little closer.

And then a little closer again.

No reaction.

He was torturing her.

She edged forward. Need driving her on.

She came to a stop less than six inches away.

Other than devouring her with his eyes, he didn't respond.

Inside, she yelled for him to touch her, to kiss her again. To reach out for her. To complete her.

On the outside she didn't move a muscle. Determined not to be the first to move. Determined to prove—to herself as much as him—that she was tough. Determined to believe that she could walk away from him whenever it suited her.

He reached forward and slowly drew down the zip of

her padded jacket. Need pooled in her core. She wriggled a little, trying to ease its beautiful pressure.

'Mi piace come baci.'

Oh, Lord, she was going to lose her mind. Did he *have* to speak in such a low, sexy whisper? She swallowed hard, her throat's tightness an alarming contrast to the loose panic of her heart.

'What does that mean?'

'Mi piace come baci—I love how you kiss me.'

'Oh.'

His hand snaked beneath her jacket. Then a finger curled around the belt loop of her jeans and yanked her between his legs. He leaned in towards her, only inches separating them.

The heat of his body encircled her, sending her hazy thoughts off into recess.

'Adoro come mi fai sentire.'

He really wasn't playing fair. 'What does *that* mean?'

'I love the way you make me feel.'

Oh, crikey, she was going down. And fast.

Despite herself, she closed the gap between them. Her hip inched towards his lap. Her mouth was almost touching his.

'Ho bisogno di te.'

His breath smelt of mint, of toothpaste. His fingers were slowly untucking her tee shirt from her jeans. Slow, unrushed movements, sensual in their laziness. Sensual in the knowing confidence that she wouldn't object. That this was exactly what she wanted.

'And that?'

His head angled perfectly to align with her mouth. 'I need you.'

With a groan she landed her lips on his. She wanted to cry out when he didn't respond at first. But quickly she realised he was happy for her to be in control now. For her to lead the way. She captured his head in her hands and deepened the kiss. Then her hands moved down to his, and silently she urged him to touch her.

Within minutes she was standing before him, her jacket and tee shirt gone, only her jeans and red satin bra remaining.

They made love on the floor.

Hot, desperate, addictive love.

Knowing their time was running out.

Outside his bedroom window darkness had settled on the city. The ball was in less than two hours. He should wake Emma. But she was lying beside him, her arms sprawled over her head on the pillow, the blankets at her waist, and he wanted more time to watch her. Watch the rise and fall of her ribcage, the perfect globes of her breasts. Watch the invitingly open lush cupid's bow shape of her mouth, the flush on her porcelain skin.

She was staggeringly beautiful.

And sleeping with her had been the most heart-wrenching, honest and tender experience of his life.

She was a gentle lover. Almost shy. And she responded to his every touch with wonder shining brilliantly from her eyes.

They had spent the past twenty-four hours in each other's arms. Ravenous for one another.

He was in love with her.

And he was lost as to what to do.

She said she didn't want a relationship, to love again. But with time would she change her mind?

And, even if she did, what if she said she did love him only to walk away one day? After he had given her his heart.

He was in love with her.

But he would never tell her.

Because to do so would mean that she would have the power to leave him.

And that he could never cope with.

Emma stabbed her brush into the almond-coloured eye-shadow. The fine powder crumbled beneath the force. She swept the brush along one closed lid. When she was done she stared at the reflection of the bedroom in the dressing table mirror. Why did she feel she no longer belonged there?

She closed both eyes and grimaced as her heart floated downwards into her stomach, where it rocked to the nervous tension already there.

She had to stop thinking.

Get through the next few hours.

Now should only be about appreciating her remaining precious hours with Matteo.

She opened her eyes in time to catch the already ajar bedroom door opening more fully in the mirror's reflection.

Matteo, dressed in a tuxedo, stepped into the room.

Goosebumps ran along her skin.

She pulled the edges of her dressing gown closer together.

Her heart, her body, her mind were all alert to him. Silently calling out to him.

Unspoken words stole into the room and beat in the air between them.

Matteo walked towards her. Her pulse raced faster with each step. He came to a stop directly behind her, a hand touching against her loose hair.

'I'll help you dress.'

She yearned to lean back, to have his fingers once again bury themselves in her hair, to have his fingertips caress her skull, her neck, her back.

Start pretending, Emma. Come on. Start acting tough. Don't you dare start believing in dreams again.

'Thanks, but it has a side zip. I'll manage by myself.'

His eyes narrowed before he turned and walked to the antique tapestry-covered chair beside her bed. 'I'll wait while you get ready.'

She wanted to say no. That to have him watch would be too intimate. That it was what somebody in a relationship would do. That it wasn't what they were about.

But she couldn't find the right words of protest.

Her dress was lying on the bed. A pink strapless floor-length silk gown, shot through with threads of peach and gold.

'Turn away.'

Engulfing the small chair he was sitting in, Matteo flashed a hand through his still damp hair. '*Per carità!* You cannot be serious. After the past twenty-four hours?'

'This is different.'

'Why?'

Because I couldn't bear to have you watch me...couldn't bear the vulnerability I would feel.

'I don't know, but it is.'

Throwing both hands up in the air, Matteo stood and walked to the bedroom window.

Emma quickly peeled off her dressing gown and stepped into the dress.

'You have a beautiful body.'

Her head shot up. Matteo still had his back to her. She pulled up the bodice to cover her bare breasts.

She gave a huff of disbelief. 'Hardly—in comparison to the naked models you see all the time.'

He twisted his head around—not enough to watch her, but enough to mark his presence, his control of the mood in the room. 'I don't care about other women, what they look like. I'm telling you that your body is mesmerising.'

There was more than a hint of annoyance to his voice.

She gave a laugh, needing to keep this conversation light and teasing. 'I believe you.'

He turned fully, his jaw set hard, a warning look flashing in his eyes. 'I never lie.'

She looked down and fiddled with her zip, wishing she *could* believe him. Wishing life hadn't taught her not to trust what anyone said.

She'd intended not to react, not to say anything, but when she looked up and into his eyes she heard herself say in a low voice, 'Is that a promise?'

Silence fell on the room. Matteo did not move a muscle. Dark and brooding, with the sharp contours of his athletic body clearly defined by the bespoke slim-cut tailoring of his tuxedo, he stared at her with an intensity that had her heart pounding in her ears, goosebumps serrating her skin.

He lifted his head in a gesture she had thought was one of arrogance when they'd first met, but now she knew it was one of intense pride and honour. 'Of course.'

She wanted to believe him. Not to be so scarred by her past. She wanted to walk to him and kiss him tenderly. She wanted to find adequate words to express the emotion pirouetting in her heart. She wanted to cancel the ball and spend these last hours alone with him, in his arms.

But to do so would mean allowing herself to hope, believe, trust, dream again.

Things she could never do.

So instead she fluttered her hands through the heavy silk of the gown's skirt and gave a single pirouette. 'Well, Prince Charming, am I okay to go to the ball?'

Matteo walked towards her, the seriousness in his eyes fading to amusement. A smile appeared on his mouth. '*Sei bellissima.* You are beautiful.'

* * *

The orchestra played 'The Blue Danube' and hundreds of masked faces twirled and spun around Matteo in the gilt and frescoed ballroom.

But he only searched for one: the delicate golden wired half-mask Emma had chosen in the atelier yesterday morning.

He smiled as Mrs Xue spoke excitedly of her trip to Verona from behind her full-faced *volto* mask, stark white with gilding around the eyes. The beauty of the Basilica... The pictures she'd taken of Juliet's Balcony... All the while he was searching, searching, searching. Needing to see Emma. Suddenly wondering how he was going to let her go.

And then he saw her. Moving towards him in the arms of Mr Xue.

She danced as though she was walking on air—fluidly, elegantly, joyfully. Her long hair lifted and bounced behind her. Those she passed turned around and stared in her direction. Captivated. Her dress sparkled beneath the lights of the Murano glass chandeliers running down the centre of the ballroom, her mask spun with gold adding to the pull of her beauty.

The music came to a stop and he led Mrs Xue towards them. He bowed to Mrs Xue and held out his hand to Emma. Silently inviting her to dance.

Below her mask her mouth gave a polite smile, but there was unrest in her eyes.

They danced slowly, but then the tempo quickened.

They danced on, to the uplifting music, but second by second her body grew stiffer in his arms. Her back arched. Her hand in his was tense.

Inside, a part of him was dying. All of a sudden he was incapable of speaking to her—even as her boss, never mind her lover. He wanted to hear her laughter. To feel that world-altering connection again. But no words came. He struggled even to look at her. It hurt too much. To know what he was about to lose. All he could do was stare blindly into the distance. Focus on the warmth and softness of her hand in his. How perfect it felt in his grasp. A perfect fit. Enticing. Nourishing. *Home.*

He heard himself ask, 'Is everything okay?'

Her response was equally polite. Impersonal. Strained. 'Yes, of course.'

He glanced down quickly and then away. Felt a dragging pain in his heart. As though it was bound by two gondolas travelling in opposite directions on a dark foggy night.

'What time do you have to leave tomorrow?'

She spoke with an edge. Was she dreading tomorrow as much as he was?

'I need to be at the airport for nine.'

She tucked her head down so that he couldn't see her eyes, but her fingers curled even tighter around his hand.

'So early?'

He grimaced at the regret in her voice. 'Unfortunately.'

Another couple moved too close to them and the woman collided hard against Emma. She gave a gasp of surprise.

The woman began to apologise, the heat in her cheeks below her half-mask showing her distress.

Emma held out her hand and touched the woman's bare arm. 'I'm fine, don't worry.'

The warmth and kindness of Emma's reassurance shifted something inside him. The way she'd touched the woman—empathetic, dignified—the gentleness of her tone. *This* was the type of woman he wanted to spend his life with. Centred. Compassionate. Caring.

He couldn't let her go.

The couple moved away.

Emma's eyes met his. Sad. Determined.

'I'll leave at the same time as you tomorrow.'

Confused, he pulled back from her. 'Why?'

Her gaze moved to the centre of his throat. He swallowed hard. Remembered her lips and tongue swirling over that tender skin at sunrise this morning.

'I've booked a hotel for my final days here in Venice.'

Not understanding, he said, 'I had assumed that you would stay in Ca' Divina.'

The hand resting on his arm tightened for a moment before her touch grew slack. 'That wouldn't be right.'

'Why?'

She shrugged. 'You've done enough for me.'

Her voice was impatient.

What was going on? Why was she springing this on him now?

Something hot and angry stirred in his stomach. She was walking out on him. He had fallen in love with her and she was walking away. He had thought she would stay. That he would leave for New York knowing that she was still in Ca' Divina. While Emma had remained there they would have had a connection. He would have had a legitimate reason to call her and see how she was doing. He had even envisaged her sleeping in his bed.

But instead she was walking away. Walking away from his home. From his hospitality. Walking away from their week together and the memories contained within the walls of Ca' Divina. Walking away from *him*.

And it didn't seem to be of any significance to her.

Anger leached from his stomach. Poisoned the rest of his body. His jaw locked. Every muscle tensed.

'Why didn't you tell me that you would be leaving?'

Her head snapped up. 'Why should I have?'

'Because it would have been polite.'

Those beautiful slender shoulders rose again. In a casual throwaway gesture that cut him in two.

'What does it matter when I leave? I thought you'd be relieved.'

The poison was in his throat. In his mind. He wanted to yell. But he forced his voice to remain cool, detached.

'Relieved?'

Emma couldn't read Matteo. There was anger in his eyes. But his voice was businesslike. Remote.

'It's time we both move on.'

She could hear herself speak…in the voice of another person. A person who was relaxed about moving on. Happy and accepting. While in truth, inside, her ribs felt as if they were going to snap under the pressure of sadness building in her chest.

Matteo gave an impatient sigh. And then fiercely, begrudgingly, he said, 'Come and work for me in Milan.'

She laughed out of confusion. A short, bitter noise.

'Work for you?'

She heard Matteo curse under his breath and then he yanked off his black half-mask.

The tips of his cheeks were red, agitated. 'I need a replacement for my event co-ordinator whilst she's on maternity leave.'

She wanted to cry. But instead she said dismissively, 'I can't work for you, Matteo.'

The redness in his cheeks spread. He lowered his head and eyeballed her. 'Why not?'

Because I will only fall in love with you even more.

She looked away, irritation layering on top of her sadness and confusion. How dared he speak to her in such a demanding tone?

She gritted her teeth, yanked off her own mask and said in an ice-cold tone, 'Because it would be too awkward— we've slept together, for heaven's sake. Anyway, I need to get back to London. Sort out accommodation, a job… I need to focus on my career. I want to go home.'

Those brown eyes were no longer soft, but as hard as rain-parched earth. 'And London is your home?'

A lifetime of hurt bubbled inside her. For the first time ever she felt a true, raw need to be tough erupting.

She inched closer to him and looked him steadily in the eye. 'Yes. London is my home. It's where my career will be.'

He nodded, but she could tell from the hard determination in his eyes that he wasn't going to leave it without a fight.

'I want you to stay. Give it six months. You don't have to commit to anything permanent. Think about what great experience you will gain. How it will look on your CV.'

Incredulously, she asked, 'You want me to give up my life in London?'

Those eyes, parched of emotion, held hers. 'I don't want you to go… I like what we have. You don't have an apartment or a job in London. Why not move to Milan? I have an apartment in Porta Venezia you can use.'

She was *so* sick of being used. First her parents. Then her ex. Now Matteo wanted to use her for his own ends. In the workplace and no doubt in the bedroom.

She planted her feet firmly on the ground. She was sick of dancing with him. Sick with herself for thinking he might be different.

She snatched her hand out of his. Jerked her other hand away from his arm. 'Because it's *my* life. I'm not some… bit on the side. I'm not interested in having a relationship with you for a few months. I can't function like that. And, frankly, I'm insulted that you would think that I would be happy being your…your kept mistress.'

He stepped closer to her and lowered his head. 'I'm asking you to *work* for me—nothing else. Why are you making such a big deal about it?' he demanded in a furious voice.

She jerked away.

What was he saying?

If he didn't want to sleep with her, was he saying that he had no interest in her? No desire for her? How could that be when attraction sizzled between them?

Or was she mistaken?

Was this all one-sided?

Pride called for her not to speak. But her pain, her hurt, her confusion were too great. 'Are you saying that you don't *want* to sleep with me again? That it would be a business arrangement only?'

He shook his head. Lifted his arms in exasperation. Confusion drifted across his features before he asked furiously, 'What do *you* want, Emma?'

Tears were forming at the back of her throat. With a cry she whispered, 'I don't know. I don't *know*, Matteo. But I certainly don't want this.'

CHAPTER TEN

EMMA RAN FROM the ball, the music and lights fading with every step, and tugged on her coat. The freezing night air was an affront to her hot anger.

She darted down the nearest side street.

Move to Milan? Work for him? Be his paid lover?

Hurt, fury, and a feeling of utter naïvety all twisted wildly in her stomach, moving upwards like a tornado until they gripped her throat. She could barely breathe.

Her ankle throbbed.

Blindly she hobbled along the maze of *calli*, cursing her exquisite pale pink Marco sandals, not made for cobbled streets. She had the vague hope that she'd finally stumble upon a recognisable landmark. But she didn't care that she was lost. Or that there were few people out at this time of night.

She wanted to be alone.

She wanted to try to understand why his proposal had stung so deeply.

She wanted to understand why it felt as though the past week had been nothing but a lie.

The connection she had thought they'd shared had been nothing more than a delusion on her part.

Their relationship was nothing more than a physical attraction for him.

Not an emotional connection.

Not the deep understanding of another person—the ability to read their needs and respond to them.

After everything she had said, how could he think that she'd be happy to uproot her life, turn it upside down for a man? A man who said he never wanted a permanent relationship.

How on earth would she manage to walk away from him after six months, a year, when it already felt so gut-wrenchingly awful to face the thought of him leaving tomorrow?

And the most infuriating, feet-stamping, tantrum-inducing part of all of this was that she didn't *want* to be in love.

But she was.

She loved him.

How could she be so stupid?

How could she be so foolish to fall in love with a man who had always said he didn't want to be in a relationship?

How could she be so reckless to allow herself to get hurt again?

On a humpback bridge she came to a stop at the apex and stared along the silent flowing water of the dark canal below.

It was snowing. How hadn't she noticed before now? Slowly swirling fat flakes dropped onto her outstretched palm. The flakes melted instantly against the heat of her skin. Just as the connection, the trust, the respect, the feeling deep in her bones that she had met her soulmate had melted tonight.

Pain radiated from her ankle. Cramping her calf muscle. She curled her toes and lifted her leg to rotate her ankle. Balanced on one leg, she wobbled and almost fell over.

She wanted to scream at life to give her a break.

She needed to get home.

Out of the cold.

But it wasn't home.

When had she even started to consider it as such?

Emptiness swept over her. She twisted away from the canal and tottered down the steep slope of the bridge on numb feet. Overwhelmed at the thought of a future without Matteo.

Before, she had clung to the hope that she would have memories to sustain her. Memories of a kind, generous, empathetic man.

Now she was no longer certain if that was who he really was.

Had be just been playing her? To get her into his bed?

She slipped and lurched along a narrow *calle*. The tall buildings either side seemed to be bearing down on her. Echoing the thin, stiletto fall of her footsteps.

The snow continued to fall.

A church bell rang out nearby.

She followed its sound.

And gasped when she walked into San Marco Square, blanketed in a thin layer of snow. Only a few solo, silent mysterious figures traversed the square, disappearing and appearing again from the arcades of the *procuratie*.

A sharp pain gripped her ribs. Forcing the air from her lungs.

She wanted Matteo to be here.

To witness the beauty of the square with her.

To hold her hand. To pull her tight against his body. To warm her. To hold her safe. To hold her for ever.

She turned her back on the square.

She knew her way back to Ca' Divina from here.

She would sleep and leave early tomorrow. And start her life afresh.

Her tears were pointless. She swiped at them, every muscle in her body hardening. She was furious with herself. For every single decision she had taken this past week.

* * *

She woke to feel her heart pounding a slow, heavy beat. Without opening her eyes she knew he was there. The adrenaline swamping her muscles, the tingle on her skin, the alertness in her brain—all told her that he was in the room.

Should she open her eyes? Confront him? Perhaps even manage to say goodbye in a civilised manner.

But would she run the risk of falling prey to his chemistry? To her weakness when she was around him?

She ground her teeth together. Annoyed with herself.

She snapped her eyes open.

He was sitting in the blue floral tapestry chair beside her bed, his bow tie undone, a dark shadow on his jawline and shadows below his eyes. Eyes that were studying her as if he was trying to stare into her soul.

She wanted to pull the covers over her head. To turn away from the awful compulsion invading every cell in her body to fold back the covers and silently ask him into her bed. To lose herself in him again.

Instead she pulled herself upright and hugged her knees against her.

They sat in silence. He held her gaze but she looked away. Her lips clamped shut. Her teeth aching. She was determined not to say anything.

'Why did you run out of the ball?'

His voice was low, gruff, tired.

She drew her knees tighter into her chest. Disappointment grabbed at her heart and then an even stronger, more breath-stealing sadness yanked at her chest. Her jaw ached with the pressure of trying not to let out a cry.

She swallowed time and time again, but her upset was still clear when she asked, 'Do you know me so little that you have to ask that question?'

He leaned back in his chair and folded one leg over the

other. The cold, hard expression of a CEO going in for the kill was on his face. 'You embarrassed me in front of my clients.'

She jerked back against the pillows of the bed, shock and anger erupting from her. 'Are you *serious*? Is that all that you care about?'

He leapt from his chair. Tense and dark. Prowled beside her bed. His shoulders bunched tight. A hand tore through his hair in disbelief. 'I needed you there. As my partner. And you left me.'

There was raw pain in his voice. Distressed pride in his eyes.

Speechless, she stared at him. Her mouth opening and closing. She had hurt him. How, she had no idea. But she had. And her heart ached. Ached for him. Ached for the mess they both were in.

'What's going on, Matteo?'

He glanced briefly at her. Flinging exasperation and anger at her. 'I can't stay here. Let's go for a walk. I'll meet you downstairs in twenty minutes.'

She moved forward. Trying to reach him. 'Why?'

Matteo, already at the bedroom door, twisted around to her, the ache inside him shooting out in furious words. 'Because we need to talk and I'm not doing it here.'

He gestured impatiently to the bed and then stared at her. Defying her not to understand how it was too painful a reminder of their hours spent together making slow, passionate love time and time again.

Too painful a reminder of how it was the way they had first met. In the intimacy of a bed. Inches apart. Staring into the eyes of a stranger. Who wasn't a stranger at all.

Anger flowing through his veins, Matteo stormed into his bedroom. After a rushed shower he dressed in charcoal wool trousers and a light grey shirt, both suitable for the long journey ahead in his private plane to New York.

He should have packed yesterday evening. But instead he had spent that time in bed with Emma.

He slammed some clothes into his suitcase with a carelessness that made him wonder if he was losing his mind.

Hurt convulsed through him. He steadied himself by locking his knees against the side of the bed. Doubled over above the open suitcase. Pain ripping through the centre of him.

She had walked out on him.

He had tried to reach out to her. He had given her a solution that would keep them together for a while. A solution that gave him some hope of a possible future together.

And she had thrown it back in his face.

Walked out on him.

Just like every other person he had ever been foolish enough to allow into his life, to have loved, had done in the past.

They walked in silence through alleyways and squares, over the Rialto Bridge into the *sestiere* of San Marco. The city of bridges, the city of romance, had never looked so beautiful and serene in the early-morning light, with a thin blanket of snow covering the city.

With few people about, they almost had the city to themselves.

In the pink-tinged dawn light, a blue sky was beginning to unfurl.

Words tumbled in Matteo's brain. He wanted to lash out. Pain was burning in his gut. In his heart. In his mind. He pulled his woollen hat down further over his ears, lifted the collar of his coat. The fire inside him intensified the bitter pull of the outside temperature.

'I wasn't trying to insult you last night with my job offer.'

Emma upped her pace, putting distance between them.

Her arms were folded tight across her padded jacket, her suede boots tramping the snow.

'I've upended my life for a man before. I'm not doing it again.'

He caught up with her as she entered Campo della Fava and pulled her to a stop. '*Per carità!* Are you serious, Emma? Are you comparing me to a man who *lied* to you? A *criminal*?'

Her blue-hatted head shook furiously. 'No… I'm not comparing you. But—'

He grabbed her by the arms and pulled her closer. Desperate for her to understand. 'I was trying to find a way for us to see each other for a while. I *like* you, Emma. I don't want us to lose contact.'

An incredulous expression grew on her face. 'You like me.'

It was not a question. More a statement of disgust.

With an angry huff she continued, 'And what happens in six months' time? In a year? Don't you think we're just going to hurt each other?'

He swallowed hard. Thrown by her fury. Her passion. Thrown by how much he longed to cup her pink-tinged cheeks and lower his lips to her mouth. To pull off her hat and lose his fingers in the soft weight of her hair. To inhale her rose scent once again. To know that she was his.

All that desire and want collided with the fear rampaging in his chest, in his heart. He grappled for words. The right words. *Any* words. He was about to put his heart on the line. Could he go through with it?

He swung away from the sight of her peppermint-toffee eyes searching his. Looking…waiting for an answer.

He marched towards the red-brick edifice of Chiesa di Santa Maria della Fava before twisting back again. 'In six months' time, a year, you might be ready for a relationship…a proper relationship.'

Her hands twisted more tightly about her waist. She lifted her chin defiantly. 'A relationship... What do you mean?'

His heart swivelled in his chest.

He felt sick.

He was about to put everything on the line.

His pride. His trust. His sworn promise to himself that he would never show any vulnerability, any need to another person.

What if she said no? Rejected him?

'I've always believed that I would never fall in love.'

He couldn't stand still. He paced up and down before her. Snow crunched under his feet.

He came to a stop. 'But I have.'

He gestured heavenwards, his head falling back. Looking for strength. His heart throbbing.

'I've fallen in love with you.'

Emotion caught in his throat. Suddenly he felt deflated. Empty.

His hands fell to his sides. 'With a woman who doesn't want to be in love.'

Paling, her expression aghast, she said incredulously, 'You've fallen in love with *me*?'

Was his admission so terrible? So unwanted? So wide of the mark from where she was at, what she wanted from this relationship?

Pain and pride slammed together in his chest. He needed to back off. Withdraw. Play it cool.

In a slow, indifferent drawl he asked, 'Is it really that horrific?'

She took a step closer to him. Her icy breath floated on the air towards him. 'Of course not. I'm not horrified. I'm just confused.'

Her hand reached out towards him. He jerked away.

For a moment she looked startled, wounded. But then she asked, 'Why didn't you want to fall in love?'

He closed his eyes. The ache in his chest was worse than the time when his mother had taken him away from Francesco. A thousand times worse. What was the point in answering her question? Did she really care?

He opened his eyes. Hazel eyes laced with tears held his gaze. In a low whisper she said, 'Matteo, please...*please.*'

He was so in love with her.

'When I was growing up my mother dated many men. Some for only weeks, others for longer...twelve, eighteen months. We would move into their homes. We would get to know their families, often their parents, brothers and sisters. I would pretend that I had a family of my own...a home. I would pretend that I had a father. But then my mother would sabotage the relationship. And it would end in one of two ways. Either the man I'd considered a father, and his parents who had treated me like a grandchild, would give in to her insistence that we move on with our lives and let us go, not fighting in any way to keep me a part of their lives. Or, if the break-up was particularly bitter, the man would throw us out onto the street.'

She moved forward and placed her hand on his chest. Just below his heart.

She looked at him and said gently, 'I'm sorry.' And then, 'There's no excusing the men who threw you out, but perhaps it was hard for those other men. Maybe they thought it would be easier for *you* if they let you go.'

Memories of Francesco clinging to him came back. If he'd been in Francesco's position, what would he have done? His throat tightened.

Her hand moved upwards. Now it was over his heart.

Her voice was hoarse. 'You think I'm doing the same thing? That I'm walking away from you?'

He was tired of pretending. Maybe if he had shown her just how upset he was when he was a child his mother would have changed. Those worthwhile father figures would have fought to stay in contact.

'Yes.'

Panic surged through Emma. 'It's not like that… I really like you. I really, *really* like you.'

She paused for breath. Her hand moved up from his heart and for a moment lingered on his jawline. She had an overwhelming need to lay her lips on his. To take the pain from his eyes.

'I can't imagine leaving you.'

She dropped her hand and took a step back. She looked down at the snow, tarnished now by their careless footsteps.

'But I'm scared. I've messed up so much in the past. My judgement has been so wrong. I'm scared that I'll jump into a relationship for all the wrong reasons.'

Matteo's eyes narrowed. She took some strength from the way he looked as though knowing and understanding all this was the most important thing in the world.

'I'm scared that I've fallen for you because I'm vulnerable. Because I'm confused.'

She tugged off her hat, suddenly too hot. Her brain felt as if it was sizzling. 'I came to Venice swearing that I was going to be tough and practical. Focused on my career. Determined that I was never going to dream again. And then I went and met you. And I *want* to dream. But what if it all falls apart again? I couldn't take it. I'm scared I'll lose you. That one day this dream that I'm living will fall apart.'

For the longest while Matteo stood still, drinking in what she had said. And then he moved towards her. His hand reached for her hair. Tucked some of it behind her ear.

His thumb ran down her cheek and gently he said, 'You're not ready for love. For this relationship.'

She didn't know how to answer. Tears flooded her eyes.

Tears of confusion and frustration. Tears of fear. Tears of love for this man.

'Are you?'

His hand cupped her cheek. He gave a sigh. Regret and sadness deepened his eyes to soft molten toffee. 'I'm not sure,' Emma said.

She stepped back. Away from his touch. Needing to step away from telling him how much she loved him.

'Are we just fooling ourselves? Is this just about the insane chemistry we seem to share?'

He nodded, but then stopped suddenly. 'I've never felt like this with another woman.'

His gaze was now hard, direct. Deeply honest.

She sucked in a breath. 'Nor me with another man.'

His jaw worked. He ran a hand over his hat. Repositioned it. 'We need some time apart to think.'

Her stomach flipped at his words. She couldn't bear the thought of being without him. But she continued on with her sensible routine, refusing to allow her heart to have anything to say in what *had* to be a logical conversation.

'Yes.'

'I'm returning from New York on Wednesday. If we decide individually that we want to try to make this work, let's meet. I'll be at Ca' Divina at five.'

Her head spun. An army of *what if*s marched through her brain. What if this was the last time they would meet? What if he decided he didn't want to be with her? She couldn't meet him in Ca' Divina. There were too many memories there. What if she turned up, wanting a future with him, and he didn't?

A wave of grief, rejection, embarrassment at that thought almost knocked her sideways. 'No, not there.'

'At the church in San Moisè square instead?'

She nodded. 'Okay.'

Their eyes locked. Intense, stomach-flipping, heart-faltering unhappiness, longing and uncertainty bound them together.

Matteo broke his gaze first. He quickly stretched his back in a jerking movement, muttering a curse. 'Stay in Ca' Divina while I'm gone.'

'I can't.'

He shook his head. There was a tense displeasure in the corners of his eyes. 'I need to go back there now, to collect my luggage. My plane is waiting at the airport. Come back with me. You're cold.'

Her throat frozen solid with emotion, she struggled to speak, 'I don't want to say goodbye. Please just walk away.'

For a moment he hesitated. But then he gave a brief nod.

He walked towards her. Her heart fluttered and swooped about her chest. At first she thought he was going to hold her. But his hand touched against hers only briefly before he moved away.

She longed to call out to his retreating back. To halt his long, determined, angry stride.

And then she heard him curse.

He turned around and made straight for her.

He grabbed her.

And kissed her hard.

His mouth, his tongue were demanding. In an instant she was falling against him. Kissing him back just as hard. Needing to feel his strength, his warmth, every single essence of his being.

Her head whirled.

She was losing herself to his taste. To his scent of musk. To the feel of his cashmere wool coat.

She couldn't let go.

And then he was gone.

Pulling himself away. Cursing lowly. Walking away without a backward glance.

But not before she saw the tears in his eyes.

CHAPTER ELEVEN

Wednesday. Four thirty.

MATTEO STOOD AT the entrance to what had been Emma's bedroom. Now it was an empty shell. Just like the rest of the *palazzo*.

He entered the room and walked around it. Restless. Searching. Just as he had searched the rest of the *palazzo*. Searching for some sign of her.

He had hoped that she would have left a note. Some indication of her thoughts before she had walked out.

In the wardrobe he'd found all the clothes he had selected for her. She hadn't even taken the blue hat; he'd found it poking out of the pocket of her navy coat. As if waiting, hoping for her to return.

He propped his head against the carved walnut of the wardrobe door. Weak with weariness and disappointment. She had wanted no reminder of their time together.

Four forty-five.

Across from her bedroom window, on the roof terrace of the house opposite her hotel, an elderly lady tended to her patio garden. She was planting bulbs in flower boxes. Her hands unsteady, she moved slowly but with care. A contented smile on her face.

Had her neighbour ever struggled with a decision? Had she ever been so scared that she felt paralysed with fear?

Emma's fingers stroked the threadbare pelt of Snowy, her toy polar bear, sitting in the palm of her hand. He was staring out of the window too. Looking as bewildered and lost as she felt.

She had rung her best friend Rachel earlier, but hadn't been able to speak to her about Matteo, too upset, her fears too deep inside her to expose them.

What if she went to San Moisè Church and he wasn't there?

What if she went and he *was* there? Waiting. And he said things she didn't want to hear?

Five o'clock.

Emma stopped at one side of the main entrance to San Moisè Church, indecision dancing and colliding with anxiety in her stomach. She steadied herself against a square plinth, the cold stone electrifying her fingertips. The dark green outer double doors were slashed with peeling paint, pushed back to reveal glass-panelled inner doors.

She pulled one of the inner doors open, the fear in her stomach exploding into the rest of her body, leaving her trembling and uncertain if she would have the strength to carry on.

What if he hadn't come? What if he had decided in their time apart that it wasn't love he felt for her after all?

Dusk was settling on the city and the empty church was lit by pale wall lights and hundreds of votive candles, placed in racks and trays in front of bye-altars.

She went and stood by the first pew, her hand touching the grain of the wood. Her heart slowed. She closed her eyes and drank in the calming, distinct and yet light scent of the church: incense, flowers, melting wax.

Centuries of prayer hung in the silent atmosphere. The prayers of the hopeful. The desperate. The fearful.

Her footsteps echoed on the marble aisle. The sound of her aloneness.

She stopped and winced.

Unable to go any further.

Unable to bear the sound of her footsteps.

Knowing he wasn't there to hear them.

She dropped down onto a wooden pew and bent her head.

She had lost him.

What had she done?

And then she heard them.

Other footsteps.

Her head snapped up.

A figure moved behind one of the two thick stone columns that sat before the main altar.

Matteo?

His steps faltered as he approached her where she sat, halfway down the aisle.

Bruised eyes met hers.

His expression was as sombre, as arresting as the knee-length black wool coat, the black cashmere jumper and stark white shirt he wore. He was freshly shaven, and his hair was shorter than it had been before. She wanted to touch him. To feel his smooth skin, hard muscle. She wanted his arms around her. His hands in her hair. The pressure of his body.

Her heart moved beyond her throat to lodge between her ears. Where it pounded to a deafening beat.

His head dropped in a barely discernible nod.

She gave a wan smile in response.

Her bones, her every muscle, her mind all felt weak—powerless onlookers in this event. Her heart had drained every ounce of energy from the rest of her body in a bid to keep working.

She slid along the seat.

Please sit with me. Please let me have a few moments with you.

She didn't look up. Too vulnerable. Too scared he wouldn't sit.

He moved forward, reached her pew. But then stopped.

From the corner of her eye she saw his black trousers, the high polish of his black leather shoes. The neat bows in his laces.

Not moving. Not joining her. A sign of what was to come?

A jolt of pain shuddered through her lungs. A silent wound.

But then he sat. His long legs, muscular thighs grazing against hers.

They swung away from each other at the same time.

He bunched his hands together.

She dared a quick glance.

He was staring towards the altar at an elaborate sculpture showing Moses receiving the Ten Commandments.

She bit down on her bottom lip and closed her eyes. Searing hot pain torched her stomach. She *hated* this distance. This isolation.

And then her breathing slammed to a stop.

His hand was over hers. Holding it. Lifting it up to rest on his leg. His warm, protective, solid hand was holding hers. And not letting go.

Tears filmed her eyes. But she couldn't open them. Not even when the tears ran down her cheeks.

She couldn't stop herself.

His arm went around her shoulder. He drew her in closer. She bent her head and sobbed against his chest.

She couldn't stop herself.

* * *

Emma's shuddering body shook against his. He held her closer. Wishing her tremors and tears away.

She had looked at him with distress, sadness, unease as he had walked down the aisle towards her.

Why?

He tugged her closer. Closed his eyes to the slightness of her body. To the jumble of memories that came.

The first time they had made love. The beauty of her porcelain skin in the pale afternoon sunshine. How they had made love later that night in the shower, with a fast and furious need. Urgent, hungry, teeth-nipping lovemaking. As though they were both desperate to leave a mark on the other. Both afraid of how soon they would have to leave one another.

He buried his head into the softness of her thick curls. Inhaled her rose scent.

Her tears stopped. But still he sat there, Emma in his arms. Reluctant to leave the sanctuary of the church.

With slow movements Emma pulled away. She inhaled a deep breath. The breath of emotional exhaustion.

Pink rimmed her eyes, and the tip of her nose was a deeper hue.

She gave an embarrassed smile, her gaze barely touching his. 'I'm sorry—that wasn't supposed to happen.'

'How have you been?'

Her mouth fell downwards before she attempted a smile. 'Honestly? Not great. It's been difficult, these past few days.'

'Me too.'

She blinked hard. Her throat worked even harder. 'I thought you hadn't come… I thought… I thought…'

Her upset slammed into him. Adrenaline and regret mixed nauseatingly in his stomach. He held her hand for a few seconds longer, reluctant to break away, before he stood. They needed to end this agony.

'Let's go and talk.'

At a small boutique hotel, in a tiny courtyard nearby, he ordered a brandy for them both in the cocktail bar to the rear of the property.

They sat in an alcove, away from the few other customers there.

When their drinks arrived he took a slug of his brandy.

Emma stared at her drink absently before she unzipped and removed her black padded jacket to reveal a cream blouse, with a matching camisole beneath the translucent silk. On her neck hung the fine gold necklace she often wore, scattered with five tiny pendants in the shape of the moon, stars and flowers.

He shuffled in his seat, pushing away the temptation to reach forward and trace a finger along the delicate chain, to feel the pulse at the base of her neck. To be close enough to hear nothing but her breath. To hear her whisper his name. To hear her cries that had wrenched open his heart.

She grasped her glass and drew it in a slow arc across the black lacquered surface of the table. 'Why did you come, Matteo?'

He wanted to turn the question back on her. Have her explain first why *she* came. Still he was uncomfortable at letting his guard down after so many years of building a fortress around his heart.

But he could see the panic, the apprehension, the fear in her eyes. See how she had paled since they had sat down opposite one another.

Her body was curved towards him. Begging him to speak. To explain.

'I thought asking you to come and work with me would be enough. I told you that I was in love with you. I thought that would be enough. But in our time apart I realised that both of those things would never be enough.'

Her head tilted to the side, as though the weight of her questions was too great.

He answered her by adding, 'I'm guessing that you heard from your ex, from your parents, that they loved you. But that they never proved it.'

Regret tingled at the tips of his fingers and toes.

'There's so much more that I should have told you. I should have found the right words to prove my love. I should have proved it by being courageous enough to say those words. To really open my heart to you. To show you what was deep inside me. But I didn't because I was scared. Scared that by talking I would have to fully face up to just how deeply I love you. And how much it would hurt when you walked away.'

He paused for a moment and looked at her. Tried to garner the energy from her to continue on. A small encouraging nod was all it took.

'All those times the men I'd considered to be a father to me walked away, they took a part of me with them. The innocent, optimistic kid who trusted others was pulled apart bit by bit, until I had nothing left but cynicism and a determination never to be hurt again. I closed down. Refused to love. Refused to ever allow myself to feel that pain again.

'But last night, before my flight, I attended a dinner at a friend's apartment. There was a couple there who reminded me of us. They laughed and chatted together constantly. They were so in tune with one another, so happy. And, watching them, I realised that I wanted what they had. A partner in life. A family of my own. Emma, I want *you*.'

A hand dashed up to cover her mouth, which was dropping open. Her eyes were narrowed with caution and doubt.

'But is it me you want or the *idea* of a partner, a family?'

That was the easiest question he'd ever had to answer.

He moved his hands across the smooth table. He opened his palms to her. 'You. Most definitely you.'

She stared down at his hands. And then into his eyes. Still about-to-bolt cautious.

'Why?'

Was this going to work? How had he messed up so spectacularly that she was asking him why he wanted to be with her?

'I wish you didn't have to ask me that question. I wish I'd had the courage to tell you before now. I want you in my life. I love you. I fell in love with you the moment I lay down beside you in my bed. I'm deeply attracted to you, but it's much more than that.'

His heart was throbbing in his chest. Pleading with him—with her—not to let what they had together go. He jerked his hands off the table and curled one fist. He banged it against his throbbing heart. Needing to connect with it. Needing to acknowledge the feelings he had denied for so long.

'It's in *here*—in my heart. A recognition, a familiarity, a sense of belonging together—I don't know what it is, but I know that when I'm with you I'm *me*. There's no pretence. There's no pressure to be something I'm not. I love your elegance, your voice. I love how you mutter in your sleep. I love how you stand with your feet angled, as though you are about to dance at any moment. I love your humour, your touch. I love how you try to act tough when really you're as soft as a marshmallow. You are kind, intuitive…yet strong. I *know* you would fight for those you love.'

He paused. The emotion pouring from his heart was overwhelming his throat. About to drown him in all those words that had been building, building, building in him.

'I love you. I know that might not be enough, but I can't

let you go without telling you all this. You need to know that I will always love you, whatever your decision.'

Emma nodded, and nodded again. As if the forward and back momentum would give her the energy to speak. His words were magical. Beautiful. But she was still scared.

Across from her Matteo, pale, drawn, waited for her to speak.

Deep inside her the truth began to unfurl. She had to open her heart to him. Ask for his support. Trust in him.

But what if he thought she was weak, stupid, needy? What if he didn't like her when she spoke about every deep fear in her heart?

But wasn't that what a true relationship was about?

Hadn't he just been honest with her? And instead of thinking him weak it had made her love him all the more.

On a deep breath she said, 'I came to Venice to heal. To build a wall around myself that nobody would ever penetrate again. I was so tired of being let down. Of my dreams falling apart. And on my first day I met you. Protective, sexy you. A man who didn't want love either. And I immediately fell for you.'

She could not help but smile as a brief, satisfied smile broke on Matteo's mouth.

Then with a shaky exhalation she admitted, 'But it scared the life out of me. I didn't *want* to be in love. So I tried to bury it. Ignore it. But deep within me I knew I was in love from the moment we first kissed. I did everything in my power to tune out the voice telling me that. I told myself that you weren't interested. That *I* wasn't interested. That it was all a rebound fantasy. I looked and looked for a way to find you out, to prove to myself that you would hurt me as much as my ex and parents had.'

She breathed out a guilty sigh. A sigh full of regret.

'When you proposed that I go to Milan and work for you it was the perfect excuse for me to hang on to and justify my fears. Justify walking away when in truth I was in love with you.'

His arm resting on the table, Matteo opened his hand to her, silently asking her to take it. Her fingers curled around his. Her whole body vibrated to a low beat. *Home.*

His voice was low, thick with emotion, when he spoke. 'That's the first time you've said that you love me.'

Was it really? What had she been *thinking*? Had she been so terrified of saying those words out loud?

'I should have told you before but I was scared…scared of dreaming again. I'm petrified something will go wrong. That I'll end up losing you. That something will happen to destroy what we have.'

His fingers tightened on hers, pulled her forward in her seat. He leaned across the table, those brown eyes boring into hers. 'I won't let anything destroy what we have.'

'Do you mean it?'

'Emma, I love you. I want you in my life. Beside me. My mother has spent her life wishing she had done something different. That she hadn't let the love of her life get away. Wondering if he feels the same. Wondering where he is now…what he is doing. If he is happy. I won't live with that regret. I won't let *you* live with that regret.'

'Where do we go from here?'

'I don't want to be without you. Since you came into my life I've realised just how lonely and empty I was before. I'm a happier, better person because of you. I *need* you. I want us to be together. I want us to get married. To be a family. To have children together. Curly-haired, hazel-eyed *bambini.*'

She couldn't help but smile at that image: soft-eyed babies with his golden skin and sucker-punch smiles that would leave her faint with love.

'Are you serious?'

His expression grew stern, as though she had affronted him.

'Do you think I would say those words unless I meant them?'

Her heart skipped a beat at the low, formidable tone of his question, the thin line of his mouth. 'I'm sorry...of course you mean what you say.'

Pain, tenderness, aloneness...all flickered in his eyes.

A bubble of love floated from her heart to her throat, where it popped when she swallowed hard in a bid to concentrate.

Was this really happening?

She had thought they might agree to date, at best.

This was everything she had ever dreamed of. *More* than she had ever dreamed of.

But would she have the courage to say yes?

The courage to believe in such a spectacular, staggering, mind-blowing dream?

To spend her life with the sexiest, kindest, most honourable man alive?

She had come to Venice hoping to harden her heart. But wouldn't doing so—hardening herself, closing herself off to others—mean that her ex, her parents had won? All the people who had hurt her would win?

And *she* would be the loser in all this. She would lose the love of an incredible man. Lose a future full of love. A future of being the mother of Matteo's children.

She would lose the love of her life.

She looked across at him.

He was watching her. Believing in her.

She smiled.

He raised a single eyebrow. Silently asking, *Well...?*

Her smile grew wider. As wide and spectacular as a

Dolomites' snow-covered valley. And then she gave a definite nod.

A tentative smile broke on Matteo's mouth, but happiness was carved into the landscape of his face.

He raised his hand and beckoned her to slip along the seat, to sit beside him.

Which she did.

His brown eyes raked over her face, waiting for her to speak.

'I came to Venice to heal, and I did because of *you*. Dancing with you, being held in your arms healed me. Laughing, kissing, making love with you, every tender touch, every eternal gaze healed me. Your compassion, your wisdom healed me. I would be honoured and proud to be your wife. I love you. With you I feel protected, safe, exhilarated. I want to care for you. Love you. I want to spend my life proving to you how much I love you. How deserving you are of love. I promise I will never hurt you. I want to make up for each time your heart was broken as a boy. I want to complete you.'

His hand touched her hair. Then gently he pulled her mouth closer and closer, his eyes packed with love, desire, joy.

In a low whisper, he breathed against her mouth, '*Voglio stare con te per sempre*. I want to be with you for ever.'

Reluctantly, wanting to stare into those magnificent eyes until the end of eternity, Emma closed her eyes. And lost herself to him.

EPILOGUE

THE HOTEL CIPRIANI's motor boat sliced through the water and Emma giggled and held firmly on to her veil. Rachel, her bridesmaid today, tried to capture it as it flew behind the boat—a fine net sail, catching the attention of the summertime tourists seeking shade from the late-afternoon August sunshine under the awnings of the cafés lining the Grand Canal.

Beads of nervousness exploded in her stomach when the boat slowed to motor up a side canal. They had both wanted to marry in Venice. And what better place than San Moisè Square and Church? The place where they had first kissed. Where they had both found the courage to dream.

With a nervous hand Emma smoothed down the lace skirt of her gown. Tears blinded her vision. What if she hadn't had the courage that day to believe in her love for Matteo? How empty her life would be now.

In the bare six months she had been with him she had gathered a lifetime of memories. Weekends spent here in Venice, in Paris, on Lake Garda, sometimes alone, sometimes with his friends...*her* friends now too. The nights he would arrive in her office, a floor beneath his executive offices, and kiss her neck and earlobes, kiss her into submission so that she would leave early with him—much to the amusement of her new colleagues, who were captivated by the sight of their boss head over heels in love.

What would Matteo think of her dress? Created by the head designer at VMV, the strapless gown had a full voluminous skirt overlaid with fine lace.

At the landing stage, Matteo's grandmother Isabella was waiting for her, shouting instructions to the driver of the boat, who was pretending not to hear her.

Beside Emma, Aurora, her five-year-old flower girl—daughter of Matteo's Marketing Director and her first pupil in the small ballet school she was opening after the summer—hopped up and down with excitement until the driver lifted her with many giggles to deposit her on the landing stage.

When Emma disembarked, Isabella pulled her into a tight embrace, loudly proclaiming, *'Sei bellissima!'* countless times.

Isabella—the woman who had rescued her. The woman who had brought Matteo into her life. She would walk her down the aisle today. Emotion caught in her throat.

Isabella drew her towards the church, her hand at her elbow, saying quietly, *'Lui ti adora.* He adores you, Emma. Thank you for making him truly happy.'

And then Emma was giggling, because a long pink carpet led the way into the church. Not red. But pink. A gift, she suspected, from Matteo. The same ballet-slipper-pink VMV shade as the thousands of roses lining the aisle of the church. The still air sweetened by their heavy scent.

She smiled at the familiar faces beaming back at her from the packed pews. She deliberately sought out Matteo's mum, at the top of the church, knowing how emotional she would be feeling. Knowing that today she was thinking of Matteo's father. They shared a look of understanding, of fondness, of friendship.

And then, inhaling a deep breath, she moved her gaze across the aisle. To Matteo. Who was standing, turned in her direction.

Waiting.

Her steps faltered for a moment.

She felt overwhelmed by how imposing, how handsome he looked in his tuxedo.

He watched her intently. As though this was the most important moment of his life.

When she reached him he didn't move.

For a moment she wondered if he was having second thoughts. But then, his eyes sombre, he leant towards her and whispered, '*Voglio sognare insieme a te per sempre.* Let's dream together for ever.'

She smiled her answer.

And a dazzling smile—a smile that had her heart floating in her chest, that said, *you are the one*—broke on his mouth.

Emma turned to the priest, impatient to become his wife. His best friend. His partner in dreams.

* * * * *

BEAUTY AND HER BOSS

JENNIFER FAYE

PROLOGUE

"THIS CAN'T BE HAPPENING."

Gabrielle Dupré frowned as she perched on the edge of a hard, black plastic chair. The room was small with gray walls. Outside the little room, there was the buzz of voices and phones ringing. But inside the room, a tense silence hung in the air like a dense fog. This was a place she'd never been in her life—a police station. How had things spiraled so far out of control? Her head pounded and her stomach churned.

After being here for more than two hours, the situation wasn't looking good. Not good at all. She'd just played her final card and she'd been praying ever since that it would pay off.

"Don't worry, daughter." Her father stared at her from across a black nondescript table. "Everything will be all right."

"All right?" She struggled not to shout in frustration. "Things are so far from all right." With each word, her voice crept up in volume. Realizing that losing her cool right now would not help their cause, she paused and swallowed hard. "Father, do you know how much trouble you're in?"

"Gaby, don't you understand? If I got word out about that monster, then it was worth it." His voice was filled with conviction. "Sometimes a man has to do what he has to do."

"And sometimes he needs to think before he acts," she said in a heated whisper. Anger pulsed through her veins, but it wasn't her father that she was upset with—it was herself.

Her father reached out and patted her hand. "You'll see. This will all work out."

She blamed herself for not being there to reason with her father. And to stop him from acting rashly. For the past six months, she'd been working two jobs to pay their outstanding bills but she was still losing financial ground. Things were so bad she was considering taking on a third job. With her father's health declining and him now in a wheelchair, it was up to her to make ends meet.

And through it all, she'd made sure to be there for her father every single day. He had been grieving ever since her aunt's deadly car accident almost four months ago. And it didn't help that the police had failed to release the truth about the accident. Although, that didn't stop the gossip sites from pointing fingers, including the magazine she'd recently started doing an admin job for, *QTR*. By way of some unnamed source, they were accusing an award-winning movie star, Deacon Santoro, of being at fault.

Gaby was still trying to figure out the how and why of her father's actions. "So you've been sneaking off to Deacon Santoro's estate all week?"

His gaze narrowed. "I wasn't sneaking. I didn't want to bother you so I took the bus."

She shook her head in disbelief. "I thought you had a girlfriend that you weren't ready to tell me about. If I'd have known what you were up to, I would have stopped you."

With her father's elbows resting on the table, he leaned toward her. His bloodshot eyes pleaded with her. "Don't you want the truth?"

"Of course I do. How could you question that? I loved her, too. She was like a second mother to me. But there are better ways to get to the truth. You shouldn't have staged a loud, disruptive protest in front of the man's house and accosted his staff."

Her father expelled a heavy sigh as he leaned back in his wheelchair. "Nothing else has worked. I've made phone call after phone call to the authorities. All I get is the runaround. They keep saying the accident report will be released as soon as the investigation has been completed."

Gaby couldn't believe what she was about to say, but someone had to reason with her father. With her mother and now her aunt gone, the responsibility landed squarely on Gabrielle's straining shoulders.

"Do you even realize how much power Mr. Santoro wields?"

Her father's bushy, gray eyebrows drew together. "Why do you think I went there? The police aren't helping us get the truth because he bought them off."

Gaby shushed her father. "Don't say those things."

"So I thought the media might help. After all, they'd do anything for a big headline."

"You certainly got their attention." Sadly, she didn't think this tactic was going to work, but she sure hoped she was wrong because the not knowing was eating at her, too. "There were so many reporters standing outside the police station that I had to be escorted through the back entrance."

Her father's tired face, with its two days' worth of

stubble, lifted into a satisfied smile. "It's working. You'll see."

Her father had a bad habit of acting first and thinking later. And she was left with the task of cleaning up his messes. But this was his first and, if she had any say in it, his last arrest. "And is it worth you going to jail or paying a stiff fine that will financially wipe us out?"

Before her father could answer, the door swung open. A tall police officer with salt-and-pepper hair stepped just inside the room. "We've contacted the complainant."

"And…" Gaby knew this was the time for restraint but there was so much on the line.

The officer shook his head. "He refused to meet with you."

That was not what she'd wanted to hear. She was hoping to plead with the man and hopefully get him to drop the charges. Her father was not physically well and punishing him would not help anyone, least of all Deacon Santoro. "Surely there has to be some way I can speak with him."

The officer cleared his throat. "I was about to tell you that he's on the phone. You may speak with him at my desk."

That was all the invitation she needed. In a heartbeat, she was on her feet and rushing out the door. She didn't so much as pause to assure her father that she'd straighten out this mess—because in all honesty, she wasn't sure she could fix things this time. But she was willing to do anything to protect her father—even from his own misguided sense of justice.

The police officer led her to his desk, where he handed over the receiver. Before she got a word out, the officer was called away to help with an unruly arrestee, who appeared intoxicated and quite belligerent.

Turning her back to the scene, Gaby said, "Hello."

"I am not dropping the charges." Deacon Santoro didn't even so much as utter a greeting, friendly or otherwise.

And yet his voice caught her attention. It was deep and rich, like a fine bourbon. She didn't need to verify who she was speaking to. After watching each and every one of his movies countless times, she would recognize Deacon's voice anywhere.

"I would really appreciate if we could talk this out."

"I've done all of the talking that I intend to do." His sexy voice was short and clipped. "Now, I've spoken to you. That is all I agreed to. I must go—"

"Wait!"

"This is a waste of time. Your father is guilty. He will have to take it up with the judge."

With each syllable the man spoke, her body betrayed her by being drawn in by the deep timbre of his voice. Logic dictated that he was the absolute last person she should be fantasizing about, but there was another more primal part of her that wanted to hear his voice again.

Gaby gave herself a swift mental jerk. She had to stay on point. Her father's future was depending on her getting this right.

"But he didn't do anything serious—"

"I'd call stalking a serious charge."

"Stalking?" This was the first she'd heard of this allegation. She couldn't help but wonder what else her father had failed to tell her.

"Yes. He's been making harassing phone calls, skulking outside my residence with binoculars and hounding my entire staff."

"I'm sorry. He hasn't been himself lately. He wouldn't hurt a soul. If you knew him—"

"I don't. And I don't plan to. None of this is my problem."

Mr. Santoro was right on that point, but would it hurt him to be a little generous? Perhaps she needed to explain the situation better. "My father, he isn't young. And his health is failing."

"Again, not my problem."

This man wasn't going to give an inch. His stirring voice ceased to affect her as she went into protective mode. "Listen, Mr. Santoro, I am sorry for the trouble my father has caused you, but pressing charges against him won't fix anything. Surely there has to be another way to work this out."

"Your father should have thought of all of this before he decided to cause trouble for me."

Why did this man have to act as though he was the innocent party here? If it weren't for his actions on that fateful night, her father wouldn't have bothered him. Angry accusations bubbled up within her and hovered at the back of her throat. It would be so easy to lose her cool—to tell this man exactly what she thought of him, which wasn't much.

What good would that do her? Yes, it'd temporarily make her feel better.

But in the long term, would it do anything to help her father? Definitely not.

Gaby's jaw muscles clenched. Her back teeth ground together.

"If that's all, I must go."

"It's not all." He wasn't getting off that easy. "My father was doing what he thought was best for my aunt."

"What does your aunt have to do with this? Or was she one of those misguided people that he coerced into shouting lies and throwing garbage onto my property?"

Gaby wasn't going to let this man go on about her father and aunt. Did he really not know who her father was? "My aunt wasn't outside your house. She—she died in the car accident."

There was a swift intake of breath as though at last he understood the gravity of the situation. A long silence ensued. Was it possible she'd finally gotten through to him?

Still, she didn't breathe easy—not yet. In just the short period of time that she'd spoken with this man, she'd learned that he didn't change his mind easily. And yet, she couldn't give up.

Every muscle in his body tensed.

Deacon Santoro didn't utter a word as he processed this new piece of information. How was this the first he'd heard of the woman in the accident having a family?

He searched his impaired memory for an answer. And then he latched on to the vital information. The police had said the woman had no family—no living parents, no ex-spouses and no children. Just a surviving brother. Deacon had never thought to ask about nieces and nephews.

Deacon swallowed hard. "You're her niece?"

"Yes. My name's Gaby."

"As in Gabrielle?"

"Yes. My aunt was the only one who called me Gabrielle."

Take care of Gabrielle.

Those words haunted him each night in his short and troubled sleep. Until now, he'd never understood what they meant. He didn't know anyone named Gabrielle. But suddenly a jagged piece of a memory from the accident came back to him. It wasn't an image but rather a voice. The woman from the accident had told him to take care of her niece.

And it was his chance to make sure the woman's final words were fulfilled. The need to help Gabrielle was overwhelming. But how? He needed time to absorb this revelation—to form a viable plan.

Deacon cleared his throat. "I didn't know she was your aunt. No one told me."

"Now you can understand my father's actions. He's grieving for his younger sister. He isn't thinking clearly."

"But that still doesn't make up for what he's cost me." Thanks to her father, another in a string of employees had quit. And thanks to the negative publicity, associates were shying away from doing business with him.

"I will do whatever I can to make this right."

He applauded her for trying to clean up a mess that wasn't hers. "How much are you talking about?"

"You want money?" Her voice took on a note of distress.

No. He had enough of his own, but he didn't want this conversation to end—not until he knew a bit more about this woman. "You did offer to make things right and I lost a lot of money when two promising business ventures fell through thanks to your father's actions."

"I—I don't have any money. Please believe me. I work two jobs to keep us afloat."

"Us?" The word rolled off his tongue before he could stop it. Suddenly he pictured this woman with a husband and children—her own support system.

"Yes. Me and my father."

At this point, Deacon should just hang up, but he couldn't do it. The father may have stepped over the line, but the daughter hadn't. And those words kept haunting him—*take care of Gabrielle.*

"What do you have in mind?" he asked.

"I could go outside and talk to the media. I could explain my father's actions—"

"Don't. The less said the better." All the while, he was considering how best to help this woman, who obviously had too much on her plate.

"So if my father and I agree not to say another word, you will see that the charges are dropped?"

"No. Not only has my name been slandered in the news, but my assistant was coming back from lunch when your father's protest was at its height. She was verbally assaulted and had things thrown at her. She has quit. And the temp agency doesn't want to send anyone else."

"Oh." Gabrielle paused. "I don't know what you want me to do to make this right."

"You don't need to do anything. You did not cause this mess." Something told him this wasn't Gabrielle's first time cleaning up after her father. Perhaps taking care of Gabrielle meant freeing her from being constantly at her father's beck and call. "Your father must face up to what he's done."

"But he's in no physical condition to go through the legal process—"

"This isn't your first time fixing things for your father, is it?"

"No." She quickly added, "But he needs me."

"Your father, can he cook for himself?"

"Yes, but—"

"Do his own laundry and shopping?"

"Yes, but—"

"You do most everything for him, don't you?"

"Of course I do. I'm his daughter. Now tell me what I can do to remedy things."

In that moment, Deacon knew what needed to be done.

Without giving himself a chance to back out, he said,
"There is one thing and it's nonnegotiable."

"Name it."

"Come work for me."

CHAPTER ONE

Two days later...

WHAT EXACTLY HAD she agreed to?

Gabrielle Dupré's heart beat faster as she turned into the gated drive of the Santoro estate. Her gaze shifted to the clock on the dash. The drive from Bakersfield had taken more than four hours. She definitely wouldn't want to deal with that long commute each day. Thankfully Newton, an old friend from the neighborhood, had recently moved back to town and was renting a room from her father and had agreed to keep an eye on him while she worked here at the estate. Newton had changed since she'd last seen him, but he was happy to be there for her father, and they seemed to get on.

Deacon had offered her more money to work here than both of her jobs combined. It also included free room and board. Under different circumstances, she'd be excited about the opportunity. But with her father convinced that Mr. Santoro was the reason her aunt had died, being here felt uncomfortable to say the least.

She swallowed hard and reached out the driver's side window, pressing a finger to a button on the intercom. She waited for someone to speak to her. However, without a word the gate swept open. She had to admit she was curious to see what awaited her on the other side of the wall. She'd done an internet search, but it hadn't turned up any pictures of the estate.

Gabrielle eased her father's vintage red convertible onto the overgrown grounds. It certainly wasn't the grand estate that she'd been anticipating. Perhaps at one time this place might have been beautiful, but now it was woefully neglected. The grass appeared not to have been cut in ages. The bushes were overgrown and gangly. The flower gardens were overrun with weeds that were strangling out the few remaining flowers.

The internet sites said that Deacon Santoro had become a recluse since he'd been involved in the deadly accident. Apparently for once, the paparazzi hadn't been totally wrong. There was definitely something amiss on this estate.

The Malibu beach house was a stunning piece of mid-century architecture. Gabrielle slowed the car to a stop to have a better look around. Feeling as though someone was staring at her, she glanced up at the massive white mansion. There was no one standing in any of the windows. But there was a window on the top floor where the sheers moved. Cold fingertips inched down her spine.

Stop it. You're just being melodramatic. It's not like this is a haunted mansion.

No matter what she told herself, she couldn't shake her uneasiness. If it wasn't for her father, she'd turn around and leave. But a deal was a deal.

When she'd handed in her immediate resignation at the library, they'd refused to accept it. The staff was small and they were all close, like a family. So, she was on sabbatical leave until her deal with Deacon was concluded. She was so grateful to have a job to return to. It was one less thing she had to worry about.

However, when she'd resigned at the tabloid, she'd made the mistake of letting Deacon Santoro's name cross her lips. That spiked everyone's interest. She'd been passed up the chain of management until she'd been sitting across from the managing editor. And when the whole sordid truth came tumbling out, the editor had assured her that she didn't need to quit. In fact, they'd increased her pay.

The editor was putting Gaby on an assignment. The money was most welcome as her father's mounting medical expense were beyond her means. She had been shocked until it became clear that they wanted her to feed them every bit of dirt she could dig up on Deacon Santoro. She'd initially refused. Finding out the truth about her aunt's death was one thing. Digging up information about his private life just for sensational headlines was something else.

In the end, they'd all agreed that she would remain on the payroll and submit a daily report with information regarding the deadly accident. After all, if the legal system wouldn't do anything about it, someone had to seek justice in whatever way possible. And so Gaby had come here not only to protect her father, but also to uncover the truth about the accident and to expose Deacon's actions to the world.

At the time, the plan had seemed so easy. She'd play along as his assistant and befriend the man, which from the looks of the desolate place wouldn't be hard. Then she'd get him to open up about the accident. She would prove that he was responsible for her aunt's death. At last the world would know the truth, just like her father had wanted for so long. And then she could return to her life—a life that was temporarily on pause.

Gabrielle wheeled the car into a parking spot next to

a late model gray sedan. She'd arrived early this morning as she'd wanted to make a good impression on Mr. Santoro. She didn't want to give him any reason to go back on his agreement to drop the charges against her father, and that included keeping her connection with *QTR* magazine hush-hush.

She climbed out of the car and lifted her head to the blue sky. There was a gusty breeze. The forecasters said there was a storm brewing over the Pacific, although it hadn't reached them yet. But there was an ominous tension in the air.

She turned to head inside, but she wasn't sure where to go. There was yet another fence surrounding the building. There were numerous gates but no signs indicating where each led.

A movement in the corner of her eye caught her attention. Her gaze strayed across the outline of a figure in the distance.

"Excuse me," Gabrielle called out as she rushed forward.

The man's back was to her.

She called out again.

The man straightened from where he was bent over a rosebush. He was wearing jeans, a black long-sleeved shirt and a ball cap. He didn't turn around. Did he hear her?

"Hey, could you tell me where to go?" Not about to continue screaming across the grounds, she started down to a set of stained concrete steps leading to the garden.

By the time she reached the bottom step, the man was gone. Perhaps he hadn't heard her. He could still be around here somewhere. She started walking around in hopes of spotting him again. However, he was nowhere to be found. How was that possible? He was just here a second ago. She turned around in a circle. Where had he gone so quickly?

She sighed and was about to walk away when she paused to take in her surroundings. She stood on the edge of an expansive rose garden with a winding footpath. Unlike the rest of the overgrown yard, this section was neat and tidy. She found this shocking. What made this garden so special? It was just one more question that she had for Mr. Santoro.

Gaby headed back up the steps to the parking area. If worse came to worse, she would try all the gates and open all of the doors she encountered until she found where she belonged. You really would think Mr. Santoro would greet her or at the very least call her.

Time was getting away from her. If she didn't hurry, she was going to start off this arrangement by being late. Talk about making a bad situation worse. She picked up her pace.

At the top of the steps, she glanced around. On both sides of the parking area were doors. There was the large main house and there were six garage doors with what appeared to be a guesthouse atop them. Would he have put the office in the guesthouse?

Her gaze moved back and forth between the two structures as she tried to make up her mind. Just as she decided to try the main house, a gate swung open. At last, Mr. Santoro had come to greet her.

She rushed toward the door, but she came to a halt when an older woman with white hair and a round, rosy face came hurrying out. The woman was muttering something under her breath and shaking her head, but Gaby wasn't able to make out what she was saying.

When the woman's gaze met hers, a smile softened the woman's face. She had kind eyes and a warm smile.

"Ah…hello, dearie. You must be Mr. Santoro's new assistant."

Gaby smiled back at the woman. "I am. My name's Gaby Dupré."

"Welcome Ms. Dupré. And you can call me Mrs. Kupps. Mr. Santoro, he likes formality."

"I'm pleased to meet you, Mrs. Kupps." Gaby held out her hand to the woman. "But please feel free to call me Gaby."

The woman giggled and placed her hand in Gaby's for a brief shake. "I'm pleased to meet you, too," she whispered, "Gaby."

"Will you be showing me what I need to do?"

The woman shook her head. "Not me, dearie. I wouldn't have a clue. I'm the housekeeper and cook."

Gaby was disappointed. Working with Mrs. Kupps would have certainly made her workday interesting. "Do you know who will be showing me what I need to do?"

"I assume that would be Mr. Santoro."

"Oh, will he be out soon?"

The woman clucked her tongue. "Mr. Santoro does not get out much these days."

"Not even on his own estate?"

The woman shook her head as a serious look came over her face. "He prefers to stay in his suite of rooms."

This arrangement was getting stranger by the minute.

"But how will I be able to work with him?"

"He will phone you."

And then Mrs. Kupps pointed out the way to the office. Gaby made it there with ease. Once inside, she glanced around the office, taking in the white walls and two desks that faced each other from across the room. They were both sparsely set up, but the one to her left looked a bit haphazard, as though the person had been in a rush to get out the door.

The room was adorned with beach decorations and a couple of prints of the ocean. It was pretty, but there was nothing of the man that owned this spacious estate. There were no movie posters, no snapshots of Mr. Santoro with costars and no awards. It was though he'd purposely removed himself from the room. But why?

Gaby moved to one of the desks and placed her purse as well as her pink-and-white tote on the desk chair. Her gaze scanned the desk as she searched for any instructions of what was expected of her or a number that she was supposed to call upon arrival.

Then the phone rang.

He should have never agreed to bring Gabrielle here.

The decision had been made in haste.

And it was a mistake.

Deacon paced back and forth in his private study. This woman with the honeyed voice was dangerous, as she was poised to be a distraction from the stark reality of his situation. She would make him think about all of the damage that had been done. If only he could remember the accident—remember if he was at fault.

He would need to be on constant guard around her. With her being the niece of the woman who had died in his arms, she would be out to finish what her father started—destroying him.

And then he'd almost been caught by Gabrielle while he was in the rose garden.

It was his oasis. His chance to feel like a normal person, not a man hunted and hounded for the truth—something he didn't possess. How exactly had she missed the sign that explicitly said Do Not Enter?

Luckily he'd had enough time to make a clean escape. But as her sweet voice called out to him, he'd hesitated. An overwhelming urge came over him to capture a glimpse of the face that went with such a melodious voice.

In the shadows, he paused and turned back. He'd been awestruck. He didn't know how long he'd stood there in the shadows watching her move about the garden searching for him. Her long hair had bounced around her slim shoulders. Her face—it was captivating. It wasn't the type of beauty that was created with powder and makeup. No. Hers was a natural, undeniable beauty.

Her creamy complexion was flawless. He was too far away to catch the color of her eyes. He imagined they would be blue. His gaze strayed down past her pert nose and paused on her lush, rosy lips. Oh, she was definitely going to be a big distraction.

He jerked his meandering thoughts to an immediate halt. What was done, was done, as his mother would say. Now he had to deal with the consequences.

Deacon Santoro gripped the phone in his good hand and pressed the number for the office. He lifted the receiver to his ear. Two rings later, Gabrielle answered. The tone of her voice was a sweet blend of vanilla and caramel with a touch of honey.

He did not have time to get caught up in such nonsense.

Focus.

Deacon resumed pacing. "I see you decided to abide by our agreement."

"I don't see how I had any choice?"

"Everybody has choices—"

"Not in this case."

"And you were able to find someone to check in on

your father?" He didn't know why he'd asked except that when he'd first made this proposal, Gabrielle had been quite hesitant to leave her father.

"I have a friend staying with him. Newton just moved back to the area and my father had a spare room. It seemed like a good idea at the time."

"I take it you've since changed your mind about this Newton."

Gabrielle hesitated. "Let's just say I've gotten to know him better and he's not the same as I remembered."

"I see." Deacon's curiosity spiked, but he forced himself to drop the Newton subject. "At least you won't have to worry about your father."

Deacon was impressed by her allegiance to her father, but that wouldn't be enough to sway him to concede. Her father had cost him more than just bad press, a mess in his yard and upset employees—her father had stirred up the paparazzi. Once again, there were news reports on television and the internet. His phone—with its private number—was now receiving calls from journalists wanting "the truth."

The little sleep he did get was once again riddled with nightmares—fiery, jagged dreams. But when he woke up, the images blurred and the memories receded to the back of his mind. With each dream, he hoped he'd be able to latch on to the elusive truth of what happened on that deadly night. But try as he might, his memory had holes the size of craters and images blurred as if in a dense fog.

The doctors had warned him that the memories might never come back to him. That was not the answer he'd wanted to hear. He needed the truth—even if it meant he was responsible for taking another person's life. Trying to live with the unknown was a torture that had him knotted up inside.

"If you would just tell me where to meet you, we can sit down and go over what is expected of me." Gabrielle's voice cut through his thoughts.

"That won't be necessary."

"Of course it is."

He could hear the confusion in her voice. She wasn't the first assistant that had been uncomfortable with his distant style of management, but it was the way it had to be. He didn't need anyone eyeing him with pity. He didn't deserve anyone feeling sorry for him. It was best for him to keep to the shadows. The accident had left permanent scars on him both inside and out. His career as an actor was over. And he was now struggling to find a new position for himself in the background of Hollywood.

He cleared his throat. "All of your instructions are on your computer. The password is capital B-e-a-c-h."

"Will you be stopping by the office later?"

"No."

"I don't understand—"

"We will conduct our business via the phone or preferably by email."

"But what if I have papers for you to sign? Or mail. I'm assuming that I'll be receiving your business correspondence."

"You will. And if you check next to the interior door, there is a mail slot. Drop whatever correspondence needs my attention in there and I'll get to it."

"But that doesn't seem very efficient. I don't mind bringing it to you—"

"No!" His voice vibrated with emotion. He clenched his jaw and swallowed hard. He didn't want to have to explain himself. After all, he was the boss. In a calmer voice, he said, "This is the arrangement. If you don't like it, you are free to leave. Our deal will be null and void."

"And my father?"

"He will face the judge and pay for the trouble he caused."

"No. I can do this." Her words were right, but her voice lacked conviction.

In all honesty, if she quit, he didn't know what he'd do for help. The temp agencies had blacklisted him after he'd gone through a dozen temps in the past couple of months. But he'd make do, one way or the other. He always had in the past. "You're sure?"

"I am."

"Then I will let you review the document that I've emailed you. It should explain everything including the fact that I work late into the night, but I don't expect you to. However, I will have work waiting for you each morning." When sleep evaded him, he found it best to keep his mind busy. It kept the frustration and worries of the unknown at bay.

"Does anyone else work in the office?" she asked.

"No."

She didn't immediately respond.

He hadn't considered that she wouldn't like working alone. It had been one of his requirements through the temp agencies, but Gabrielle hadn't given him time to get in to specifics when they'd spoken on the phone. Maybe this was his way out—even if the voice inside his head kept saying that he needed to watch out for her.

He cleared his throat. "If working alone is going to be a problem, we could end this now."

The silence on her end continued. He really wished he could look into her eyes. For the first time, he found communicating via the phone frustrating.

"No. It won't be a problem." Her voice sounded confident. "But I have a stipulation of my own."

"And that would be?"

"I need to speak with my father at least once a day—"

"That's fine."

"Would you reconsider letting me visit him? He will miss me."

This separation was to punish her father—not her. He'd cost Deacon and now the man had to pay a price—even if it wasn't dictated by a judge. Her father would learn not to take Gabrielle for granted.

"He should have thought of that before he allowed you to pay the price for his actions. Our arrangement will hold. You will stay here and work for three months."

Deacon knew what it was like to be alone. Both of his parents had passed on and he had no siblings. Other than Mrs. Kupps, the housekeeper, he was alone in this big rambling estate—except now Gabrielle was here. And somehow her mere presence seemed to make this place a little more appealing and less like a prison.

"My father didn't make me do anything. I volunteered." Her indignation came through loud and clear.

"Now that everything is settled, I'll let you get to work." Deacon disconnected the call.

Something told him this was going to be a very, very long three months. But it definitely wouldn't be boring.

CHAPTER TWO

THIS DEFINITELY WASN'T her best first day on the job.

In fact, it ranked right up there as one of the worst.

And the day wasn't over yet.

A loud crack of thunder shook the windows at the same time as lightning lit up the sky around the guest-house. Gabrielle rushed to close the French doors. Some-how the weather seemed rather fitting.

She had one more piece of business before she curled up with a book and escaped from reality. She had to file her first report with *QTR*.

Gaby sat down at the granite kitchen bar and opened her laptop. She stared at a blank screen with the cursor blinking at her...mocking her. What would she say? She didn't even know what format to use. Did they expect her to tell a story or stick to bullet points?

Sure, she'd earned a bachelor's degree in journalism, but with a downturn in the economy, she hadn't been able to land a position in publishing, so she'd returned to school. She'd gone on to get a second degree in library science. Books had always been her first love.

And as much as she loved words, right now they wouldn't come to her. She typed a couple of words, but they didn't sound right. She deleted them.

This is ridiculous. It's not an article for the public to

read. It doesn't have to be perfect. It just needs to be the
facts. So start writing.

The man has closed himself completely off from
others. Is it the result of guilt? Or something else?

As she pressed Enter to begin the next point, the land-
line rang. That was odd. She hadn't given anyone that
phone number. Her father had her cell phone number.

She picked up the phone. "Hello."

"Did you find everything you need?" Not a greeting.
Just straight to the point.

"Yes, I did."

"I wasn't sure what you like to eat, so I had Mrs.
Kupps prepare you a plate of pasta, a tossed salad and
some fresh baked bread. You will find it in your kitchen."

Outside the storm raged on with thunder and howling
wind. Gaby did her best to ignore it. "Thank you." Had
he called purely out of courtesy? Or was this his way of
checking up on her? Perhaps this was her opportunity to
flush him out of the shadows. "Will you be joining me?"

"No." His voice was firm and without hesitation. He
was certainly a stubborn man. "In the future, you can
let Mrs. Kupps know what you eat and don't eat, so that
she can plan the menu appropriately."

"I—I can do that." She hesitated. "The guesthouse
is nice." There was some sort of grunt on his end of the
phone. She wasn't sure what it was supposed to mean, so
she ignored it. "What time would you like to get started
in the morning?"

"I start before the sun is up. You can start by eight.
Will that be a problem?"

"No. Not at all." She was used to opening the library

at eight each morning. "I have a few things that I'd like to go over with you. Shall we meet in my office?"

"I thought you understood that this arrangement is to be by phone or email. I don't do one-on-one meetings—"

"But—"

"There are no exceptions. Good night."

And with that terse conclusion, he'd hung up on her. She stared at the phone. She could not believe that this man was so stubborn. Working for him was going to be difficult, but trying to get information about the accident from him was going to be downright impossible—unless she could get past this wall between them. And she hadn't come this far to give up.

Gaby hung up the phone and turned her attention back to the report for *QTR*. She'd lost her concentration after speaking with Deacon. She was back to staring at the blinking cursor and wondering what she should write.

QTR had assured her that before anything was published, they would get her approval. She wouldn't have agreed to the arrangement otherwise. After all, she didn't want them getting the facts wrong.

Although at this point, there wouldn't be much to write about the elusive Mr. Santoro. Giving herself the freedom to write about anything she'd learned so far, she resumed typing.

His estate in in disarray with overgrown vegetation. Was it always this way?

He's run off multiple assistants. What has happened? Has he fired them? If so, for what?

Locked door between the office and the rest of the house. What is he hiding?

The man lacks social niceties. Has he always been this way? Or is this a new thing?

It certainly wasn't a stellar first report. Would they be upset that it contained more questions than answers? Or would they appreciate her train of thought and look forward to the answers?

Accepting that it was the best she could do now, she proofread the email. Gabrielle pressed Send and closed her personal laptop.

She moved to the French doors and stared at the sky—the storm had now moved away. She opened the doors, enjoying the fresh scent of rain in the air. In the distance, the lightning provided a beautiful show. Was Mr. Santoro staring at the sky, too? She instinctively glanced in the direction of the main house, but she couldn't see it as it sat farther back than the guesthouse.

Still, she couldn't stop thinking about her mysterious boss. There had to be a way to break through the man's wall. She would find it, one way or the other.

CHAPTER THREE

TWO DAYS...

Forty-eight hours...

Two thousand, eight hundred and eighty minutes...

One hundred seventy-two thousand and eight hundred seconds...

No matter how Gaby stated it, that was how long she'd been at the Santoro estate and how long she'd gone without laying eyes on her new boss. It was weird. Beyond weird. What would that be? Bizarre?

Gaby sighed. Whatever you called it, she wasn't comfortable with this arrangement. Not that her accommodations weren't comfortable. In fact, they were quite luxurious. And unlike the estate's grounds, the guest suite was immaculate, thanks to Mr. Santoro's housekeeper, Mrs. Kupps. The woman had even written her a note, welcoming her.

Gaby glanced at her bedside table and realized that she'd slept in. She only had five minutes until she was due at the office. She had to get a move on. She slipped on a plain black skirt to go with a gray cap-sleeve blouse. There was a jacket that went with the outfit, but she rejected it. It was a warm day and she was more comfortable without the jacket. After all, it wasn't as if she had any business meetings. When Mr. Santoro said that he would limit their interactions to strictly email with the rare phone call, he hadn't been exaggerating.

She stepped in front of the full-length mirror and slipped on her black stilettos. With her height of only five foot two, the extra inches added to her confidence.

A knock sounded at the door, startling Gaby. She knew who it was without even opening the door. It would be Mrs. Kupps trying to lure her into eating breakfast. Gaby already explained that she didn't eat much in the mornings. In all honesty, she loved breakfast but never had time for it. She'd grown used to her liquid diet of coffee, with sugar and milk. It was easy to grab when she was on the run. Upon learning this, Mrs. Kupps had clucked her tongue and told her that she would end up with an ulcer if she didn't take better care of herself.

Gaby rushed to the door. "Good morning."

Mrs. Kupps stood there with a bright smile, a tray full of food and a carafe of coffee. "Good morning to you, too. I just brought you a little something to eat." Mrs. Kupps rushed past her and entered the small kitchen, placing the tray on the bar area. "I know you're in a hurry, but I'm determined to find something you can eat quickly."

"Mrs. Kupps, you don't have to do that." And then, because she really didn't want to hurt the woman's feelings, she added, "But it is really sweet of you. And the food looks amazing."

Mrs. Kupps beamed. "Oh, it's nothing, dearie. I enjoy having someone around here to spoil. Lord knows Mr. Santoro doesn't let anyone fuss over him since the accident. He's like a big old bear with a thorn in his paw."

"So he wasn't always so standoffish?"

Mrs. Kupps began setting out the food. "Goodness, no. He was always gracious and friendly. Perhaps he was a bit wrapped up in his acting career, but that's to be expected with his huge success. But now, he lurks about all alone in that big mansion. He doesn't see guests and rarely takes phone calls. I cook all his favorites, but his appetite isn't what it used to be. I'm really worried about him."

"Do you know what's wrong with him?" Gaby couldn't help but wonder if the guilt over the accident was gnawing at him.

Mrs. Kupps shrugged. "I don't know. And I really shouldn't have said anything. I just don't want you to leave. We need someone young and spirited around here. Lord knows, we've gone through assistant after assistant. He's even tried to run me off but it's not going to happen." The woman smiled at her. "You're a breath of fresh air. I have a good feeling about you."

Mrs. Kupps checked that everything was as it should be and then made a quick exit. It wasn't until the door shut that Gaby thought of a question for the very kind woman. Why did she stay here? Mr. Santoro was not the easiest person to work for. In fact, he was demanding and expected nothing but perfection with everything that Gaby did. And when she messed up, there was a terse note telling her to fix said error. And he didn't spare the exclamation points.

Still, she had agreed to this arrangement to save her father—a father who was now more eager to know what dirt she had dug up on her boss than worrying about how she was making out in such strained circumstances. It was all he'd wanted to talk about on the phone. His full attention was on making Mr. Santoro pay for the accident.

Gaby's gaze scanned over the croissant and steaming coffee. There was also a dish of strawberries. Okay. So maybe she had enough time to enjoy a few bites. Her stomach rumbled its approval. Perhaps some nourishment would help her deal with the stress of the day.

She couldn't help but wonder if this would be the day that Mr. Santoro revealed himself to her. He couldn't hide from her forever.

Deacon awoke with a jerk. His gaze sought out the clock above the door. He'd slept for more than two hours without waking. That was a new record for him, but it had come at a cost. He'd had another nightmare and, even worse, he was late.

It'd been another night spent in his office. He preferred it to staring into the dark waiting for sleep to claim him. Because with the sleep came the nightmares.

A couple of months after the accident, his nightmares had started to subside. But then Gabrielle's father had staged his protest with a megaphone, and he'd shouted horrible accusations. It was then that the nightmares had resumed. Sometimes Deacon remembered bits and pieces. There were brutal images of fire, blood and carnage. He had to wonder how much was real and how much had been a figment of his imagination.

Other times, he was left with a blank memory but a deep, dark feeling that dogged him throughout the day. It'd gotten so bad that he dreaded falling asleep. That's when his insomnia had set in with a vengeance. After spending one sleepless night after the next, he'd given up sleeping in his bed. In fact, he'd given up on sleep and only dozed when utter exhaustion claimed him.

It'd helped to keep his mind busy. And so he'd become a workaholic. Knowing the movie industry inside and out, he was working on starting his own production business. But being the man behind the curtain meant he had to find people he could rely on to do the legwork for him. That was proving to be a challenging task.

He'd just sat down to read over the lengthy letter that

Gabrielle had typed up for him. It had been late in the night or early in the morning, depending on how you looked at it. He'd made it to the last page when his eyes just wouldn't focus anymore. Blinking hadn't helped. Rubbing them hadn't made a difference. And so he'd closed them just for a moment.

He jumped to his feet and gathered up the papers that he'd reviewed. If he didn't get these on Gabrielle's desk before she arrived, it would have to wait until lunchtime. Because the mail drop in the wall only went one way. There was no way for him to deliver any documents anonymously for his assistant. He would have to see about rectifying that, but for now, he had to beat Gabrielle to the office.

He strode toward the door. When he reached out his hand for the doorknob, he couldn't help but notice the webbed scars on the back of his hand. They were a constant reminder of the horror he might have caused that impacted so many lives—especially Gabrielle's.

It was no secret that he'd liked his cars fast and he'd driven them like he was on a racetrack. He couldn't remember the details of that fateful night, but it wouldn't surprise him if he'd been speeding. If only the police would just release their findings. Gabrielle's father wasn't the only one anxious for that report.

His attorney had told him there were a number of complications. There had been an intense fire that destroyed evidence followed by a torrential downpour. Deacon didn't care about any of it. He just needed to know—was he responsible for taking a life?

Deacon moved through the darkened hallway, past the dust-covered statues and the cobwebs lurking in the corners. He didn't care. It wasn't like there was anyone in the house but him. Not even Mrs. Kupps was allowed in this part of the house. She kept to the kitchen and the office suite.

He descended the stairs in rushed steps. When he reached the locked door that led to the office area, he paused. There was no light visible from under the door and no sounds coming from within. He hated sneaking around his own home, but he didn't have any other choice. He didn't want to startle her with his appearance.

He recalled what had happened when his friends, or rather the people he'd considered friends, had visited him in the hospital right after his accident. They were unable to hide their repulsion at seeing the scars on his face, neck and arms. And then he'd held up a mirror to see for himself. The damage was horrific. After numerous rounds of plastic surgery, his plastic surgeon insisted the swelling and red angry scars would fade. Deacon didn't believe him. He'd already witnessed the devastating damage that had been done. It was so bad that he'd removed all the mirrors in the house as well as any reminders of how he used to look.

Deacon banished the troublesome thoughts. What was done, was done. He moved into the office and placed the stack of papers on Gabrielle's desk. That would definitely keep her busy today and probably some of tomorrow.

He noticed that her desk was tidy. However, there were no pictures or anything to tell him a little about her. It was though she wasn't planning to be here one minute longer than necessary to repay her father's debt. Not that Deacon could blame her—no one wanted to be here, including him. But he couldn't go out in the world—not until the accident was resolved and answers were provided.

Without tarrying too long, he turned to leave. He was almost to the door when he heard a key scrape in the lock. For a moment, he wondered what it would be like to linger in the office and have a face-to-face conversation with Gabrielle. In that moment, he realized how much he missed human contact. Maybe if he were to stay—maybe it would be different this time. Maybe she wouldn't look at him like he was a monster—a monster that killed her aunt.

He gave himself a mental shake. It was just a bunch of wishful thinking. He moved with lightning speed to the other door. He grasped the doorknob and, without slowing down, he gave it a yank, slipped into the outer hallway and kept moving. He needed distance from the woman who made him think about how one night—one moment—had ruined things for so many people.

CHAPTER FOUR

Didn't this man sleep?

It was almost lunchtime and Gaby hadn't even scratched the surface of all the tasks her boss had left for her. It didn't help that the phone rang constantly. Most calls were from reporters wanting to speak with Deacon. She had been left strict instructions to tell them "no comment" and hang up. With business associates, she was left with explaining that Deacon didn't take phone calls. When she explained that they would have to deal with her, it didn't go over well. Still, Gaby persisted. She had a job to do.

With a sigh, Gaby pressed Send on an email requesting the script for a film that Deacon was considering backing. But from what she could gather from prior correspondence and the files in the office, he had requested a lot of screenplays, but had yet to back one. She wanted to ask him how he decided which would be worth his money and which wouldn't.

Gaby got up to place the mail in the allotted slot for Mr. Santoro. When she approached the mail slot, she noticed the connecting door was slightly ajar. She slipped the papers into the slot and then turned back to the door. It beckoned to her.

What would it hurt to go see what was on the other side?

She knew if Mr. Santoro caught her, he would not be happy. In fact, it could very well blow up their whole deal. But if she didn't take a chance now, would she ever find out what he was hiding?

And to be fair, she was never told that she couldn't enter the house—only that mail was to go in the slot and communication would be phone or email. She had a hard time believing that he was as bad off as Mrs. Kupps had let on. This place wasn't exactly a dungeon by any means. He probably was just avoiding all the unanswered questions about the accident. And it was high time he stopped hiding from the truth and faced up to what had happened.

With a renewed determination, Gaby placed her hand on the doorknob and pulled the door open. It moved easily and soundlessly. There were no lights on in the hallway, but a window toward the back of the house let in some sunshine, lighting her way.

She didn't know what she expected when she crossed the threshold—an enraged Deacon Santoro, or a dark, dank house?—but she found neither. The house was done up in mainly white walls and marble floors. What she did notice was all of the empty spaces on the walls. There were mounted lights as though to illuminate a work of art or a framed photo, but there was nothing below any of the lights, as though even the hangings had been removed. *How odd.* The oddity was beginning to become a theme where Mr. Santoro was concerned.

The first set of doors she came to had frosted-glass inserts. One door stood ajar. She peered inside, wondering if at last she'd come face-to-face with Deacon Santoro, the larger-than-life legend. But the room appeared to be empty—except for all of the books lining the bookshelves.

Her eyes widened as she took in what must be thousands of titles. She stepped farther into the room, finding the bookcases rose up at least two stories. Like a bee to honey, she was drawn to the remarkable library. There was a ladder that glided along a set of rails to reach the top shelves. And a spiral staircase for the second floor of shelves with yet another ladder. It was truly remarkable.

She didn't know whether she had walked onto the set of *My Fair Lady* or the library of *Beauty and the Beast*. She'd never seen anything so magnificent. She moved to the closest bookshelf and found an entire row of leather-bound classics. It was then that she noticed the thick layer of dust and the sunshine illuminating a spiderweb in the corner. Who would neglect such a marvelous place?

Gaby ignored the dust and lifted a volume from the shelf. She opened the cover to find that it was a first edition—a *signed* first edition. It was probably priceless or at least worth more than she could ever pay.

And then she realized that if it was so valuable, she shouldn't be holding it in her bare hands. When she reached out to return it to the shelf, she heard footsteps behind her. She paused, not sure what to do. She moved the book behind her back. The time had come to face Mr. Santoro and suddenly she was assailed with nerves. It probably wouldn't help her case to be found hiding a collector's item. Her hand trembled and she almost dropped the book, but with determination, she gently placed it back on the shelf.

She leveled her shoulders, preparing for a hostile confrontation, and turned. The man had just entered the library and caught sight of her at the same time she had spotted him. He wore jeans and a long-sleeved shirt, which struck her as odd considering it was warm outside. And then she realized he was the man she spotted the first day that she'd arrived. He was the mysterious man from the rose garden.

"Who—who are you?" She didn't take her eyes off him.

His dark eyes narrowed. "I'm the one who should be asking questions here."

The voice, it was familiar. Was it possible that this was Deacon Santoro? She peered closely at him, trying to make up her mind. She supposed that it could be him. But it was his hair that surprised her. It was a longer style, if you could call it a style. The dark strands brushed down over his collar and hung down in his face.

She'd never seen him wear his hair that long in any of the movies he'd played in and yes, she'd seen them all. At one point, she'd have been proud of that fact, but after the accident, she'd wondered what she'd ever seen in the man.

When her gaze returned to his face, she had to tilt her chin upward. He was tall, well north of six feet.

And by the downturn of his mouth, he was not happy to find her in here. Her heart picked up its pace. She should turn away, but she couldn't. She needed to size up the man—all of him. She swallowed hard and jerked her gaze from his mouth. She really had to get a grip on herself. After all, he was the enemy, not some sexy movie star... Okay maybe he was that, too.

Ugh! This is getting complicated.

Her gaze took in the full, thick beard. It covered a large portion of his face. Between the beard and his longer hair, his face was hidden from view, for the most part. Except for his eyes. Those dark mysterious eyes stared directly at her, but they didn't give away a thing.

"What are you doing here?" His voice was deep and vibrated with agitation.

"I was looking for you." She refused to let on that his presence unnerved her. She clasped her hands together to keep from fidgeting. "I thought it was time we met." She stepped forward and held out her hand. "Hello, Mr. Santoro."

His eyebrows drew together and he frowned as he gazed at her hand, but he made no move to shake it. "I told you I don't do face-to-face meetings. And you may call me Deacon."

Gaby recalled what Mrs. Kupps had said about him preferring formality and was surprised he'd suggest she call him by his given name. Perhaps he wasn't as stuck in his ways as she'd originally thought.

"And I don't like to be kept isolated." Ignoring the quiver of her stomach, Gaby withdrew her hand. "If I am going to work with a person, they need to have the decency to meet with me—to talk one-on-one with me."

"You've seen me. Now go!"

She crossed her arms, refusing to budge. It was time someone called him out on his ridiculous behavior. "Does everyone jump when you growl?"

"I don't growl."

She arched a disbelieving eyebrow at him.

"I don't." He averted his gaze.

"You might want to be a little nicer to the people who work for you." And then she decided that pushing him too far would not help her cause, and said, "I have a request that just came in today for you to make an appearance at the upcoming awards show to present an award—"

"No."

"No? As in you don't want to attend? Or no, as in you won't be a presenter?"

"No, as in I'm not leaving this house. And no, I'm not presenting any awards. Have you looked at me? No one would want me in front of a camera."

The fact that he'd dismissed the idea so quickly surprised her. For some reason, she thought he would enjoy being in the spotlight. Isn't that what all movie stars craved?

Deciding it might be best to change the subject, she said, "You have an amazing library."

At first, he didn't say a word. She could feel his gaze following her as she made her way around the room, impressed that the books were placed in the Library of Congress classification system. Was it possible Mr. Santoro... erm, Deacon loved books as much as her?

"I see you have your books cataloged." She turned back to him. "Do you also have a digital catalog?"

He nodded. "The computer that houses the database is over there."

She followed the line of his finger to a small wooden desk next to the door she'd entered. "This place is amazing. I've never known anyone with such an elaborate private library."

His dark eyebrows rose behind his shaggy hair. "You like books?"

"I love them. I'm a librarian and..." Realizing that she was about to reveal that she was an aspiring journalist would only make him more wary of her.

"And what?"

"I was going to say that I read every chance I get." She turned back to him. "I take it you read, too."

He shrugged. "I used to. These days my reading is all work-related."

"That's a shame, because books are the key to the imagination. You can travel the world between the pages of a book. Or visit another time period. Anything is possible in a book."

"What is your favorite genre?"

"I have two—suspense and romance. And cozy mysteries. And some biographies." She couldn't help but laugh at herself. "I have a lot of favorites. It depends on my mood." Perhaps this conversation was her chance to get past his gruff exterior. "How about you?"

"Mysteries and thrillers." He turned toward the door but paused. Over his shoulder, he said, "You—you may make use of the library while you are here." Then his voice dropped to the gravelly tone. "But do not wander anywhere else. The rest of the house is off-limits."

He certainly growled a lot, but she was beginning to think that his growl was much worse than his bite. So far, so good. Now if she could just get him to open up to her, perhaps she could find the answers to the questions that were torturing her father.

But before she could say another word, Deacon strode out the door.

Why had he gone and done that?

Later that afternoon, Deacon strode back and forth in his office. He never gave anyone access to the house. Even Mrs. Kupps, who had been with him for years, had restricted access. Now, his house was being overrun by women and he didn't like it.

He'd rather be left alone with his thoughts. His repeated attempts to uncover the truth had been unproductive. He kept coming back to one question: had he been responsible for Gabrielle's aunt's death?

As long as Gabrielle stayed in the library and the office, he could deal with her unwelcome presence. If he wanted a book to distract him from reality, he would make his visits late at night, when he was certain that Gabrielle would be asleep.

The thought of having that beauty staying on the estate gave him a funny sensation in his chest. It wasn't a bad feeling. Instead, it was warm and comforting. Dare he admit it? The sensation was akin to happiness.

It was wrong for him to be excited about Gabrielle's presence. He didn't deserve to be happy. But there was something special about her and it went beyond her beauty. She was daring and fun. He admired the way she stood up to him. He could only imagine that she was just as fiery in bed.

In that moment, his imagination took over. The most alluring images of his assistant came to mind. He envisioned Gabrielle with her long coppery hair splayed over the pillow while a mischievous grin played on her lips. With a crooked finger, she beckoned him to join her.

Eagerness pulsed through his veins as he shifted his stance. He'd been alone so long and she was an absolute knockout. He imagined that she could see past his scars and—

Knock. Knock.

Immediately his lips pulled down into a distinct frown. Who was disturbing his most delicious daydream? Wait. Who was in his private area?

Deacon spun around. Heated words hovered at the back of his mouth. And then his gaze landed on Gabrielle. A smile lifted her glossy red lips. Her eyes were lit up like they had been in his fantasy. He blinked and then peered into her eyes once more. Instead of desire, there was uncertainty.

"What are you doing here?" His words came out much gruffer than he'd planned.

"I—I have some correspondence for you to approve, and I have an idea I want to run by you."

"And for that you marched up here to my private office? You couldn't have emailed me?"

Her lips lowered into a firm line just as her fine eyebrows drew together. "I didn't think you were serious about resuming that ridiculous nonsense of emailing each other. I thought now that you've granted me access to your home, we could start working together like two professionals instead of being pen pals."

His prior assistants never would have been so bold. His respect for Gabrielle grew. And that observation caught him off guard. If he wasn't careful, her tenacity would lead them into trouble. However, she certainly did liven up his otherwise boring existence. Maybe he could risk having his life jostled just a bit.

"Well, you're here now, so out with it. What's your idea?" He had to admit that he was curious.

"I've been thinking over your concern about your public image. And I know that my father didn't help with that. But I've thought of something that might help—"

"Help?" He was utterly confused. "You want to help me?" When she nodded, he asked, "Why?" He was certain there had to be some sort of catch. There was no way she would want to help the person that was involved in an accident that killed her aunt. No one had that good of a heart.

Gabrielle lifted her chin. "During our first phone conversation, you appeared to be upset with the negative publicity, and I've thought of a way to negate some of it."

Some people may call him a pessimist, but the possibility of countering the bad publicity was definitely too good to be true. There was a catch and he intended to find it. "And what's in it for you?"

Her eyes widened. "Why does there have to be more?"

"Because you aren't here out of choice. There is absolutely no reason for you to help me. So out with it. What do you stand to gain?"

She sighed. "Fine. There is something—"

"I knew it." He felt vindicated in knowing that behind that beautiful face was someone with an agenda. "Well, by all means, don't keep me in suspense. What do you want in exchange?"

She frowned at him. "Why do you have to make it sound so nefarious?"

"And why are you avoiding the answer?"

"If my idea works, I was hoping you'd see fit to shorten my time here."

He smiled. "I was right. There is a catch."

"I just think we can help each other is all. Would you consider sponsoring a fundraiser?"

A fundraiser? He had to admit he hadn't seen that coming. "I am the last person who should be asking people for money."

Gabrielle shrugged. "I don't agree. People know who you are. You're up for a couple of awards for your latest movie release. And you have another movie about to be released. I think you'd be surprised by the public's support."

Deacon shook his head. "It's not going to happen."

"Consider it your way to put some good back in the world."

"You mean my penance."

She shrugged and glanced away. "I suppose you could put it that way."

There was no penance big enough, generous enough or selfless enough to undo his actions. "No."

"Because you don't want to do something good?"

Why did she have to keep pushing the subject? He had to say something—anything—to get her to let go of this idea. And then he thought of something that might strike a chord with her. "Have you looked at me?"

"Yes, I have." Her gaze was unwavering.

"Then you know that I have no business being seen in public."

Her gaze narrowed. "I think you're trying to take the easy way out."

"Easy?" His hands clenched. "There is nothing easy about any of this. You of all people should know that."

"You're right. I'm sorry. That didn't come out the way I meant."

He wanted to know what she had meant but he decided the subject was best left alone. "I need to get back to work."

"I think with a haircut and a shave that you'd look…" She stepped closer to him. At last, she uttered softly, "Handsome."

Too bad he didn't believe her. There wasn't a stylish enough haircut to distract people from his scars. And a shave would just make those imperfections obvious. He shook his head. "It isn't going to happen."

"What isn't? The haircut or the shave? Or the fundraiser?"

"All of them." Why couldn't she just leave him alone? It would be better that way.

She crossed her arms and jutted out her chin. "I can do this. And you can participate as much or as little as you want."

"What do you know about fundraisers?"

"Enough. I've organized one for my library each of the past five years."

"A library fundraiser?"

She nodded. "Funds are being withheld from libraries across the country. Lots of them are closing. In order to keep doors open, libraries have become creative in raising money. So many people need and use the resources made available by the library, but the government is of less and less help at keeping the lights on. It's a real struggle."

"I didn't know." It'd been a very long time since he was in a public library. "My mother used to take me to the library when I was very young. I remember they had reading time where all the kids sat around in a circle and they read a story to us. I think that's when I got the acting bug. I'd listen to the librarian use different voices for the various characters and it struck a chord in me."

Gabrielle's smile returned and lit up the room. "As a librarian, that's the best thing I could hear. I love when we are able to make a difference in someone's life, big or small."

"So, what you're saying is that you'd like me to do a fundraiser for your library."

She shook her head. "Not at all. The library is what is close to my heart. You need to find what's closest to yours."

He took a second to think of what charity he'd most like to help and the answer immediately came to him.

"You've thought of something. What is it?" She stared at him expectantly.

"Breast-cancer research. *If* I were going to have a fundraiser, that's what I would want it to be for."

"Why?" she asked, curiosity ringing from her gaze.

He shook his head. He wasn't going to get in to this. Not with her. Not with anyone. It was too painful and still too fresh in his mind.

After a few moments, Gabrielle asked, "Will you at least consider the idea?"

It would be more efficient and less hassle to just write a hefty check, which he did every year in memory of his mother. But Gabrielle seemed to have her heart set on this. Perhaps if he didn't readily dismiss the idea, with time she'd forget about it.

"I'll think about it." When a smile reappeared on her face, he said, "But don't get your hopes up."

She attempted to subdue her smile, but there was still a remnant of it lighting up her eyes as she placed some papers on his desk. Those eyes were captivating. They were gray, or was it green? Honestly, they seemed to change color. And they had gold specks in them. They were simply stunning, just like Gabrielle.

And then as he realized he was staring, Deacon turned away. "I'll get these back to you by morning."

He gazed out the window at the cloudless sky until he heard the clicking of her heels as she walked away. It was then he realized he'd forgotten to tell her something.

He turned around but she was out of sight. He was going to tell her not to enter this part of the house again—that it was out of bounds. But something told him she would have just ignored him anyway.

CHAPTER FIVE

THE NEXT MORNING Deacon couldn't concentrate.

He should be working, if he was ever to get his fledgling company firmly ensconced in the movie business. He'd made a lot of inroads so far. The legal documents were all signed and filed with the appropriate agencies. Financial business accounts were opened. Sunsprite Productions was at last ready to do business.

In front of him sat a stack of proposed movie scripts to read. However, every time he sat down, his mind would venture back to Gabrielle. Why had he agreed to keep the door unlocked? To give her access to his space?

He'd avoided the library like the plague and, so far, she hadn't returned to his office. The way she'd looked at him—well, it was different than others. She hadn't shuddered. And she hadn't turned away. If anything, she'd been curious. In fact, she'd even stepped closer to him. What was he to make of that?

No one who'd come to see him in the hospital, people who were supposed to be his friends, had been able to look him in the eye. Most had hovered at the doorway, unwilling to come any closer. But not Gabrielle. She was different. And his curiosity about her kept mounting.

He had to wonder why her aunt had found it necessary to use her last breath to tell him to take care of her niece. He had to be missing something. Gabrielle Dupré was quite capable of taking care of herself.

She hit things straight on and treaded where others feared to go. And she was smart, as she'd demonstrated by coming up with that idea to improve his public image—though he doubted it would work. He needed to tell Gabrielle that he wasn't going to take her up on the offer; he just hadn't gotten around to telling her yet. It wasn't like he had to worry about letting her down. Gabrielle was no damsel in distress. She was sharp and would always land on her feet. Deacon wondered if her father knew how lucky he was to have her by his side.

He halted his train of thought. Listing all of her positive qualities was doing him no favors. No matter how much she intrigued him, nothing could ever come of it.

Because there was a look in her eyes, one that was undeniable. She looked at him with anger. She blamed him for her aunt's death. And for all he knew, she might be right.

Feeling the walls closing in around him, Deacon made his way down to the rose garden. It was the one place where he found some solace. With the gentle scent of the roses that reminded him of his mother and the sea breeze that conjured up memories of sailing, his muscles relaxed. It was here that the pulsing pain in his temples eased.

He moved about the garden. His doctor and physical therapist had told him to make sure to get plenty of movement as that would help heal the injury to his leg caused by the crash. He wasn't about to venture outside the estate gates. He knew the press would soon catch up to him. And then the probing questions would begin.

And so he spent time here in the spacious rose garden. He hadn't spared any expense creating this retreat. The garden ran almost to the edge of the cliff overlooking the ocean. Wanting a wide-open feel, he'd declined building a wall around the garden. He used to think that this garden was a little piece of heaven on earth.

Deacon took a deep breath, enjoying the fresh air. Out here he could momentarily forget the guilt that dogged him. Out here, he could pretend there wasn't the most amazing yet unobtainable woman working for him. For just a few precious moments, his problems didn't feel so overwhelming.

He followed the meandering brick path to the far edge of the garden. He paused to prune a dying purple rose from a newly planted bush. He'd surprised himself by finding that he didn't mind gardening. In fact, he found the whole process relaxing. Who'd have ever guessed that?

A glint of bright light caught his eye. He glanced around, finding an idle speedboat bobbing in the swells not far off the shoreline. The light must have been a reflection. It wasn't unusual for the water to be filled with boats on these beautiful sunny days. And today, with the brilliant sunrise, it wasn't surprising that people were out enjoying the warm air and the colorful sky.

He didn't give the boat any further attention as he turned back to his task. He continued to trim the dead blooms from the bush when a movement out of the corner of his eye caught his attention. Was it animal? Or human?

Deacon swung around. He didn't see anything. Perhaps it was just his exhaustion catching up to him. With a shake of his head, he returned to his task.

"Good morning."

The sound of Gabrielle's voice startled him. He turned with a jerk. "You shouldn't be here." Did she have to invade every part of his life? Frustration churned within him. "Go!"

Her eyes widened. "I… I'm sorry."

She stepped back. Her foot must have struck the edge of a brick because the next thing he knew, her arms were flailing about and then she was falling. He started toward her, but he was too far away to catch her. And down she went. Straight into a rosebush.

Deacon immediately regretted his harsh words. He didn't mean to scare her. He inwardly groaned as he rushed over to her.

The first thing he spotted was blood. Little droplets of blood dotting her arms and legs from the thorny vines. And it was all his fault. Since when had he become such a growling old bear—so much like the father that he swore he would never turn into. And yet it had happened…

Take care of Gabrielle. There it was again. Her aunt's last dying wish. He was certainly doing a dismal job of it.

As he drew near her, he watched as Gabrielle struggled to sit up. Her movements only succeeded in making the situation worse and a pained moan crossed her lips.

"Don't move," he said, coming to a stop next to her.

This was one of the rosebushes he hadn't gotten to. The limbs were long and unruly. He pulled the shears from his back pocket and hastily cut the bush. He worked diligently to free her.

And then he had her in his arms. Her eyes glistened with unshed tears. She sniffled but she refused to give in to the pain. Her strength impressed Deacon. He was used to women who lashed out or gave in to the tears. Gabrielle was stoic—or perhaps stubborn fit her better.

He started toward the house with her in his arms.

"I can walk," she insisted.

"I've got you."

"Put me down." There was steely strength in her voice and the unshed tears were now gone.

He hesitated, not wanting to put her down. To his detriment, he liked holding her close. She was light and curvy.

And she smelled like strawberries. His gaze lowered to her lips. They were berry-pink and just right for the picking. He forgot about their awkward circumstances and the fact that he hadn't shaved or had a haircut in months.

In that moment, all he wanted to do was pull her closer and press his mouth to hers. Her lips were full and shimmered with lip gloss. It had been so very long since he'd been with a woman—

"Now." Her voice cut through his wayward thoughts.

When his gaze rose up to meet her eyes, she stared up at him with determination. Did she know where his thoughts had drifted? He hoped not. Having her know that he was attracted to her would just make this uncomfortable arrangement unbearable. He lowered her feet to the ground.

"Come with me." This time he was the one issuing orders and he wasn't going to take no for an answer.

He led the way into the darkened house. He knew that in its day the house was impressive, but now the blinds were lowered and dust covered most everything. But it didn't matter to him. He never spent time on the first floor. He stuck to his suite of rooms. And that's where he led Gabrielle.

Into the expansive foyer with its white marble floor and large crystal chandelier. He turned toward the sweeping staircase that curved as it led to the second floor.

"Where are we going?" she asked.

"To get you cleaned and bandaged."

"I'll be fine."

She didn't trust him. That was fine. She had no reason to trust him. He wasn't even sure he trusted himself now that he had a faulty memory and tormenting dreams. But this wasn't about her trusting him. This was about her welfare and making sure she didn't have any serious injuries.

"You need someone to help you." He turned to her at the bottom of the stairs. "You can't reach the cuts on your back. And as fate would have it, today is Mrs. Kupps's day off."

He started up the steps, hoping she would see reason and follow him. The very last thing he needed on his conscience was her being injured because of him and then getting an infection. He may have royally messed up the night of the accident and no matter how much he wanted to go back in time, it was impossible. However, right now he could help Gabrielle. If only she would allow him.

At the top of the steps there were three hallways— one to the left, which was where his mother had had her suite of rooms, another hallway to the right, where the people he'd considered friends used to stay, and then the hallway straight back, which led to his suite of rooms and his office that overlooked the ocean.

He stopped outside the last door. He hadn't made his bed. He hadn't straightened up in forever. And it hadn't mattered to him for months. But now, it mattered. Now he was embarrassed for Gabrielle to see his inner sanctuary. Later tonight he would do some cleaning.

"Is something wrong?" she asked. "If you changed your mind, I can go."

"No. Nothing's wrong." And with that he swung open the door. It wasn't like he was trying to impress her. That ship had sailed a long time ago. In fact, he'd lost any chance to impress her before they'd even met.

The room was dark as the heavy drapes were drawn as they always were, but he knew his way around without bothering with a light. However, he realized that Gabrielle would have a problem, and he reluctantly switched on the overhead light.

"Why is it so dark in here?" she asked. "You should open the curtains and let in the sun."

"I like it this way."

"Maybe the sun would give you a cheerier disposition."

Why did she want to go and change him? He didn't want to be changed. This was now his life and he would live it however he chose. "My disposition is fine."

"Really? And you think it's normal to go around scowling at people and barking out warnings for them to go away?"

"I do not bark and I do not growl." He turned on the bathroom light.

"Apparently you don't listen to yourself very often."

"You are—" he paused, thinking of the right word to describe her "—you are pushy and…"

"And right about you."

He sighed. "You don't know everything."

"But I do know that you're going to turn down my offer to help you."

He arched an eyebrow and stared at her, finding that she was beautiful even with her hair all mussed up from the rosebush and cuts crisscrossing her arms. It was then that he recognized just how much trouble he was in. There was something about Gabrielle that got under his skin, that made him feel alive again. And made him want to be worthy of her affection.

And if he wasn't careful, he was going to fall for her—head over heels. And that couldn't happen. She would be crazy to fall for him after the car accident. And he didn't deserve to have love in his life—not that he was falling in love with her. He wouldn't let that happen.

But knowing that it was even a possibility had him worried. The best thing he could do for both of their sakes was to keep her around here for as little time as possible. Maybe he should accept Gabrielle's offer to plan the fundraiser. Not that he relished having more attention cast upon him, but he could shorten her time on the estate without arousing her suspicions. She would never know how she got to him.

"What are you smiling about?" Gabrielle was eyeing him suspiciously.

"Who, me? I don't smile. Remember, I growl."

"Oh, I remember. But I saw a distinct smile on your face, so out with it."

What did he have by holding back? He'd strike the deal, set the timetable and soon his life would return to the way it used to be. Why did the thought of his quiet, lonely life no longer sound appealing?

"I accept your offer," he blurted out before he had an opportunity to change his mind.

Her eyes widened. Today, they looked more blue than green. "You do?"

He nodded. "How long do you need?"

"A few months would be ideal."

Months? He was thinking in terms of weeks. "You'll need to do it faster than that."

She thought about it. "How grand do you want to make it?"

"That's up to you."

"Instead of say a grand ball, we could do a garden party."

"That might not be enough of a draw."

"Okay. Give me a little time and I'll come up with some other ideas."

"Just don't take too long. I'd like to do this in the next few weeks."

Her eyes widened. "You don't give a person much room to work, do you?"

"If you're not up to the challenge—"

"I'll do it."

"Good. Now let's get you cleaned up." He led her into the bathroom and set to work cleaning and medicating her injuries.

He felt terrible that she'd been injured because of him. He would work harder in the future not to be so abrasive. He'd obviously been spending too much time alone.

He stood in front of her as she sat on the black granite countertop. He'd just used a cloth to wash the wounds on her arms with soap and water. Now that they were rinsed off, he was gently patting them dry.

As he stood there, he could sense her staring at him. He glanced up to say something, but when his gaze caught hers, he hesitated. And then her gaze lowered. Was she staring at his lips?

CHAPTER SIX

WAS THAT DESIRE reflected in her eyes?

Deacon swallowed hard. Suddenly the walls seemed to close in around them and the temperature was rising... quickly. He should turn away because if she kept staring at him, he was going to start to think that she wanted him—almost as much as he wanted her.

"You shouldn't do that," he said.

"Do what?" Her voice carried a note of innocence.

He inwardly groaned. "You know what."

"If I did, I wouldn't ask."

Surely she couldn't be that naive. Could she? "Look at me like—like you want me to kiss you."

She didn't blush, nor did she look away. "Is that what you think I want? Or is that what you want?"

Why did she have to insist on confusing matters? He was already confused enough for both of them. "Forget I said anything."

"How am I supposed to do that now that I know you're thinking about kissing me?"

"That's not what I said." He huffed in exasperation. "Turn around."

"Why?"

"Do you have to question everything?"

She shrugged. "If I didn't, I wouldn't know that you want to kiss me."

"Would you quit saying that?" Heat rushed up his neck and settled in his face, making him quite uncomfortable. "Turn around so I can tend to the wounds on your back."

For once, she did as he said without any questions. Thank goodness. He wasn't sure how much longer he could have put up with the endless questions. It would have been so much easier to smother her lips with his own. And then he'd know if her berry-red lips were as sweet as they appeared.

But this was better. With her back to him, he could get a hold on his rising desire. They were oh, so wrong for each other. She was pushy and demanding. She was definitely not the type of woman he normally dated. If he hadn't been alone all these months, he wouldn't even be tempted by her. He assured himself that was the truth.

And then she lifted her shirt, stained with thin traces of blood, to reveal the smooth skin of her back. His assurances instantly melted away. All he wanted to do was run his hands over her body and soothe away her discomfort with his lips, fingers and body.

"Is something the matter?" she asked.

His mouth suddenly grew dry. He swallowed and hoped when he spoke that his voice didn't give away his wayward thoughts. "I—I'm just figuring out where to start."

"Is it that bad?"

He wondered if she was referring to his level of distraction or the cuts and punctures on her back. He decided that she'd given up flirting with him and was at last being serious. "It could be worse."

"That's not very positive."

He was beginning to wonder if along with his memory

loss he'd lost his ability to talk to women. He used to be able to flirt with the best of them without even breaking a sweat, but talking to Gabrielle had him on edge, always worrying that he'd say something wrong, which he seemed to do often.

"I didn't mean to worry you." He grabbed a fresh washcloth from the cabinet and soaked it with warm water. He added some soap and worked it into a lather. "Let me know if this hurts."

"It'll be fine."

He wanted to say that the skin on her back was more tender than that on her arms or hands, but he didn't want to argue with her. It was then that he noticed how her skirt rode up her legs, giving a generous view of her thighs. His hand instinctively tightened around the washcloth as his body tensed.

With great reluctance, he glanced away. It took all of his effort to concentrate on the task at hand. And it didn't help that the task involved running his fingers over her bare flesh. Talk about sweet torture.

He pressed the cloth gently to the first wound. When he heard the swift intake of her breath, he pulled away the cloth. "I'm sorry."

"It's okay. Just keep going."

"Are you sure?"

"Keep going. I obviously can't do it myself."

And so he kept working as quickly as he could. When her wounds were cleaned, rinsed and dried, he grabbed the antibiotic cream, which, thankfully, had something for pain relief. A few of the cuts had required bandages. The others had already started the healing process.

He lowered her top. "There. All done."

She turned to him. "Thank you."

"Don't." He waved off her gratitude. "I don't deserve your thanks."

"Yes, you do. You fixed me all up."

"I'm the one who caused your injuries." He just couldn't seem to do anything right these days.

"No, you didn't. I stumbled and fell. End of story."

"You stumbled because I startled you."

Her green-gray eyes studied him for a moment. "You do have a way of growling—"

His voice lowered. "I don't growl."

She laughed. "You just growled at me."

Had he growled? No, of course not. He wasn't some sort of animal. He was human—a damaged human, but human nonetheless. Still, his tone might have been a bit gruff.

She stepped toward him. "I see the doubt in your eyes."

He narrowed his gaze on her. "If I growl so much, why are you still here?"

"Good question. I guess I'm just holding up my side of our agreement."

For a moment there, he'd forgotten that she was there at his insistence. He knew that if she had a chance, she'd be anywhere else. And he couldn't blame her. He definitely wasn't the most hospitable host.

But when he was this close to Gabrielle, he wanted to be someone else. His old self? No. He'd been too selfish—too self-absorbed. Right now, he wanted to be someone better.

"I'm sorry that I startled you earlier." He made sure when he spoke that his voice was soft and gentle. He would not growl at her. "I never meant for you to get hurt."

She stared into his eyes. "You really mean that, don't you?"

"Of course." His voice took on a rough edge again. He swallowed hard. And when he spoke, he made sure to return to a gentle tone. "I'm not used to having anyone out in the gardens."

"The rose garden is beautiful. That's why I was out there. I could see them from my bedroom window and I wanted to get a better look. Unlike the rest of the grounds, they are well-maintained. They must be special to you?"

"They are. I had them planted for my mother." He missed his mother. She had been kind and gentle. She had been the exact opposite of his brutal father. "Roses were her favorite. She used to spend hours out there. It's where she spent her last days."

Gabrielle's eyes filled with sympathy. She reached out to him. Her fingers wrapped around his hand. She gave him a squeeze. "I know that saying I'm sorry isn't enough, but it's all I have."

He continued to stare into her eyes, and he saw something more than sympathy. There was…understanding. He searched his memory and he recalled her mentioning that she'd also lost her mother. "You understand?"

She nodded. "My mother died giving birth to me, so I never knew her."

Instead of offering her the same empty words, he nodded and squeezed her hand back. It was then he realized her hand was still in his. The physical contact sent a bolt of awareness through his body.

He should let her go. He should step away. But he could do neither of those things. It was as though she were a life-sustaining force and without her, he would cease to exist.

His gaze lowered to her lips. Today they were done

up in a striking purple shade. Against her light skin, her lips stood out. They begged for attention and he couldn't turn away.

This wasn't good—not for his common sense. Because right now, all he could think about was her mouth—her very inviting mouth. He wanted to kiss her. He needed to kiss her. He longed to feel those lush purple lips move beneath his. A groan swelled in the back of his throat, but he choked it back down. He didn't need Gabrielle realizing how much power she had over him.

Because there was no way her kiss could be as amazing as he was imagining. Nothing could be that good. Not a chance.

He needed a heavy dose of reality to get her out of his system. And then he'd be able to think clearly. Yes, that would fix things.

Without giving his actions further thought, he dipped his head. He captured her lips with his own. At first, he heard the swift intake of her breath. She pulled back slightly and he thought she was going to turn away.

Then her hand lifted and smoothed over his beard. It must have caught her off guard. He should shave it, but it never seemed like the right time, until now.

And then her lips were touching his again. Tentatively at first. She didn't seem to know what to make of this unlikely situation. That made two of them, because kissing her was the absolute last thing he thought he'd be doing this morning.

As if he were acting in a trance, he drew Gabrielle closer and closer. He expected her to pull away. To slap him. Or at the very least stomp away.

Instead her hands came to rest on his chest. Her lips began moving beneath his. Her hands slid up over his shoulders and wrapped around his neck as her soft curves leaned against him. Mmm…she felt so good. And she tasted sugar-sweet, like the icing on a donut. And he couldn't get enough of her.

Their kiss escalated with wild abandon. It was as if she were the first woman to ever kiss him. No one had stirred him quite the way she did. He never wanted to let her go.

In the background, there was a noise. He couldn't make it out. And then it stopped. Their kiss continued as his body throbbed with need.

And then the sound started again. He wanted it to stop—for them to be left alone to enjoy this very special moment. The next thing he knew, Gabrielle braced her hands against his chest and pulled back.

It was too soon. He wasn't ready to let her go. And yet she moved out of his embrace. She reached for her cell phone, which was resting on the countertop.

"Hello, Dad. Is something wrong?" She turned her back to Deacon.

He ran the back of his hand over his lips. Instead of getting Gabrielle out of his system, he only wanted her more. He was in so much trouble.

Gabrielle turned back to him. She didn't have to tell him how much she loved her father. It was there in her voice when she spoke of him. It was in her eyes. It was in her actions by coming here and working for Deacon. She was a devoted daughter. Deacon just hoped her father deserved such devotion.

When she ended the call, Deacon asked, "Is everything all right with your father?"

She nodded her head. "He's fine."

Deacon noticed how her gaze failed to meet his. "But he's not happy about you being here."

"No. He isn't." She sighed. "My father used to

be such an easygoing guy. But the accident, well, it changed everything—for both of us."

Right then the wall went back up between them. Deacon could feel the warmth slip away. The chill was as distinct and real as the kiss they'd shared—the kiss that would not be followed by another. He would be left with nothing more than the memory.

"I know how death can change people." His mother changed after his father's death. Even though the man didn't deserve her undying love, she'd given it to him anyway. When his father passed away, his mother was cloaked in sadness. She moved on with her life, but it was never the same. She was never the same again.

Gabrielle's gaze briefly met his. "About what happened between us—"

"It was nothing." He was a liar. A bold-faced liar. "We lost our heads for a moment. It won't happen again." At least that part was the truth.

Gabrielle glanced away. "You're right. It was a mistake."

Her sharp words stabbed at him. He didn't know how much more of this he could take. It was best that they parted ways until he got his emotions under control.

He wasn't mad at her. He was angry with himself for losing control—for complicating an already messy situation.

"I should go." She just turned and walked away.

This situation was such a mess. An awful mess. How in such a short time had Gabrielle taken his dark hopeless life and filled it with light? He didn't know how he'd go back to the dark again.

CHAPTER SEVEN

THE SUN WAS sinking into the sky when Gaby called it quits for the day. Deacon had made himself scarce the rest of the day and perhaps that was for the best—for both of them.

Things were confusing enough. That kiss only intensified the conflicting emotions within her. She had no business flirting with him—coaxing him into kissing her. She should keep a respectable distance from this man. He was trouble.

Wait. Was that the answer? Could she be drawn to Deacon because he was so different from the other professional men she'd dated? Did Deacon's dark side act like a magnet?

Whatever it was, she had to get a grip on it. Because her reason for being here had absolutely nothing to do with becoming romantically involved with Deacon Santoro. And she'd do well to remember the circumstances that had led her here.

Gaby sighed as she let herself inside the guesthouse. There was still enough light filtering in from outside that she didn't turn on the lights. Instead she kicked off her heels and moved to the couch.

Her cell phone rang. She didn't recognize the number.

She was about to ignore it when she thought of her father. Something might have happened to him.

Needing to be certain her father was all right, she answered the call. "Hello."

"Gabrielle Dupré?" The male voice was unfamiliar to her.

Concern pumped through her veins. "Yes."

"My name's Paul. I'm with *Gotcha* magazine. Do you have a comment on the photo?"

"Photo?" She had no idea what this man was talking about. Thinking it was probably a scam, her finger hovered over the end button.

"The one of you in Deacon Santoro's arms. Would you like to comment on why you're in the arms of the man that *allegedly* killed your aunt?"

"There is no photo."

"If you don't believe me, go to our website. It's on the home page, front and center. I'll wait," he said smugly.

Gaby pressed the end button. It didn't matter what they had posted on their website, she wasn't giving a comment. But she wanted to see what had prompted the reporter to call her.

Her fingers moved rapidly over the touch screen and then the website popped up. She gasped. It was true. They did have a photo of her and Deacon.

Her face felt as though it was on fire. That man had made the situation sound so scandalous. Deacon had only been helping her after she'd been an utter klutz.

She studied the photo more intently. She didn't recall Deacon looking at her like—like he desired her. Surely they'd done something to alter the photo. She'd heard they do that all the time to make people thinner or prettier.

Thankfully there hadn't been any cameras in Deacon's house. Her face burned with embarrassment when she recalled how she'd flirted with him and then that kiss—oh, that heated kiss had been so good.

And yet, the kiss could not be repeated.

No matter how good it was, it was a one-time thing—a spur-of-the-moment thing. It didn't matter if his touch had been so gentle and so arousing. There could be no future for them. It was impossible. She was the niece of the woman who'd died because of Deacon's actions. There was no way they could get around that.

And she wouldn't do that to her father. She owed everything to her father—a man who'd always stood by her and who'd encouraged her to follow her love of books and sacrificed so that she could go to college.

She needed to talk to Deacon. She needed to tell him about the photo. She headed out the door. She also needed to make sure he'd heard her when she said that she regretted that soul-stirring, toe-curling kiss—because she did, didn't she?

Now that she had full access to the house, she knew her way around. She knew where Deacon would be, where he spent most of his time—in his office. It was like a one-room apartment. From what she could tell, it was where he took his meals, where he slept—when he slept—and where he worked.

Her footsteps were silent over the carpeting. When she reached his office, the door was open and the soft glow of the desk lamp spilled out into the hallway. But there were no sounds inside.

She stepped just inside the door. Her gaze scanned the room, with its long shadows. The desk chair was empty and so was the leather couch. Her gaze continued around the room until she spotted him standing in the open French doors that overlooked the ocean.

He didn't move. He must be lost in thought. She wondered if she was too late. Had he seen the photo?

She softly called out, "Deacon."

He didn't turn to her as she'd expected. Instead he said, "You shouldn't be here."

"We need to talk."

"If it's business, it can wait."

She crossed her arms and leveled her shoulders. "If you're going to talk to me, you could at least have the decency to face me."

He turned to her. His face was devoid of expression. She didn't know how he managed that when she was certain he was anything but calm—not after that spine-tingling kiss. She supposed that was what made him such an accomplished actor. She, on the other hand, wore her emotions on her sleeve. She didn't like it, but she didn't know how to hide her emotions.

"I'm facing you," he said matter-of-factly. "Now, why are you here?"

"I just had a phone call from a reporter. There's a photo of us on the internet."

A muscle in Deacon's jaw twitched. "Let me see it."

Recalling how the photo made it seem like there was something going on between them, she didn't think Deacon would take it well. "I don't think you want to see it."

He approached her and held out his hand.

She pulled up the picture on her phone. The headline read: Evading the Police in the Arms of a New Lover. Maybe bringing it to Deacon's attention wasn't a good idea after all.

She handed him the phone and waited for his reaction.

For a moment, he didn't speak. He scrolled through the article. With a scowl on his handsome face, he returned her phone.

"I don't even know how they got the photo," she said.

"I do. There was a boat not far off the shoreline. I hadn't thought much of it at the time, but there must have been a photographer on board."

"How can they publish this stuff? The headline is a lie."

"Welcome to my world. The tabloids will do anything for headlines. They are vultures."

"But they know it's not true."

"They don't care about the truth. It's whatever makes them money. I'm sorry you got caught up in it." He raked his fingers through his hair. "Until the police report is released, I'll be in the headlines."

They'd both been dancing around the subject of the car accident for far too long now. She needed some answers and she didn't know how to get them other than being direct. "Deacon, tell me about the accident."

"No." He moved to his desk and started moving papers as though he were looking for something.

"Don't dismiss me. I need to know—I need to know if what my father is saying about you is true."

Deacon straightened and his dark gaze met hers. "Why would you doubt him?"

"Because I feel like I'm missing something. And yet I keep thinking if you were innocent, you would have given your statement to the police. You would have cleared up this mess. Instead you remain tight-lipped about the facts, which says you're guilty. Is that it? Are you guilty?"

His jaw tightened. "I know in part you agreed to this arrangement to get information, but I'm not talking about the accident. Not now. Not ever. So if that's what you're after, you can go back to Bakersfield."

"So you can say I broke the arrangement and have

you press charges against my father? No thank you. I'm staying until my time has been served."

"This isn't a prison." His voice rumbled. "You're free to go."

"When our deal is fulfilled and not a minute sooner."

She paused and studied his face. "You might feel better if you talked about it."

"That subject is off-limits," he said with finality.

She sighed. "Okay then. I'll go work on the plans for the fundraiser. I'll let you know how it goes."

"At this hour?"

"It's not like I have much else to do around here. This place is so big and yet so empty."

His eyes grew dark. "It's the way I like it."

She didn't believe him. He didn't live alone in this big house because he wanted to. There was so much more to him closing himself off from the outside world. How would she get him to open up to her?

Gaby moved to the door. She paused in the doorway. She still hadn't told him the other reason she'd sought him out. She worried her lip. With him standing there looking so cold, it wasn't easy to talk to him. He reminded her of the man she'd met that not-so-long-ago day in the library, but tonight he hadn't told her to get out. Nor had he growled at her. Maybe he was changing.

"What?" he prompted.

"I just wanted to make sure that things were straight between us. You know, about the kiss."

He brushed off her concern. "It's already forgotten. I won't be kissing you again if that's what you're worried about."

"Oh." She wasn't sure what she'd wanted him to say, but that wasn't it.

Without a word, he turned his back to her and stared out at the moon-drenched ocean.

She had been dismissed, quickly and without hesitation. And so had their kiss. Was it just her that had been moved when his lips touched hers?

As she walked away, she felt as though she had lost her footing with Deacon. Her fingers traced her lips, recalling the way his mouth had moved passionately over hers, bringing every nerve ending to life. Her lips tingled at the memory.

He may deny it, but he'd felt something, too. And for the life of her, she didn't know what to do about this attraction that was growing between them.

CHAPTER EIGHT

HE COULDN'T STOP thinking about that picture.

The next morning, Deacon set aside his pen and leaned back in his desk chair. Although he didn't like the invasion of privacy, that wasn't what was eating at him. Nor was it the inflammatory headline. It wasn't any of that stuff.

He pulled up the photo on his computer with the larger monitor. The part that he couldn't get past was that she looked good in his arms. In fact, if he didn't know better, he'd swear they were lovers. And he was certain that's what anyone who caught a glimpse of the photo would think.

He scrolled down, finding there were hundreds of comments. He knew he shouldn't read them, but he couldn't help himself. There were, of course, mean, nasty comments, but to his surprise, there were others in support of them. They commented that sometimes love comes at the most unexpected times. Those people were all wrong—very wrong. Others said he was taking advantage of Gabrielle. That, too, was untrue. He was trying to help her, both financially, with an inflated salary, and so that she could gain her independence from her father. And it certainly had nothing whatsoever to do with love.

Deacon shut down the site. He'd read enough. He

checked the time. It was almost time for him to leave for his appointment.

He moved to his bedroom to change clothes. Still, he couldn't stop thinking about Gabrielle.

He knew she wanted answers, but he didn't think she'd buy his amnesia story any more than the police had bought it. There had been the skeptical looks followed by the prodding questions that went on and on with the same answers. It was as if they believed that if they asked the same questions a hundred and one times, his answers would change from "I don't remember" to something they could use against him.

In the short amount of time he'd spent with Gabrielle, he'd come to respect her. And having her upset with him for not opening up about the deadly accident was better than the look she would give him upon hearing that he couldn't remember it. In her shoes, he probably wouldn't believe him, either. He couldn't bear to have her look at him as if he were a liar. He was a lot of things in life, and some of them were not so good, but he wasn't a liar.

Maybe today he would get those elusive answers. His attorney had said he had news, but he wouldn't say on the phone whether it was good or bad. Something told Deacon that it wasn't good news. But he didn't want to say anything to Gabrielle until after his meeting, when he'd hopefully have more information.

Once he left the attorney's office, he had a doctor's appointment, where they'd run some tests to make sure he was healing properly. The accident had done significant damage to his body. If he were to pass through the metal detectors at the airport, he'd surely set them off with his newly acquired hardware.

In the end, he'd spend most of the day in Los Angeles. He didn't like these outings. They were fraught with the stress of being hounded by the press and wondering if the attorney and doctors would have more bad news for him.

Refusing to dwell on the unknowns awaiting him, he gathered the screenplay he'd finished reading. He was on the fence about this one. It was a mystery and he recalled Gabrielle mentioning that she enjoyed reading mysteries. He'd like to get her take on this one before he went any further. He did have a few changes he'd like to see incorporated when the screenplay was rewritten, but he'd run those past Gabrielle after he got her initial reaction.

However, when he opened the door to the office, Gabrielle wasn't at her desk. He walked farther into the room and found the outer door slightly ajar. He dropped the stack of papers on her desk and headed out the door. Once outside, he spotted Gabrielle at the end of the walk.

Deacon called out to her, but she must not have heard him as she kept moving. She turned the corner away from the beach and the guest cottage. Where was she going?

As he followed her, the sidewalk soon became surrounded by overgrown bushes, tall grass and weeds. He frowned. To be honest, he never walked toward the front of the house. It was too close to the road for his comfort with the paparazzi lurking about.

Surely she couldn't be enjoying a leisurely stroll through this thick vegetation, could she? He kept walking. His steps were long and quick as he hustled to catch up with her.

He turned a corner and there she was on the opposite side of the house. She stood in the shadows with a legal pad in one hand and a pen in the other. She was so intent on writing something that she didn't appear to notice his presence.

Once he was within a few yards of her, he called out to her.

Her head jerked up.

"Oh. It's you." And then she flashed him a smile that filled his insides with warmth. "Good morning."

"I stopped down to speak with you and didn't find you at your desk."

She turned back to the legal pad and continued writing. "I had an idea and I needed to check it out. Now, I'm not sure how to make it work."

An idea? Suddenly he grew uncomfortable. If he knew anything about Gabrielle, it was that she wasn't afraid to shake things up. And the fact that she was standing in his overgrown yard making notes didn't sit well with him.

She sent him a mischievous grin that lit up her eyes and intensified that fuzzy warm feeling in his chest. He swallowed hard. "Gabrielle, dare I ask what you have in mind?"

She glanced around. "This used to be a golf course, didn't it?"

He glanced over the neglected grounds and a fresh wave of guilt washed over him. "At one point, it was a private course."

"Wow." Her gaze was glued to the lush green grounds. "How many holes?"

"Nine." He used to spend a lot of time out here entertaining friends and associates. They said he had the best private course in the country. "But it doesn't matter anymore."

"Of course it matters. Why don't you golf anymore?"

"After the accident, my injuries made it impossible."

"And now, can you play?"

"I don't know. I haven't tried." He rotated his left shoulder. There was a dull pain, but thanks to lots of therapy, his range of motion was almost one-hundred-percent. "Not that anyone could golf out here."

"It looks like at one point it was beautiful."

"It was." His mind conjured up an image of the golf course in its prime. It had come with the house and it had been gorgeous, with water hazards and sand bunkers. It might have been a short course, but it had been a fun way to while away a lazy summer afternoon with friends. Those carefree days seemed like a lifetime ago now.

"It's a shame to let it go to ruin. Have you ever considered restoring it?"

He shook his head. He just couldn't imagine golfing when he had so much uncertainty and guilt weighing him down. "I stopped by to let you know that I need to go out for a while."

Her eyes widened and her mouth gaped open, but she quickly recovered her composure. "I didn't know you ever left here."

"I don't unless it's necessary."

Unasked questions filled her eyes, but she was smart enough to leave them unspoken. "Is there anything you need from me while you're gone?"

"Yes. I put a screenplay on your desk. I know you enjoy mysteries and I was interested in your thoughts. The sooner, the better."

"Thoughts? As in a pro-con list?"

He hadn't thought of that, but it wasn't a bad idea. "Sure. That works for me." And then he added, "I'd really appreciate it."

"Well, when you put it so nicely, I'd be happy to do it."

So nicely? He didn't think he'd said it in any special manner. Perhaps she meant since he didn't growl at her. Was Gabrielle having that much of an effect on him?

"I'll be gone most of the day." He turned to walk away.

"Do you mind if I ask where you're going?" When he turned back to her, she added, "You know, in case something comes up while you're gone."

"I'll have my cell phone. The number is listed on your computer."

"Oh, okay." She tried to hide it, but he caught the hint of a frown. "But there's something I want to discuss with you."

He checked the time on his phone. "It'll have to wait."

When he turned to walk away, Gabrielle said, "But it won't take long—"

"I can't be late. I'll talk to you when I get back."

Without another word from either of them, he strode away. He could have told her about his meeting with his attorney, but he didn't want to get her hopes up. He felt the pressure every time she looked at him. She wanted the truth as much as he did. If only he could remember.

This was pointless.

Gaby sat behind her desk later that afternoon. Deacon still hadn't returned. The fact that he'd been gone for hours worried her. Perhaps she should have pushed harder to learn his destination, but she doubted there was anything she could say to get him to open up.

She was quickly coming to the conclusion that no matter what she tried, Deacon wasn't going to let his guard down with her. He was a very determined man. But at least he didn't growl at her any longer. That had to mean something, right?

And now that she had him considering the fundraiser, she had to make it extra special. It was her ticket out of here without jeopardizing the deal for her father.

The fundraiser needed to be something different. Something that would attract big names with big money and also attract the press. She told herself that concluding their deal early was the only reason she was so invested in these plans that kept her up at night. Because there was no way she was trying to improve Deacon's image.

Her gaze scanned across the manuscript that Deacon wanted her to read. It could wait until later. Right now, she was wound up about the fundraiser. It could help so many people, not just Deacon.

After making some notes, Gaby looked up the name and number of the printing company she'd used for the library fundraiser. Lucky for her, she could use a lot of the same contacts for this event. It would cut down on her workload because getting this estate ready for the event was going to take a lot of time.

Gaby recalled seeing a list of estate employees on her first day here when she'd been checking out everything. Now where had she seen it? Her gaze scanned her desktop. Nothing there. Then she turned to the bulletin board behind her desk. No names and numbers.

She logged on to her computer. Maybe they were in here. A lot of pertinent information was stored on the network. She clicked on directory after directory. And then she stumbled across a file titled Personnel Listing. Under Grounds Crew, there were six names listed. Was it possible they were still employees? She knew it was a long shot, but hope swelled within her.

She reached for the phone and then hesitated. Should she do this without checking with Deacon?

She worried her bottom lip. He did give her the lead on this fundraiser. And it wasn't like he had much interest in the plans. But if she could show him what she had in mind, she was certain he would agree. She hoped.

Without letting any more doubts creep into her mind, she picked up the phone and dialed the first number on the list.

CHAPTER NINE

IT HAD NOT been a good day.

Not at all.

Deacon stepped out of the dark SUV and sent the door flying shut with a resounding thud. He pulled the baseball cap from his head, scrunched it with his hand and stuffed it in his back pocket. He removed his dark sunglasses and hung them from the collar of his shirt. He was done with disguises for today.

For all of the good it had done him, he might as well have stayed home. His attorney didn't have any good news for him. In fact, it was quite the opposite. The television network he'd been negotiating with had pulled out of the deal. They felt he brought too much bad publicity to the table and it would ruin their chances of having a hit. Apparently they didn't subscribe to the notion that there is no such thing as bad publicity.

Perhaps Gabrielle was right. Maybe he needed an image makeover. But would that work before the police report was released?

People might think that he'd refused to answer the officer's questions, but it was quite the opposite. In fact, at his meeting with his attorney, he told him in no uncertain terms to light a match under the powers that be. If he was innocent, he needed to be cleared ASAP. And if he had caused the tragedy, then he'd deal with the consequences.

When he'd moved on to his doctor's appointment, he grilled his physician about the gaping holes in his memory and the nightmares that plagued him. The doctor said the memories might all come back to him at once, or they might come back in pieces. His dreams were indicative of them coming back to him bit by bit. The doctor did warn him that the dreams might be real memories or they could be figments of his imagination. Or a combination of both.

When Deacon stepped out of the garage, he ran straight in to Gabrielle. He was not in the mood to be social right now. "What are you doing here? Shouldn't you be working?"

Her eyes widened. "I am going up to my rooms. And no, I shouldn't be working as the workday is over."

He pulled out his phone. It was much later than he'd been expecting. His appointments had taken up his entire day and he still didn't know any more than he had when he'd left that morning.

"I—I didn't realize the time." Not wanting to chitchat, he said, "I'll just be going."

"Wait. I wanted to talk to you."

"About?"

"The fundraiser. I've come up with some really good ideas. I was hoping for your input."

Deacon shook his head. He was in no frame of mind to deal with Gabrielle or the fundraiser. "I don't think this evening is a good idea."

"Are you feeling all right?"

"As good as can be expected. I just…" He paused as he grasped for any excuse to make a quick exit. "I'm just hungry."

"Then I have the perfect solution. It's Mrs. Kupps's night off, so I'll cook us up some dinner."

"I don't want you to go to any bother."

"It's no bother. We both have to eat, don't we?"

Her insistence surprised him. Of course, he realized that her interest was purely for business reasons. And she was right, they did have to eat. So what would it hurt to combine food and work?

"Okay. Count me in." He arched an eyebrow at her. "I take it this means you know how to cook."

She nodded. "Does that surprise you?"

"It's just that I don't know much about you."

"What would you like to know?"

A bunch of questions sprang to mind, like was she seeing anyone? If circumstances were different, would she go out with him? He immediately squelched those inquiries. They were none of his business—no matter how much he longed to know the answers.

He swallowed hard. "How well do you cook?"

A smile lifted her pink lips. "Don't you think you should have asked before agreeing to this meal? Now you'll just have to find out for yourself. Come on."

She didn't even wait for his reply before she started up the steps to the guesthouse. He watched the gentle sway of her hips as she mounted each step. No one had a right to look that good. And oh, boy, did she look good.

He hesitated. Right now, he was truly regretting agreeing to this meal. And it had absolutely nothing to do with his bad day or his uncertainty about her cooking skills and everything to do with how appealing he found the cook.

She glanced over her shoulder. "Well, come on."

Not wanting her to notice his discomfort, he did as she said. He started up the steps right behind her. A meal for two. This was a mistake. And yet he kept putting one foot in front of the other.

He'd spent so much time alone that he wasn't even sure he remembered how to make small talk. Just stick to business. It wasn't like she wanted to have this dinner for them to get closer. She was just anxious to get on with this fundraiser—a fundraiser that he was certain would fail if it had his name attached to it.

What had she done?

Gabrielle entered the galley kitchen. It was small and cozy. If Deacon were to be in here with her, they'd be all over each other—as in bumping in to each other. But now that the seed had been planted, she started to think of other things they could cook up together that had absolutely nothing to do with food.

Her imagination conjured up a shirtless Deacon in her kitchen. Oh, yes, things would definitely heat up. And then she'd be there in him arms. Her hands would run over his muscled chest. And there was a can of whipped cream—

Heat rushed to Gaby's face. This was a mistake.

But as she heard Deacon's footsteps behind her, she knew that it was too late to change her mind. She just had to keep her attention focused on the main course and not the dessert.

She moved to the fridge and pulled the door open. There on the top shelf sat the whipped cream. She ignored it. "What are you hungry for?" She was hungry for... The image of licking cream off Deacon came to mind. She gave herself a mental jerk. "Maybe I, ah, should tell you what I have ingredients for and, um, then we can go from there."

"Are you okay?"

"Um, sure." If only she could get the image of having him for dessert out of her mind. "Why?"

"You're acting nervous. If it's dinner, don't worry. We can order in."

"No." Her pride refused to give up. "I've got this."

Deacon took a seat at the kitchen counter. "I'm not a picky eater. So anything is good."

"Let me see what's in here." Mrs. Kupps had kindly offered to fill her fridge for the times when she was off and for the evenings when Gabrielle might get hungry.

"I've found a steak." Gaby opened the produce drawer. "There are some fingerling potatoes. And some tomatoes, onions, Gorgonzola cheese and arugula."

Her gaze skimmed back over that tempting whipped cream, but she absolutely refused to mention dessert. When he didn't respond, she glanced over her shoulder. "What do you think?"

"Sounds good. I'll just look over this information about the fundraiser while you cook the food."

She closed the fridge and turned to him. "I don't think so."

His dark eyebrows drew together as his puzzled gaze met hers. "What?"

"I'm not cooking us dinner. We're both doing it."

He shook his head and waved off her idea. "That is not a good idea. I don't know my way around a kitchen. That's what takeout menus are for."

"It's about time you learned your way around it." She wasn't about to wait on him. She didn't care how much money he had or how famous he was. "Come on. You can wash the potatoes and get them ready to go in the oven while I get out the ingredients for the salad."

And so with a heavy sigh, he got off the bar stool and made his way into the kitchen. She gave him detailed instructions and they set to work. This wasn't as bad as she'd been imagining.

Gabrielle finished rinsing the lettuce and turned to grab a bowl from one of the cabinets over the counter when she ran in to Deacon. To steady herself, she reached out with both hands. They landed on his chest—his very firm chest. The breath caught in her throat.

He reached out, catching her by the waist. His hands seemed to fit perfectly around her. It was though they fit together. But how could that be?

Deacon was the man who was responsible for her aunt's death. At least that's what her father and the papers were saying. But there was a voice deep inside her that said there was so much more to this man. Was she only seeing what she wanted to see?

Neither of them moved as her gaze rose from his chest to his full beard to his straight nose. And then she noticed his hair. It looked like it hadn't been cut in months. It fell just above his eyes. When their gazes at last connected, her heart pounded. Each heartbeat echoed in her ears.

Was it wrong that she wanted him to kiss her again? That kiss they'd shared was stuck in her mind. No man had ever made her feel so alive with just a kiss. And she hadn't gotten enough. Maybe it was the knowledge that it was wrong that made this thing—whatever you wanted to call it—between them that much more enticing. Deacon was the bad boy and she was the good girl.

Her gaze slipped back down to his mouth. It was surrounded by his mustache and beard. Though they were both well kept, she wasn't sure she was a fan of so much facial hair. Still, she wouldn't pass up the chance to kiss him, beard or no beard.

At that moment, Deacon stepped back. He released her. When she glanced at him, he turned away. Did he know what she was thinking? Did he know that she'd almost kissed him again?

"I just need the olive oil," he said, as though nothing had happened between them.

"I think I saw some in the cabinet to the right of the stove."

"Thanks."

And that was it. They were both going to act as though sparks of attraction hadn't just arched between them like some out-of-control science experiment. Well, if he could pretend nothing happened, so could she. After all, it was for the best.

Refusing to let her mind meander down that dangerous road, she focused on preparing a delicious dinner. In no time, Gaby filled their plates with seared steak, roasted potatoes and a fresh salad tossed with a wine-and-cheese dressing. They took a seat at the kitchen bar and ate in silence. In fact, Deacon was so quiet, she couldn't tell if he was enjoying the meal.

"Do you like it?" she asked.

"Yes." His gaze met hers but then he glanced away as though he wanted to say more but wasn't sure if he should. He stabbed a potato with his fork. "It's the best meal I've had in a long time."

"I doubt it. Mrs. Kupps is a marvel in the kitchen. But thank you for the compliment." It'd been a long time since anyone had taken notice of her cooking, including her father.

She was truly happy he was enjoying the meal. This is the point where she should once again probe him about the accident, but she just couldn't bring herself to ruin the moment. The questions had waited this long, surely they could wait a little longer.

They continued to eat in a comfortable silence. Deacon

emptied his plate first. He politely waited for her to finish before he carried both of their plates to the sink. Together they cleaned up the mess they'd made in the kitchen.

After the dishes were placed in the dishwasher, Deacon said, "I should look over those notes for the fundraiser."

Gabrielle spied a beautiful sunset splashing the sky with brilliant pinks and purples. "Or you could go for a walk with me."

He shook his head. "I don't think so."

"Oh, please? It's such a beautiful evening."

He shook his head.

"Do you ever get out of this estate?"

He frowned at her. "Of course I do. I was just in the city today."

"I don't mean for business or whatever drew you away. I mean get out of here and do something relaxing."

"Not since the accident."

"Because of the paparazzi?"

He nodded. "It stirs up interest in me. And it's not my reputation so much as the people closest to me being harassed. When the reporters start their feeding frenzy, Mrs. Kupps can't even go to the grocery store without being harassed in the parking lot. I thought staying out of public sight would help and it did for a while."

"And then my father stirred things up."

Deacon lowered his gaze and nodded.

"I'm sorry." So he wasn't hiding out here for purely selfish reasons. "Is that why you gave your grounds crew time off?"

"Yes. It just got to be too hard on everyone. Although Mrs. Kupps refused to take paid leave. She said she wasn't going to let the reporters bully her."

Gaby glanced away. Guilt settled over her like a wet,

soggy blanket. Here he was telling her how hard the media had made the life of those around him and she was writing daily reports for *QTR*. She was starting to wonder if her idea to publicly out him was the best approach.

"What's the matter?"

Her gaze lifted and she found him studying her. Apparently the guilt was written all over her face. "It's nothing."

"You're upset because I don't want to go for a walk."

It was best to let him think that was the source of her distress. "Oh, come on. There's no one out on the beach. Let's go."

"I thought the fundraiser stuff needed to be dealt with."

"It does. But there's plenty of time for it. Right now, I'd like to see more of this area. I must admit I'm not used to hanging out in Malibu. And the beach here is so nice. Come on." She reached out and grabbed his hand. "Show me around." She started toward the door, hoping that he'd give in to her tug of his arm.

"But there isn't much to show. It's a beach."

"A beautiful beach with a gorgeous sunset."

He followed her to the door and then stopped. "But I have work to do."

"Don't you ever just want to play hooky?"

There was a twinkle in his eyes. "So that's what you do? Play hooky instead of working."

The smile slipped from her face. She couldn't decide if he was being serious or if he was just giving her a hard time. She removed her hand from his. "I promise you that I work all day. I do a lot—more than what you've asked—"

"Slow down. I was just teasing you." He sent her a small smile.

She studied him for a moment, determining if he were serious or not. "Don't do that."

"Do what? Harass you a little?"

"Yes. Because I don't know you well enough to know if you're being serious or not."

"Perhaps I am too serious these days."

"You think so?" The words slipped across her lips before she could stop them.

His eyes widened. "I didn't know I was that bad."

"Let's just say that a bear with a thorn in its paw is more congenial than you."

"Ouch." He clasped his chest. "You really know how to wound a guy."

"Well, if you want to make it up to me, let's go for that walk."

He hesitated. She waited for him to say no, but instead, he said, "Fine. Lead the way."

She didn't say a word, not wanting to give him a chance to change his mind. Instead, she headed down the steps as quickly as her legs would carry her.

CHAPTER TEN

WHY EXACTLY HAD he agreed to this walk?

Deacon pulled the navy blue ball cap from his back pocket and settled it on his head. And even though evening was descending upon them, he put on the sunglasses that had been dangling from the neck of his shirt. These days, he always took precautions.

He shouldn't be out here, in the open for anyone to approach him—especially the press. The thought of being hounded with question after question about one of the most horrific events in his life almost had him turning around. Instead he pulled the brim down a little farther on his forehead. But the lure of stepping outside of his self-imposed confines was almost too tempting for him.

How could he resist walking along the sandy shore with the most beautiful woman he'd ever known by his side? The truth was, she'd cast a spell over him and he'd follow her most anywhere. And so he kept moving—kept in step with Gabrielle—as they made their way down to the beach.

He scanned the beach, looking for any signs of trouble. There was a man jogging along the water's edge. And coming from the other direction was an older woman walking her dog. Other than that, the beach was quiet.

Before his life had crashed in on him, he would jog on

the beach each morning. And sometimes in the evening, if he had time. He'd come out here to clear his head. It was funny to think that he'd ever taken those simple liberties for granted—

"Don't you think?" Gabrielle's voice cut through his thoughts.

He had no idea what she'd been saying. "What was that?"

"I said the sunset is exceptional tonight. I wish I'd have grabbed my phone from the kitchen counter so I could take a picture of it."

Deacon stopped. This was one small thing that he could do for her. "I've got mine."

He pulled out his phone and snapped a picture. And then he handed it over so Gabrielle could forward it to her phone. When she was done, she returned the phone and that's when their fingers touched. How could such a small gesture get to him? And yet, a zing of nervous energy rushed up his arm and settled in his chest, making his heart beat faster.

"Thank you." When she smiled at him, it was like having the sun's ray on his face.

"You...you're welcome." It'd been a long time since he'd used his manners, but it made him feel more human—she made him feel like a man again. He didn't want this evening to end. "What are you waiting for? Surely you don't want to turn around already."

Her eyes lit up with surprise. "Certainly not."

They set off again at a leisurely pace. Every now and then they passed someone else with the same intention of enjoying such a perfect evening. Deacon couldn't recall the last time he was able to let go of the guilt, the remnants of the nightmares and the worry of what tomorrow would bring long enough to enjoy the here and now.

"I can see why you live here," Gabrielle said. "If I had the opportunity, I'd get a little place along here and wild horses couldn't drag me away."

"Actually I've been considering moving. It's time for a change. Maybe I could move someplace where they don't recognize me."

"I don't think that place exists."

He shrugged. "Perhaps."

"You aren't returning to the movies?"

Was she just being polite? Or had she not really looked at him? He stopped walking and held out his hand in front of them. "With scars like these, no one would want to hire me."

"These are from the accident?"

"Yes."

She reached out and ran her fingertip ever so gently over his skin. "It's not so bad. Maybe some makeup could hide what's there from the camera if you're self-conscious about it."

But makeup could not hide the scars in his mind. They were there—they kept him up at night, walking the halls in the dark. "It's not going to happen."

"Why not try?"

"Because…" Because he didn't deserve to be in front of those cameras any longer. She of all people should understand that. "Why are you being so nice to me?"

She shrugged and then started to walk again. "How am I supposed to act around you?"

"Like you hate me."

"Should I hate you?"

He inwardly groaned. Why did she have to keep turning things around on him? "It's not for me to say how you should feel. It's just that if circumstances were reversed, I'd probably act more like your father."

"And what has that accomplished? He has broken the law and has his daughter bailing him out."

Deacon really wanted to understand her. "So you think by taking the high road that you'll accomplish more?"

"Such as you telling me what happened the night my aunt died?"

"There it is." He stopped next to an outcropping of rocks. "I knew that's why you dragged me out here. You wanted to get me someplace where you could interrogate me."

"That's not true. I didn't drag you out here—"

"But you can't deny that you didn't think about questioning me. You were hoping to wear me down into a confession."

Her gaze searched his. "Do you have something you need to confess?"

He should turn and leave. That's what he'd do if he were thinking clearly. That's what his attorney would advise him to do.

But his feet wouldn't cooperate. He stood there staring into Gabrielle's eyes and could only imagine the pain that she'd been through. And the not knowing, well, he knew all about that. Much too well.

He swallowed hard. "If I told you, you wouldn't believe me."

"Try me."

He wanted to trust her. He wanted to believe that whatever he said would stay between the two of them. But he hardly knew her. And right now, he could count on one hand how many people he trusted.

Instead he turned and climbed up on the rocks. He made his way to a large boulder on the water's edge. He sat down, letting the sea breeze fan his face, and hoped the lulling sound of the ocean would ease the storm raging inside him.

He sat there for the longest time, trying to get his thoughts in order. By then the sun had sunk below the horizon. It was an overcast night with the moon peeking out here and there. Deacon found comfort in the long, dark shadows. He glanced around and found that Gabrielle hadn't left. Instead, she was sitting just a few feet away. She was too far away in the dark to make out her face. As she sat there with her knees drawn up to her chest, he couldn't help but wonder what she was thinking. He hated the thought that he continued to cause her pain. But nothing he could say would fix things.

"If you're waiting for a confession, you're wasting your time." He turned back to the ocean.

Gabrielle moved to settle on the rock next to him. "Is that because you didn't cause the accident?"

Why was he holding back? So what if she didn't believe him. Once he said it, it would be out there. Perhaps she'd believe him. Perhaps she wouldn't. But it was time he told the truth.

"I don't remember." Somehow it was easier having this conversation under the shelter of darkness.

"What don't you remember?"

"The accident." He could feel her intense stare.

"What part don't you remember?"

"All of it. They called it retrograde amnesia or some such thing."

"That's pretty convenient." She said it as a fact.

He turned to her and now that she was closer, he could make out the disbelief written on her face. "Actually, it isn't. I want to remember the accident as bad as you need me to remember. I need to know what I've done." His voice cracked. "I—I need to know if I'm responsible."

For a moment, Gabrielle didn't say anything. "So you're not holding out and trying to bury the events?"

His jaw tightened. He knew that she wouldn't believe him. But then again, why should she?

"No. I'm not lying." He shook his head. "I knew you wouldn't believe me."

"And the delay with the police report?"

"I've had my attorney pressing for its release, but without camera footage or an eyewitness account, it complicates matters. Once the police have finalized the report, it must go up the chain of command, ending with the DA's office. When my attorney checked yesterday, he was told the report should be released soon." When Gabrielle didn't say anything, he glanced over at her. "I'm sorry. I know that's not what you want to hear."

Her gaze met his and she placed a slight smile on her lips. "It's the truth and that's what matters."

"You believe me?" If she did, she'd be the first person to do so.

"Are you saying I shouldn't?"

"I'm just surprised is all."

Gaby paused. "So tell me more about yourself."

"You don't really want to hear about me?"

She nodded. "I do."

"Where do I start?"

"How about at the beginning."

"Well, I was born on Valentine's Day. My father died when I was thirteen. My mother finished raising me on her own. I split my time between the fishing boat and watching movies."

"Fishing and movies. Those are two diverse interests."

"The fishing wasn't a hobby. It was my job. I started when I was thirteen, getting paid under the table, in order to help my mother pay the bills." It hadn't been an easy life and his schooling had paid the price, but he'd graduated by the sheer willpower of his mother. "The movies were my passion. I drove my mother crazy telling her that one day I would be a movie star. And do you know what she told me?"

Gabrielle shook her head.

"She used to say, 'Deacon, you're a smart boy. You can be anything you want to be as long as you work hard and don't give up.'"

"She sounded like a smart lady."

"I thought so, too. And then she met my stepfather. In the beginning, he wasn't so bad. And then they got married. That was when I decided to move to California. I just couldn't stick around and watch those two argue. I tried to talk my mother in to coming with me, but she insisted that her place was with her husband."

"I'm sorry. That must have been tough on you."

"And what's even worse is that when she first found a lump in her breast, that—that man told her it was her imagination. By the time I talked her in to going to the doctor, the cancer was advanced. I brought her here to California. Oh, they tried to help her, but by then the cancer had spread."

Gabrielle reached out, taking his hand in hers. She gave a firm squeeze. It shouldn't, but it meant a lot to him. And it even meant more because she wasn't supposed to be here giving him support. She was supposed to hate him—hate his very existence. The fact that she didn't confused him, yet also intrigued him. There was definitely something different about Gabrielle.

CHAPTER ELEVEN

SHE DIDN'T MOVE.

Gabrielle left her hand securely within Deacon's hold. His hands were large and his fingers long. And his hand fit perfectly around hers. It was as though they were made for one another. Not that she was letting her heart get ahead of her mind. She knew that nothing could ever come of their relationship, whether he'd caused the accident or not.

Because in her father's mind, Deacon would always be responsible for her aunt's death. And she highly doubted that anything would change her father's mind. He was a very stubborn man. She'd inherited his stubborn streak. Or at least that's what her aunt had told her.

However, Deacon was far from the spoiled movie star that her father and Newton had accused Deacon of being. There was a lot more to this man than anyone would guess. He was like an onion, with layer upon layer, and she had an overwhelming desire to keep peeling back the layers until she reached his heart.

"Maybe we should head back." Deacon released her hand and got to his feet.

"So soon?"

He laughed. "We've been out here a long time. It's getting late."

"But we have the whole beach to ourselves." And then she dropped her voice. "We can do whatever we want and there's no one around to see."

"Be careful. Or I just might take you up on the invitation."

A shiver of excitement raced through her. She knew she shouldn't be flirting with him, but she couldn't stop herself. There was something about Deacon that she couldn't resist.

"Maybe I *want* you to take me up on the invitation."

Deacon stood there in the shadows. She wished she could make out his eyes. He was so quiet. Was he considering taking advantage of her suggestion? Her heart thudded against her ribs.

"Gabrielle, don't make offers you aren't ready to fulfill. Let's head back before something happens that we'll both come to regret. I don't want to hurt you."

He held out his hand to her and helped her to her feet. For a moment, they stood there face-to-face. Her pulse raced and her heart pounded. With darkness all around them, a few moonbeams silhouetted Deacon's face. She wanted to tell him that she wasn't fragile. But her tongue refused to cooperate.

Instead of turning and heading back to the estate, Deacon continued staring at her. Was he considering kissing her again? Was it wrong that she wanted him to pull her against his chest and lower his head to hers?

And then he turned away and started climbing down off the rocks. When he was standing on the sand, he turned back to her and held out his hands in order to catch her. Even though she could make it down on her own, she didn't resist his offer of assistance.

He placed his hands on her waist and lowered her ever so slowly. Her body slid down over his. It was tantalizing and oh, so arousing. She was so caught up in the crazy sensation zinging through her body that she never noticed when her feet touched the ground.

Beard or no beard. Scars or no scars. Long hair or short. There was something magnetic about this man. She knew that it wasn't rational. And right now, she didn't care.

Her heart pounded so loud that it drowned out rational thought. She was going to live in the moment and damn the consequences. She tilted up her chin and lifted up on her tiptoes. Her mouth pressed to his.

His lips were warm and smooth. And the kiss, it was full of emotion, of need, of desire. Her hands slid up over his broad shoulders and slipped around his neck. She could get used to this.

Except for the beard. It tickled her. And when he moved to trail kisses down her neck, it tickled so much that she pulled away. A smile lifted her lips as she struggled not to laugh. He sent her a concerned look as though wondering if he had done something wrong.

"It's not you." But when he went to press his lips to her neck again, she placed her hands on his shoulders and held him back.

"What?"

She wasn't sure if he would take offense or not. And so she stood there not saying a word.

He frowned. "Just tell me."

"It…it's your beard. It tickles."

His eyes twinkled with mischief. "It does?" He leaned toward her. "How much?"

Before he could tickle her again, she yanked away from him. "Catch me if you can."

And with that taunt, she ran up the beach. A big smile was plastered across her face. For once, she wasn't the dutiful daughter working two jobs to keep the bills paid and she wasn't answering her father's numerous phone calls to check up on her. She was just Gabrielle Dupré, a woman with a dangerously handsome man chasing her. She could hear Deacon calling out to her, but she didn't stop until she was out of breath.

When she turned around, she fully expected Deacon to be standing there, but he wasn't. She squinted into the shadows. He was quite a way down the beach. What in the world? Hadn't he wanted to catch her?

Disappointment socked her in the gut. They'd been having so much fun. Where had it gone wrong?

Her wounded pride urged her to keep going. But another part of her wanted to wait and find out what was up. The curiosity in her won out. She started to walk back to him.

When she was within a few feet of Deacon, he said. "Sorry. I couldn't keep up. My leg is getting better, but it's not that good yet."

And suddenly she felt foolish. She was worried about him being upset with her when in fact he had an injury. It never even dawned on her that the injuries he'd sustained to his face, arms and hands had extended further.

"I'm sorry. I didn't think."

"It's not your problem. And how would you know?"

They started to walk side by side. She felt awful. She'd just assumed that he was fine. "Are you okay to walk back?"

"Yes. I'm just not up for running. Maybe one day, if I keep going to therapy and doing the exercises."

"You go to physical therapy?" She hadn't noticed him leaving on a regular basis, but then again, she hadn't been here that long.

"Not anymore."

"Why not?" She knew from her father's accident how important physical therapy could be to making a full recovery. "It's really important."

"I'm fine." His dismissive manner bothered her.

"If you were fine, you would have kept up with me or surpassed me. You are not fine. Your therapy is important. You can't just dismiss it because you don't want to do the work."

He arched an eyebrow. "And since when does my welfare matter to you?"

"It—it doesn't." Did it? She glanced away from him, not wanting him to read anything in her eyes. "But that doesn't mean it shouldn't be important to you."

"I don't think it's going to matter. All I do is haunt that place." He gestured toward the mansion in the distance.

"If you refuse to leave home, I can help you with the exercises."

"I don't need help." His voice rumbled with agitation, letting her know that she'd pushed as far as he was going to let her go.

And so they walked in silence. She wasn't sure what to say now. He'd made it clear he didn't want her help and he refused to go anywhere to get help. She couldn't believe this, but she'd met someone who was as stubborn or perhaps more stubborn than her father. They at least had that in common.

The thought of who could be more stubborn made her smile and the more she thought about it, a giggle started to form. And before she knew it, she was laughing. Maybe it was her nervousness or maybe it was the stress, but it felt good to laugh. Talk about a cathartic moment.

Beneath one of the estate security lights, Deacon stepped in front of her. "What's so funny?"

The frown on his face just made her laugh some more. It was almost like an out-of-body experience. She couldn't help herself. And it just felt so darn good.

"Stop it. Right now." His eyebrows were drawn into a firm line.

"I—I can't." She laughed some more.

She could see that the more she laughed the angrier he was getting. She really had to pull herself together. She had no idea what had come over her, but she needed to get a grip.

With a frustrated groan, Deacon turned and started to walk away. That was definitely not a good sign, at all. The elation in her started to ebb.

"Wait." She rushed to catch up with him, all the while trying to catch her breath.

"I don't care to be laughed at."

"I wasn't laughing at you. Not really." And then she thought about it a little more. "Well, maybe some. But it really wasn't that bad."

"I don't want to be laughed at."

Totally sober now, she said, "I just started thinking about you and my father and what you two have in common."

Deacon came to a stop and she almost ran in to him. "You were comparing me to your father?"

"Yes, in a way."

"What way?"

"You are both so stubborn. I was trying to figure out which one of you is the worst, but I couldn't decide."

"And that made you laugh."

"Yes, I guess it did."

He shook his head. "I don't understand you."

"That's okay. I don't really understand myself, either." It was the truth. She understood the parts of her that were like her father, but the other parts, the silly parts, sometimes surprised her. "I honestly don't know why I laughed. But once I did, it felt good. It's been a very long time since I laughed like that. You should try it some time."

He looked at her like she'd just grown an extra head. "You want me to laugh for no reason at all."

She shrugged. "Don't put it down until you've tried it."

He shook his head again. "It must be a woman thing."

Before they went their separate ways, Deacon asked for the fundraising plans. She ran upstairs and retrieved the papers. She was kind of hoping he'd follow her upstairs. His kisses were more addictive than the squares of chocolate with caramel centers that she enjoyed each night while reading.

She hurried back down the steps. "This is everything I have so far."

When she handed over the papers, their fingers touched. To her surprise, he didn't rush to pull away. Neither did she. Their gazes met and her heart careened into her throat.

Her gaze lowered to his mouth. She'd never been so tempted by anything in her life. What was it about this man that muddled her thoughts? It was as though he had some sort of magnetic force and anytime she was near him, she was drawn in.

And then he stepped back. "Thanks for these. I'll look them over tonight."

She choked down her disappointment. "Good. The sooner I jump on these plans, the better."

"Then how about a breakfast meeting?" When she didn't immediately respond, he asked, "You do eat breakfast, don't you?"

At last, she found her voice. "Yes, I do."

"Good. We'll discuss this in the morning." He gestured toward the papers. "Good night."

She stood there for a moment watching him retreat to the main house. What was wrong with her? She knew better than to fall for him. It was the ocean breeze and his deep voice that caused her to lose focus for just a few moments. She was fine now. Realizing that she shouldn't be standing around staring at Deacon like some besotted schoolgirl, she turned and headed up the steps.

Before it got much later, she needed to file her daily report with *QTR*. She carried her personal laptop to a chair on her private balcony and sat in one of the comfy chairs.

She opened the laptop and typed in her password. Once she had her email open, the words came pouring out of her.

Tonight we walked on the beach. It was like a scene right out of a movie, with the lull of the water in the background and the gentle breeze. It was amazing.

Beneath the moonlight, we kissed. I don't think my feet were touching the ground. His touch—it was amazing. I know that I shouldn't feel anything for him because of the accident, but the harder I fight it, the more attracted to him I become.

His kiss awakened a part of me that I'd forgotten about. There was a rush of emotions unlike anything I've ever experienced before. It's all so confusing. Maybe I'm just lonely. It has been over a year since I dated anyone. Work and caring for my father has consumed my life. When I leave here perhaps I need to revisit the dating scene and update my online profile. Because there's no way what I'm starting to feel for Deacon is real. It can't be!

She read back over what she'd written. What was she thinking? She could never tell anyone her most intimate thoughts—most especially a tell-all magazine. Talk about creating sensational headlines.

With a shake of her head, she highlighted it all. Then she pressed the delete key. But she still had to find something to write in her report.

And after what she'd learned today, she was beginning to suspect there was no story here. But she had promised that she would document the details relating to the accident. And she liked to keep her word. So she started to write out in as much detail as she could what little Deacon had told her about the night of the accident.

But with every word she typed, guilt weighed on her. How could she betray Deacon's trust? Even if now it was to help *clear* his name?

Her emotions warred within her. She knew how Deacon felt about the paparazzi and tabloids. He would consider what she was doing as an utter betrayal. Could she blame him?

She hadn't taken any of this into consideration when she'd agreed to this plan. Getting close to Deacon, gaining his trust, was changing everything. And now she was utterly confused. More than anything, she wanted to leave. Each day that passed, her confusion over where she stood with Deacon grew.

Gaby saved her report to the drafts folder. She wanted more time to consider her actions. In the meantime, she jotted a brief email stating that there was nothing new to report.

She closed her laptop and leaned back in her chair. Her presence on the estate had nothing to do with the accident and everything to do with protecting her father from prosecution. And so she would keep her word to

Deacon and stay until the fundraiser. And once it was a huge success, she could return to her life. A life without a brooding movie star with the ability to make her laugh and feel lighter than she had in years. Suddenly, returning to her prior life didn't sound so appealing. But life here on this Malibu estate wasn't reality. It was some sort of dream and soon she'd wake up—probably about the time the police report was released. And she worried about the steep fall back to earth.

CHAPTER TWELVE

MAYBE THIS HAD been a mistake.

Deacon sat across the table from Gabrielle. The table was done up with a light blue linen tablecloth. Fine china was laid out. The yellow napkins were folded into the shape of bow ties. A vase of yellow roses had been placed in the center. This was Mrs. Kupps's doing. The last time the table had been so fancy had been before the accident. These days, he ate at his desk with a tray of food. No flowers. No company.

What had he been thinking to invite Gabrielle to breakfast? Perhaps it was the fact that when she smiled, the whole world was that much brighter. And when they talked, she didn't hold back. She was filled with optimism. He gave himself a mental jerk. That line of thought could get him into trouble—big trouble. It was best to focus on the business at hand.

But that would be easier said than done with the table all decked out to impress Gabrielle. When he'd mentioned all the needless fuss to Mrs. Kupps, she'd clucked her tongue at him. She told him he needed to do everything he could not to run off Gabrielle, as she was the sunshine in his otherwise gloomy world. It was as if she was worried that he'd grow old alone. He was not some beggar, desperate for anyone's attention.

Is that what Gabrielle thought of him, too? Did she think that he was pathetic and deserving of her sympathy? He would show her. He did not need anyone's pity. He was not some charity case.

"You know this isn't going to work." His words came out terser than he'd intended.

Gabrielle glanced up from where she unfolded the yellow napkin and placed it on her lap. "Which part doesn't work?"

"All of it. Every single last piece of it." That wasn't exactly true, but he was in no mood to be generous. If they were adversaries, then perhaps she wouldn't feel obligated to be nice to him—to let him kiss her.

He watched her closely. He was waiting for her to leave. However, the only visible sign of her discomfort was in her eyes. They widened, but she didn't move. He knew a lot of people would have turned tail and fled by now. But not Gabrielle. She was made of sterner stuff. But he should have figured that when she'd volunteered to take her father's punishment.

She adjusted her napkin and at the same time avoided his gaze. When she glanced back up at him, she said, "I'm assuming you are referring to the fundraiser plans and not the meal."

"Of course."

She nodded. Then she set about removing the lid from the dish of scrambled eggs. She was going to eat? He was setting up for an argument and she was acting as though everything was perfectly fine. Everything wasn't fine.

He couldn't take her lack of reaction any longer. "Are you just going to sit there and ignore me?"

"I'm not ignoring you, but Mrs. Kupps went to a lot of work to prepare this meal and I think it'd be a shame to let it go to waste."

"You're hungry?"

She smiled at him. "Of course I am. I'm sure you'll feel better after you eat."

He wanted to disagree, but his gaze moved to her plate. The food did look good. "But what about the problems with the fundraiser?"

"They aren't going anywhere. We can deal with those later." She scooped up some bacon and added it to her plate. When he didn't move, she said, "Do you want some bacon?" When he didn't respond fast enough, she added, "If you don't hurry, there might not be any left. I love bacon."

He did, too. He held out his hand for her to pass the serving plate. She hesitated as though she weren't so sure she wanted to share, but in the end, she passed it to him.

It was really hard staying upset with her. She was either a very good actress, good enough to be in the movies with him, or she tried not to let things ruffle her. Either way, he was going to have to figure out a different way to deal with her. Because all his huffing and puffing didn't appear to deter her.

Gabrielle continued to fill her plate. "I can't believe Mrs. Kupps made us all of this food."

"She was more than happy to do it. For so long now, she's been begging me for things to do and I've been putting her off."

"I take it you don't have breakfast like this very often."

"No. Not at all. Not since, well, you know." He didn't want to bring up the accident. Not this morning. But since Gabrielle had entered his life, his appetite was back.

Gabrielle buttered her toast. "Well, I will make sure to tell Mrs. Kupps just how good this is."

"I'm sure she would love to hear it. I must admit that I've been lacking on the compliments lately."

"I'm sure she understands that you've been going through a lot."

When they'd finished their meal, which took much longer than he was accustomed to taking to eat, he found himself in a better frame of mind. He assured himself that it had nothing to do with what Gabrielle had said about him needing to eat, and more to do with the fact that he was right about this fundraiser and he would prove it to her.

Mrs. Kupps brought more coffee and then cleared the empty dishes. Both of them complimented Mrs. Kupps on the delicious food. The woman's cheeks grew rosy as she thanked them.

After Mrs. Kupps departed, Gabrielle turned to him. "Now, what were you saying about the fundraiser?"

"I don't think people are going to attend."

"Why would you think that? Are my plans that bad?"

He shook his head. "It isn't anything you've done." Surely he didn't have to spell this out for her. "I'm the problem."

"Oh." Her good mood seemed to have diminished a bit. She sat there and stared off at the shimmering ocean for a moment. When she turned to him again, she had a glint in her eye. "Actually, I think all of your notoriety will work to our advantage."

He had a feeling he wouldn't like where she was going with this line of thought. But it was too late, he'd already been drawn down the rabbit hole. "How's that?"

"You forget that in addition to the car accident, you also have a movie being released next month."

"What about it?"

"I couldn't sleep last night, so I turned on the television. And guess what I saw?"

He sighed. "I don't know, but I'm sure you're going to tell me."

"I saw the promo for your movie. Your name and face were all over the ad. Your movie sponsors aren't backing down from using your brand and you shouldn't, either."

If only people still thought he was that man. Now they all questioned him and his actions—including himself. "I'm not that man anymore."

"Which makes people all the more curious about you—"

"I'm not going to be some sort of freak show for them to come here and stare at."

"Relax." She reached across the table and placed her hand on his. "I promise you, it won't be like that. I believe that people will come out for the event. They will want to get behind a great cause because so many lives have been touched in one way or another by breast cancer."

When she put it that way, he felt guilty for making such a big deal about his circumstances. Some people had it much worse. "So you'll make sure to keep the emphasis of the event on the reason for it and not on the sponsor?"

"Um, yes." Worry clouded her eyes. "Does that mean you don't want to be mentioned at all?"

"That is what I'd hoped."

She worried her bottom lip but didn't respond.

"Go ahead and say it."

"It's just that without your name, I don't know how to make the event stand out."

He reminded himself that raising funds would help save other families from having to go through the pain, the uncertainty and, for some, the loss of a loved one, like he'd experienced. And when it came down to it, if using his name would help raise awareness of the event, didn't he owe that to his mother's memory?

"Okay. You can use my name, if you think it will help."

"I do." Gabrielle pulled out a legal pad from a colorful bag she had on the ground next to her chair. There were handwritten notes on the top sheet. It was a long list. It appeared they were going to be here a while. She sent him a sideways glance. "You aren't going to change your mind after we get this all started, are you?"

He knew once news of the fundraiser was out there that his world would get a lot smaller, with paparazzi hanging from trees and sneaking onto the property. It would be chaos and he'd want to back out. "No. I'll manage."

"Good." A smile eased the worry lines bracketing her beautiful face. "And I think they are really going to have a great time."

He filled his coffee cup, then added a dash of sugar. He'd forgotten how much he enjoyed sitting outside in the morning with the bright sunshine and the cool breeze. He could feel Gabrielle's gaze on him. She was anxious to hear his thoughts, but he didn't think that she'd like what he was about to say.

As he stirred the coffee, his gaze skimmed down over the printout that Gabrielle had given him the night before. She had certainly paid attention to details and made certain that there was plenty of entertainment.

He took a drink of the dark brew and then returned the cup to the saucer. "You do realize that you have so many events listed that it dilutes the entire event."

Gabrielle's eyebrows drew together. "But people need something to do."

"True. But not this many things. This is more like an amusement park than a fundraiser." Before she could argue with him, he intended to prove his point. "You have golfing, amusement rides, clowns, artists, dancing and games. That's a lot. A whole lot."

"But with each of those things, we can raise money."

"How much money are we talking? Really?"

She sighed and gazed down over the list of events. "What are you proposing?"

"That you narrow the list down to two or three things."

She frowned at him. Then she shook her head and looked away.

"What?"

Her gaze met his as she worried her bottom lip.

"Gabrielle, just spit it out." He wasn't good at guessing, especially where women were concerned.

"I was just wondering if it is the money. You know, if sponsoring the event is too much for you."

Oh, that was all. This was something he could deal with.

"It isn't the money." Though this fundraiser would cost a small fortune to pull together, he could handle it. He'd had a number of blockbuster movies and he'd carefully invested the money. When her gaze told him that she still wasn't reassured, he said, "I promise. I'm good financially."

His main concern was for Gabrielle. She had invested herself completely in making this fundraiser a huge success. She had her hopes so high that when it all fell apart, she would have a long way to tumble.

In the short time he'd gotten to know her, he'd learned that she had a big heart—big enough to even care about his welfare, which was more than he'd ever expected. He didn't want her to get hurt because of him and his now tarnished reputation.

"That's good to hear." There was a catch in her voice

as though there were something more she wanted to say, but she decided to refrain.

"You know it's not too late to pull out—"

"No. I really want to do this."

He knew what she meant. She was anxious to get away from him. And he couldn't blame her. She blamed him for what had happened to her aunt. And as much as he wanted to deny it, he couldn't. He didn't know. And his nightmares only confused him even more.

He thought about just calling off the deal. But he knew Gabrielle would take it personally. She had a lot of pride and would think he didn't believe in her ability to pull it all together. He didn't want to do anything else to hurt her. So he would do what he could to help Gabrielle— even at the expense of his privacy.

Deacon cleared his throat. "The events should either be big draws in order to up the ticket price or garner large donations once the guests are in attendance." And he had another observation. "Perhaps keep this an adults-only event. Without children around, people will relax and perhaps they'll be willing to spend more freely."

"That's the exact opposite of how I ran my fundraisers for the library. I did a lot of activities to draw in the kids and by extension their parents." She frowned. "I suppose you're going to want to remove all of the fun events."

He really did hate to disappoint her, but he'd been around these affairs many times in the past. And he knew a lot of the big fish she was hoping to hook would appreciate something more low-key.

"Trust me." He knew that was a poor choice of words where she was concerned, but they were already out there and he couldn't undo them. So he kept going with the point he wanted to make. "I do know what I'm talking about."

"But it'll be boring."

He had to admit some of the charity events he'd attended were boring, but he didn't want to tell her that. He knew Gabrielle would use any excuse to keep her current lengthy list of events.

"Ah… I see. I'm right." Her face lit up.

"What are you talking about?"

"The look you just made when I said that it would be boring. You couldn't deny it."

"I was thinking is all."

"Uh-huh. What if we compromise?"

Oh, no. He had a bad feeling about this. His experience of compromising with a female in his private life consisted of him giving up on what he wanted, so the woman wouldn't be mad at him any longer.

With great trepidation, he asked, "What sort of compromise?"

And so they started with the first activity on the list—dart toss. They discussed it and the type of atmosphere they'd like to present to the people. In the end, it was cut in an effort to make the fundraiser more sophisticated.

After they made it through a quarter of the list and had nixed all but one item, Gabrielle said, "Okay. So we should stick to just a handful of entertainments."

"Or even less. For the most part, the affluent people you'll be inviting will want to be seen." He explained a little more of his understanding of the elite of Hollywood.

Gabrielle nodded. "Okay. I can work with this."

"Now, what were you considering for the main focus of the event?"

She took a moment, as though considering everything he'd told her. "I think we should make it a golfing event. Lots of people golf, both men and women. And you do have an amazing golf course."

"How would you know? It's a mess."

"Mrs. Kupps showed me some pictures. The course needs some TLC, but I talked to your head groundskeeper. He said that with the help of the entire grounds crew, they could pull it together. They might have to bring in some turf, but it is possible to have it together in time."

He arched an eyebrow at her. "You really have worked hard on this."

"I saw an opportunity and I took it. This fundraiser will be great—if you'll agree to it."

His gut told him not to do it. But he saw the gleam of hope in Gabrielle's eyes. He just didn't have it in him to turn her down. What would it hurt to get this place cleaned up? He wasn't even sure if he wanted to live here any longer. It would have to be restored if he were to put it up for sale. So he would let Gabrielle move ahead with her plans and when no one bought the tickets, he would still abide by their agreement. Once the planning was over, he would let her go back to her life.

He told her to take what they'd discussed and refine her list. Include a few more details and they'd go over it tomorrow. And then he would give her his decision about whether they should move forward with it or not.

He had a gut feeling that he'd dug himself a hole. Gabrielle had a determined look in her eye that said she would never give up on the fundraiser. And he was going to have to find a way to be okay with all those people being here on his estate.

Unless…no one bought a ticket or showed up. But then Gabrielle would be crushed and he would be to blame. Either way he would be in trouble.

CHAPTER THIRTEEN

THE PLANS WERE coming together.

Later that afternoon, Gaby straightened her desk. It had been a very productive day. She recalled her breakfast with Deacon. He hadn't been very congenial at first, but once he realized she wasn't going to give up, he became helpful.

And though she hated to admit it, he was right. This event needed a different vibe than the events she'd planned at the library. This was his world and he knew these people, so she'd follow his lead.

It may not be the type of event she was used to planning, but she would work to make it perfect. People would come. They would enjoy themselves, and they would donate to a worthy cause.

By five o'clock she'd also finished reading the screenplay Deacon had given her. She'd made a list of pros and cons and sent it to him in an email. With her tasks done for the day, she shut down the computer and then made her way to the guesthouse.

She brought the fundraising plans with her. She was too excited to stop now. The plans were coming together really well and instead of this event being her get-out-of-jail-free card, it was turning into an event she believed in and wanted to see succeed.

Mrs. Kupps had placed some dinner in the fridge with a note for reheating it. Gaby smiled. The woman was the absolute sweetest. She wondered if Deacon knew how lucky he was to have someone so kind and thoughtful in his life.

Gaby settled at the table with her laptop, a legal pad and all the notes she'd taken during her talk with Deacon. She didn't know how much time had passed when there was a knock at the door.

She couldn't imagine who it might be. Mrs. Kupps had left long ago. And no one could get access to the private estate.

Gaby ran a hand over her hair and a finger around her mouth, making sure there weren't any crumbs from the chocolate chip cookies that Mrs. Kupps had left her. And she rushed to the door. Gaby peered through the peephole and was shocked to find Deacon.

What was he doing here?

Her heart started beating faster. She glanced down at her white shorts and old Support Your Library tank top. Not exactly the most attractive outfit, but it'd have to do.

She swung the door open. "Hi."

Deacon looked uncomfortable as he shifted his weight from one foot to the other. "Never mind. I shouldn't have bothered you."

"It's fine. Do you want to come in?"

He shook his head. "I saw your light on and figured you couldn't sleep, either."

Either? As in he didn't sleep at night? Interesting. "I was going over more plans for the fundraiser."

"At this hour?"

"You gave me until tomorrow to come up with a revised plan."

"I did, didn't I?" When she nodded, he frowned. "If you need more time, it's not a problem."

"Actually, I'm just about finished. Tomorrow works fine to go over the agenda." She was certain that wasn't why he stopped over. "What did you need?"

He glanced down. There was a book in his hand. When his gaze rose and met hers, there was uncertainty in his eyes. "It was nothing."

"Obviously it was something or you wouldn't be here. Are you sure you don't want to come inside?"

He shook his head. "I—I just finished reading this new book and thought you might enjoy it."

The fact he'd thought of her and wanted to share something personal filled her chest with a warm sensation. A smile lifted her lips.

She held out her hand. "What type of book is it?"

He handed it over. "It's a suspense book. But I'm sure you have other books you're already reading."

"Actually, I just finished one last night. So you have perfect timing."

"I do?"

She couldn't help but smile at his awkwardness. When it came to business, he was very sure of himself. But here, with it just being the two of them, he was nervous. And that bit of knowledge chipped away at the wall she'd erected to keep him out of her heart.

He shifted his weight from one foot to the other. "Usually I can figure out what's going to happen in the end, but this book kept me guessing until the last page."

She turned over the book and quickly read the blurb. "It sounds intriguing. I can't wait to read it. Thank you."

"I, uh, should be going." And with that he walked away.

As Gaby closed the door, she was struck by the gesture. It was so small and yet, it said so much about the man. The fact that he liked to read checked off a big box for Gaby—not that she was looking at him as a prospective boyfriend. But the fact that he used his mind for more than just work meant a lot.

And what meant even more was that he was thoughtful. The more she got to know him, the less he seemed like the monster that others had made him out to be after the accident. It was getting harder and harder to view him as the enemy.

"Okay. You have yourself a fundraiser," Deacon said the next day after going over her revised plans for the event in his office.

"I do?" Gabrielle smiled.

He tried to ignore the way her smile warmed his insides. *Focus on the fundraiser.* He cleared his throat. "Do you have a name for it?"

"Actually, I've given this a lot of thought. And you can change it, but how about the Diana Pink-Rose Tournament?"

The title that Gabrielle had chosen couldn't have been more perfect. His mother's name. She would have loved it. He was touched that Gabrielle had included her name in it. A lump of emotion swelled in his throat and for a moment he didn't trust himself to speak.

Misinterpreting his silence, Gabrielle said, "If you don't like it, I could work on some other titles."

He shook his head and swallowed hard. He wasn't the type to let himself get emotional, but Gabrielle was the first person to do something so kind and thoughtful in honor of his mother. She probably didn't even know how much it meant to him and perhaps it was better that way.

It's too bad the fundraiser would never become a reality. He thought it would definitely have been a great event.

His gaze met hers. "It's perfect. Thank you. What made you choose the pink rose for the title?"

She shrugged. "I guess because pink is the color of breast-cancer campaigns."

"Do you know what else pink rose means?"

She shook her head.

"Then come with me." He led her down to the rose garden, where he'd purposely planted a rosebush in every color that he could track down. As they made their way down the steps in the back of the house, he said, "My mother loved roses. And so I made a point of buying as many colors as I could find. I loved watching her face light up with every color that was added to the garden."

"That was very sweet of you. She was lucky to have you."

"No. I was the lucky one." And he meant every word of it. His mother had loved him even when he hadn't made the wisest choices. And she cheered him on when he reached for the stars. "I couldn't have asked for a better mother."

When they stood in the rose garden, Gabrielle's eyes searched his. "What are we doing here?"

"Did you know that each rose has a meaning?"

"I know that red roses mean love. But that's all."

"Ah, but not any love—true love. I'm sure you must get them all of the time."

"I must admit that I've never received any."

The fact that no man had given her roses really surprised him. Gabrielle was so beautiful. Her beauty started on the inside and radiated outward. He'd like to be the first to present her with one. "You should have roses and daily."

Color filled her cheeks. How was it possible that she grew more beautiful each time he saw her? His heart picked up its pace. He couldn't help but stare. He never got enough of looking at her. Was it possible for her to look even more radiant?

It was with great effort that he turned away. He walked down the brick path and stopped next to a white rose. "This one is the traditional rose of weddings. And it represents purity and virtue."

"How do you know all of this?"

"Each time I ordered a new rose, I would do my research. Roses are quite intertwined in history. I would distract my mother from her discomforts with stories that included the various roses."

Gabrielle gazed at him but didn't say anything. Yet there was a look on her face and he couldn't read it.

"What?"

"It's just that you continually surprise me."

"You mean you thought I was nothing but a conceited partygoer."

"Um, no. I don't know why you think that. It's just that I don't know any men who know so much about flowers."

His body tensed. It was even worse than he'd thought. "You think I'm a wimp—"

"No. Not at all. I think what you do here is wonderful." There was sincerity in her voice. She continued down the walk and stopped in front of a pink rosebush. "And how about these? What do they mean?"

"The dark pink petals mean gratitude and appreciation." He moved to a neighboring light pink rose. "And this one means sympathy."

He continued walking through the garden. When he came across his gardening supplies, he grabbed a pair of shears. He moved to some long-stemmed yellow roses. He searched for a perfect bloom and then cut it. He turned and presented it to Gabrielle.

A bright smile lit up her face. "Thank you." She lifted it to her nose and inhaled. "What does it mean?"

"Friendship."

She sniffed the petals again. "Is that what we have here?"

He hadn't tried to define what was going on between them until now. It was more complicated than friendship, but that title was safe and easy, so he went with it. "That's what I'd like to think."

Her eyes reflected her approval. "Me, too."

She'd slept in!

The next morning, Gabrielle awoke with a start. It was Deacon's fault that she'd been awake until the wee hours of the morning. He'd loaned her that book and it was good—no, it was great. She raced through her bedroom, trying to get ready for work as fast as she could. It wasn't that Deacon would be standing there by the office door waiting for her to arrive. It was more a matter of how much she wanted to accomplish that day.

She opened the door of the guesthouse and found a bud vase with a single yellow rose. She glanced around for Deacon, but he was nowhere to be seen. What had happened to the man who used to growl at her? She knew where she stood with his former self, but with this new version of Deacon, she was constantly losing her footing.

Deacon wasn't all good or all bad—he was both, but she was quickly learning that there was a lot more good in him than bad. She picked up the rose and lifted it to her nose. Its perfume was gentle but delightful. She'd never smell another rose without thinking of him.

She loved that each color of rose had a meaning. What

impressed her more was that Deacon had learned the meanings in order to delight his mother.

As she carried the flower into the guesthouse to find just the perfect spot for it, her aunt's words came back to her: *if you find a man that is good to his mother, he will also be good to you.* Gaby had only been a know-it-all teenager when her aunt had given her these sage pieces of advice, but somehow they'd stuck. Someday, some woman was going to be very lucky to have Deacon by her side.

But it wasn't going to be her.

Even if she were drawn to him, the cards were stacked against them. There was just too much baggage between them. Relationships were hard enough under normal circumstances, but theirs was outside the bounds of normal.

As she tried to dismiss the profound meaning of Deacon making this gesture, she recalled what he'd said about yellow roses: *they meant friendship.*

Did that mean he considered her a true friend? The acknowledgment stirred a rush of emotions. She tried to tamp down her reaction, but her heart refused to slow. She once again breathed in the flower's gentle perfume.

The fact that it wasn't her birthday and it wasn't a holiday made this gesture all that much more special. He'd done it just because he could. This was the most thoughtful thing a man had ever done for her.

She knew then and there that she was in trouble. Deacon was working his way through all the barriers she'd built around her heart. Why did it have to be him that got to her? He was the absolute last person she should be interested in and yet, he was the one that kept her awake at night. And when she did fall asleep, he was the one that filled her dreams.

She was still puzzling over what to do about her feelings for Deacon when he materialized in the doorway of the office. He looked quite handsome. The dark circles under his eyes were fading and when he smiled, it eased the worry lines bracketing his eyes.

"I hope you had a good night," he said.

Gaby yawned. She didn't know if there was enough coffee in the world to keep her awake today. "Morning."

His eyebrows gathered. "Don't tell me you were working all night."

"No. I was reading." She recalled the book, so she grabbed it from her purse and handed it to him. "Thank you. It was just as good as you said it would be. It had me guessing right up until the last chapter."

He accepted the book. "I'm glad. But you didn't have to read it so quickly."

"Yes, I did. Once I started reading, I had to keep going. It's the way I am when I get into a book."

When he nodded in understanding, their gazes met and held longer than necessary, and her heart began racing. Her stomach shivered with nerves. She'd never had a problem speaking with anyone until now. When she glanced away from him, her gaze skimmed over the yellow rose. "Thank you for the rose. It's beautiful."

"I'm glad you like it." He stepped back and leaned against the desk opposite hers. "I've been thinking that you have everything pretty much planned out for the event except for the menu."

"I guess I need to do that sooner rather than later so I can give the caterer the menu." She pulled out a pad of paper. "Do you have a preference for the format? Sitdown? Buffet? Finger foods?"

He paused as though giving each option due consideration. "This is going to be more of a garden party than anything else, correct?"

Gaby wouldn't exactly classify the event that way, but for the lack of a better term, she went with it. "Sure." Following his line of thought, she said, "So the finger foods might be best." When Deacon nodded, she added, "And we could have the wait staff mingle with trays."

"Sure, sounds good."

There was one more thing that she'd thought of. She didn't know how Deacon would feel about it since he was in favor of streamlining the event. But she thought that it would add a bit of fun to the event and it could be a big revenue raiser during the afternoon.

"I've been going over the plans and I think there's one more thing we should do."

Deacon's face grew serious. "What would that be?"

"A Chinese auction."

"No."

She frowned at him. "How can you just readily dismiss the idea?"

"Because the basis of the Chinese auction is to ask others to donate items or services. I don't want to ask anyone for anything."

She dropped the pen to the desk and lifted her chin. "Maybe that's your problem."

"What's that supposed to mean?"

"It means that you're trying to get through this difficult part of your life by yourself—by putting a wall up between you and everyone else."

He arched a dark eyebrow. "I let you in."

"No, you didn't. I made my own way past your walls in spite of you."

"This is my life, my choices—not yours."

She glared at him. "And this is my fundraiser and I'm telling you that there will be a Chinese auction."

His voice lowered and rumbled with agitation. "Are you always so stubborn?"

"My father says so, but I don't believe everything he says." She no longer believed what he said about Deacon.

"And you're going ahead with this auction no matter what I say?"

"Yes."

"Then I won't waste any more time trying to talk you out of it." He muttered under his breath as he strode out the door.

Something told Gaby that he regretted giving her that flower. But she wasn't backing down. That was Deacon's problem. When he growled, everyone backed away. He needed to learn that life was about give and take.

CHAPTER FOURTEEN

THERE WAS SOMETHING different about Gabrielle.

Something not quite right.

Deacon had kept his distance from her since their disagreement last week. He didn't know exactly why he'd taken such a strong opposition to her idea of the Chinese auction. It wasn't a terrible idea. He could think of much worse.

He was left with no choice but to admit the truth to himself. He'd created the disagreement on purpose to put some distance between them. And it was all because of that rose and the other ones he continued to leave at her door each morning.

He had mixed emotions about leaving her yellow roses. Part of him said that it was just a friendly gesture, but another part of him wanted them to mean more. And that made him uncomfortable.

Logic said that there was a fifty-fifty chance he was responsible for the car accident. If he were responsible, Gabrielle wouldn't want anything to do with him. But even if he were found innocent, would that really do much to change their circumstances? He was still the other party in a two-party accident.

But when he was outside in the rose garden, he would catch glimpses of Gabrielle. And when she didn't think he was watching, the smile vanished from her face. A glint of worry reflected in her eyes. Was it his fault? Had he upset her that much?

This time he didn't need to hear her aunt's voice in his head to know he needed to somehow fix things. Mrs. Kupps was right about Gabrielle being a ray of sunshine in his otherwise gloomy life. And when her light was dimmed, the darkness and shadows were too much for him.

He approached Gabrielle where she was sitting on the patio. She had pen and paper in hand, but she wasn't looking at either. Instead she was staring out over the ocean with a faraway look in her eyes.

"Mind if I join you?" He stopped next to the table.

She blinked and turned to him. "I don't mind, if you don't."

It wasn't exactly the invitation he'd been hoping for, but he sat down anyway. "Something is bothering you. I'd like you to tell me what it is."

She shook her head. "I'm fine."

"No. You're not. You haven't been happy in a while."

She sighed. "I didn't know that it was that obvious."

"Maybe not to others, but I've gotten to know you pretty well and I know when you have something on your mind. Is it the fundraiser? Are you worried—"

"No. It's not that. Things are going well. In fact, I'm already getting RSVPs to the digital invitations."

Frankly, that was quite a surprise to him. He'd assumed the event would be a failure. Actually, he'd been counting on it. The thought of opening his home to all those people was not something he relished, but it was a problem he'd deal with later. Right now, he was concerned about Gabrielle.

"If it's not the fundraiser, what it is? Maybe I can help."

Her tentative gaze met his. "It's my father."

"Your father? I don't understand. Did something happen?"

"No. At least not that I know of."

He should probably leave it there. It wasn't like he was friends with her father. But the sadness on her face had him searching for the truth. "Then what is it?"

"We've just never been apart for this long. It's always been just the two of us against the world."

Deacon hadn't expected this. "But isn't it nice not to be responsible for caring for him on a daily basis?"

She shrugged. "It never really bothered me. Maybe it should have. I guess I like being needed."

She did? "You mean you don't mind taking care of your father even to the extent of you not having a life of your own?"

"Is that what you think?"

"Well, when was the last time you had a date?"

She glanced away. "It's been a while."

"And when was the last time you did anything with your friends?"

"Lindsay and I went to the movies the other month."

"Other month? That sure doesn't sound like a busy social calendar."

"Why do I need a busy social calendar? So what if I don't have time to hang out. I have two jobs to hold down. And the cleaning and shopping to do." She paused as though she realized that she'd said too much. And then she frowned at him as though he was now the one in trouble.

He drove home his point with one final comment. "Maybe you take on too much."

"I do what I need to do."

There was no talking to her. She obviously couldn't see that she did so much for others that there wasn't any time left for her. He felt bad for her, but his persistence on this subject was only upsetting her more. "I didn't mean to upset you."

She sighed. "It's not you. I'm just frustrated. I'm not sure my father is taking proper care of himself."

This was Deacon's chance to pay her back for all the generous things she'd done for him. And he knew exactly what he must do.

When he looked at Gabrielle, he knew he didn't have any other choice. "Go to your father."

Her head jerked around until her puzzled gaze met his. "But our agreement—"

"I know about our agreement and I don't care. I won't stop you. Go to your father. Make sure he's okay."

"Really?" Immediately her face lit up. "You don't mind?"

"No." He was lying.

He knew that once she passed beyond the estate gates that she would not return. Why should she? She had a life that had nothing to do with him. She had a father that loved her. Friends to do things with. She had a full life.

And what did he have to offer her? He struggled to come up with any reason for her to return. The memory of their kisses passed through his mind. But he knew that had been a fleeting thing—a moment of pity on her part for a man who looked and sounded like some sort of beast.

"Do you mind if I go now?" She looked radiant, like Dorothy about to click her red heels.

He, however, didn't feel like the Wizard. "No. Go."

She ran over to him and hugged him. The moment passed much too quickly and then she pulled back.

He refused to let her see how much her departure bothered him.

Without another word, Gabrielle rushed away. He wasn't even sure that her feet touched the ground, she was so happy to get away from there. How could he take that happiness away from her? He sighed in resignation.

He was happy for her, but he was sad for himself. He just couldn't believe in the short amount of time that they'd been together that she'd come to mean so much to him.

And now he was on his own again.

CHAPTER FIFTEEN

IT HAD BEEN a lovely visit.

The weekend had flown by. It had been so good to see her father. The time with him had been exactly what she'd needed. And best of all, Newton had been out of the house. Everything had gone smoothly so long as she stayed away from the subject of Deacon.

She'd tried a couple of times to let her father know that Deacon was treating her really well, but her father hadn't wanted to hear any of it. All he'd wanted to hear regarding Deacon was if she'd gained any information to help move along the legal process. He was still convinced that Deacon had paid off people to bury the accident report. In the end, Gaby had given up because she didn't want to spend the short amount of time she had with her father arguing. Though she didn't believe Deacon was a monster, she couldn't confidently claim his innocence, either. They still didn't know exactly what had happened in the accident. To say she was confused was putting it mildly.

While she was home, she'd cooked for her father. She'd spent quite a bit of time in the kitchen preparing healthy meals. By the time she left, the fridge was full. The freezer was stuffed with meals that just needed re-heating. And her father's prescriptions were refilled.

Her father begged her not to return to Deacon's estate, saying that he could take whatever punishment the judge was likely to throw at him. But Gaby told him this was about more than just him. She was doing important work with the fundraiser and she needed to see it through until the end. And that soon she would be back home. With a hug and a kiss, she'd left for the long drive back to Malibu, knowing her father was doing quite well on his own. Perhaps she did fuss over him more than necessary.

Thanks to Deacon, both she and her father were finding that they didn't need each other quite so much. When her time was over at the estate perhaps she could stick her foot back in the dating pool. But as soon as she thought of dating, Deacon's image came to mind.

She tried to imagine him with his hair cut and his face shaved. He'd look like a whole new man and perhaps he'd feel like one, too. Maybe it was time to see how he felt about a makeover.

Monday morning, she opened the door to the guest-house of Deacon's estate and paused to look around. After waking up for the past week to find a yellow rose at her door, today there was none. It saddened her, but she knew eventually they had to stop. Still, she'd come to look forward to them. And now she tried not to read in too much to their absence.

It wasn't until later that morning, with a check in hand for his signature, that she went in search of him. At that hour of the morning, Deacon was usually tending to the roses. But when she went to the garden, there was no sign of him and it didn't look as though he'd been there that morning. That was odd.

She went to his office, thinking he was working on an important project, but the office was empty and the lights were off. Concern started pumping through her veins.

In the kitchen, she tracked down Mrs. Kupps. "Do you

know where Deacon is?" The woman nodded, but her face said that something was definitely amiss. "You're worrying me. Where is he?"

"He's closed in his rooms."

"His rooms. But why?"

"I don't know. He hasn't said a word to me." Mrs. Kupps shrugged. "He went in there after you left and he hasn't come out. I'm worried about him."

Gaby recalled their last conversation. She thought things had been fine between them, but then she recalled how Deacon had been eager for her to go visit her father. She'd missed her father so much at the time that she hadn't paid much attention to Deacon's reaction, but looking back on things, she should have realized something was off with him.

"Leave it to me. I'm used to dealing with stubborn males."

A weak smile lifted the worry lines on the woman's face. "I knew as soon as I laid eyes on you that you would be the ray of sunshine this house needed. I was just preparing him a late breakfast. You could take it to him, if you like."

"Thank you. I would."

Mrs. Kupps put together a tray of eggs, bacon, toast, fruit and juice. When she handed it over, she said, "Good luck."

"Thank you. I'll need it."

Remembering the day that Deacon had taken her to his room to clean her wounds from falling in the rose garden, Gaby made her way upstairs. The tall double doors were closed, but that wasn't going to stop her.

She leveled her shoulders and then gave a quick knock. Without waiting, she opened the door. She was surprised to find the room so dark. She squinted into the shadows, looking for him.

"Go away!" His deep voice rumbled through the room.

It seemed that he'd regressed. "Your growl isn't going to scare me."

Suddenly he was standing in front of her. Frown lines were deeply etched upon his face. "You're back?" He seemed surprised.

"Of course."

His face quickly returned to its frown. "Well, since you aren't going to leave until you've had your say, get it over with. Quickly."

"I hear that you've been in your room since I left. What's the matter? Are you sick?"

"No."

"Something must be the matter." Now that her eyes had adjusted to the low lighting, she moved to a table and placed the tray. "You have things to do. There's no time for slacking."

"I'm not slacking." Again his voice rumbled. "Now go away. Shouldn't you be with your father?"

So *that's* what was bothering him? She worked to subdue a smile. He had missed her. Who'd have guessed that? In truth, she'd missed him, too. But she wasn't ready to admit it.

She moved past him with sure, steady steps. At the window, she stopped and threw open the heavy drapes, letting the bright morning sun into the room. She turned to find Deacon squinting and trying to block the sun's rays with his hand.

"Close that."

"And let you sit in here in the dark? I don't think so."

He grunted his displeasure. "I'm your boss. You're supposed to do what I say."

"I'm your friend, remember? And I'm doing what's best for you."

"No, you came back because your father probably kicked you out for working here. I bet you don't listen to him any better than you do me."

"When both of you make poor choices, I don't mind calling either of you out on them."

Deacon frowned at her. "I didn't make a poor choice."

"You mean sitting around in the dark is your way of being productive?"

He opened his mouth and just as quickly closed it again. He sighed and glanced away. "If you're going to stay here, shouldn't you be in your office doing some work instead of harassing me?"

"I will just as soon as you start eating that delicious meal Mrs. Kupps prepared for you." He looked at her but he didn't move. She crossed her arms and tapped her foot. "I have all day."

With a look of resignation, he moved to the small table and sat down. "You are certainly something."

"I'll take that as a compliment."

He took a bite of egg. It was followed by a half a slice of toast. Partway through his meal, he stopped and looked at her. "Why do you care?"

"Because you apparently need someone to care about you. You don't seem to do a very good job of it on your own."

"How am I supposed to, when I know what I've done?" The worry and stress lines etched his handsome face.

"I thought you said you didn't remember the accident?"

He let out a heavy breath, causing her heart to lodge in her throat. Did he know more than he'd told her? Had the police report been released? Her mind rapidly searched for the reason for his despair.

"Talk to me," she prompted, needing him to tell her that the worst hadn't happened.

"The nightmares are getting worse. It's hard to tell the truth from the products of my imagination."

"And…" She waved her hands as though trying to pull the information from him.

"And I remember bits and pieces, like the fire burning my skin. I remember your aunt. I remember her saying 'Take care of Gabrielle.'"

"What? She did?" When he nodded, she asked, "Is that why you gave me this job?"

His gaze met hers. "Yes."

Gaby had been right about him. Deacon was a good man—buried beneath a mountain of unnecessary guilt. Her aunt's words were the proof of his innocence that she needed.

"Why are you smiling?" His dark eyes searched hers.

"Don't you understand? You're innocent."

His eyebrows drew together and his forehead wrinkled. "Why would you say that?"

"Because if you were guilty, my aunt never would have asked you to reach out to me and take care of me—not that I need you to." Gaby smiled at him, feeling as though a huge weight had been lifted. When he didn't look convinced, she asked, "What's wrong?"

Deacon rubbed the back of his neck. "Your theory is not proof—not legally."

"It's enough for me. It'll all work out. You'll see." There was one more thing bothering her. "But if you really wanted to fulfill her wishes, instead of having me work here, you could have just offered me money or something, but you didn't. Why?"

Deacon hesitated. "When you went on and on about how you cared for your father after telling me that he could take care of himself, I wanted you to know that you could have a life of your own and you didn't have to sacrifice everything for him."

"It was more than that and you know it."

"Perhaps."

"Perhaps nothing. You wanted to separate me from my father in order to punish him for the pain he caused you."

Deacon's gaze lowered and he nodded. "Yes, I did. I suppose that makes me a bad person."

"No. It just makes you human." She eyed him as he returned to eating. "Speaking of making you more human. What would you say to a haircut and shave?"

"I don't think that's a good idea."

She wasn't going to let him wiggle out of this. He'd been hiding behind all of that hair long enough. "Really? You like having your hair hang in your eyes?"

"No, but it's better than seeing what's beneath it."

So he was worried about the scars. He couldn't hide from them forever. Maybe facing up to them would be his first step back to the life he'd left behind after the accident.

She stepped closer to him. "I'd like to see you. The real you beneath all of that hair."

He looked at her as though gauging her interest. "And what if I'm a scary mess?"

"I'll still think you're handsome." Now where had that come from? She couldn't believe she'd uttered those words, even if it was the truth.

His eyes widened with surprise. "Really? You're not just saying that because you pity me? Which is ridiculous considering I lived and your aunt didn't. Listen to me. I just keep rambling…"

She kneeled down next to him. With her hands, she smoothed his hair back from his face. "There you are. Yes, you're definitely the most handsome man I know."

There she went again, saying the first thing that popped into her mind. But this time, when Deacon reached up and wrapped his hand around her wrist, she didn't regret speaking the truth.

"Okay. I'll do it," he said, "as long as *you* do the haircut and shave."

That wasn't exactly what she'd imagined when she'd proposed the idea. Still, if he was willing to take this big step with her, who was she to deny him?

CHAPTER SIXTEEN

HER HEART POUNDED in her chest.

After gathering the supplies she needed, Gabrielle stood there in Deacon's bathroom holding a razor.

What if she messed up? She wasn't a barber or a hairdresser. Sure she could trim her own bangs when her hairstyle dictated. But there was a big difference between trimming bangs and trimming a man's entire head, on top of giving him a shave.

But with his dominant hand still not working well enough for him to manage a razor, what choice did she have?

Call a professional? The idea was so appealing and yet, she knew that it was an impossibility. Deacon was so certain that beneath all of that hair that he was a monster. And this was her one chance to prove him wrong.

The truth was she didn't know what she'd find beneath his beard. She prayed that in his mind, he'd made the scars much worse than they were in reality. No matter what he looked like, she had to let him know that he wasn't some sort of beast.

The fact that he trusted her enough to allow her to shave and trim him wasn't lost on her. They had come a very long way since she'd started working at the estate. She remembered how awkward it felt working in that office, knowing that he was on the other side of a locked door.

But at the time, she hadn't understood that he had such significant injuries from the accident. That certainly wasn't how the accident was portrayed in the news. In fact, she was beginning to think that nothing in the media was as it seemed.

"Did you change your mind about revealing the real me?"

Deacon's voice jarred her out of her thoughts. "No. Of course not. I'm just trying to decide if I should start with your hair or your beard."

"The hair. That way after you're done shaving me, I can jump in the shower."

"You're sure about this?" She had to hear his answer one more time.

"I am." He studied her for a moment. "If you are."

"I am." She sucked in a calming breath. It didn't work, but she focused on the task at hand instead of her lack of experience.

Trading the razor for a pair of scissors, she set to work. She drew on her memories from her own haircuts and her experience trimming her dad's hair when he was in rehab. Gaby took her time, not wanting to mess up. She knew there was a lot riding on this particular haircut.

Her stomach was a nervous, jittery ball of nerves. Lucky for her, her hands remained steady. A cut here. A cut there. The trimmed locks of hair piled up on the floor. And all the while, Deacon remained quiet.

She walked around his chair, checking for any uneven spots. There was one by his left ear. With great care, she trimmed it.

And in the end, he retained both ears, and no blood

was shed. It wasn't the most stylish haircut, but considering his hair before, it was a large improvement.

Deacon lifted a hand and ran it over the short strands.

"Do you want to look in the mirror?"

"I don't have any mirrors. I got rid of them."

"But I have one." She held up a hand mirror.

He turned away and shook his head. "I'll see it when you're all done."

After the trimmings were swept aside, she grabbed a comb and the scissors. Then she set to work trimming his beard as short as she could. She'd never trimmed a man's beard before. Sure, she'd shaved her father when he'd been in the hospital but his stubble was nothing compared to Deacon's full-on beard.

But what got to her more was being this close to him. There was something special about him. It was more than him being a famous movie star. It was an air of strength and power that exuded from him. And she was feeling herself being drawn closer and closer to him.

She'd never experienced such an intense attraction and it scared her. Not the part about her father or the accident. No—it was the fact that she didn't know how she was going to return to a world without Deacon's reluctant grin, or seeing the way his eyes twinkled when he was happy.

As the fundraiser grew closer, her time with Deacon was running out. She wanted this time to count. If all she had left when this was over were the memories, then she wanted them to be earth-shattering, pulse-quickening memories.

Deacon didn't know how much time had passed.

His eyes were closed as he focused on Gabrielle's gentle touch. He didn't know that a haircut and shave could be so tantalizing. Thank goodness she didn't attempt to make small talk because he wasn't sure he'd be able to follow along.

Each time her fingertips brushed over his skin, it short-circuited his thoughts. And each time her body brushed up against him, he longed to reach out and pull her onto his lap. He ached to press his mouth to hers. He smothered a groan.

"Are you okay?" Gabrielle paused.

He opened his eyes to find her staring directly at him. "Um, yes."

"You're sure?"

She'd heard him moan? He smothered a curse. He thought that he'd caught himself. Deciding it was best that he change the subject, he asked, "How's it going?"

"Before I go any further, I need to soften your beard." She turned on the water.

He couldn't see, but he could imagine Gabrielle letting the water get hot and steamy. And the next thing he knew, she was draping a hot towel over his jaw. The heat gave him a bit of a start, but he soon adjusted to it.

All the while, he was tempted to ask for her mirror just to make sure his hair wasn't an utter mess, but then he decided at this point, it didn't matter. If worse came to worse, he'd shave his entire head. At one point in his life, his hair had only been touched by the finest stylist in the movie business, but that felt like a lifetime ago. These days his hair didn't matter to anyone.

Gabrielle moved in front of him. "I have to admit I've only ever shaved my father when he was in the hospital."

"Don't worry. I trust you." It wasn't until the words crossed his lips that he realized what he'd uttered. He would retract the words if he could. But now they were out there. They filled the room with silence as the heavy impact settled in.

Gabrielle immediately turned away so he was unable to read the emotions filtering through her expressive eyes. When she turned back, she removed the hot towel from his jaw.

He didn't know why he'd said such a thing. That wasn't exactly the truth. He knew. He just didn't want to admit it to himself or to anyone else.

He was a man who prided himself on relying on no one. He told himself during all these months of solitude that he was fine on his own because he couldn't trust anyone else in his life. And then Gabrielle burst into his world and little by little she'd chipped away at the crusty shell that he'd armed himself with. And now he was starting to care about her. He didn't know what to do with these feelings.

But it was getting difficult to ignore his body's strong reaction to her with her fussing all about him. And when she stood in front of him to shave him, he had to close his eyes to keep from staring at the most tantalizing view of her firm breasts. But it was too late. The image of her curves straining against the thin cotton top when she leaned toward him was permanently tattooed upon his mind.

Think of something else—anything else.

He didn't want to let Gabrielle know just how much this session of playing barbershop was getting to him. The truth was he was letting himself get too close to Gabrielle. And no matter how he tried to hold her at arm's length, she ended up getting so much closer. But that would all end as soon as Gabrielle revealed his scars.

He told himself that he was ready for her to be repulsed, but he wasn't. One look at him and she wouldn't be able to pack fast enough. The truth was that before Gabrielle, he'd forgotten how to smile—how to laugh. He'd forgotten what it was to sleep at night for more than two hours. She had totally turned his life upside down and made him think of all the things that he could still do.

"Relax." Gabrielle's voice drew him back to the present.

"I am relaxed."

"No, you're not. Your jaw is rigid and so are the muscles in your neck. If you don't trust me—"

"I do trust you. Keep going. I have things to do." The truth was he didn't have any other place that he wanted to be other than right here with her hands moving gently over his skin.

"Look at me when you say those words."

He opened his eyes and found her staring straight at him. "I trust you."

With that admission hanging between them, she continued shaving him. Her motions were slow and deliberate. He banished the worries and drew in a deep, calming breath. The more she worked on him, the more relaxed he became under her skilled hands. He sat there with his eyes closed, enjoying the way her fingers felt on his skin. Her touch was gentle, but it ignited a fire within him.

She ran a towel over his face. "You can open your eyes. I'm done."

When his eyes opened, she was smiling at him. "You're already done?"

"Already? That took close to an hour."

"It did?"

She nodded. "And it was worth every minute. Because just as I predicted, you're amazingly handsome. You'll have all of the women swooning at your feet," she added softly.

"I doubt it." He ran a hand over his smooth jaw. It felt so good to have all that hair removed. The beard had been itchy and too warm.

However, he refused to let himself buy in to Gabrielle's compliment. He'd seen the damage to his face at the hospital. He'd been a mess of angry scrapes and nasty gashes. She was just being nice.

"If you don't believe me, have a look for yourself." She handed him a hand mirror.

He really didn't want to look. He knew that he'd find an angry red map of scars. Still, it couldn't be avoided forever. He might have removed all the mirrors from his home, but he was quickly learning just how many surfaces were reflective.

Not allowing himself an easy out, he lifted the mirror. He blinked. Surely he wasn't seeing clearly. He turned his head to one side and then to the other. Where were all the ugly scars?

"See, I told you." Gabrielle continued to smile at him. "You're as handsome as ever."

"I can't believe it." He ran his fingers over his face. "I know that when they transferred me to another hospital, they mentioned something about bringing in a world-class plastic surgeon, but I didn't think there was any hope of salvaging my face."

"I'd say that surgeon is quite gifted."

The angry red lines had faded. The surgeon had hidden most of the scars. Others were fine white lines, but they didn't make him look like Frankenstein. He'd never be the way he used to be, but at least now he wouldn't scare children.

He turned to Gabrielle to thank her for helping him through this difficult step. But when he faced her, the words caught in the back of his throat. She looked at him differently. Not in a bad way. More like a woman who desired a man. Was that possible? Or was he reading what he wanted in her eyes?

As though in answer to his unspoken question, she bent over and pressed her lips to his. At first, he didn't move. He didn't want to do anything to ruin this moment. And yet she pulled back, ever so slightly.

Need and desire pumped through his veins in equal portions. When she looked at him, he felt like a whole man. Not like a man haunted by his past and worried about his bleak future. She looked at him as if she couldn't imagine him doing anything bad. And he so wanted to believe it, too.

Giving in to the urgent need consuming his body, he slipped his arms around her waist and gently pulled her back to him. Her warm, soft curves pressed against his hard muscles and a moan formed in the back of his throat.

He didn't know why fate had brought them together, and in this moment, it didn't matter. The only thing he cared about was Gabrielle's happiness. He wanted to give her a good memory—something to overshadow some of the pain he'd caused.

In all honesty, the memory they were creating would be something he'd cherish, too. He'd never known anyone as generous of heart, as understanding and as bossy as Gabrielle. And he knew no matter how long he lived, he'd never find anyone else like her.

As their kiss deepened, he longed to have all of her. But he had to be sure she wanted the same thing. He wouldn't rush her.

With every bit of willpower, he pulled back and waited until her gaze met his. "Are you sure about this?"

She nodded.

That wasn't good enough, he had to be absolutely sure

she wanted him as much as he wanted her before he carried her into his bedroom and laid her down on his king-size bed. "Gabrielle, do you want to make love?"

"I thought I made my desires clear just a moment ago."

"I need to be sure. I... I don't want to do anything to upset you."

Her eyes reflected the desire warming his veins. "Then let me make this perfectly clear. I, Gabrielle Dupré, want to make love to you, Deacon Santoro."

That was all he needed to hear. He scooped her up in his arms and carried her to the bedroom. He laid her gently on the bed. Nothing had ever looked so good—so right.

He knew after tonight that nothing would ever be the same for them, but he would deal with the aftermath later. Much, much later...

CHAPTER SEVENTEEN

THE NEXT MORNING Gaby awoke alone.

She reached out, running her hand over Deacon's pillow. It was cold to the touch. Her gaze searched the bedroom. There was no sign of him.

The convergence of disappointment, embarrassment and sadness left her grappling to keep a lid on her emotions. He regretted their night together. A sob caught in the back of her throat.

No. Don't lose it now. You're stronger than this.

As she looked to see the time, her gaze stumbled across a yellow rose on her bedside table. It hadn't been there last night. She was certain of it.

She withdrew the rose from the vase. As she stared at its velvet petals, she wondered what Deacon was trying to tell her. Did he want to go back to being friends? Or was she reading too much in to it? Maybe, in this case, a rose was just a rose.

She glanced at the clock. She realized if she didn't hurry, she'd be late to work. Finding out where her relationship now stood with Deacon would have to wait until later. She was expecting phone calls that morning about the fundraiser. And no matter what happened between her and Deacon, she intended to do her best job.

She scrambled out of bed and rushed to get dressed.

There was something else she needed to do that morning—conclude her arrangement with *QTR*. She may not know the exact circumstances of the accident, but she knew Deacon hadn't been at fault and didn't deserve any further bad press.

When she returned to the guesthouse, she knew she'd made a big mistake. Not the night she'd spent with Deacon. One minute, he'd been so tender and loving. Then in the next moment, he'd been hot and passionate. It was a night of surprises and delights. No, her problem was agreeing to do an exposé about him. Now that she knew about her aunt's request, she was certain he was innocent. Her aunt would never have asked a killer to look after her. And now Gaby had to try to undo some of the damage.

So far *QTR* hadn't printed anything that she'd given them, not that there was anything noteworthy. Hopefully it wasn't too late to call off the arrangement.

Gaby retrieved the number of the editor at *QTR*. The phone rang and rang. She began to worry that no one would answer.

Suddenly there was a male voice. "Hello."

Gaby was startled. This certainly wasn't the perky young female editor that she'd been assigned to. "I'm sorry. I must have rung the wrong number."

"This is Elle McTavish's desk."

Gaby swallowed down her nervousness. "I was hoping to speak with her."

"And who is this?"

"Gaby, um, I mean Gabrielle Dupré. And who is this?"

"Thomas Rousseau."

As in Quentin Thomas Rousseau II. Gaby's stomach clenched. Oh, boy. She'd heard stories about the man. None of it was any good. He was legendary. She wasn't sure what was going on, but she had the feeling that it wasn't going to be good.

She gripped the phone tighter. "Could I leave a message for Ms. McTavish?"

"I've taken over for her."

But he was the owner, not an editor. Gaby clenched the phone tighter. "I see. Then perhaps you are the person I should speak to."

"I'm listening."

"I've changed my mind about doing the story about Deacon Santoro."

"I see." His voice was smooth and patient. "But my understanding was that's what you wanted—for the world to know about Santoro—and how he's evading the law."

At the beginning, that was exactly what she had wanted. But now she knew that her aunt hadn't blamed Deacon and, therefore, neither should she. He was not the beast she'd originally thought. He was just a man—a man who had punished himself needlessly.

"That was before—"

She stopped herself from saying too much. The less she told this man, the better. She had learned firsthand how words and images could be twisted into something they're not.

"Before what?"

"It was an accident. That's all."

"Have the police said this?"

"No, but they will."

"Miss Dupré, what changed your mind about gaining the truth and forcing the police's hand in delivering their findings about the incident?"

She worried her bottom lip. What was she supposed to say now? She didn't want to break Deacon's confidence. She didn't want to share her aunt's last words with the world.

"Miss Dupré?"

"I want to end our arrangement."

"Is that because you're now romantically linked with Mr. Santoro?" The man's voice took on a hard edge. "Yes, I saw that photo of you in his arms. I was not happy to be scooped by another magazine."

"It wasn't the way it looked." At least at *that* moment, everything had been innocent. Now everything was exponentially more complicated.

"Tell me about it." His tone was more congenial. He wanted her to give him a story but she refused to do it.

"You and I don't have a signed agreement. Remember, your magazine wanted to wait until you could ascertain what information I would provide."

"There was a verbal agreement, was there not?"

"Sounds like a case of 'he said, she said.'"

Regretting the deal she'd struck with the magazine, and now this man that she didn't trust in the least, she said, "I am calling off the arrangement. Besides, I never gave you anything you could use."

The line went dead.

She had to admit that had gone a little better than she'd expected. And as she set aside her cell phone, she felt a bit lighter. She didn't care how hard up she was for money, she was never working for a gossip rag again.

Now she had to deal with Deacon. She had no idea what to make of his disappearance that morning. He did say that he didn't sleep much. Maybe he'd just gotten up early.

And to complicate matters, she needed to come clean about her liaison with *QTR*. She felt now that her relationship with Deacon had shifted, she needed to be completely open and honest—even if he didn't like what she was about to say.

How was he supposed to face her after last night?

Deacon moved to the window in his office. She was going to look at him differently. She was going to expect things of him—things he couldn't give her.

And yet he didn't want to lose her. He told himself that it was the fact she was the best assistant he'd ever had. And this fundraiser, if it worked out, might help fund a breakthrough in the fight against breast cancer. There was too much riding on them continuing to work together.

Was it possible to wind back the hands of time? If they didn't talk about it, could they pretend that amazing night of lovemaking had never happened?

"Deacon, we need to talk."

He didn't move as he stared out the window of his office. She'd just said the five words he'd been dreading. It was time he put his plan in action.

Deacon turned to her. "I wanted to talk to you, too. I have another screenplay and I'd like to get your thoughts on it."

"It can wait—"

"No, it can't. If I don't get the rights to it, someone else will. I know it."

"But what I have to say—"

"Can wait." He saw the frustration reflected in her eyes. He owed her more than a quick brush-off. He swallowed hard. "I wasn't expecting last night. It wasn't something I planned."

"Me neither."

That was good to hear. It meant she had to be as confused as him. "Then you'll understand when I say I need time to process this. My life—it's not the best time to start anything serious."

Disappointment dimmed her eyes. "I understand. But I feel I owe you the truth about something."

Revealing secrets and truths were things people did when they were establishing a relationship. When they were building a foundation. He didn't intend to do any of those things with Gabrielle. Because when that police report was released—when he was sure his whole world would come crashing down—he didn't want Gabrielle hurt any more than she already would be.

Whatever she'd done or thought she'd done, it wouldn't compare to his transgressions.

"Now isn't the time for sharing." He averted his gaze. "We can talk another time."

"But—"

"Please." She didn't know how hard she was making this for him.

Because in a different place, at a different time, under different circumstances, he would have welcomed her into his life with both arms. Turning her away was the hardest thing he'd ever done.

As he watched her walk away, he felt the distance grow between them. It was like the sun had been eclipsed from his life. And as much as he wanted to go after her—to pull her into his arms—his feet remained rooted to the floor.

He clung to the fact that she was better off without him.

CHAPTER EIGHTEEN

IT WAS ALL coming together.

Beneath the blue skies, Gaby stood to the side of the golf course and gazed out over the estate grounds. Deacon's grounds crew were miracle workers. Of course, it helped that they'd enjoyed months of paid leave and were now anxious to get back to work. Gaby couldn't imagine what it would be like to have all that free time. Right now, she didn't have enough hours in the day to do everything that needed done.

And ever since they'd made love, Deacon had held her at arm's length. She didn't understand it. Had she done something wrong? Had he not enjoyed it? Whatever it was, he wasn't talking and she was left with nothing but doubts and worries. Thankfully the fundraiser was only a couple of days away and there were so many last-minute details to attend to that she didn't have time to get lost in her thoughts.

Every last ticket for the event had been sold. Now if only they'd all show up. The food had been ordered. The catering service had been reserved. The rose garden was already in order. Deacon had seen to that. But there was something she was forgetting. She just couldn't put her finger on it.

"You wanted to see me?" Deacon's voice came from behind her.

"I did." She tried to hide her surprise at him actually seeking her out instead of calling her on the phone. "What do you think?"

"About what?"

She subdued a sigh. What was wrong with him? "Look around. The grounds are done. The men have been working on it every day from dawn until dusk."

Deacon remained quiet as he took in his surroundings. His expression was masked behind a look of indifference. How could that be? Didn't he notice what a mess the estate had been? Even she had been out here every day going over the details to make this place spectacular.

"It looks good." He still didn't smile.

"Good? That's it. This place is amazing. Anyone would be amazed by the transformation." There was something more to this. Something that he wasn't telling her. "Deacon, we need to talk about the other night—"

"There's nothing to talk about."

She was tired of being patient—of thinking he just needed time to adjust to the change in their relationship. "I don't believe you."

"What?" He gave her an innocent look.

"Don't go acting like you don't know what I'm talking about. You've been avoiding me at all costs ever since we made love."

"I've been busy." His phone chimed. He withdrew it and held it up as proof of his business. Then he silenced it and slipped it back in his pocket.

"Fine. We'll play it your way."

"I'm not playing. What happened was a mistake. One we shouldn't repeat."

She managed a shrug as she wasn't so sure she trusted

her voice. It took her a second to swallow the lump in the back of her throat. With a blink of her eyes, she mustered up what she hoped was a blank expression. He wasn't the only actor here.

Willing her voice not to waver, she said, "And the golf course? What do you think of that?"

"It's good."

She planted her hands on her hips. "After all this work, *good* is all you have to say?"

His gaze didn't meet hers. "I don't know what you want me to tell you."

"More than that. My lunch was good. Your haircut is good. But the transformation of this estate from an unruly jungle to a work of art is spectacular."

He sighed and then proceeded to rub the back of his neck. "I just can't shake the feeling that something is going to go terribly wrong." He turned to her and apparently her thoughts were reflected on her face because he said, "What happens if the report on the accident comes out between now and then?"

"We deal with it."

"What if it says I'm to blame?"

In all honesty, she wasn't sure how she'd cope if the report really did say that Deacon was responsible for the accident that stole away her aunt, no matter how sure she was that he was innocent. But now Gaby understood why he'd pulled away from her. The accident was like a deep chasm between them, and try as they might, it was hard to cross.

She wanted to believe she would be able to move past the accident—to not hate him if the truth turned out to be different than what she imagined. But she knew that emotions could be tricky. Her father was a prime example— who'd have thought he would be arrested for stalking and harassment? Her father had never been in trouble with the law before in his life.

Not wanting to get caught up in the what-ifs and may-bes, she said, "Would you like to give it a go?" She gestured toward the golf clubs that were all spiffed up and standing next to the house in a special shed. "The clubs are just waiting to be used."

He hesitated and she was certain he was going to turn her down. And then he said, "I'll do it, if you do."

She shook her head. "Not me."

"Why not?"

"I—I prefer to watch." She really didn't want to admit that she didn't know a putter from an iron. Those were terms she'd heard the groundskeepers throwing around.

Deacon arched an eyebrow as he stepped closer to her. "Are you afraid I'll beat you?"

He was challenging her? Oh, boy. Maybe it was time for her to fess up. "No. I'm not worried." There was a glint of excitement in his dark eyes. He definitely had the wrong idea and so she said, "I don't know how to golf."

His eyes widened. "But you're the one who suggested making this a golfing event."

"I know I did. You did happen to notice that most of your yard is taken up by a nine-hole golf course?"

"But usually when you host an event, you know how to do the said event."

Now she understood his confusion. "But see, I'm not the host, you are. The fundraiser is in your mother's name. This is your home. And the people are coming here because of you—"

"No. They are coming because they are curious to see the recluse and find out if I'm an ugly, scarred mess like the tabloids have portrayed."

"Whoa! Whoa!" She waved away all his worries.

"That isn't why they're coming here. They're attending the event to support a worthy cause."

"And I think you see only the good in people."

"What's that supposed to mean?"

"Look at you. You're always so positive. Wanting to believe people are truly good. But they aren't."

She didn't know where all of this was coming from. "I'm not some Pollyanna."

"Yes, you are. You're all smiles and sunshine."

She hadn't meant to mislead him. "I'm human just like you. I have my share of doubts and worries. I just try not to dwell on them."

He rolled his eyes.

"Don't do that. Don't make me out to be like someone up on a pedestal."

"Then tell me that you aren't doing everything you can to convince yourself that I'm innocent. Go ahead. Deny it."

"But my aunt—"

"She was probably in shock. She probably hadn't even understood what had happened. The only thing she could think about was her love for you."

She shook her head, refusing to believe his version of events. "Now that I've gotten to know you, I just can't believe you would be reckless with your life and that of others."

"But see, that's the point. I have been in the past. I've bought super cars and I've taken them out on the road to see how fast they could go—to push the envelope. Doesn't that make me reckless?" When she couldn't argue with him, she remained quiet. His gaze implored her to affirm his actions. "Go ahead, say it."

"No." She wasn't going to help convict him when there wasn't any evidence. Because if he were guilty—if he did act recklessly—she would have lost not one but two people that she cared deeply about in that accident.

"Gabrielle, you can't bury your head in the sand and pretend the accident didn't happen. The reality is my nightmares grow stronger every night. You have to accept that—that I'm responsible for what happened. No amount of positivity will be able to overcome the fact that I—I killed your aunt."

Each word he threw at her was a blow at her heart. Tears pricked the back of her eyes. "Why are you doing this?"

Deacon hated hurting her.

But he didn't have a choice. More of his memories were starting to come back to him. He remembered being in the car. He recalled the blinding headlights headed straight for him. The rest was bits and pieces, but he couldn't shake the guilt mounting within him.

And now he was making a mess of things with Gabrielle. He'd only wanted to help her. He should have done it from a distance. Bringing her here to his estate was his first mistake. The second mistake was getting caught up in her greenish-gray eyes and letting himself be drawn in by her pouty lips. Now he had to untangle the ties that bound them together. It was best for Gabrielle.

He cleared his throat. "I never should have let things get this far. You and I need to part now, before either of us gets hurt."

"Are you saying you never cared? That this thing between us is all in my imagination?"

Why did she have to make this harder on herself? He couldn't tell her what she wanted to hear—not if he wanted her to leave, if he wanted to save her from more pain.

"It was fun and nice." He glanced away, unable to

stand the hurt reflected in her eyes. "But it wasn't real. It would never last."

His phone vibrated again. What in the world was going on? His email was busier than ever. Using his phone as an excuse not to face the pain he'd caused Gabrielle, he pretended to check it. In truth, he couldn't care less about business right now—right when he was sending away the woman that he'd come to care about deeply—

The breath caught in his throat as his gaze strayed across a bit of news. There was a distorted picture of him with ugly scars, next to a photo of Gabrielle. The headline read, The Beast Wins Beauty?

"What is it?" Gabrielle asked. When he didn't respond, she asked again, "What's the matter?"

He ignored her as his gaze skimmed down over the slanderous piece of trashy journalism. The fact that Gabrielle was *quoted* in the article stabbed him in the chest. Each breath was painful.

All this time, he'd thought she was so amazing with her ability to see the good in him. At first, he hadn't wanted to believe in her generous heart, but she'd worn him down and snuck past the wall around his own heart. And it'd been a lie. All of it.

"Deacon, I'm getting worried. What's wrong?"

His gaze narrowed in on her. "Why? Are you hoping I'll give you another headline?"

"What?" She reached for his phone. The color drained from her face as she read the article. When she looked up at him, worry lines bracketed her eyes. "I can explain."

"Don't bother." His angry words died in his throat when he realized she'd done what most anyone would have done in her situation. "I probably would have done the same thing in your place."

"But you don't understand. I—I backed out of the deal.

Once I knew you better and you told me what my aunt said to you, I backed out."

He wanted to believe her but he couldn't allow himself. "It looks like you gave them plenty to work with."

"This isn't my stuff. They did a hatchet job on the information I supplied them. Please. You have to believe me."

Anger pulsed through his veins. He was angry at the tabloid for printing outright lies. And he was furious with himself for not listening to his gut. Instead, he'd let down his guard with Gabrielle. He'd let himself fall for her and it'd all been a lie.

"Just go." His voice rumbled.

"But the fundraiser—"

"Is taken care of. You said so yourself. All the arrangements have been made. Now that your end of our deal has been fulfilled, it's time for you to leave."

When she didn't move but rather stood there with tears glistening in her eyes, he said with a low guttural growl that he knew she hated, "Go now. And don't come back."

He turned his back to her because it was killing him to send her away. He would try to forget the happiness that Gabrielle had brought to his life. He would banish the image of her warm smile—a smile that she would get when he walked in the room.

Because none of it had been true. While he'd been falling in love with her, she had been figuring out how best to twist the knife. And she'd succeeded. Worst of all, he deserved it and more after causing the accident.

His last little bit of hope that his name would be cleared was also gone. The future looked bleak. He just hoped the article brought Gabrielle and her father some sort of satisfaction.

CHAPTER NINETEEN

THIS WAS THE absolute last place he wanted to be.

Deacon stood off to the side of his newly manicured lawn. Despite what he'd said to Gabrielle, the estate did look spectacular. She hadn't overlooked a single detail. And his staff had gone above and beyond to make everything perfect for this occasion.

After Gabrielle left, it had been too late to cancel the fundraiser. He knew it was up to him to see it through to the end. Only things weren't turning out quite as he'd imagined.

With not one, not two, but three scandalous headline articles in as many days that featured him in the worst light, he didn't think anyone would attend. Instead, everyone was in attendance. He didn't know if they'd come in spite of the article or to find out if any of the lies were true.

The only person not there was the one person he longed to see—Gabrielle. He knew he should be angry with her, yet when she said that she'd backed out of the arrangement with the magazine, he'd believed her. But it didn't mean they belonged together.

He drew his thoughts up short. Today he had to be a gracious host.

He really couldn't believe all of these people had

shown up. There were fellow actors, directors, pillars of the music industry and people he didn't recognize, but what they all had in common was that they were happy to be here. All were smiling, talking and greeting each other. Food and drink flowed freely. The golf course looked better than it ever had, thanks to Gabrielle's insistence.

He'd already had compliments and slaps on the back that his scars had healed so well. After that doctored photo in *QTR*, where they'd made him to look like some sort of monster, people were pleasantly surprised by his normal appearance. It felt surprisingly good to greet friends and acquaintances. And he had Gabrielle to thank.

A mariachi band played in the background as well-dressed people mingled. Deacon worked his way past the crowd. He was headed for the rose garden, hoping to gain a moment alone. Though people had been accepting of him, it was all a bit overwhelming.

And then Gabrielle appeared in the distance.

Deacon came to a halt. It couldn't be her, could it? Not after the way they'd ended things. He blinked and looked again.

She was gone.

He expelled a disappointed sigh. It must have been someone that resembled Gabrielle. He assured himself it was for the best. She would soon forget him and move on with her life.

And then Gabrielle came back into view. She had on a yellow crocheted dress. The spaghetti straps showed off her slim shoulders. The plunging neckline hinted at her voluptuous breasts. He swallowed hard. A slit ended high up on her thighs, letting the crocheted high-low

skirt show off glimpses of her long legs. She really was
a looker.

It was then that he noticed a man next to her. The guy
was chatting her up. Deacon stood too far away to overhear what was being said, but Gabrielle was smiling.
However, it wasn't an easy smile. It looked forced. Yet,
the guy acted as though he didn't have a clue she was
only putting on a show of being nice to him.

Deacon's body stiffened as this man had the audacity
to reach out and put his hand on Gabrielle's upper arm
as though they knew each other intimately. If Gabrielle's
body gestures were anything to go by, the attention was
unwanted. Deacon started forward. Before he reached the
two, the guy leaned over and whispered something in Gabrielle's ear. She pulled away. What did the man think he
was up to? Couldn't he tell Gabrielle wasn't interested?

Deacon's steps quickened. He would step in. Or should
he? He slowed down. Was it his place to step in? After
all, he had told Gabrielle to go away. What would he be
telling her if he were to step in now?

Yet, this was his estate. He had a right to see that
none of his guests were unduly harassed. Determined
that he had a right to make sure things were all right, he
continued in Gabrielle's direction. He could see that she
was no longer smiling and her gaze was darting around
as though to find an excuse to slip away from the guy.

Deacon was almost at her side, when someone stepped
in his way, blocking his view of Gabrielle. "Excuse me."

"Deacon, old boy. It's so good to see you."

Deacon focused on the man speaking to him. It was
his agent. A man he used to speak to at least once a day,
but since the accident, his agent hadn't bothered to call.
The man had obviously given up on Deacon, figuring
his pretty face was gone forever. Now that his face had

healed, Deacon wondered if his agent realized he'd given up too soon.

"Harry, it's good to see you." Deacon did his best to smile, even though he didn't feel like it—not for a man who, for all intents and purposes, had told him in the hospital that his future in Hollywood had gone up in flames along with his good looks. Of course, Harry had been smart enough to put it in friendlier terms, but that's what it amounted to.

"You know I've been trying to reach you—"

"I've been busy." Deacon knew whatever Harry wanted would be what was good for Harry and not something that would help Deacon. "Could you excuse me for just a moment—"

"Not so fast. We should talk. This fundraiser was a brilliant idea. It certainly squashes those rumors of you becoming some sort of recluse. I've never seen the estate look better. And you, well, it's remarkable. If I hadn't seen you in the hospital, I'd never believe the extent of your injuries."

"The plastic surgeon did an amazing job," Deacon murmured tightly.

"Indeed. And this event is a great chance to get you back in the swing of things. Everyone seems to be having a great time."

"My assistant gets the credit. This fundraiser was her brainchild." It wasn't until the words were out that he realized Gabrielle was no longer his assistant. She was... well, they no longer had any sort of official relationship, but it sure didn't feel that way to him when he saw that other guy hanging all over her. Where had she disappeared to?

"This assistant, she sounds like a miracle worker,"

Harry said. "Perhaps I should try to steal her away from you."

The forced smile slipped from Deacon's face. "I don't think so."

"Well then, I'll get straight to the point of my calls. I have a part in a movie that I think you'd be perfect for—"

"No."

"No?" The agent's mouth gaped. "But surely you want to get back to work."

"I am working. I'm finding that I like being behind the camera more than I like being in front of it."

"So the rumor is true?"

"Yes. I'm starting to back some movies, and I'll see where things go from there."

The agent nodded as he digested the information. "If you change your mind, give me a call."

"I don't think that will happen." Deacon had to admit it felt good to know what he wanted in life. And what he wanted most was Gabrielle—even though he couldn't have her.

The agent's eyebrows rose with surprise before his face settled into a smile. "I knew you weren't one to hold a grudge. Glad to hear all of the ugliness is in the past." And then as though the man didn't know what else to say, he said, "Well, I should be moving on. I have other people that I need to speak to."

Deacon didn't say a word, not wanting to waylay the man. After the man moved on, Deacon's gaze scanned the area for Gabrielle. He didn't see her. But there were so many people that she could be anywhere.

He started moving through the crowd, but it was slow going with so many people wanting to greet him. He did the obligatory handshakes and pasted a smile on his face.

But he didn't linger. He needed to find her. He needed to—to what? Make sure she was okay? And then what?

He wouldn't know the answer to that until he caught up with her. He stopped and turned in a circle looking for her. She had to be here. And he wouldn't stop until he found her.

CHAPTER TWENTY

SHE SHOULDN'T BE HERE.

But she couldn't stay away.

To Gaby's surprise, the morning after she'd left the Santoro estate, the complaint against her father had been formally withdrawn. He was free and clear. There was no reason for Gaby to ever see Deacon again—but seeing him was exactly what she had planned.

She owed Deacon an apology. Instead of helping him with this fundraiser, she'd only made things worse for him. *QTR* had issued a series of malicious articles about Deacon. She recalled the morning's headlines on the *QTR* magazine. It was all over the newsstands, grocery stores and internet: Beast Hides from Public & Justice.

It appeared that *QTR* was intent on running a series of damning articles about Deacon. It killed her to read how they'd stolen her words. *QTR* had twisted the facts and made up other things. They'd embarked on an all-out campaign against him. No wonder she hadn't spotted Deacon amongst his guests. The fact that he had even let the fundraiser go forward amazed her.

When he'd banished her from the estate, she'd worried that he would once again hide away in his darkened office and keep everyone outside the tall estate walls. And after those atrocious headlines, she wouldn't blame him if he cut himself off from the outside world.

She didn't care what Deacon said, she knew he had a good heart. She couldn't—she wouldn't—accept that he'd recklessly taken her aunt's life. It had been a horrible accident. End of a very sad story.

She'd been talking frankly with her father—something she should have done before things had gotten out of control. And the fact that her father had agreed to attend the fundraiser with her was the first step on the road to forgiveness, even if her father would vehemently deny it. He said he was only here because Gaby had planned the event. He refused to acknowledge that the event had anything to do with Deacon.

Her gaze scanned the enormous crowd of finely dressed people. Was Deacon really somewhere among them? She had to try and fix things. She at least had to try. She didn't like the way they'd left things.

"Hey—" Newton nudged her "—isn't that the guy that acts in *The Screaming Racers*?"

She hadn't seen the action movie, but she had seen the previews on the television in her father's living room. "Yes, I think it is."

"What do you think he's doing here?"

"Supporting a good cause."

"I don't know. He's a big star. Why would he come here to the beast's lair?"

"Newton, don't start."

"Hey, it's what they called him in the headlines. You know, the story you helped write."

She gave Newton a stern look. "I only agreed to bring you here because you insisted that my father might need help getting around. But we could leave now—"

"Okay. Okay."

He pressed his lips together into a firm line. But his eyes told a different story. If she wasn't careful with him, he would make a scene. She sincerely regretted bringing him. As soon as she placed some tickets in the raffle baskets, she'd gather her father and Newton and they would go.

"Go find my father. You know, the reason you're here?" she said. "I need to go buy some raffle tickets."

"I'm hungry. Maybe we'll get some food." Newton walked away.

With Deacon nowhere in sight, Gabrielle made her way over to the table where they were selling the tickets for the twenty-five elaborate baskets that had been generously donated by area businesses.

Gabrielle couldn't help but smile as she observed all of the people gushing over the beautiful baskets and buying an arm's length of tickets at a time. This event was turning out better than she'd ever imagined. She wished Deacon could find some comfort in knowing that these people were in attendance in spite of the nasty headlines. That had to mean something, right?

With guests still streaming through the gates and the press along the road photographing the event, this was certainly going to give Deacon some positive spin. She pulled her cell phone from her purse. She clicked through to the different social-media sites to find that Deacon's name was trending. And this time, his name was linked with positive news.

Her lips lifted into a broader smile.

She'd done it. She'd kept her word to Deacon. The fundraiser appeared to be a smashing success. But this event wasn't nearly enough to make up to him for the lies that were lining every grocery store checkout and splattered on the internet. If only she could explain properly, maybe he'd believe her.

But where was he? She'd already worked through the crowd of guests and walked the whole way around the estate. And now, she was back where she'd started, in the garden. There had been no sign of Deacon amongst the pink tea roses, the purple climbing roses and the many other varieties of blooms that took root in the impressive garden.

The truth was she shouldn't have left when he'd told her to. She should have...well, she wasn't sure what she should have done. But leaving hadn't been the right answer. Because every minute she was away from him, the gap between them yawned even wider. She hoped it wasn't too wide for her to cross. Because she missed him with every fiber of her body. Life wasn't the same without him in it.

And then she remembered something her aunt had told her way back when she was in elementary school. There had been some trouble between her and another girl. Her aunt's sage advice was that a gentle word or a kind action could be more powerful than the strongest objection or the harshest retaliation. Her aunt had been a gentle soul. And Gabrielle had a feeling that her aunt would understand why she was doing what she was doing with Deacon. Or at least she hoped so.

"Hey, Gaby! Wait!"

It wasn't Deacon.

Her heart sunk a little.

With a forced smile, she turned to find Newton running back over to her again. "I thought you went with my father to find the food."

"Your father found someone to talk to and I decided to bring you a drink."

She realized now that he must have had more than one himself. He lurched toward her, spilling the drink on her bare arm, and then making as if to pat her dry with his free hand, surprising her.

Gaby turned, jerking away from his touch. "Stop. I'm fine…"

It was then that she spotted Deacon. He noticed her at the same time. Newton was still talking, but she was no longer paying attention. Her full focus was on Deacon.

"Excuse me." She moved past Newton and headed straight for Deacon.

Please let him listen to me before he throws me out.

CHAPTER TWENTY-ONE

GABY'S STOMACH SHIVERED with nerves.

As Deacon approached her, she forgot about everyone else around them. In that moment, it was just the two of them. She started moving toward him. Although the closer she got to him, the more she noticed the tenseness of his body and the rigid set of his jaw. She braced herself for a confrontation. She understood how he'd think that she'd turned against him.

They stopped in front of each other. At the same time, they said, "I'm sorry."

Gaby's gaze searched his. "Do you mean it?"

He nodded. "I never should have told you to leave like that."

"And I should have stayed. I need to tell you how sorry I am—"

"You!" Newton wedged himself between her and Deacon. "You killed her aunt. You should be in jail."

A hush fell over the growing crowd.

"Newton! Stop." Gabrielle saw the pain that his words had inflicted on Deacon.

Newton turned on her. "How can you defend him?"

Gabrielle's gaze went from Newton to Deacon. If there were ever a time to be honest with herself and everyone else, it was now. "I'm defending Deacon because I've come to know him. I know that he's a good man with a big heart. He would never intentionally harm a person." She turned to Deacon. She stared deep into his eyes. "I know this because I love him."

"You can't. He's a killer." Newton shouted the accusation.

By then a crowd had formed around them. People were pulling out their cell phones and filming the scene. This mess had gone from bad to worse.

"He's my best friend," she countered.

"Don't," Deacon said. "I can defend myself."

"I'm only speaking the truth," Gaby said, feeling very protective of him.

Before Newton could say another word, Gaby's father rolled his wheelchair between them. He turned to Newton. "That's enough."

"But he is a—"

"Hero," her father said.

"What?" Newton stared at her father like he'd spoken another language.

Her father cleared his voice. "I should have said something earlier. The official accident report was released this afternoon. There is irrefutable proof that Deacon is innocent."

"What evidence?" Deacon approached her father.

"I'll admit my protest in front of your place may have been rash, but it garnered a lot of attention." He held up a hand, staving off Deacon's heated words. "Before you say anything, it was that protest and those interviews that brought forward a reluctant witness. They have a video of the accident. It has cleared you, Deacon. My sister was the one that swerved into your lane."

Gaby reached out and took Deacon's hand in hers. She

smiled through her tears. At last this long, hard journey was over.

She turned to Deacon. "Did you know about this?"

He shook his head. "I haven't touched my mail or listened to my voice mails today. I was busy making sure all of your plans for the fundraiser were carried out."

Gaby's father turned to Deacon. "And I owe you a big apology. Instead of accusing you of horrible things, I should have been thanking you." He held out his hand. Deacon hesitated and then he withdrew his hand from Gaby's grasp in order to shake her father's hand. "Gaby tells me that you don't remember much of the accident, but the witness reported that at great risk, you attempted to save my sister."

Deacon visibly swallowed. "I'm sorry for what you've gone through."

"Thank you." Her father's gaze moved to Gaby and then back to Deacon. "As long as you keep my daughter happy, we'll get along just fine."

Gaby glanced around to find that Newton had disappeared. She scanned the crowd for any sign of him. Thankfully she didn't spot him. She hoped he just kept going. The farther away, the better.

When she finally turned back to Deacon, he presented her with a single, perfect red rose. The simple gesture had a profound effect on her heart and love spilled forth.

Gaby lifted up on her tiptoes and looped her arms around his neck. "There's something else I came here to say."

At the same time, they said, "I love you."

As the crowd of onlookers cheered, Gaby leaned into Deacon's embrace. He claimed her lips with a kiss that promised love and happiness.

EPILOGUE

Six months later...

"I NEED TO talk to you." Gabrielle smiled at her new husband in the back of a black limo.

"Really?" The smile he'd been wearing all day slipped from his face. "I wanted to talk to you, too."

"You did?" Gaby sat up straighter. She couldn't imagine what Deacon had on his mind. "Maybe you should go first."

"Wipe that worried look from your beautiful face. Or else I'll have to put up that privacy divider and give you something to smile about." His eyes twinkled with mischief.

She knew exactly what direction her husband's mind had taken and she shook her head as a smile returned to her face. "That will have to wait." When Deacon made a point of pouting, she added, "There's no time. We're almost to the airport."

He nodded in understanding. "As usual, my wife is right."

"Make sure you remember those words the next time we have a disagreement." The lights of the Los Angeles skyline rushed past the window in a blur as their limo headed for LAX. They were hopping a private plane to Fiji. Their honeymoon was going to be a new adventure for the both of them.

"But if we disagree, we get to have make-up sex."

She couldn't help but laugh at her husband's unabashed eagerness. "Do you ever think of anything besides sex?"

"Not when you're around. You've ruined me." He pulled her closer until she was sitting on his lap. Then he closed the divider. "We should probably save Charles from all of this naughty talk. And this way, I can show you what I was thinking about."

He drew her head down to him and claimed her lips with his own. It didn't matter how many times he kissed her, he still made her heart race. His lips moved hungrily over hers, making her insides pool with desire.

She knew where this kiss was headed and it wouldn't leave time for them to talk before the flight. And there were some things they'd put off discussing for too long. It was best to clear the air now before the honeymoon began.

It took every bit of willpower to place her hands on her husband's muscular chest and push back, ending the kiss. "Deacon, wait."

His eyes blinked open and she could read the confusion in his expression. "What's the matter?"

She moved back to the seat beside him. "You're distracting me."

"But in a good way, right?"

"Of course. But we still need to talk."

The color drained from his face. "What's wrong?"

She couldn't help but laugh at the utter look of panic on his face. "Relax. Nothing is wrong."

"You're sure?"

Gaby nodded. "I know we should have talked about this before now, but I was wondering how you felt about children."

"Children?" His gaze narrowed as he eyed her. "I must say I like them. I happened to be one not so long ago."

"Hah! I've seen your six-bay garage with all those sports cars. You're still a kid at heart."

"Busted. But I do make time for business. Speaking of which, remember how I sued *QTR* for that pack of lies they printed about the car accident?"

She nodded. "How's the lawsuit going?"

"It's over. I got the news yesterday, but with the wedding festivities, I didn't want to ruin anything."

Gaby braced herself for bad news. "Did they get it thrown out of court?"

"It never went to court. *QTR*'s board stepped in and between our combined legal teams we hammered out a reasonable deal. The gist of it is they will be revising their editorial guidelines."

Gaby's mouth gaped as she digested the ramifications of the deal. "You mean no more hatchet jobs?"

"Exactly."

"Deacon, that's wonderful." She rewarded him with a kiss, but before it got too heated, she pulled back.

"Why did you stop again? I have a piece of paper that says we must kiss multiple times a day."

She laughed. "I didn't see that on our marriage certificate."

"It's in the fine print."

"Oh. Okay. I'll have to look closer." She smiled. "And did it say anything about how many kids we're supposed to have?"

"No. How many were you thinking?"

"At least one… Since it's already on the way."

For a moment, her husband didn't speak. He didn't move. She wasn't even sure that he was still breathing.

"Deacon, did you hear me?"

"Say it again." His voice lacked emotion and she was

beginning to wonder if he was having second thoughts about having children.

"We're having a baby."

"That's what I thought you said." He lifted her back onto his lap. Then he placed his large hand over her abdomen. "You're going to be a mom."

"And you're going to be a dad."

A big smile lit up his eyes. "I love you."

"I love you, too."

She reached out, placing her hand behind her husband's head, and drew him toward her. She claimed his lips with her own. No matter how old she got to be, she would never tire of his kisses. And she planned to grow very old with this wonderful man by her side.

* * * * *

MILLS & BOON
MEDICAL
Pulse-Racing Passion

Set your pulse racing with dedicated, delectable doctors in the high-pressure world of medicine, where emotions run high and passion, comfort and love are the best medicine.

LET'S TALK
Romance

For exclusive extracts, competitions
and special offers, find us online:

f facebook.com/millsandboon

y @MillsandBoon

O @MillsandBoonUK

Get in touch on 01413 063232

For all the latest titles coming soon, visit
millsandboon.co.uk/nextmonth

 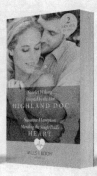